OXFORD WORLD'S

CANDID

AND OTHER STORIES

VOLTAIRE was the assumed name of François-Marie Arouet (1694–1778). Born into a well-to-do Parisian family, he was educated at the leading Jesuit college in Paris. Having refused to follow his father and elder brother into the legal profession he soon won widespread acclaim for *Œdipe* (1718), the first of some twenty-seven tragedies which he continued to write until the end of his life. His national epic *La Henriade* (1723) confirmed his reputation as the leading French literary figure of his generation. Following a quarrel with the worthless but influential aristocrat, the Chevalier de Rohan, he was forced into exile in England. This period (1726–8) was particularly formative, and his *Letters concerning the English Nation* (1733) constitute the first major expression of Voltaire's deism and his subsequent lifelong opposition to religious and political oppression. Following the happy years (1734–43) spent at Cirey with his mistress Mme du Châtelet in the shared pursuit of several intellectual enthusiasms, notably the work of Isaac Newton, he enjoyed a brief interval of favour at court during which he was appointed Historiographer to the King. After the death of Mme du Châtelet in 1749 he finally accepted an invitation to the court of Frederick of Prussia, but left in 1753 when life with this particular enlightened despot became intolerable. In 1755, after temporary sojourn in Colmar, he settled at Les Délices on the outskirts of Geneva. He then moved to nearby Ferney in 1759, the year *Candide* was published. Thereafter a spate of tragedies, stories, philosophical works, and polemical tracts, not to mention a huge number of letters, poured from his pen. The writer of competent tragedies had become the militant embodiment of the Age of Enlightenment. After the death of Louis XV in 1774 he eventually returned to Paris in 1778 for the performance of his penultimate tragedy *Irène*. He was acclaimed and fêted by the entire capital as the greatest living Frenchman and as one of the most effective champions of freedom, tolerance, and common sense the world had ever seen. He died there on 30 May 1778.

ROGER PEARSON is Professor of French in the University of Oxford and Fellow and Praelector in French at The Queen's College, Oxford. He is the author of *Stendhal's Violin: A Novelist and his Reader* (1988), *The Fables of Reason: A Study of Voltaire's 'Contes philosophiques'* (1993), *Unfolding Mallarmé: The Development of a Poetic Art* (1996), *Mallarmé and Circumstance: The Translation of Silence* (2004), and *Voltaire Almighty: A Life in Pursuit of Freedom* (2005). For Oxford World's Classics he has translated Zola, *La Bête humaine* and Maupassant, *A Life*.

OXFORD WORLD'S CLASSICS

VOLTAIRE

Candide
and Other Stories

Translated with an Introduction and Notes by
ROGER PEARSON

OXFORD
UNIVERSITY PRESS

OXFORD
UNIVERSITY PRESS

Great Clarendon Street, Oxford OX2 6DP

Oxford University Press is a department of the University of Oxford.
It furthers the University's objective of excellence in research, scholarship,
and education by publishing worldwide in

Oxford New York

Auckland Cape Town Dar es Salaam Hong Kong Karachi
Kuala Lumpur Madrid Melbourne Mexico City Nairobi
New Delhi Shanghai Taipei Toronto

With offices in

Argentina Austria Brazil Chile Czech Republic France Greece
Guatemala Hungary Italy Japan Poland Portugal Singapore
South Korea Switzerland Thailand Turkey Ukraine Vietnam

Oxford is a registered trade mark of Oxford University Press
in the UK and in certain other countries

Published in the United States
by Oxford University Press Inc., New York

Translation and editorial material © Roger Pearson 1990, 2006

First published as an Oxford World's Classics paperback 2006

British Library Cataloguing in Publication Data

Data available

Library of Congress Cataloging in Publication Data

Voltaire, 1694–1778.
[Short stories. English. Selections]
Candide and other stories / Voltaire; translated, with an introduction and notes,
by Roger Pearson.
p. cm.—(Oxford world's classics)
Includes bibliographical references.
1. Voltaire, 1694–1778—Translations into English. I. Pearson, Roger. II. Title.
III. Oxford world's classics (Oxford University Press)
PQ2075 2006 843'.5—dc22 2005034736

Typeset in Ehrhardt
by RefineCatch Limited, Bungay, Suffolk
Printed in Great Britain by
Clays Ltd, St Ives plc

ISBN 0–19–280726–9 978–0–19–280726–7

1

CONTENTS

INTRODUCTION

THIS edition presents a selection of the best of all possible stories by Voltaire: *Candide, Micromegas, Zadig, What Pleases the Ladies, The Ingenu*, and *The White Bull*. Each of them is a classic; but if ever a work deserved to be called a World's Classic, it is *Candide*. Published simultaneously in Paris, Geneva, Amsterdam, London and probably Liège on or around 20 February 1759, it soon became *the* bestseller of the European book trade in the eighteenth century. Cramer, its Genevan publisher, printed an initial run of 2,000 copies, the norm for a book that was expected to sell well: within a month, after further printings and many pirated editions, at least 20,000 copies had been sold. After a similar period even Swift's *Gulliver's Travels* (published on 28 October 1726) had sold only half that number. The first English translation came out within six weeks and sold at least 6,000 copies. Since then the work has been published in countless editions. It has been translated into all the world's major languages, and repeatedly so in some cases as renewed efforts are made to capture the elegance and vitality of Voltaire's prose. Candide and Pangloss are as well known as Don Quixote and Sancho Panza; and Leonard Bernstein turned them into the protagonists of a successful comic opera.

The original publication of *Candide* was a carefully calculated coup. Unbound copies of the work (in pocketbook duodecimo format) were discreetly dispatched from Geneva on 15 and 16 January 1759; 1,000 to Paris, 200 to Amsterdam, and others to London and Liège. They were then bound at their respective destinations and published on a previously agreed date, the idea being to circulate as many copies of the original edition as possible throughout Europe before pirated editions usurped and corrupted it (and, in those days before the laws of international copyright, siphoned off Voltaire's potential profits). The aim, too, was to create the maximum stir in as many countries as possible before the authorities could suppress this subversive tale. In the event, although the police were quick to seize all the copies they could and to smash any press on which a new edition was being printed, the flood was too great for them to stem. The damage was done—and long before the Vatican got round to placing *Candide* on its Index of forbidden books on 24 May 1762.

Voltaire himself observed great secrecy about the work, as indeed he did about many of his stories. There is no mention of *Candide* in his extant correspondence before the date of publication, and afterwards he is to be found denying authorship and dismissing the tale as nothing but a schoolboy joke. Sometime in 1758 he sent a manuscript version to the Duchesse de la Vallière in Paris, which is now preserved in the Bibliothèque de l'Arsenal in Paris; but he kept no manuscript or printed version in his own library (which was subsequently bought by Catherine the Great and is today still conserved in St Petersburg). Nor did his publishers retain their printer's copies. By now ensconced in his chateau at Ferney on the French side of the Franco-Genevan border, Voltaire was already to some extent proof against police attention; but his circumspection over the publication of *Candide* in part accounts for the fact that the authorities in Paris and Geneva took no action against Voltaire personally even if they did try in vain to contain the diffusion of his latest and most explosive piece of writing.

For explosive it was—and is. Wordsworth may have called it the 'dull product of a scoffer's wit', but he is considerably outnumbered by those who have seen *Candide* as one of the key texts of the Enlightenment. Moreover it is the supreme example of the *conte philosophique*, or philosophical tale. Whether or not Voltaire invented this genre is a moot point: admirers of Rabelais and Swift, and even of Boccaccio and Cervantes, might dispute the claim. Unquestionably, however, he devised a unique blend of shorter fiction and philosophy (in its broadest sense). It is also clear that, whether or not the *conte philosophique* already existed, Voltaire would have had to invent it: for it proved the perfect medium of expression for the sceptic and empiricist that Voltaire was. Deeply suspicious of metaphysics and 'systems', he was constantly appealing to the facts: fiction, paradoxically, allowed him to show the ways in which the muddle and miseries of life could not be reduced to neat, abstract theories. He was able to avail himself variously of the traditional narrative structures of chivalric romance, of the traveller's tale, and of the Oriental tale, and to present a human being, usually a young man, beginning to make his own way in life and learning the lessons of experience.

In this he was following the lead of the one work which influenced his thinking perhaps more than any other: Locke's *Essay concerning Human Understanding* (1690; translated into French by Coste in 1700). Locke describes his own philosophical method as being 'historical' and 'plain' (I, i. 2); 'historical' because ideas are not innate but arrived at by stages ('the steps by which the human mind attains several truths': I, ii. 15, 16); and 'plain' because, in its uncorrupt state, it is untrammelled by prejudice and preconception. 'Candide' and 'candidement' ('candid' and 'candidly', from the Latin meaning 'white') recur frequently in Coste's translation to convey this state of openness to experience and readiness to base one's judgements on empirical evidence, to reason inductively rather than deductively.

For Voltaire, therefore, there was great narrative potential in the discovery of truth, and no better way to present the process of its discovery than as the voyage of a naive or 'candid' observer. Half of the twenty-six prose tales he wrote employ the narrative device of the journey, including all his major ones and four of the five presented in this edition. Indeed this is how his career as a writer of *contes philosophiques* began, for in 1739 Voltaire sent Frederick of Prussia a manuscript copy of his *Voyage du baron de Gangan*. This manuscript has been lost, but from the correspondence between Voltaire and Frederick it is possible to infer that this work was essentially a prototype of *Micromegas*, which was eventually published thirteen years later.

Micromegas

Micromegas dates originally, therefore, from the period when Voltaire was living, in a *ménage à trois*, with Mme du Châtelet and her husband at their home at Cirey some fifty miles from Nancy in eastern France. Life with his mistress was as energetically intellectual as it was amorous, and together they read, studied, and wrote over a whole range of mathematical, scientific, philosophical, and literary subjects. In fact they were being *philosophes*, or philosophers, in the special eighteenth-century French sense of the word: namely, they thought freely (i.e. independently of all religious or political authority) throughout the entire field of human intellectual enquiry. They were, as the etymology of the word indicates, lovers of knowledge and, in those days before the specialist, rightly believed themselves capable of understanding and contributing to the latest scientific

debates. A particular enthusiasm of theirs was the science, or natural
philosophy as it was then called, of Isaac Newton (1642–1727). Voltaire had 'discovered' Newton during his stay in England (1726–8)
and introduced his work to the French in his *Lettres philosophiques*
(1734; originally published in English in 1733 as the *Letters concerning the English Nation*). Indeed it is Voltaire who was responsible for
circulating the story about Newton and the apple, which he claimed
to have heard from Newton's niece.

Newton's *Principia Mathematica* (1687) made a deep impression on
Voltaire, not least because it offered him as a deist empirical evidence
and philosophical proof to sustain the 'argument from design' (i.e.
that the order in the universe points to an intelligent Creator: the
workings of the clock prove the existence of a clockmaker). Here,
too, was a new method of scientific enquiry, comparable with Locke's
philosophical method published three years after it, and based on
observation and induction (where, for example, Descartes's had been
based on logic and deduction). Newtonian physics filled the empti-
ness of interplanetary space with the order and harmony of gravi-
tational law, where Pascal (1623–62) had seen only the void left by a
God who had withdrawn from Creation, and Descartes (1596–1650)
a system of vortices, or whirlpools, of ethereal fluid (*materia subtilis*)
which supported and conveyed the celestial bodies within a *plenum*.
In 1738 Voltaire presented French readers with a full, accurate, and
intelligible account of Newtonian science in his *Éléments de la philosophie de Newton*, which had a considerable impact on contemporary French thinking (and was largely responsible for Voltaire's
election in England as a Fellow of the Royal Society in 1743).

It was in 1738 also that he began the first version of *Micromegas*,
the only one of his stories to be described by him explicitly as 'philosophical'. Imagine someone setting out to rewrite Jules Verne's *De
La Terre à la lune* (*From the Earth to the Moon*) having met Neil
Armstrong; for this, in part at least, is what Voltaire was doing. He
took the device of the interplanetary journey which had been used in
such works as Godwin's *Man in the Moon* (1638) or Cyrano de
Bergerac's *États et empires de la lune* (*States and Empires of the Moon*;
1657); combined it with elements of the imaginary journey used in
the quasi-scientific, Utopian travel literature of the seventeenth and
early eighteenth centuries (such as Bacon's *Nova Atlantis* of 1627);
and added the technique of the alien visitor which Montesquieu,

among others, had put to such good use in his *Lettres persanes* (*Persian Letters*; 1721). The originality of *Micromegas* lies partly in having a being from another planet come to have a 'close encounter' with us (in the hope of finding Utopia . . .). Further Voltairean twists include the fact that this extraterrestrial being travels because he has been exiled for writing about biology and microscopy, and that he sees himself—inhabitant (rather than man) of the world that he is—as being on a kind of educational Grand Tour of the universe.

In *Micromegas*, as Candide will subsequently remark, 'travel's the thing'. The Sirian travels, the Saturnian travels, earthly philosophers travel: it is the only way to discover anything—by a change of perspective. For the Sirian, as for Voltaire at Cirey, the universe exhibits a wonderful profusion of difference and variety within a framework of orderly proportion and harmony. The Great Chain of Being extends from the *mega* to the *micro*, and man, much further down this chain than he imagines, can see only a small part of it (just as the Saturnian cannot see several stars which are visible to the Sirian). Ridiculous in his *mega*, anthropocentric pride (especially the person in academic dress), and absurdly wretched in his warring, man may be physically *micro* but his capacity for precise scientific observation (with a quadrant and microscope) suggests *mega* potential for discovery. But only if he will learn humility, and to eschew metaphysical absurdities about the soul. He should not jump to conclusions, like the far-from-'candid' Saturnian, but proceed in the judicious manner of the Sirian—and of the little follower of Locke. *Micromegas* is a eulogy of Newtonian physics and Lockean epistemology, of divine power and man's potential for enlightenment. As its moral lesson it teaches the virtues of the measured response.

It is also a comedy, and it entertains as it instructs. Human intellectual hubris is here punished, not by the nemesis of tragedy (though ending up in the Sirian's pocket is a near-tragedy) but by the nemesis of deflation. Some of the comedy shows the clear influence of Swift, whom Voltaire met when in England and whose *Gulliver's Travels* were published while he was there. Voltaire elaborates on the Swiftian (and Rabelaisian) comedy of size by creating a further comedy of measurement. He includes as many different units of measurement as he can (fathoms, leagues, and geometrical paces, not to mention the French feet that are longer than English ones), and he makes considerable play with methods of measurements,

juxtaposing the analogical reasoning of the Saturnian ('nature is like
a flower-bed', etc.) and of the narrator (the lapdog and the Prussian
guards officer) with the exact calculations of algebraists and geometers. Conjecture and vague speculation are fruitless: what is needed
is accurate observation—with a microscope, a diamond, a quadrant,
or indeed the naked eye. Seeing is all, as long as one is careful not to
be deceived by appearances. Newtonian physics may seem fantastical, but it proves to be borne out by the facts: metaphysics may
seem profound, but it reveals itself as pure fantasy. The real mystery
lies not in interstellar space but in the heart of man.

   And the story itself exemplifies some of its own lessons by providing a change of perspective, by presenting a different way of seeing.
It is a distorted mirror, even a kind of inverted microscope, in or
through which man can see himself in all his pettiness. *Sub specie
siriani*, if not *aeternitatis*, the Russo-Turkish War (1736–9) becomes a
squabble between men in hats and men in turbans over a few lumps
of earth, and the metaphysics of Aristotle, Descartes, Malebranche,
Leibniz, and Aquinas so much nonsensical gobbledegook. In the end
there are seemingly no answers: the Sirian's nice book of philosophy
is blank. But we have the full pages of the story itself: imagination
and fiction have provided their own kind of answer where metaphysical logic fails. Where reason falls short, the fable provides.

Optimism

Micromegas reflects the mood of comparative serenity and optimism
which prevailed at Cirey, and which Voltaire enjoyed up until the
mid-1740s. Both he and Mme du Châtelet warmed to the philosophical Optimism which had been expressed in Alexander Pope's
Essay on Man (1733–4; translated into French prose in 1736 and
French verse in 1737):

> Submit.—In this, or any other sphere,
> Secure to be as blest as thou canst bear:
> Safe in the hand of one disposing Pow'r,
> Or in the natal, or the mortal hour.
> All Nature is but Art, unknown to thee;
> All Chance, Direction, which thou canst not see;
> All Discord, Harmony not understood;
> All partial Evil, universal Good.

And, spite of Pride, in erring Reason's spite,
One truth is clear, 'Whatever is, is RIGHT'.
(Epistle i. 285–94)

In 1736 they came into contact with the work of the German philosopher Leibniz (1646–1716) as expounded, and distorted, by his follower Christian Wolff (1679–1754). Mme du Châtelet was enthusiastic, but Voltaire preferred the less metaphysical approach of Pope (1688–1744). Nevertheless, although he found Leibniz's theory about monads and pre-established harmony difficult to swallow (and parodies it in *Micromegas*), he was sufficiently preoccupied with Leibnizian Optimism to make it the focal point of both *Zadig* and *Candide*.

In his *Essais de théodicée*, written in French and published in 1710, Leibniz addressed the age-old question: what is the nature of divine Providence and how can we reconcile it with physical and moral evil and with the idea of free will? The traditional Christian answer to the problem of moral evil is, of course, that God, in his goodness, endowed man with free will but that, since Adam's original sin, man has abused this freedom with evil results. In respect of physical evil the traditional Christian response has been to posit satanic forces inimical to God, but this in turn poses further problems: if God is benevolent, why does he permit these forces to operate? and if God cannot prevent them, then he is not omnipotent. It is but one step from this to the so-called Manichaean heresy (after the third-century Persian thinker Manes who sought to reconcile Christianity with the philosophy of Zoroaster) which argues that the universe is governed by two equally powerful forces of Good and Evil. (This is the position adopted by Martin in *Candide*.)

In his *Dictionnaire historique et critique* of 1697 Pierre Bayle had given this heresy a fairly vigorous airing, duly condemning it but also using it as a powerful weapon in his attack on all attempts to construct a theodicy. For Bayle the demands of human reason and the content of the Christian revelation were not to be reconciled. Leibniz, on the other hand, sought to do just that, and to refute Bayle in the process.

One of the basic axioms in Leibniz's system is the so-called Principle of Sufficient Reason, which holds that there must necessarily be some logical reason why anything is as it is. According to this axiom even God must have, or have had, a sufficient reason for his actions, and since he is by definition perfect, it must always be, or have been, the right reason. If God is perfect, however, why is he not sufficient unto himself? In other words, why did he create? The answer lies in the traditional ontological proof of God's existence. According to this, if one can conceive of a being uniting all possible perfections, this being must necessarily exist, since for it not to exist would be an imperfection. If existence is a perfection in God, then it must be a perfection in created beings. Hence (or so Leibniz argues) the more different kinds of created beings there are, the more God has demonstrated his divine power.

Since God is perfection, and since God was creating something separate from himself, it follows that what he created had necessarily to be imperfect. At the moment of Creation he had to decide between an infinite number of possible (i.e. imperfect) worlds. Following the Principle of Sufficient Reason he necessarily chose the best of all possible worlds (i.e. the least imperfect), namely that in which the greatest diversity might obtain and in which there would be the greatest excess of good over evil. By this token a world without evil, were it even logically possible, might be less good than a world with evil since some great goods are inevitably bound up with certain evils. Thus, for example, free will is a great good but entails the possibility of sin. By this reasoning, then, the presence of evil in the world may be said to offer no argument against the benevolence or omnipotence of God. On the contrary, all evil is for a greater good (though it does not follow, as Pangloss proposes in *Candide*, that the more evil there is, the better . . .). Thus, all is for the best in the best of all possible worlds.

Finally, as to the question of man's soul and the nature of the interaction between matter and spirit, Leibniz rejected the Cartesian theory that the soul was located in the pineal gland and posited the existence of what he called monads, spiritual units which were in perfect, divinely 'pre-established' harmony with the material universe in the manner of two clocks keeping perfect time with each other. Voltaire thought this completely daft.

Zadig

It may be seen from this account of Leibniz's system that it informs the Sirian's view of the universe in *Micromegas*, which suggests that

Voltaire, in 1738–9 at least, was in sympathy with some of Leibniz's thought even if he did not take to the monads or the clocks. And Leibnizian ideas are further expounded by the angel Jesrad towards the end of *Zadig* (written between 1746 and 1747 and published in 1748). *Zadig*, like *Micromegas*, is essentially an intelligent story about the limits of intelligence. Zadig has all the talents, all the virtues: he is 'the one human being who most deserved to be enlightened'. He has had a good education, he can think straight, he displays a considerable gift for inductive reasoning, especially in the episode of the dog and the horse (in a manner anticipating Sherlock Holmes), and he puts the lessons of experience to good use. But even his superior intelligence and virtue are no guarantee of happiness, and he spends most of the story as the bewildered plaything of destiny (or Providence, which is the subtitle Voltaire wanted for the story but felt was too inflammatory).

Once he is finally reduced to railing (blasphemously) against Providence, the angel Jesrad intervenes, rather in the manner of divine grace, and explains all in familiar Leibnizian terms. After the usual Voltairean reminder of the need for intellectual humility, Jesrad gives the sufficient reason for the existence of evil people and argues the case for the necessary interconnection of good and evil. He further alludes to the theory of possible worlds and to the notion of diversity as a sign of divine power, and concludes by asserting that everything is as it has to be, as it should be.

Voltaire's originality in *Zadig* lies in his use of the structure of the Oriental tale as a model for the Providentialist view of history. On the face of it, events in the narrative seem random and haphazard, and the worlds of Babylon, Egypt, and Arabia appear fantastical and absurd. Yet there is order: the conventions of the Oriental tale, and perhaps of all traditional storytelling, mean that everything is leading, by a roundabout route, to the Happy Ending. As readers we have a sense of inevitability: we may feel that the author is playing with us as destiny plays with Zadig, but in the end all will be well.

Or will it? *Zadig* has two endings, corresponding to the hero's two reactions to Jesrad's pronouncements. On the one hand, Zadig submits to Providence, and the story ends with the chapter entitled 'The riddles'. Zadig wins Astarte, justice and love prevail: 'The people glorified Zadig, and Zadig glorified heaven.' On the other hand there is Zadig's 'But . . .': Jesrad's Leibnizian explanation is perhaps

inadequate, a trifle glib even? We note the irony that Zadig wins
Astarte by solving the riddles: yet these riddles are mere party
games, and he has been unable to solve the riddle that really matters—the riddle of Providence. And then *Zadig* continues after the
happy ending; and the Appendix, like the three dots after Zadig's
'But . . .' (and like the blank pages in Micromegas's book of
philosophy), leaves the reader in a state of suspense.

The two chapters in the Appendix to *Zadig* were added by Voltaire
probably in 1752 towards the (unhappy) end of his three-year stay at
the court of Frederick the Great of Prussia and so may reflect his
own anxiety about the future. Within the context of *Zadig* they are
the two chapters which perhaps most resemble the *Thousand and
One Nights*, and as such they refer the reader back to the Epistle
Dedicatory at the beginning, where there is explicit reference to the
Thousand and One Nights and which is written as a pastiche of the
latter's Oriental style. (The *Thousand and One Nights* had first been
translated into French by Antoine Galland (1646–1715) and
published between 1704 and 1717.)

A kind of framework of Oriental narrative is thus created outside
the main story, providing a measure of formal order to offset the new
'untidiness' which the Appendix brings to the plot. For these last
two chapters detract from the happiness of the ending, and throw
the emphasis back on to Zadig's role as a playing of fate. The work
now concludes in a much more open-ended way: 'Let us depart, and
we shall see what my sorry destiny still has in store for me.' Living
happily ever after becomes life as ongoing uncertainty, life as an
endless journey of experience. There is a note of Stoic acceptance
here, but heaven is no longer to be blessed and glorified.

The inconclusiveness of the revised *Zadig* is further underlined by
the (purely fictional) editorial revelation at the end that the manuscript of *Zadig* is incomplete. Perhaps there are gaps that have to be
filled. Again one is reminded of the Epistle Dedicatory, in which
Sadi warns the Sultana Sheraa that this is 'a work which sayeth more
than it may appear to say'. Indeed we may even be put in mind of the
Seal of Approval (preceding the Epistle), which implies that the only
way to get the truth across is to say the opposite of what one means.
And we may wonder too about the lesson to be learnt from the story
of the broken writing tablet in Chapter 4. Half a text may mean the
direct opposite of what the whole text says, and to judge an author by

half his text may have fatal consequences. So, like Micromegas, we must proceed judiciously and without jumping to conclusions: Jesrad's explanation may be only half the story.

Yet destiny itself is a book, which Jesrad can read but Zadig cannot. And it comes in two halves: the past and the future. Jesrad knows the content of both halves and so can explain and justify the past in terms of the future. Zadig blasphemes against Providence because he has read only, as it were, the left-hand side of the tablet of history. And what the story of *Zadig* teaches us is, as the narrator of *Micromegas* puts it, that 'in this world people never know the half of it'. (*Zadig* was actually published in this dual manner. In order to limit the initial print run to 1,000 copies, and because he did not trust his printers to do this, Voltaire gave one half of the manuscript to one printer and the second to another. All he had to do then was have the two bound together.)

Candide

Zadig thus returns an open verdict on Leibnizian Optimism: *Candide*, on the other hand, sentences it to death. Generally, *Candide* is said to be a satire on Optimism, but this is only partly true. It would be more accurate to say that it is a satire on systems. The philosophy of Optimism, nevertheless, is one such system, and it is the one most savagely attacked in *Candide*.

Between writing the main part of *Zadig* in 1747–8 and beginning *Candide* in 1757, Voltaire cannot be said to have had the most Leibnizian time of it. His brief period of favour at court following his appointment as Historiographer to the King at Versailles in 1745 ended in November 1747 some two months after the publication of *Zadig*; Mme du Châtelet died on 10 September 1749, a week after giving birth to the child of another man (that Voltaire was by that stage in love with his niece, Mme Denis, made the event no less distressing); his stay at the court of Frederick the Great, begun in June 1750, ended in acrimony, and Voltaire and Mme Denis (who had come to meet him) were actually arrested in Frankfurt, beyond Prussian jurisdiction, by agents of his erstwhile patron, friend, and co-philosopher.

Most especially perhaps, Voltaire's faith in God had been severely shaken by the Lisbon earthquake on 1 November (All Saints' Day)

1755, which killed 20,000 or more people; and his poem on the subject, published in 1756, is a devastating *cri de cœur* against Pope and Leibniz, not to mention the Almighty. Subtitled 'An Examination of the Axiom: All is well', the poem begins by asking, first, how such carnage can be in accordance with the eternal laws of a good and free God and, second, how it can be a punishment from God. Why Lisbon? Why not London or Paris? ('Lisbon lies in ruins, while in Paris they dance.') Did the volcanic activity that caused the earthquake really have to be part of the Creation? Is it any consolation to the people of Lisbon to be told that their 'partial evil' is contributing to the universal good? And, says Voltaire, it is no good talking about the immutable laws of necessity and the Great Chain of Being. The question remains: 'Why do we suffer under a master who is just?' Is God powerless? Or not beneficent? Is he punishing us? Or is he indifferent and letting his original decrees run their course? Is evil inherent in matter and not subject to God's control? Or is God testing us? Seeking the guidance of others, Voltaire rejects Plato and Epicurus in favour of the scepticism of Bayle. Finally he admits defeat and submits:

> I can but suffer, and in silence.

The poem ends with the brief story of a caliph who, after death, offers up to God all that he, in his immensity, does not have: deficiency, regrets, ill fortune, ignorance—and hope. This, the last word of the poem, shows Voltaire's refusal to abandon himself to nihilism, but it represents an act of blind faith rather than the outcome of any reasoned argument.

By the time Voltaire came to write *Candide*, his own personal circumstances had improved with the purchase in 1755 of a home near Geneva (called Les Délices: he acquired and moved into the nearby chateau at Ferney roughly at the same time as *Candide* was published) where he could settle down and indeed cultivate a garden. But the extensive work which he carried out in writing a history of the world, his *Essai sur les mœurs* (*Essay on the Manners and Spirit of Nations*; published in 1756), had made him even more aware of the evils of the human condition. Given man's inhumanity to man since the dawn of time, he was now even less ready to accept the philosophy of Optimism than before.

In *Candide* Voltaire evidently satirizes Leibniz's Optimism not only by the illogical travesty of it which Pangloss parrots throughout the story, but also by juxtaposing it with the various atrocities and disasters of which the story provides such a seemingly inexhaustible catalogue. Rape, pillage, murder, massacre, butchery, religious intolerance and abuse, torture, hanging, storm, shipwreck, earthquake, disease, prostitution: all is well. Yet it is not just the particulars of Leibniz's system which Voltaire objects to, but even more so the belief, which he felt to be characteristic of the rationalism of his age, that logic and reason can somehow explain away the chaotic wretchedness of existence by grandly and metaphysically ignoring the facts. (Hence the name 'Pangloss'.) After all, even Martin, whose views seem so much more persuasive than Pangloss's, is said by the narrator to have 'detestable principles'. They are detestable not because they are Manichaean, but because they are principles. Martin, no less than Pangloss, has a system, and he makes the facts fit the system rather than keep an open, 'candid' mind. Thus he predicts that the faithful Cacambo will betray Candide, which in the event he does not.

As in *Zadig*, it is this human desire to impose order on experience which is the mainspring of the story. Where Voltaire had previously availed himself of the Oriental tale and its associations with Eastern fatalism and the philosophy of Zoroaster, here he exploits the traditions of chivalric romance. The hero, in pursuit of his beloved (both Cunégonde and, by extension, happiness), undergoes a series of ordeals by which he proves himself worthy of her. Part of the comedy in *Candide* lies, of course, in the exaggerated and incongruous nature of these accumulated ordeals and of the quest itself. This time there is no question of the Providentialist view being taken seriously. At the end of *Candide* both Pangloss's description of the foregoing chain of events and his definition of happiness as eating candied citron and pistachio nuts are plainly absurd. Indeed they are mere words: 'That is well put,' says Candide, but what he wants is practical action, gardening. (In fact it is almost as if Voltaire himself were saying here: 'well, now you've read my fine words, stop reading and get on with it.')

But the fact that Pangloss's conclusion is ridiculed does not mean that the world of *Candide* is without order, and in this respect *Candide* is a more optimistic work than *Zadig*. The final version of the latter leaves the reader with a major question mark hanging over the nature of Providence and offers no positive solution other than a rather weary, and passive, 'Oh, well, let's see what's going to happen next'. In *Candide*, on the contrary, there is indeed order, and it is the order of education. As far as Candide himself is concerned, things happen to him suddenly and surprisingly, without rhyme or reason; and yet all the time he is turning his experiences to account. Gradually he perceives and comes to terms with the disparity between Pangloss's system and the facts of life; not only of his own life, but also of the lives of Cunégonde (Chapter 8) and the old woman (Chapters 11 and 12). By Chapter 13 he is questioning Pangloss's philosophy explicitly, and on reaching Eldorado in Chapter 18 he is in no doubt that Pangloss was wrong, at least about the optimal virtues of Thunder-ten-tronckh. He finally renounces Panglossian Optimism in Chapter 19 when he sees the effects of slavery in Surinam, and when he hears the applicants for the job as his companion.

Thereafter Candide tries to think and act for himself. At the end of Chapter 20 he begins to perceive that truth may be unattainable in the abstract, and that more comfort may be derived from the human intercourse of inconclusive conversation. For all his new independence of mind, however, Candide is not yet a sure judge, and he is constantly deceived by appearance, be it the attempted fraud of the abbé from Périgord, or the seeming happiness of Paquette and Giroflée, or the contentment of Pococurante. The temptation to adopt Martin's Manichaeanism in place of Panglossian Optimism is great, until in Chapter 26 Cacambo undermines it by proving faithful. After this, Candide's rejection of systems is bolstered by the renewed evidence of the sterility of intransigence: first, in Chapter 28, the comic refusal of Pangloss to change his mind ('I am a philosopher after all'), and second, in Chapter 29, the rather less comic persistence of the Baron in refusing to allow his sister to marry the unsuitable bastard Candide. In the concluding chapter he learns: (*a*) from the old woman, that simply opting out may be no answer, since boredom may be the greatest evil of all; (*b*) from the dervish, that it is best to bracket the metaphysical problem of evil; and (*c*) from the kindly old man, that work offers the possibility, if not of happiness, at least of a tolerable *modus vivendi*. Martin speaks for all of them when he suggests they 'get down to work and stop all this philosophizing', but even this is an abstraction, a sweeping statement.

Candide's manner of expression is less dogmatically exclusive, more practical, more environmentally sound: 'we must cultivate our garden'.

It is education, then, the process of enlightenment, which gives shape to experience, and not only for Candide. Cunégonde learns that there are finer castles than that of Thunder-ten-tronckh, and the old woman learns from being digitally explored by pirates that travel broadens the mind . . . Indeed her mind has been so broadened, and she has learnt so frequently not to trust to appearances, that she seems almost unwilling to blame the monk for robbing them in the inn at Badajoz when he is most blatantly the culprit. Worrying whether you have a leg to stand on (or a buttock to sit on) breeds futile, incapacitating caution.

At the end of *Candide*, therefore, retrospect should suggest not the absurd chain of events described by Pangloss but the Lockean 'steps by which [Candide's] mind attains several truths'. By the same token, the hilarious spoof of chivalric romance conceals a symbolic narrative order of a more serious kind: the journey from one Garden of Eden to another via Eldorado, or from falsity to reality via the ideal. The castle of Thunder-ten-tronckh, supposed microcosm of the best of all possible worlds, is, of course, a fool's paradise. It is characterized by pretension—be it aesthetic (specifically, architectural), genealogical, intellectual, or even horticultural ('the little wood they referred to as their "parkland" ')—and the Fall occurs as Cunégonde witnesses Pangloss giving Paquette 'a lesson in applied physiology' (during which, one later infers, he contracts syphilis). Armed with the apple of her new sexual knowledge, this Westphalian Eve seduces her Adam.

The farm outside Constantinople is a pragmatist's paradise: not some abstract garden of 'good works' as Pangloss theologically and uselessly suggests; nor a garden like Pococurante's which you simply install at vast expense and then want to replace; but a garden of human beings in which the talent of each is a plant to be nurtured so that society as a whole benefits while the individual finds fulfilment. In this paradise male chauvinism still prevails, as the women make pastry, sew, and do the laundry, but Teutonic snobbery and Jesuit arrogance are sent back to the galleys, while Pangloss, forever imprisoned within his own risible metaphysical system, is retained. His talent, for academic debate, will at least give them something to laugh at: every paradise needs a fool. Candide's talent, of course, turns out to be that of moral leadership.

This journey from falsity to reality leads, at the centre of *Candide*, via the authentic Garden of Eden of Eldorado. Here there is true merit—aesthetic, social, intellectual, and even agricultural ('the land had been cultivated as much to give pleasure as to serve a need'). Deism is the only religion; there is a liberal monarchy; commerce is encouraged by the funding of free restaurants for tradesmen and waggoners; intellectual freedom is permitted; the spirit of scientific enquiry is fostered; the arts are encouraged; public buildings are praised (even, one assumes, by the royal family); women can join the Guards; . . . and the King's wit survives being translated. Eldorados, it would seem, do not date.

Nor does human nature change. Sex and vanity are the instruments of the Fall as Candide and Cacambo leave Eldorado in pursuit of their sweethearts and in order to show off their riches and surpass the wealth of all the world's monarchs put together. Experience will tell that neither ambition was worth the sacrifice: Cunégonde has become ugly and shrewish, and kings are either deposed and turned into carnivalesque lookalikes, or else they meet a bad end in the manner of those whom Pangloss so eruditely lists. It would have been better not to leave, and this is the lesson they should have learnt in Eldorado. Travel may broaden the mind, but wanderlust may blow it. The Incas who once lived there left to 'go and conquer another part of the world', rather as Candide and Cacambo want to go off and lord it. But, says the King, 'when one is reasonably content in a place, one ought to stay there'. And this is the right way to think of the matter, not negatively like Martin who 'was firmly persuaded that one is just as badly off wherever one is'.

Just as *Zadig, or Destiny* returns an open verdict on the nature of Providence, so *Candide, or Optimism* comes to no clear-cut conclusion about optimism. About Optimism, yes: as a philosophical system, Optimism is discredited, not so much (and certainly not only) because its tenets are shown to be implausible in the light of the evidence, but essentially because it is a system. As such it is as inhuman and as dangerous as all the other systems which are ruthlessly satirized in the story: the military system, the Church system, the colonial system, the caste system, and indeed the system of logic itself.

And yet the picture is not unrelievedly bleak, and there may be some grounds for optimism. First, human beings may be admirable for their will to survive, their refusal to commit physical, and what Albert Camus later called 'philosophical', suicide. As the old woman says: 'A hundred times I wanted to kill myself, but still I loved life. This ridiculous weakness for living is perhaps one of our most fatal tendencies. For can anything be sillier than to insist on carrying a burden one would continually much rather throw to the ground? Sillier than to feel disgust at one's own existence and yet cling to it? Sillier, in short, than to clasp to our bosom the serpent that devours us until it has gnawed away our heart?'

Secondly, human beings may be admirable for this very awareness of their ridiculousness, indeed for their capacity to laugh at adversity. Perhaps, even, there is some value in adversity. After all, Pococurante is the man who has everything and, precisely, is bored. He seeks to improve his garden by having a bigger and better one, but without personal effort. He never travels: people visit him (and without difficulty, unlike Eldorado). Perhaps some measure of deprivation, some evil, actually is beneficial, because it lends purpose and contrast to life. Perhaps Pope and Leibniz are not entirely wrong. And purpose would lie in developing one's own individual talents, apparently self-centredly, but ultimately to the benefit of society. (Presumably Cunégonde does not scoff all her pastries herself.)

But in the end there is only the semblance of a solution to the problem of evil in *Candide*. The dervish's view simply minimizes it but does not remove it; and the kindly old man's advocacy of work leaves much out of account. Work may prevent boredom, vice, and need, but what about intellectual and emotional fulfilment? Martin says we should stop philosophizing, but an enquiring mind is one of the more desirable human attributes. And what is happiness? Merely the avoidance of things? And what of love?

To the random chaos of existence *Candide* brings not the order of Jesrad's Leibnizian Providentialism but the literary order of a symbolic journey from a false, Germanic Eden to a state of rather muted Turkish delight. But the story offers only an illusion of closure: the final, famous aphorism fails to hide much uncertainty and gives on to as much of a blank page as those which fill Micromegas's book of philosophy or that which, metaphorically speaking, follows Zadig's tentative 'But . . .'. *Candide* is ostensibly translated from the German of one Doctor Ralph, but consists also of the addenda found in his pocket when he died at the battle of Minden. Were all the addenda found? Perhaps the final page was lost. Where reason fails, the fable provides—if nothing else, an excuse for the absence of an answer.

What Pleases the Ladies

For, as we discover in *What Pleases the Ladies*, finding answers is only possible in fairy tales. In this, the longest and most famous of Voltaire's verse tales, our chivalric hero Messire Jean Robert (here translated, in part for the rhyme, as 'Sir John Roebear') has to find the answer to the age-old question: 'What do women most desire?' . . . and it would, of course, be most unchivalrous of an Introduction to reveal the answer in advance. But knowing readers will perhaps already have been reminded of Chaucer's 'The Wife of Bath's Tale', since it was indeed on John Dryden's version of this tale, published in 1700, that Voltaire based his own rather more risqué version when he came to compose it—in about a day and a half—during the winter of 1763–4. And as usual he had a very particular reason for doing so.

Verse, of course, was as natural a medium as prose for educated gentlemen of Voltaire's time, an accomplishment to be acquired like swordsmanship or the ability to dance a minuet. Except that Voltaire did it better. He had made his name at the age of 24 with *Œdipe* (1718), a verse tragedy in the neoclassical style, and written over twenty verse plays since. In 1723 he had immortalized his name with a verse epic in the Virgilian mould, soon to be known as *La Henriade*. Set at the time of the French Wars of Religion, it relates the exploits of Henri IV (1553–1610), the first Bourbon King of France and a Protestant who converted to Catholicism in order to unite his country ('Paris is well worth a Mass,' as he put it). Simultaneously Voltaire had been making himself notorious with a stream of verse satires, and his subversive rhymes had circulated by mouth, memory, and manuscript throughout the coffee houses and taverns of early eighteenth-century Paris. He was a poet for all seasons, and—by the lights of his day—a great one at that. Not a poignant lyricist like the sixteenth-century sonneteer Pierre de Ronsard (1524–85), nor a master of subtle and economical expression like the seventeenth-century tragedian Jean Racine (1639–99), but a versifier of wit and fluent elegance with a particular gift for the sound-bite.

Much of Voltaire's poetry belongs to the more elevated genres of epic and drama, the epistle and the ode, but he had a considerable talent—and taste—for comic verse. For many years, from his late thirties onwards, it was his habit to regale trusted guests with readings from *La Pucelle* (*The Maid*), a mock epic about Joan of Arc. The crux of its plot caused him much hilarity: 'If saving a city is something you should, | Of what possible use is your maidenhood?'; and the ever-growing number of its cantos were filled with similar 'unpatriotic' irreverence, not to mention much topical satire, anti-clerical sentiment, and no little bawdy. Small wonder that his mistress Mme du Châtelet kept his manuscript copy firmly under lock and key at Cirey: people were regularly hanged for less.

As to the particular genre of the *conte en vers*, or verse tale, Voltaire wrote approximately twenty (depending on the criteria of definition). Barely fewer than his prose tales, therefore, but many are relatively short (a hundred lines or less) and only one or two come near them in wit or narrative invention. Broadly speaking they fall into three groups. In the first, dating from the mid-1710s, the libertine *contes en vers* of Jean de La Fontaine (1621–95) are clearly the young poet's model, with their characteristic mix of Graeco-Roman mythology and restrained smut. In *Le Cocuage* (*Cuckoldry*; 1716) we learn that Cuckoldry is the name of a new god. Born of Vulcan, that ugly thunderbolt-forger married to an unpredictable Venus, he is also the only god the young poet can trust. In *Le Cadenas* (*The Padlock*; 1716) we learn how the chastity belt was invented by a jealous Pluto and is currently being employed by the curmudgeonly 60-year-old husband of the poet's would-be mistress to ensure his beautiful young wife's fidelity. But love, the poet assures us, will find a way to unpick the lock.

In its first edition this verse tale included a reference to a certain Monsieur de Rochebrune, the author of popular verse lyrics of uncertain propriety. This was the man that Voltaire claimed to be his real father: the chevalier Guérin de Rochebrune (d. 1719), an impecunious songster of ancient if unexalted aristocratic lineage (rather like the verse tale itself). It is likely that Voltaire met him during his teens, for he is known to have lived in his near neighbourhood in 1707 (and quite possibly for much longer). What is certain is that Voltaire much preferred to proclaim his own filiation to a high-born pop star rather than to the serious, upper-middle-class lawyer and tax official, François Arouet, who was his official father. And this has an important bearing on Voltaire's return to the genre of the verse tale in the winter of 1763–4, shortly before his seventieth birthday.

Ce qui plaît aux dames (*What Pleases the Ladies*) was the first of seven *contes en vers* composed then—and dictated to a secretary, for Voltaire suffered from snow-blindness during the winters spent at Ferney. These verse tales were then published, together with other short works in prose and verse, in a collected volume entitled *Contes de Guillaume Vadé* in 1764. There was no Guillaume Vadé. This was simply one of the many pseudonyms adopted by Voltaire in these years, a practice he adopted partly for fun, partly to offer brief protection to his publishers while yet encouraging a publicity-fostering guessing game, and perhaps partly to persuade a credulous world that the number of 'enlightened' authors was rapidly increasing. But there had been a Jean-Joseph Vadé (1720–57), a highly successful author of scabrous verse and popular comic opera. Before his early death from smallpox he had been especially noted for introducing the so-called 'style poissard' to the Opéra-Comique, that is, an allegedly vulgar 'explicitness' of language, plot, and action. In the view of his detractors he had at once dumbed down and sexed up the domain of comic opera. Formerly the Comédie Italienne (where *commedia dell'arte* had held sway for so long), the Opéra-Comique stood halfway, in terms of literary register, between the Classicism of the Comédie Française (where Voltaire's own plays were performed) and the popular culture of the Foire, or fairground. In adopting the name of Vadé Voltaire was therefore associating himself with anti-establishment irreverence and 'vulgarity', and his principal purpose in so doing was to upset that sector of the Catholic Church known as the Jansenists (see note to p. 54), whom he regarded at best as po-faced killjoys (like his father) and at worst as dangerous and inhumane fanatics (like his elder brother). Both these Jansenist relatives were long dead (in 1722 and 1745 respectively), but the memory remained.

The *Contes de Guillaume Vadé* open with a preface signed by a no-less fictional Catherine Vadé, who purports to be presenting this anthology of her late cousin's work. Voltaire had already used this device in his anonymously published verse satire *Le Pauvre Diable* (*The Poor Devil*) in 1760, when the death of the real Vadé was still fresh in readers' minds. Here in her preface Catherine refers to the seven *contes en vers* as harmless 'tall stories' and relates how Guillaume would entertain his family with them, a family that also numbered his fictional brother Antoine Vadé, and his 'cousin-german', Jérôme Carré, both of whom have also recently died. More broadly the preface sets the tone for the work as a whole: making distinctly anti-Catholic comments about church burial and the significance of baptismal names, debunking literary pretension, and offering mock apologies for the 'unsuitable' content to come.

This content is an apparent hotch-potch. The prose texts range widely in length and subject matter, from a relatively brief (fictional) letter from one Protestant pastor to another, to a concise biography of Molière accompanied by plot summaries of his plays. Verse is represented not only by seven distinctly various *contes* but also by a satire, *Les Chevaux et les ânes* (*Horses and Asses*), in which the poet complains contemptuously about falling intellectual and professional standards in Parisian public life. But certain common themes clearly emerge: religious hypocrisy; the question of education; the increased acceptance of 'enlightened' thought; and dubious trends in the modern world, including especially the bane of seriousness and the need for comedy. Taken as a whole the collection reflects the tensions within the 69-year-old Voltaire: on the one hand, a continuing desire to shock, to rebel, to fight the good anticlerical and anti-establishment fight; on the other, an increasingly conservative hankering after the past and a sense that the modern world, even as it becomes more liberal-minded, has also become duller and distinctly mediocre. Wit, style, and original intelligence seemed to be in short supply. The Jesuits, partly because of their perceived moral laxity and intellectual sophistry, were in the process of being ousted from their central position in French political life, and had recently been stripped of their role as the educators of the French nation. If someone did not come up with an enlightened school syllabus fast, then the Jansenists' eighteenth-century version of 'political correctness' was likely to prevail.

The polemical thrust of the *Contes de Guillaume Vadé* is made most explicit by the inclusion of a 'Discours aux Welches' ('An Address to the "Welches"'), the 'Welches' being Voltaire's latest nickname for his compatriots (and derived from German usage). By 'Welches' he meant 'the enemies of reason and merit, the fanatics, the stupid, the intolerant, the persecutors and the calumniators'; as opposed to the real 'Français', by which he meant 'the *philosophes*, good company, real writers, artists, in fact anyone who is nice'. His agenda is clear. And by 'Welches' he principally meant the Jansenists, the party of earnestness and moral austerity, the enemies of fun. Hence Voltaire's ventriloquial insistence throughout the collection on the delights of both popular and ancient culture (in which the Jansenists found evidence of pagan immorality), and hence the recurrent theme of education—but education of a resolutely unorthodox and irreverent kind. If the 'Welches' were the French who had forgotten how to laugh, Voltaire would draw on a long and venerable European tradition—Boccaccio (1313–75), Chaucer (?1343–1400), Ariosto (1474–1533), Rabelais (?1493–1553)—to remind them of the humanistic virtues of romance narrative and bawdy.

And hence *What Pleases the Ladies*: derived from Chaucer via Dryden, but thereby heir to a whole body of Arthurian legend that centres on the so-called 'loathly lady' tradition. Be it the late four-teenth-century *Sir Gawain and the Green Knight*, which features the unappetizing crone Morgan le Fay and is contemporary with 'The Wife of Bath's Tale', or the thirteenth-century *Roman de la Rose* (itself translated by Chaucer) with its character of La Vieille (The Old Woman), Voltaire's verse tale boasts a proud pedigree. But it also bastardizes its material. King Arthur becomes the Merovingian monarch Dagobert (*c.*603–639), who did much to unite the Frankish kingdom and had become a popular and quasi-mythical figure in French legend and song. Guinevere, for her part, is transformed into Berthe. Dagobert had a number of wives (sometimes simultaneously) with splendid Frankish names: Gomatrude, Nantechilde (or Nanthilde), Ragnetrude, Wulfgunde, Berchilde (or Berthilde). But no Berthe. La Reine Berthe, on the other hand, was also a real historical figure (being Charlemagne's mother) who had become the subject of many legends and proverbs, not least on account of her large feet. Voltaire's, therefore, is a marriage made in myth. The knight errant in the tale remains nameless in both Chaucer and Dryden, but a playful rhyme on Dagobert gives Voltaire his plain and simple 'Messire Jean Robert'. As to the knight's elderly bride, again only Voltaire gives her a name, Urgele, the origins of which remain veiled in mystery.

But there is no mystery about the choice of subject. Already in Chaucer and Dryden the tale begins by lamenting the long-departed days of elves and fairies, banished by exorcizing friars. As Dryden puts it:

> For priests, with prayers, and other godly gear,
> Have made the merry goblins disappear;
> And where they play'd their merry pranks before,
> Have sprinkled holy water on the floor.
> ('The Wife of Bath, her Tale', ll. 25–8)

Compare the end of *What Pleases the Ladies*:

> O happy times of fairy deed,
> Of elves and sprites and stories tall,
> And kindly spirits tending mortal need.
> People heard these marvellous tales, and believed,
> . . .
> And now they've banished spirits, fairies too;
> Reason rules, a story must be true.

Where the medieval tale lamented the vanished fairies themselves, Voltaire now expresses regret that people no longer listen to fairy *stories*. But the cause is still the same: an interfering Church that thinks it has a monopoly on virtue and truth. Hence his own impish embellishment on the idealized Chaucer/Dryden vision of the past:

> People heard these marvellous tales, and they believed,
> Seated round the hearth in every castle hall:
> The chaplain was the teller, and father, mother,
> Friend and daughter, neighbour, brother,
> Listened rapt: for how could interest pall?
> No matter what the fable, it held them in its thrall.

In better days the chaplain (in the original French 'aumônier', or almoner) tolerated fairy stories and realized that there were many ways of communicating God's truth. Just as Voltaire does. His own tale is presented as a fireside entertainment (see ll. 1–10), and he is thus our 'chaplain'. And our good fairy, too, for Sir John's new wife is a skilful storyteller:

> She lent her tales the personal touch,
> With maxim, comment, and opinion much,
> Delighting him even when instructing,

And never once the story's flow obstructing.
She gave her listener food for thought,
Teaching him, though he knew not he was taught. (ll. 297–302)

But what does this verse tale teach us? As so often in Voltaire it is
the medium rather than the message that matters. As far as the
message is concerned, we 'learn' that chivalric values of honour and
gratitude will be rewarded, that qualities of mind and heart count for
more than superficial and ephemeral good looks. We all know, of
course, what pleases the gentlemen, but in time-honoured fashion
the lustful male reader is being cautioned that in a marriage ' 'tis
better woman wise than woman fair' (l. 247). As to what it is that
really pleases the ladies, the modern woman may or may not agree
. . . But what should please all readers of this verse tale is the pastiche of chivalric romance. Already in Chaucer the chivalric code is
called into question by the fact that his anonymous knight is a rapist
('full of youthful fire, | By force accomplished his obscene desire', as
Dryden has it (ll. 56–7)), but Voltaire veils this 'obscenity' in the
playful nonsense of broken eggs (not to mention the fact that the
victim seems more concerned about money than about her virtue).
What he really wants to do is amuse and shock by focusing
unashamedly on the young man's 'chivalric ordeal' of having to make
love to such an old, ugly, dirty, smelly woman. In the end *What
Pleases the Ladies* is a piece of relatively harmless nonsense, a simple
spoof with a few moments of discreet titillation. Above all it presents
itself as an antidote to earnestness.

As do the remaining six *contes en vers* in the *Contes de Guillaume
Vadé*, and also the seven or eight that Voltaire wrote during the last
ten years of his life (1768–78). But between these two groups of
verse tales, he produced a prose tale that ranks almost alongside
Candide as a masterpiece of similar irreverence and pastiche: *The
Ingenu*. Ostensibly 'A True Story taken from the manuscripts of
Father Quesnel', nothing more unlikely could have been found
among the papers of this leading Jansenist theologian (1634–1739).

The Ingenu

It is possible that Pangloss is a caricature not only of Leibniz but also
of Rousseau (1712–78). Pangloss preaches both the natural goodness

of primitive man and the inequity inherent in the unequal distribution of wealth. Together with a somewhat lubricious sexuality, these articles of faith may well have put a reader of *Candide* in mind of Jean-Jacques. In *The Ingenu* (1767) Rousseau is quite definitely at the centre of Voltaire's attention, along with the favourite seventeenth- and eighteenth-century myth of the noble savage.

So too is the question of religious intolerance. This had long been a target of Voltairean vituperation, but since he had established his 'safe house' at Ferney in 1759, Voltaire had embarked on a sustained and vigorous anticlerical campaign for which, in correspondence with the mathematician and thinker D'Alembert, he coined the famous battle-cry: 'Écrasez l'infâme!' (Literally, 'Crush the infamous!' or, less literally, 'An end to vile oppression!' His model was Cato's 'Delenda est Carthago', that is, 'Carthage must be destroyed'.) Part of this campaign centred on his efforts to clear the name of Jean Calas, a Protestant merchant in Toulouse, who had been found guilty and broken on the wheel in 1762 for allegedly murdering his son because the latter wanted to turn Catholic. Thanks to Voltaire, Calas's name was posthumously cleared in 1765. Another *cause célèbre* concerned the Protestant Elizabeth Sirven, a young woman with a history of mental illness who was found dead in a well on 4 January 1762. Orders were given for the arrest of her parents, along with their two remaining daughters that they might witness their parents' execution. The family was tipped off and fled to Switzerland before they could be arrested. Again, thanks to Voltaire, their name was cleared, though not until 1771. Most horrific of all for Voltaire personally perhaps—and there were many other such cases that occupied his attention—was the execution in July 1766 of the young Chevalier de la Barre, a Catholic, who had been found guilty of sacrilege and the blasphemous disregard of a religious procession. Voltaire felt particularly implicated since a copy of his own *Dictionnaire philosophique* had been found among the Chevalier's possessions.

To illustrate his theme Voltaire set *The Ingenu*, the most historically based of his stories, in 1689—that is, four years after the Revocation of the Edict of Nantes, which had ended such tolerance as had been exercised towards the Protestant, or Huguenot, minority since 1598. At this period Jesuits like Père La Chaise enjoyed considerable power and influence (as, of course, did the other real historical figures who appear in the story, such as his assistant, Friar Vadbled, or

Louvois, the Minister for War, Saint-Pouange his deputy, and Alexandre, one of his senior officials): while the Jansenists would some years later suffer the persecution which Voltaire here, with some historical licence, depicts. At the time when *The Ingenu* was written, however, the Society of Jesus had just been expelled from France (in 1764) and the Jansenists were in the ascendant. Positions were reversed, but the intolerance remained.

In *The Ingenu* the portrait of religious persecution (and of religious superstition and ineptitude as manifested in Lower Brittany, that traditional French equivalent of Rutland or Hicksville) serves as a foil to the ideals of humanity and civilization which Voltaire illustrates in the character and experiences of his protagonists. As in *Candide*, education is all. Indeed it is because so many of the characters undergo some kind of development, or even metamorphosis, that this story comes closest among all Voltaire's stories to being a novel.

Where previously Voltaire had borrowed the established formats of interplanetary and Utopian travel, the Oriental tale, and chivalric romance, and given them each an original and ironic twist, here he takes the myth of the noble savage which dates back at least as far as Gabriel Sagard Théodat's *Grand Voyage au pays des Hurons* (*Great Journey to the Land of the Hurons*) of 1632. For those either jaded with or morally repelled by the sophisticated 'civilization' of the age, the North American Indian represented dignified humanity in its original, untainted form. The noble savage was a child of nature, a free spirit able to roam the plains of God's Creation, untrammelled by authority or convention. It was a nice idea, particularly if you wanted to highlight the corruption and hidebound artificiality of your own society. But it was not exactly a faithful representation of the facts, as Voltaire doubtless knew already in 1725 when he interviewed four savages who had been brought all the way from Mississippi to the court at Fontainebleau and asked one female savage what it was like to eat human flesh.

The twist in *The Ingenu*, of course, is that the savage in this case may actually be a Frenchman who has been spared the mind-warping obfuscations of a French education. Like Candide he is a naive, not to say militantly literal-minded, observer of 'civilization' and religion, and he exposes their absurdities, inconsistencies, and inequities with rugged determination. Yet for all his natural, noble, good sense, he is a savage, and his instinctive reactions, be they of a libidinous or bellicose kind, do not always persuade of the merits of absolute spontaneity. As the Abbé de Saint-Yves says: 'without the conventions established between men the laws of nature would scarcely amount to much more than natural skulduggery'. After further discussion the Ingenu accepts the point, thus siding with Voltaire (and Hobbes) against Rousseau's view that man is naturally good.

Hurons are said, like Pangloss the philosopher, never to change their minds. But Hercules de Kerkabon has fluff on his chin and is therefore educable. After a course in geometry, metaphysics, history both ancient and modern, and classical tragedy, the Ingenu outstrips his Jansenist tutor and even educates him. Like Zadig before him, 'whom nature had endowed with a fine disposition on which education had improved', the Ingenu is the Enlightenment hero *par excellence*. As he puts it himself: 'I have been changed from a brute into a man': which is Voltaire's answer to Rousseau's notorious (and generally misinterpreted) statement in the *Discourse on Inequality* that 'the man who meditates is a depraved animal'. Indeed in many ways *The Ingenu* is an answer to the pedagogical theories which Rousseau had recently expressed in *Émile* (1762).

While the Ingenu is undergoing his intellectual metamorphosis, his beloved Saint-Yves is developing emotionally, and by the time she has paid her appalling price for the release of the Ingenu, 'sentiment had developed as far in her as reason had in the mind of her unfortunate lover': 'She was no longer that simple girl whose mind had been narrowed by a provincial education. Love and misfortune had moulded her.' Here we see one of the important lessons of *The Ingenu*, as well as one of the commonest themes in eighteenth-century literature. True humanity and 'civilization' depend not only on reason but on sensibility. This is the lesson which the Ingenu teaches Gordon in prison, and it is a lesson which the Ingenu re-learns by experience at the end of the story. His soul is fired in the kiln of Saint-Yves's tragic death, and he emerges, glazed and polished, ready to be an ornament to French society as both expert on war and intrepid philosopher. And most of the other characters, with the exception of the magistrate and his son, undergo some kind of transformation which improves them materially, and in some cases morally: 'It is an ill wind that blows nobody any good.'

But this cliché, following on so quickly at the end of the story after the one about time being a great healer, suggests ambivalence on Voltaire's part. *The Ingenu* goes further than *Candide* with the idea that evil may be educative and suggests, in an almost Christian manner, that evil may ennoble man by testing his reason and tempering his sentiment. But the abrupt way in which the Ingenu's reaction to Saint-Yves's death is passed over and the rather perfunctory form of 'prize-giving' in respect of the secondary characters culminate in the deflation of Voltaire's parting shot: 'An ill wind blows nobody any good.' So human suffering may not be so beneficial after all.

But in literature it can be. *The Ingenu* is about the education 'of hearts and minds', that phrase which Voltaire so frequently mocks in his stories. This particular cliché had considerable currency during the eighteenth century, but Voltaire is thinking specifically of its use in the title of a book on how to study literature or, more especially, on how to use literature as an instrument of moral improvement. This book was the *Traité des études* (*Treatise on Study*) by the historian and Jansenist pedagogue Charles Rollin (1661–1741), published in 1726–8, and of which the full title was *Of the manner of studying and teaching belles-lettres in relation to the heart and the mind*. Voltaire doubtless hated the cliché *qua* cliché, but he also despised the suborning of literary masterpieces for the inculcation of a pious and simplistic morality, no less indeed than he scorned the banal use of fable, apologue, or so-called 'moral tale' (the *conte moral* that was so popular in the 1750s and 1760s) to a similar end.

Voltaire's own aims are also, of course, didactic, but his didacticism is of a more subtle kind. In this he is to be compared with the fairy Urgele in *What Pleases the Ladies*: 'She gave her listener food for thought, | Teaching him, though he knew not he was taught.' *The Ingenu* describes the education of the hearts and minds of Hercules de Kerkabon, Mlle de Saint-Yves, and Gordon, but it also imparts its wisdom by working on the intellectual and emotional reactions of the reader too. Broadly speaking, the story falls into two halves: the first half being a laughter-provoking, satirical juxtaposition of common sense and religious practice, while the second is a tear-inducing, tragic account of noble self-sacrifice. In the first, Voltaire uses his familiar techniques of caricature and *reductio ad absurdum*, while the second includes many explicit comparisons with the presentation of theatrical scenes as well as repeated reference to the emotions of pity and fear which are at the centre of the Aristotelian and neoclassical definition of tragedy. As the Ingenu is moved by the plays of Racine, so we are having our heartstrings tugged by the man who wrote some twenty-seven tragedies (from *Œdipe* in 1718 to the posthumous *Agathocle* of 1779) and whose plays were performed at the Comédie Française more times throughout the eighteenth century than those of either Racine or Corneille (and in England more often than those of Shakespeare).

But whereas the Aristotelian theory attributes a cathartic, or purgative, function to tragic pathos, it is in fact the comedy of the first half (and of the whole of *Candide*) which may be said to purge our emotions (of anger, bewilderment, and despair at the presence of evil), while the pathos of the second half may arouse and ignite protest against the absurdity and inhumanity of certain religious proscriptions and against the cruel abuse of ecclesiastical and ministerial power that characterizes the court at Versailles.

The Ingenu may teach us the value of education, of 'growing up', of civilization (even the villainous Saint-Pouange is transformed by his experience into a penitent sinner bent on making reparation); but it also preserves and stimulates our capacity for outrage. In *Candide* evil is constantly being put down to experience so that, for all the final emphasis on active cultivation, the story may leave a residual sense of passive acceptance. That is how things are, and we must make the best of this only possible world. But *The Ingenu*, for all its final emphasis on the way in which its hero has reached an accommodation with life and society, remains a powerful indictment of the abuse of office and draws a clear line between one kind of accommodation and another. Controlling your emotions and looking before you leap (the Huron enters the story, of course, by leaping before he looks) is one way of being civilized: having to sleep with a government minister as the only means of redressing injustice is quite another. In the view of the nineteenth-century novelist Stendhal (1783–1842), theatre audiences and readers are more readily moved to tears if first they have been made to laugh. Exactly this happens in *The Ingenu*: satire gives way to pathos, and a pathos that turns us against the unacceptable face of so-called 'civilization'.

But Voltaire cautions us against pathos, too. The eighteenth century was as much the Age of Sensibility as it was the Age of Reason, and by the 1760s it had become—in Voltaire's eyes at least—an Age

of Sentimentality. Despite his reputation in some quarters as a heart-
less cynic, Voltaire was a deeply emotional man, but he despised all
heart-on-sleeve displays of emotion as ill-bred and unintelligent.
Indeed both these facts account in part for his very deep love of the
theatre. He was never happier than when acting with friends at home
in one of his own tragedies, and often he would reduce himself to
tears as he performed some of his poignant set-piece speeches. For
the theatre legitimized what was otherwise unacceptable within
polite and civilized social intercourse.

He was particularly irritated by the combination of excessive sentiment with an extravagant display of virtue, and the sentimental
novel of the mid-eighteenth century was thus a favourite bugbear.
One such was Samuel Richardson's best-selling *Clarissa* (7 vols.,
1747–8; translated into French by the Abbé Prévost in 1751), in
which the virtuous heroine, having been raped by her immoderate
aristocratic suitor, Robert Lovelace, dies—at very considerable
length—of shame. Similarly the heroine of Jean-Jacques Rousseau's
long novel *Julie ou la nouvelle Héloïse* (1761), having 'fallen', becomes
a model of virtue and dies a noble self-sacrificial death. In Voltaire's
view this type of moral example was pernicious in that it helped
foster a wholly unrealistic and ultimately incapacitating conception
of 'goodness'. Thus in *The Ingenu*, where the vocabulary of the
sentimental novel is much in evidence, Mlle de Saint-Yves's death is
pointedly unidealized: 'Let others seek to praise the ostentatious
death of those who enter destruction with impassivity. That is the
fate of animals' (Ch. 20). Instead the heroine 'felt the full horror of
her situation, and communicated it in dying words and glances that
speak with so much authority'. Accordingly the modern reader may
find Mlle de Saint-Yves's passing all the more convincing.

But need she have died? In sacrificing her 'virtue' to save the man
she loves, she has in fact been more virtuous than the 'virtuous'. And
yet she herself, partly because of the novels she has read during her
convent incarceration (like an eighteenth-century Emma Bovary), is
convinced that she is irredeemably worthless. Such a reaction, while
authentically moving, is nevertheless also gently ironized. 'I, your
wife!' she exclaims to the Ingenu: 'Ah, my dear love, that word, that
happiness, that prize, they were not for me. I am dying and I deserve
to. O God of my heart! O you whom I have sacrificed to infernal
demons, it is all over. I have been punished. Live and be happy.' As

the narrator observes: 'These tender, terrible words made no sense.' For all that Mlle de Saint-Yves has undergone the education of experience, her mind remains tragically blinkered by an absurdly literal-minded ethics that equates sexual intercourse and sin. In Voltaire's view, Richardson, Rousseau, and of course the despicable Jansenists with their dire and unforgiving view of man's sinfulness are all in their way responsible for the death of this most altruistic and pragmatic heroine. And that indeed should make us cry.

The White Bull

Quite how a story affects its reader is a question which is very much at the centre of *The White Bull*, one of Voltaire's last stories and written when he was approaching the age of eighty. (He lived till he was 84, at a time when life expectancy was about half that. Given that he very nearly died of smallpox when he was 29, and that he suffered ill health for most of his life, one does indeed begin to wonder at the ways of Providence.) Published in three instalments in Grimm's manuscript periodical, the *Correspondance littéraire*, in November and December 1773 and January 1774, *The White Bull* is superficially an entertaining send-up of the Old Testament. It contains within one story many of the jokes and biblical absurdities which had studded Voltaire's anticlerical writing (and conversation too, no doubt) for more than half a century, and combines them in a *faux naïf* story of a young Princess's forbidden love for Nebuchadnezzar during the period in which the latter had the misfortune to be turned into a bull. As an Oriental tale devoted to the Bible it is unique not only among Voltaire's stories but also among all eighteenth-century Oriental tales.

By the time the story was written, the anticlerical campaign of Voltaire and the younger generations of deists and atheists had succeeded to the point where the Old Testament was hardly a very daunting target any more. Nevertheless the polemical thrust is as subtle and unlaboured as ever. The authority of the Old Testament as an historical document is implicitly rejected by the presentation of many of its more famous and often miraculous moments as mere fables, akin to the metamorphoses of Ovid. Hence the concentration on animals and, the white bull apart, on animals that speak (not to mention animals that don't eat prophets). On several occasions in his works, most notably in another of his stories, *The Princess of Baby-lon*, Voltaire fancifully supposes an original, prelapsarian world in which animals could speak—in other words a world where fables would have constituted an accurate depiction of reality. Such a world is Voltaire's own fabulous version of a primitive pre-Enlightenment era where all sorts of superstitious nonsense were believed. In *The White Bull* this world is Egypt, and once again Voltaire draws on a whole tradition of more or less implausible fiction (about the 'wise Egyptian' this time, rather than the noble savage or the Utopian traveller or the Oriental potentate, etc.) and creates a marvellous realm of idiotic credulity as a backdrop to the triumph of reason.

One of the many delights Voltaire must have had in writing *The White Bull* was the inclusion of two tongue-in-cheek self-portraits in the guise of the old prophet Mambres and of the serpent himself. There is Mambres, coming up to his thirteen-hundredth birthday, a bit slow on the uptake now but still a wily and cogitative old bird once he gets going. With all the wisdom of his many years he exploits and manipulates the religious beliefs of King Amasis and the people of Tanis to his own ends. In one way, of course, he acts no differently from the Jesuit confessors in *The Ingenu*, using a position of religious and political authority for personal ambition. But, as with Voltaire, Mambres's ambition is a humanitarian one, and in this respect he provides a portrait of Voltaire, the Patriarch of Ferney, saving the victims of 'l'infâme' from execution by manipulating public opinion and outwitting a corrupt and intolerant judiciary in its own law courts (the 'parlements').

In his undertaking Mambres relies on his friend the serpent and on the latter's talent for storytelling. Like Mambres, the serpent too seems to be a little over the hill, but appearances may be deceptive. In Amasida he has a very demanding audience. She has read the philosophy of Locke and the fables of La Fontaine: not for her, therefore, the various amorous exploits related in the Old Testament. They may have done for her distant ancestors, but her own requirements are more exacting: 'I require a story to be essentially plausible, and not always sounding like the account of a dream [even Nebuchadnezzar's, presumably]. I prefer it to be neither trivial nor far-fetched. I particularly like the ones which, from beneath the veil of the plot, reveal to the experienced eye some subtle truth that will escape the common herd.' 'That's rather a tall order,' replies the serpent, but she insists. 'Tell me a fable that is perfectly true and well attested, one that really is moral, and that I haven't heard before, one "to complete the education of my heart and mind", as our Egyptian pedagogue Linro would say.'

Voltaire's own story obeys this prescription, for beneath the veil of biblical absurdity and the pretty tale of Amasida's love for Nebuchadnezzar may be seen both a warning to all despots and a word of commendation for Louis XV. The biblical Nebuchadnezzar dreamt of being turned into an ox, and in the event he was driven out of Babylon into the wilderness for seven years as a punishment for his abuse of power. He should have heeded Daniel's advice: 'Wherefore, O king, let my counsel be acceptable unto thee, and break off thy sins by righteousness, and thine iniquities by shewing mercy to the poor; if it may be a lengthening of thy tranquillity' (Daniel 4: 27). Perhaps, for their own sakes, the ageing Louis XV (who died on 10 May 1774) and, more especially, his successor Louis XVI might have done well to heed the hidden message of *The White Bull*. The French Revolution was only just over fifteen years away when it was first published, and the story's thematic insistence on cutting people's heads off looks what in the circumstances can only be called prophetic.

Not that Voltaire was anti-royalist. On the contrary, he felt that a strong monarchy was crucial if social order was to be preserved in the face of what he saw, with the conservatism of old age, as mounting anarchy. The latter he saw especially in the ever-increasing power of the 'parlements', which Louis XV himself had sought to curb by his famous harangue against the 'parlement' of Paris at the so-called *séance de flagellation* on 3 March 1766 and by the appointment of Maupeou as Chancellor in September 1768. With royal support Maupeou set about reducing the powers of the magistrature (one of whose representatives Voltaire had caricatured in *The Ingenu* in the character of the compulsively cross-questioning bailiff); and by the time *The White Bull* was written, Voltaire may well have felt that Louis XV deserved a pat on the back for trying to reassert his control over his kingdom: 'Long live our great King who is no longer dumb!' Indeed it was roughly seven years since the Breton 'parlement' (in 1764) supported a move not to levy the royal tax known as the *corvée* and thus precipitated open conflict between the magistrates and the crown which was to lead to the attempts by Louis XV and Maupeou to reassert control.

But what of the serpent's own storytelling? Does it also fulfil Amasida's requirements? Only too effectively. After her first admonishment he lulls her into a false sense of security by telling her the story of King Gnaof and Queen Patra. His narrative ploy (to get her to ask him what the priest whispered in the Queen's ear) is so blatant that she 'can guess what's coming'. After her second objection he undertakes to tell her a fable than which, he says, 'there's none more authentic'. The story of the three prophets, with its traditional and relatively unveiled message that one should be content with one's lot, lulls her still further by its seeming irrelevance to her own position; so much so that she drops her guard and is beguiled into uttering the forbidden name of Nebuchadnezzar. For its devilish narrator, the veiled point of his 'authentic' story lies less in its content than in its effect. By manipulation of his listener's vicarious interest in the sex life of a king and by exploiting her readiness to interrupt his narrative (about which this most gentlemanly serpent has warned her), he induces her to break a taboo and to speak the unspeakable. The serpent thus precipitates the crisis which wise Mambres had sought to forestall and which only the ageing prophet's superior foresight will in the end resolve to the benefit of his loose-tongued ward. Never let your daughter read fiction; and never let your subjects, or your congregation, read Voltaire. It is the work of the devil.

Tales of a Serpent

Like the serpent's fable in *The White Bull*, all Voltaire's stories are an onslaught on taboo, and not least the taboo that theological, metaphysical, scientific, moral, political, and aesthetic debate must be conducted with earnest reverence in dry-as-dust language that only the initiated can understand. For Voltaire, supper-party conversation was the epitome of civilized human intercourse, and the anecdote its principal ingredient. He himself was a brilliant raconteur, and narrative verve is to be found throughout his work, especially in his historical works but also in more supposedly abstract or analytical writings. At Cirey with Mme du Châtelet a magic lantern had been purchased and, by way of after-dinner entertainment, Voltaire would improvise stories to accompany the projected images: hence, perhaps, the episodic and cumulative manner of his written stories,

Hence, too, their similarity to the modern comic strip; and, in particular, it may not be too fanciful to see certain parallels with the adventures of Asterix, notably the clash of highbrow allusions and lowbrow Gallic humour, and the recurrent trading on national and professional stereotypes (the Celt with his mistletoe, the glum Briton, the arrogant Teuton, the proud and multinominal Iberian, the doctor who's bad for your health, etc.).

For Voltaire the *conte philosophique*, or philosophical story, was an invaluable and effective weapon in his long campaign against bigotry and intolerance and in favour of open-minded enquiry and debate. In his hands it is a kind of fallen fable: where the fable of old appealed to a childlike credulity and fostered the passive acceptance of incontrovertible moral truths, his modern fable is like an apple plucked from the Tree of Knowledge and handed to us by the Serpent himself that we should 'gorge' ourselves (as he advises Eve in *The White Bull*) and feel the nakedness of our prejudice. We should eat, question, and consider.

For the polemicist the *conte* offers many advantages. It is short; and so, as Edgar Allan Poe later put it when defining the tale in his review of Nathaniel Hawthorne's *Twice-Told Tales*, 'avail[s] itself of the immense benefit of *totality* . . . During the hour of perusal the soul of the reader is at the writer's control.' The *conte* is easily digested; it sells well; and, mere story or tale that it is, its advertisement of its own fictionality may deceive the censor. It is essentially 'of the people', since it stems from a long oral folk tradition: it is neither the product nor the slave of the Academy with all its classical rules. It is unpretentious; and the use of such a low form as a medium by and for those with a supposedly higher education serves a dual purpose. It punctures academic self-importance, while it democratizes thought and asserts that these 'higher' issues concern human beings of all rank and condition everywhere. It subverts the idea of an intellectual and cultural hierarchy: it pokes fun at the 'big names' from Aristotle to Zoroaster, and it debunks the claims of traditional fiction. It shows that the worlds of chivalric romance and the Oriental tale are even further removed from reality than its own absurd Punch and Judy world with its only too visible puppeteer. (Note how, as in Hitchcock's films, the director likes to make a guest appearance: not only as Mambres and the serpent but also, for example in *Candide*, as the retired courtier in Eldorado, or the dervish and the kindly old man both living near Constantinople (i.e. Geneva).)

The Voltairean tale is the more real for being unreal. It defamiliarizes the familiar, renders the world and its inhabitants strange, ready to be seen and judged afresh. We are offered succeeding images of the human condition, as it were from both ends of a microscope, which alternately enlarges and reduces the specimens and behaviour under observation. More specifically, the enlargement comes from exaggeration and accumulation (as of the nature and quantity of evil in *Candide*), and the reduction from understatement and brevity (as in the old woman's story in *Candide*). It stimulates an adjustment of focus (provided we are not, like the obtuse Pangloss, blind in one eye) by incongruous juxtaposition and combination (as with Pangloss's genealogy of syphilis). Indeed the very use of the *conte* to debate and illustrate major philosophical and religious questions is an instance of this. By presenting these grander issues (such as the nature of Providence, the problem of evil, and the pursuit of happiness) via a medium more usually associated with entertainment, Voltaire makes us cast aside our usual mental perspectives on them and see them in a new light.

The choice of the *conte* as a polemical and didactic instrument thus corresponds to the use of the alien visitor and naive observer as central protagonists. The *conte* refuses to assume anything in advance: it casts aside earnestness and solemn preoccupation and looks at the facts. At the same time, in presenting the facts, it demonstrates that at every turn these major issues are always at stake. In this way it breaks down the barrier between philosophical abstraction and ratiocination on the one hand, and mere banal, day-to-day living on the other. Thus it prods the complacent non-thinker as much as it mocks the one-track mind of the bigot.

Above all, Voltaire's *contes* demonstrate that *systems* are an unwarranted and unsustainable imposition of false order on the facts of life. The certainty of earthly mathematicians that they have taken the measure of things, Zadig's automatic equation of virtue and happiness, Pangloss's Optimism and Martin's Manichaeanism, even the Ingenu's systematic spontaneity, are all subjected to the test of experience and found wanting. Each of these stories traces a coming to terms: with human ignorance (of God's mysterious ways), with bad luck (or is it destiny?), with other people, with oneself. They tend to depict an accommodation with reality, a movement from system to sagacity, from being philosophical in the sense of being abstract and unemotionally logical to being philosophical in the sense of being knocked about by life. Above all, they proclaim humanity; and they offer the reader, if not catharsis, at least a kind of therapy.

Voltaire's storytelling is not, therefore, the imparting of an abstract message or moral in a more or less palatable form, his fictions not simply the sugar-coating on a bitter philosophical pill. Horace wrote famously that 'he has succeeded who has mixed the useful with the pleasing, by delighting the reader at the same time as instructing him'. Voltaire's stories mix education and entertainment to the point where they are indistinguishable. The old-style fable was supposed to, but animals that speak are not quite the thing for a modern. Thanks to the special mix of Voltaire's 'fallen' fables, ideas may be instructive but they may also just as often be a source of fun, even those Voltaire approves of. Likewise, the element of adventure in a story may afford delight, but it is just as often the repository of a more subtle and compelling idea. More especially it may, like the philosophical dialogues which were so popular in the eighteenth century, permit the writer to leave a question open. Fiction, in this way, may sometimes be truer than logic. Equally, the story may have an emotional effect which is at once pleasurable (laughter and tears) and useful (the therapeutic function): laughter is an antidote to the poison of evil. The story civilizes us, knocks us about, turns us from brutes into men: it effects a metamorphosis. And so, as the Ingenu says: 'Ah, if we must have fables, let them at least be the emblems of truth! I love philosophers' fables, and I laugh at children's. I hate those of charlatans.' What Voltaire the serpent has given us are the authentic fables of reason.

TRANSLATOR'S NOTE AND ACKNOWLEDGEMENTS

THE translations of the prose stories in this edition are based on the text of Voltaire, *Romans et contes*, edited by Frédéric Deloffre and Jacques Van den Heuvel in the Bibliothèque de la Pléiade series (2 vols., Paris: Gallimard, 1979). The translation of the verse tale *Ce qui plaît aux dames* (*What Pleases the Ladies*) is based on the text of Voltaire, *Contes en vers et en prose*, edited by Sylvain Menant (2 vols., Paris: Bordas [Classiques Garnier], 1992). I would like to acknowledge my debt to the scholarship of these three editors, as well as to that of Giles Barber, W. H. Barber, Theodore Besterman, J. H. Brumfitt, Nicholas Cronk, M. I. Gerard Davies, Haydn Mason, Christiane Mervaud, and René Pomeau.

In translating the prose tales I have tried to remain faithful to the letter and spirit of the originals. My versions are intended to be fluently accessible to the modern reader, avoiding obtrusive anachronism (whether in relation to the original or to the current state of the English language) while yet retaining some flavour of writing that originated in a different century and in a foreign country. In translating the verse tale I have followed Voltaire's varied rhyme scheme and converted Voltaire's decasyllabic metre into lines with four stresses. I have imitated the discretion with which he pastiches the linguistic usage of medieval epic and romance, and I have hoped to recreate his knowing blend of the solemn and the naughty.

SELECT BIBLIOGRAPHY

Editions

As well as the standard French editions mentioned in the Translator's Note (see above), also recommended is *Romans et contes en vers et en prose*, ed. Édouard Guitton (Paris: Librairie Générale Française [La Pochotèque, Le Livre de Poche], 1994). See also *Les Œuvres complètes de Voltaire. The Complete Works of Voltaire*, ed. Theodore Besterman, W. H. Barber, Ulla Kölving, Haydn Mason, and Nicholas Cronk (Geneva: Voltaire Foundation, 1968–   ): especially vol. xlviii (1980): *Candide* (ed. René Pomeau).

Informative English-language editions of the French texts include:

Candide, ed. J. H. Brumfitt (Oxford: Oxford University Press [Clarendon French Series], 1968).

Candide, ed. Haydn Mason (Bristol: Bristol Classical Press, 1995).

'L'Ingénu' and 'Histoire de Jenni', ed. J. H. Brumfitt and M. I. Gerard Davies (Oxford: Blackwell, 1960; reissued London: Bristol Classical Press, 1992).

Zadig and Other Stories, ed. H. T. Mason (Oxford: Oxford University Press [Clarendon French Series], 1971).

Further reading of Voltaire in translation:

Micromégas and Other Short Fictions, trans. Theo Cuffe, ed. Haydn Mason (London: Penguin [Penguin Classics], 2002).

Philosophical Dictionary, ed. Theodore Besterman (Harmondsworth: Penguin [Penguin Classics], 1972; reissued 2004).

Political Writings, ed. David Williams (Cambridge: Cambridge University Press, 1994).

The Selected Letters of Voltaire, ed. Richard A. Brook (New York: New York University Press, 1973).

Treatise on Tolerance, trans. Brian Masters, ed. Simon Harvey (Cambridge: Cambridge University Press, 2000).

Voltaire: Selections, ed. Paul Edwards (New York: Macmillan, 1989).

Biographies in English

The most recent and comprehensive biography is Roger Pearson, *Voltaire Almighty: A Life in Pursuit of Freedom* (London: Bloomsbury, 2005).

Earlier biographies include:

Ayer, A. J., *Voltaire* (London: Faber, 1988).

Besterman, Theodore, *Voltaire* (3rd edn., Oxford: Blackwell, 1976).

Davidson, Ian, *Voltaire in Exile: The Last Years, 1753–78* (London: Atlantic Books, 2004).

Hearsey, John E. N., *Voltaire* (London: Constable, 1976).

Mason, Haydn, *Voltaire: A Biography* (London: Elek, 1981).

Mitford, Nancy, *Voltaire in Love* (London: Hamish Hamilton, 1957).

Morley, John, *Voltaire* (London: Macmillan, 1885).

Tallentyre, S. G. (pseudonym of Evelyn Beatrice Hall), *The Life of Voltaire*, 2 vols. (London: Smith, Elder & Co., 1903).

Critical Studies in English

Barber, W. H., *'Candide'* (London: Edwin Arnold, 1960).

Bottiglia, W. F., *Voltaire's 'Candide': Analysis of a Classic* (2nd edn., Geneva: Institut et Musée Voltaire, 1964).

Brumfitt, J. H., *Voltaire Historian* (Oxford: Oxford University Press, 1958; reissued with new preface, 1970).

Clouston, John S., *Voltaire's Binary Masterpiece: 'L'Ingénu' Reconsidered* (Berne: Peter Lang, 1986).

Gay, Peter, *Voltaire's Politics: The Poet as Realist* (2nd edn., New Haven: Yale University Press, 1988).

Howells, Robin, *Disabled Powers: A Reading of Voltaire's Contes* (Amsterdam: Rodopi, 1993).

Mason, Haydn, *Voltaire* (London: Hutchinson, 1975).

—— *'Candide': Optimism Demolished* (New York: Twayne, 1992).

Nablow, Ralph Arthur, *A Study of Voltaire's Lighter Verse*, published as vol. 126 of *Studies on Voltaire and the Eighteenth Century*, ed. Theodore Besterman (Banbury: Voltaire Foundation, 1974).

Pearson, Roger, *The Fables of Reason: A Study of Voltaire's 'Contes philosophiques'* (Oxford: Clarendon Press, 1993).

Sherman, Carol, *Reading Voltaire's 'Contes': A Semiotics of Philosophical Narration* (Chapel Hill, NC: University of North Carolina, 1985).

Wade, I. O., *The Intellectual Development of Voltaire* (Princeton: Princeton University Press, 1969).

—— *Voltaire's 'Micromégas'* (Princeton: Princeton University Press, 1950).

Williams, David, *Voltaire, 'Candide'* (London: Grant and Cutler, 1997).

Some Background Reading

Gay, Peter, *The Enlightenment: An Interpretation*, 2 vols. (New York: Vintage, 1966–9).

Jones, Colin, *The Great Nation: France from Louis XV to Napoleon* (London: Penguin, 2002; paperback, 2003).

Porter, Roy, *The Enlightenment* (2nd edn., London: Palgrove, 2001).

Roche, Daniel, *France in the Enlightenment* [trans. from French: *La France des Lumières* (1993)] (Cambridge, Mass: Harvard University Press, 1998; paperback, 2000).

Further Reading in Oxford World's Classics

Johnson, Samuel, *The History of Rasselas*, ed. J. P. Hardy.

Rousseau, Jean-Jacques, *Confessions*, trans. Angela Scholar, ed. Patrick Coleman.

Swift, Jonathan, *Gulliver's Travels*, ed. Claude Rawson and Ian Higgins.

Voltaire, *Letters concerning the English Nation*, ed. Nicholas Cronk.

A CHRONOLOGY OF VOLTAIRE

1694   21 Nov.: officially born as François-Marie Arouet in Paris, the second (surviving) son of a successful notary and tax official. Unofficially Voltaire himself claimed to have been born nine months earlier, on 20 February, the illegitimate son of the chevalier Guérin de Rochebrune (or Roquebrune), a writer of popular songs and scion of an ancient, aristocratic family from the Haute Auvergne. It is possible that he used his unofficial 65th birthday (20 Feb. 1759) as the secretly agreed date for the simultaneous publication of *Candide* throughout Europe.

1701   13 July: death of Voltaire's mother.

1704–11   Educated at the Jesuit college of Louis-le-Grand, the Eton of its day.

1712   Becomes a law student, but spends most of his time writing and mixing in smart, libertine company.

1713   Packed off first to Caen and then to a position in the French embassy in Holland. Brought home swiftly when on the point of eloping with his Protestant first love, Olympe Dunoyer, known as Pimpette.

1715   1 Sept.: death of Louis XIV.

1716   May–Oct.: exiled from Paris to Sully-sur-Loire, suspected of having written a satire against the Regent, Philippe d'Orléans.

1717   16/17 May: arrested and imprisoned without trial in the Bastille on account of a further political satire.

1718   Apr.: released and banished for six months to Chatenay, near Sceaux, about six miles from Paris. June: adopts nearly anagrammatic pseudonym of Voltaire. 18 Nov.: his first tragedy, and first major work, *Œdipe*, is staged and is a great and immediate success. The Regent gives him a gold medal and a pension; George I sends a gold medal and a watch.

1718–26   A period of successful financial speculation, social prestige, and literary productiveness: *La Henriade* (1723), an epic poem about Henry IV (1553–1610) on the theme of religious intolerance, is regarded as a masterpiece and establishes his reputation once and for all. Nov. 1723: almost dies of smallpox and saved only, as he commented, by drinking two hundred pints of lemonade.

1726 After responding in kind to a slur on his origins from the worthless but aristocratic Chevalier de Rohan, is beaten up by the latter's servants as the Chevalier watches from a carriage. Subsequently threatens a duel (supposedly an impertinence on the part of a bourgeois). 17/18 Apr.: the Rohan family have him thrown into the Bastille. May: goes into exile in England.

1726–8 Exile in England. Discovers the work of Isaac Newton. Mixes with Bolingbroke, Pope, and Swift.

1729–33 Literary activity in Paris, including further tragedies and his first attempt at writing history (the *Histoire de Charles XII*, 1731).

1733 Publishes his *Letters concerning the English Nation* in London.

1734 His French version of the *Letters* (with the addition of a letter on Pascal) published in Paris as the *Lettres philosophiques*. These are condemned and burnt by the Parlement of Paris. Voltaire leaves the capital to live in a *ménage à trois* with his mistress Mme du Châtelet at her home at Cirey.

1734–43 A period of happiness with Mme du Châtelet, as well as considerable philosophical and literary activity (beginning with the *Traité de métaphysique* written in 1734). Aug. 1736: receives his first letter from Frederick of Prussia. June 1739: sends Frederick of Prussia the *Voyage du baron de Gangan*, a first version of *Micromégas*.

1743 Begins to enjoy a brief period of favour at court, with the support of Mme de Pompadour and despite Louis XV's distrust. Elected a Fellow of the Royal Society in London.

1745 Appointed Historiographer to the King at Versailles.

1746 25 Apr.: elected to the Académie Française.

1747 A first version of *Zadig* published under the title *Memnon*, this being the first of his stories to appear in print.

1748 Sept.: *Zadig* published. Also *The Way Things Are* (*Le Monde comme il va*).

1749 10 Sept.: death of Mme du Châtelet of puerperal fever following the birth of a daughter, who also died after a few days. The father was the soldier and poet Jean-François de Saint-Lambert (1716–1803).

1750 June: departure for the court of Frederick of Prussia.

1752 *Micromégas* published.

1753 March: leaves Frederick's court after relations between the two become impossible. Illegally detained in Frankfurt by Frederick's men. Takes up temporary residence in Colmar.

1755   Settles at Les Délices on the outskirts of Geneva. 1 Nov.: the Lisbon earthquake, of which news reaches him before 24 Nov.

1756   Publishes the *Poème sur le désastre de Lisbonne*; and the first complete official text of his world history, the *Essai sur les mœurs* (*Essay on the Manners and Spirit of Nations*), which was to be reprinted sixteen times in the next thirty years.

1759   Jan.–Feb.: publication of *Candide*. Moves into the chateau at Ferney near Geneva, where he lived for the remainder of his life. He refurbishes the chapel and adorns its façade with the inscription: 'Deo erexit Voltaire' ('a fine word between two great names', as a waggish poet, the abbé Delille, later remarked)— the chapel being thus dedicated to God, rather than to a saint, and having a figure of Christ over the altar but not a crucifix. He arranged that his own tomb should lie half in and half out of the chapel.

1762   Beginning of the campaign to rehabilitate Calas (see Introduction, p. xxxi), and later other victims of religious intolerance.

1764   First edition of his *Dictionnaire philosophique*.

1767   Publication of *L'Ingénu*.

1773–4 Publication of *Le Taureau blanc* (*The White Bull*).

1774   10 May: death of Louis XV.

1778   Returns to Paris for the production of his penultimate tragedy *Irène* and is acclaimed and fêted by the whole capital. It is all too much: he dies on 30 May. To avoid the indignity of his being refused a decent burial by Parisian church authorities, his body is smuggled out of the capital at dead of night and later buried at Scellières in Champagne. His remains are subsequently transferred to the Panthéon in Paris on 11 July 1791.

CANDIDE
AND OTHER STORIES

CANDIDE
or
Optimism

Translated from the German of Dr Ralph

Together with the addenda which were found in the Doctor's
pocket when he died at Minden in the year of grace 1759*

CHAPTER 1

*How Candide was brought up in a beautiful castle, and how he was
kicked out of the same*

ONCE upon a time in Westphalia, in the castle of Baron Thunder-ten-
tronckh, there lived a young boy whom nature had endowed with the
gentlest of dispositions. His soul was written upon his countenance.
He was quite sound in his judgement, and he had the most straightforward of minds. It is for this reason, I believe, that he was called
Candide. The older servants of the household suspected that he was
the son of the Baron's sister by a kind and upright gentleman of the
neighbourhood, a man whom this lady had consistently refused to
marry because he had only ever been able to establish seventy-one
heraldic quarterings, the rest of his family tree having been destroyed
by the ravages of time.

The Baron was one of the most powerful noblemen in Westphalia,
for his castle had a door and windows. His great hall was even
adorned with a tapestry. All the dogs in his farmyards would combine, when the need arose, to make up a pack of hounds: his grooms
were his whippers-in, and the local vicar his great almoner. They all
called him 'Your Lordship', and laughed at his jokes.

The Baroness, who weighed approximately 350 pounds, therefore
enjoyed a large measure of public esteem; and she performed the
honours of the house with a degree of dignified aplomb that rendered her all the more respectable. Her daughter Cunégonde, being
seventeen and of a high complexion, looked fresh, chubby, and

toothsome. The Baron's son seemed in every way worthy of his father. Pangloss, the tutor, was the oracle of the household, and little Candide would listen to his lessons with all the good faith of his age and character.

Pangloss taught metaphysico-theologico-cosmo-codology. He could prove wonderfully that there is no effect without a cause and that, in this best of all possible worlds, His Lordship the Baron's castle was the most beautiful of castles and Madam the best of all possible baronesses.

'It is demonstrably true,' he would say, 'that things cannot be other than as they are. For, everything having been made for a purpose, everything is necessarily for the best purpose. Observe how noses were made to bear spectacles, and so we have spectacles. Legs are evidently devised to be clad in breeches, and breeches we have. Stones were formed in such a way that they can be hewn and made into castles, and so His Lordship has a very beautiful castle. The greatest baron in the province must be the best lodged. And since pigs were made to be eaten, we eat pork all the year round. Consequently, those who have argued that all is well have been talking nonsense. They should have said that all is for the best.'

Candide would listen attentively, and innocently he would believe: for he found Miss Cunégonde extremely beautiful, though he had never made bold to tell her so. His conclusion was that, next to the happiness of being born Baron Thunder-ten-tronckh, the second degree of happiness was being Miss Cunégonde, the third was seeing her every day, and the fourth was listening to Maître Pangloss, the greatest philosopher in the province and therefore in the whole world.

One day, as Cunégonde was taking a stroll near the castle in the little wood they referred to as their 'parkland', she caught a glimpse through the bushes of Dr Pangloss giving a lesson in applied physiology to her mother's maid, a very pretty and very receptive little brunette. As Miss Cunégonde had quite a gift for science, she noted in breathless silence the repeated experiments to which she was witness. She saw clearly the doctor's sufficient reason, the effects and the causes, and returned home all agitated, her thoughts provoked, and filled with the desire to be a scientist, musing that she might well be able to be young Candide's sufficient reason, just as he could well be hers.

She met Candide on her return to the castle and blushed. Candide blushed too. She greeted him in a choked voice, and Candide spoke to her without knowing what he was saying. The next day after dinner, as they were leaving the table, Cunégonde and Candide found themselves behind a screen. Cunégonde dropped her handkerchief, Candide picked it up. Innocently she took his hand, innocently the young man kissed the young lady's hand, and with quite singular vivacity, sensibility, and grace. Their mouths met, their eyes shone, their knees trembled, their hands strayed. Baron Thunderten-tronckh passed by the screen and, seeing this cause and this effect, chased Candide out of the castle with a number of hefty kicks up the backside. Cunégonde fainted. As soon as she recovered her senses, the Baroness slapped her. And all was consternation in the most beautiful and most agreeable of all possible castles.

CHAPTER 2

What became of Candide among the Bulgars

CANDIDE, thus expelled from paradise on earth, walked on for a long time, not knowing where he was going, weeping, raising his eyes to heaven, and turning them often in the direction of the most beautiful of castles, which contained the most beautiful of barons' daughters. He went to sleep in the middle of the fields, supperless, in a furrow. The snow fell in large flakes. Next day, soaked to the skin, Candide dragged himself as far as the neighbouring town, which was called Wald-berghoff-trarbk-dikdorff. He had no money, and he was dying of hunger and exhaustion. He stopped wistfully at the door of a small hostelry. Two men dressed in blue spotted him.

'Comrade,' said one, 'there's a fine figure of a young man, and he's the right height.'

They went up to Candide and very civilly invited him to dine with them.

'Gentlemen,' said Candide with charming modesty, 'you do me great honour, but I have not the means to pay my corner.'

'Oh, sir,' replied one of the men in blue, 'people of your looks and quality never pay. Are you not five feet five inches tall?'

'Yes, gentlemen, that is my height,' he said with a bow.

'Oh sir, come, do sit yourself down at the table. Not only will we pay for you, but we will not see a man such as yourself go short either. Man was made that he might help his fellow-man.'

'You are right,' said Candide. 'That's what Mr Pangloss always told me, and I can see that everything is for the best.'

They pressed him to accept a few crowns. He took them and wanted to make out a receipt. It was not required. They all sat down at the table.

'Don't you love . . . ?'

'Oh, yes,' he replied. 'I love Miss Cunégonde.'

'No,' said one of the gentlemen, 'what we want to know is whether you love the King of the Bulgars or not.'

'Not in the least,' he said, 'for I have never met him.'

'What! He is the most charming of kings and we must drink to his health.'

'Oh, very willingly, gentlemen,' and he drank.

'That will do nicely,' he was told. 'That makes you a supporter, a defender, a champion, nay a hero of the Bulgars. Your fortune is made and your glory assured.'

His feet were promptly clapped in irons and he was taken off to the regiment. They made him do right turns, left turns, draw ramrods, replace ramrods, take aim, fire, quick march, and then they gave him thirty strokes of the birch. Next day he performed the drill a little less badly, and he received only twenty. The next day they gave him only ten, and his comrades thought him a prodigy.

Candide, totally bewildered, could not yet quite make out how he was a hero. One fine day in spring he took it into his head to go for a stroll, simply walking straight ahead, in the belief that it was the privilege of the human, as of the animal species to use its legs how it wished. He had not gone two leagues when up came four other heroes, each six feet tall, who tied him up and carted him off to a dungeon. They asked him which, juridically speaking, he preferred: whether to run the gauntlet of the entire regiment thirty-six times, or to have twelve lead bullets shot through his brains at one go. It did no good his talking about the freedom of the individual and saying that, personally, he wished for neither: a choice had to be made. He resolved, by virtue of that gift of God called 'freedom', to run the gauntlet thirty-six times. He managed two. The regiment numbered two thousand men. For him that meant four thousand birch strokes, which laid bare every muscle and sinew in his body from the nape of his neck right down to his butt. As they were preparing for his third run, Candide, quite done for, implored them to be so kind as to do him the favour of bashing his head in. This favour was granted. He was blindfolded and made to kneel. At that moment the King of the Bulgars passed by and inquired what crime the condemned man had committed. As this King was a great genius, he understood from everything that Candide told him that here was a young metaphysician much in ignorance of the ways of the world: and he pardoned him with a clemency that will be praised in every newspaper and in every century. A splendid surgeon cured Candide in three weeks with the emollients prescribed by Dioscorides. He already had a little skin and could walk when the King of the Bulgars joined battle with the King of the Abars.*

CHAPTER 3

How Candide escaped from the Bulgars and what became of him

NEVER was there anything so fine, so dashing, so glittering, or so well-regulated as those two armies. The trumpets, the fifes, the hautboys, the drums, and the cannon produced a harmony such as was never heard in hell. First the cannon felled about six thousand men on each side. Then the musketry removed from the best of all worlds nine or ten thousand ruffians who were poisoning its surface. The bayonet, too, was the sufficient reason for the death of a few thousand. The sum total may well have come to about thirty thousand souls. Candide, who was trembling like a philosopher, hid himself as best he could during this heroic butchery.

At length, while the two Kings were having *Te Deums* sung in their respective camps, he made up his mind to go and think about cause and effect elsewhere. He climbed over the heaps of dead and dying, and came first to a neighbouring village. It was in ashes. This was an Abar village which the Bulgars had burnt to the ground in accordance with international law. In one part, old men riddled with shot looked on as their wives lay dying, their throats slit, and clutching their children to blood-spattered breasts. In another, young girls lay disembowelled, having satisfied the natural urges of a hero or two, breathing their last; others, half burnt to death, cried out for someone to finish them off. Brains lay scattered on the ground beside severed arms and legs.

Candide fled as fast as he could to another village. It belonged to Bulgars, and Abar heroes had given it the same treatment. Candide, continually stepping over quivering limbs or through the midst of ruins, eventually left the battlefield behind, taking with him some few provisions in his bag and with Miss Cunégonde never far from his thoughts. His provisions had run out by the time he reached Holland but, having heard that the people there were all rich and all Christians, he had no doubt that he would be treated as well as he had been in the Baron's castle before he had been turned out on account of Miss Cunégonde's pretty little eyes.

He begged alms of several solemn personages, who all replied that if he continued in this occupation, he would be locked up in a house of correction and taught how to earn a living.

He then spoke to a man who, all on his own, had just been address-ing a large gathering for a whole hour on the subject of charity. This orator scowled at him and said:

'What are you doing here? Do you support the good cause?'

'There is no effect without a cause,' replied Candide humbly. 'Everything is connected in a chain of necessity, and has all been arranged for the best. It was necessary that I should be separated from Miss Cunégonde and that I should run the gauntlet, and it is necessary that I should beg for my bread until such time as I can earn it. All this could not have been otherwise.'

'My friend,' said the orator, 'do you believe that the Pope is the Antichrist?'

'I've never heard that one before,' replied Candide. 'But whether he is or he isn't, I need bread.'

'You don't deserve to eat it,' said the other. 'Be off with you, you rogue! Away with you, you miserable wretch! And don't you come near me ever again.'

The orator's wife, having stuck her head out of the window and set eyes on a man who could doubt that the Pope was the Antichrist, poured a pot full of . . . over his head. Heavens! To what lengths the ladies do carry their religious zeal!

A man who had never been baptized, a worthy Anabaptist named

Jacques,* saw the cruel and ignominious treatment being meted out in this way to one of his brothers, a living being with two feet, no feathers, and possessed of a soul. He took him home with him, cleaned him up, gave him some bread and beer, presented him with two florins, and even wanted to train him for work in his factories, which produced that 'Persian' material that is made in Holland. Candide, almost prostrate before him, exclaimed:

'Maître Pangloss was quite right when he told me that everything in this world is for the best. For I am infinitely more touched by your extreme generosity than by the harshness of that gentleman with the black hat and his lady wife.'

The next day, while out walking, he met a beggar all covered in sores. His eyes were glazed, the end of his nose was eaten away, his mouth was askew, his teeth black, and he spoke from the back of his throat. He was racked by a violent cough and spat out a tooth with every spasm.

CHAPTER 4

How Candide chanced upon his old philosophy tutor, Dr Pangloss,
and what came of it

CANDIDE, again more moved by compassion than by disgust, gave this appalling beggar the two florins which he had received from his worthy Anabaptist, Jacques. The phantom stared at him, wept, and fell upon his neck. Candide, startled, recoiled.

'Alas!' said the one unfortunate to the other, 'do you no longer recognize your dear Pangloss?'

'What do I hear? You? My dear tutor?! You in this dreadful state?! But what misfortune has befallen you? Why are you no longer in the most beautiful of castles? What has become of Miss Cunégonde, that pearl of a daughter, that masterpiece of nature?'

'I'm all in,' said Pangloss.

Whereupon Candide took him to the Anabaptist's stable, where he gave him a little bread to eat and, when Pangloss had recovered, said:

'Well? What about Cunégonde?'

'She is dead,' replied the other.

Candide fainted on hearing this. His friend brought him round with some old vinegar that was lying about in the stable. Candide opened his eyes.

'Cunégonde is dead! Ah, best of all worlds, where are you now? But what did she die of? It wouldn't have been at seeing me kicked out of her father's beautiful castle, would it?'

'No,' said Pangloss, 'it wouldn't. She was eviscerated by Bulgar soldiers after they'd raped her as many times as anyone can be. They smashed the Baron's head in as he tried to protect her, the Baroness was hacked to pieces, my poor pupil received precisely the same treatment as his sister, and as for the castle, not one stone remains standing on another. Not a single barn, or sheep, or duck, or tree is left. But we had our revenge, for the Abars did exactly the same to the neighbouring barony of a Bulgar lord.'

At this account Candide fainted again. But having recovered his senses and said everything one should say in such circumstances, he enquired as to the cause and the effect and the sufficient reason which had reduced Pangloss to such a woeful state.

'Alas,' said the other, 'the answer is love: love, the solace and comfort of the human race, the preserver of the universe, the soul of all sentient beings, tender love.'

'Alas,' said Candide, 'I too have known it, this love of yours, this sovereign ruler of the heart, this soul of our soul. All the good it ever did me was one kiss and a score of kicks up the backside. How can this fine cause have had such an abominable effect on you?'

Pangloss replied in these terms:

'O my dear Candide! You knew Paquette, that pretty lady's maid to our noble Baroness. In her arms I tasted the delights of paradise, and in turn they have led me to these torments of hell by which you see me now devoured. She had the disease, and may have died of it by now. Paquette was made a present of it by a very knowledgeable Franciscan who had traced it back to its source. For he had got it from an old countess, who had contracted it from a captain in the cavalry, who owed it to a marchioness, who had it from a page, who had caught it from a Jesuit, who, during his noviciate, had inherited it in a direct line from one of Christopher Columbus's shipmates. For my part I shall give it to no one, because I'm dying.'

'O Pangloss!' cried Candide. 'What a strange genealogy! Was it not the devil who began it?'

'Not at all,' replied the great man. 'It was an indispensable part of the best of all worlds, a necessary ingredient. For if Columbus, on an island in the Americas, had not caught this disease which poisons the spring of procreation, which often even prevents procreation, and which is plainly the opposite of what nature intended, we would have neither chocolate nor cochineal. Moreover one must remember that until now this disease has been unique to the inhabitants of our continent, like controversy. The Turks, the Indians, the Persians, the Chinese, the Siamese, the Japanese, they have all yet to know it. But there is sufficient reason for them to know it in their turn a few centuries hence. In the meantime it is making spectacular progress among our population, and especially among those great armies of fine, upstanding, well-bred mercenaries who decide the destiny of nations. One can be sure that when thirty thousand soldiers are fighting against a similar number in pitched battle, there are about twenty thousand cases of the pox on either side.'

'Well, isn't that extraordinary,' said Candide. 'But you must go and get treated.'

'And how am I supposed to do that?' said Pangloss. 'I haven't a penny, my friend, and in the whole wide world you can't so much as be bled or have an enema without paying for it, or without someone else paying for you.'

These last remarks decided Candide. He went and threw himself at the feet of his charitable Anabaptist, Jacques, and painted such a poignant picture of the state to which his friend was reduced that the good fellow did not hesitate to take Dr Pangloss under his roof: and he had him cured at his own expense. In the process Pangloss lost but one eye and one ear. He could write well and had a perfect grasp of arithmetic. Jacques the Anabaptist made him his bookkeeper. Two months later, having to go to Lisbon on business, he took his two philosophers with him on the ship. Pangloss explained to him how things could not be better. Jacques was not of this opinion.

'Men must surely have corrupted nature a little,' he would say, 'for they were not born wolves, and yet wolves they have become. God gave them neither twenty-four pounders nor bayonets, and they have made bayonets and twenty-four pounders in order to destroy each other. I could also mention bankruptcies, and the courts who seize the assets of bankrupts and cheat their creditors of them.'

'That was all indispensable,' was the one-eyed doctor's reply. 'Individual misfortunes contribute to the general good with the result that the more individual misfortunes there are, the more all is well.'

While he was presenting his argument, the air grew thick, the winds blew from the four corners of the earth, and the ship was assailed by the most terrible storm, within sight of the port of Lisbon.

CHAPTER 5

Storm, shipwreck, earthquake, and what became of Dr Pangloss,
Candide, and Jacques the Anabaptist

HALF the passengers on board, weakened and near dead from those unimaginable spasms that the rolling of a ship can induce in every nerve and humour of the body by tossing them in opposite directions, did not even have the strength to worry about the danger. The other half shrieked and prayed. The sails were rent, the masts were smashed, the ship broke up. Work as they might, no one could make himself understood, and there was no one in charge. The Anabaptist was helping out with the rigging down on the decks. Furious, a sailor came up, gave him a good clout, and laid him flat on the boards. But the force of the blow jerked him so violently that he himself fell head first overboard and ended up suspended in mid-air, hanging from a piece of broken mast. Kind Jacques ran to his rescue, helped him back on board, and in the process was precipitated into the sea in full view of the sailor—who left him to perish without so much as a backward glance. Along came Candide, saw his benefactor momentarily reappear on the surface and then sink without trace, and wanted to jump in after him. Pangloss the philosopher prevented him, arguing that Lisbon harbour had been created expressly so that the Anabaptist would be drowned in it. While he was proving this a priori, the ship foundered and everyone perished, except for Pangloss, Candide, and the brute of a sailor who had drowned the virtuous Anabaptist. The blackguard swam safely to the very shore where Pangloss and Candide were also carried on a plank.

When they had recovered a little, they proceeded on foot towards Lisbon. They had some money left and hoped with this to escape hunger, just as they had survived the storm.

Scarcely had they set foot in the city, still weeping over the death of their benefactor, than they felt the earth quake beneath their feet. In the port a boiling sea rose up and smashed the ships lying at anchor. Whirlwinds of flame and ash covered the streets and public squares: houses disintegrated, roofs were upended upon foundations, and foundations crumbled.

Thirty thousand inhabitants of both sexes and all ages were crushed beneath the ruins. The sailor said with a whistle and an oath:

'There'll be some rich pickings here.'

'What can be the sufficient reason for this phenomenon?' wondered Pangloss.

'The end of the world is come!' Candide shouted.

The sailor forthwith dashed into the midst of the rubble, braving death in search of money; he duly found some, grabbed it, got drunk and, having slept it off, bought the favours of the first willing girl he met among the remains of the ruined houses, among the dying and the dead.

Pangloss, however, took him aside:

'My friend,' he said, 'this is not right. You are in breach of universal reason, and this is hardly the moment.'

'Hell's teeth!' replied the other. 'I'm a sailor and I come from Batavia. Four times I've trampled on the crucifix,* on four separate voyages to Japan. You've picked the wrong man, you and your universal reason!'

One or two fragments of stone had injured Candide. He was lying in the street covered in rubble. He kept calling out to Pangloss:

'Help! Get me some wine and oil. I'm dying.'

'This earthquake is nothing new,' replied Pangloss. 'The city of Lima felt the same tremors in America last year.* Same causes, same effects. There must be a vein of sulphur running underground from Lima to Lisbon.'

'Nothing is more probable,' said Candide, 'but for God's sake get me some oil and wine.'

'What do you mean, "probable"?' the philosopher retorted. 'I maintain that the thing is proven.'

Candide lost consciousness, and Pangloss brought him some water from a nearby fountain.

The next day, having located some food by crawling about among the rubble, they recovered their strength a little. Then they worked like everyone else at giving assistance to the inhabitants who had survived. One group of citizens they had helped gave them as good a dinner as was possible in such a disaster. It is true that the meal was a sad one, and the company wept over their bread; but Pangloss consoled them by assuring them that things could not be otherwise:

'For all this is the best there is. If the volcanic activity is in Lisbon, it means it could not have been anywhere else. For it is impossible for things not to be where they are. For all is well.'

A little man in black, an agent of the Inquisition, was sitting next to him. He intervened politely and said:

'Apparently sir does not believe in original sin. For if everything is as well as can be, there has been neither Fall nor punishment.'

'I most humbly beg Your Excellency's pardon,' replied Pangloss even more politely, 'but the Fall of man and the curse entered necessarily into the scheme of the best of all possible worlds.'

'So sir does not believe in freedom?' said the agent.

'Your Excellency will forgive me,' said Pangloss. 'Freedom can exist alongside absolute necessity, for it was necessary for us to be free. For ultimately, the will once determined . . .'

Pangloss was in the middle of his sentence when the agent nodded to his henchman, who was pouring him some port, or rather Oporto, wine.

CHAPTER 6

How they had a splendid auto-da-fé *to prevent earthquakes, and how Candide was flogged*

AFTER the earthquake, which had destroyed three-quarters of Lisbon, the wise men of the country had not been able to come up with any more effective means of preventing total ruin than to give the people a splendid *auto-da-fé*. It was decided by the University of Coimbra that the spectacle of a few people being ceremonially burnt over a low flame is the infallible secret of preventing earthquakes.

Consequently they had arrested a man from Biscay who had been found guilty of marrying his fellow godparent,* and two Portuguese who had removed the bacon when eating a chicken.* After dinner men came and tied up Dr Pangloss and his disciple Candide, one for what he had said, and the other for having listened with an air of approval. Both were led away to separate apartments, which were extremely cool and where the sun was never troublesome. A week later they were both dressed in a *san-benito*,* and paper mitres were placed upon their heads. Candide's mitre and *san-benito* were painted with flames that were upside down and with devils which had neither claws nor tails, but Pangloss's devils had claws and tails, and his flames were the right way up. So dressed, they walked in procession and listened to a very moving sermon, followed by a beautiful recital of plainchant. Candide was flogged in time to the singing; the man from Biscay and the two men who had not wanted to eat bacon were burned; and Pangloss was hanged, despite the fact that this was contrary to custom. The very same day the earth quaked once more: the din was fearful.

Terrified, confounded, thoroughly distraught, all bleeding and trembling, Candide reflected to himself:

'If this is the best of all possible worlds, then what must the others be like? I wouldn't mind if I'd only been flogged. That happened with the Bulgars. But, o my dear Pangloss! You, the greatest of philosophers! Did I have to see you hanged without my knowing why?! O my dear Anabaptist! You, the best of men! Did you have to drown in the port?! O Miss Cunégonde! You pearl among daughters! Did you have to have your stomach slit open?!'

He was just leaving the scene afterwards, scarcely able to stand up, and having been preached at, flogged, absolved, and blessed, when an old woman came up to him and said:

'Take courage, my son, follow me.'

CHAPTER 7

How an old woman took care of Candide, and how he was reunited with the one he loved

CANDIDE did not take courage, but he did follow the old woman into a hovel. She gave him a pot of ointment to rub on himself, set things out for him to eat and drink, and indicated a small, moderately clean bed, beside which lay a full set of clothes.

'Eat, drink, and sleep,' she said, 'and may Our Lady of Atocha, His Eminence Saint Anthony of Padua, and His Eminence Saint James of Compostela watch over you. I'll be back tomorrow.'

Candide, still astonished at all he had seen and suffered, and even more astonished at the charity of the old woman, wanted to kiss her hand.

'It's not my hand you should be kissing. I'll be back tomorrow. Rub yourself with ointment, eat, and sleep.'

Candide, despite so many misfortunes, ate and slept. The next day the old woman brought him breakfast, inspected his back, and rubbed a different ointment on it herself. Then she brought him dinner, and in the evening she returned with supper. The day after that she went through the same ritual again.

'Who are you?' Candide kept asking her. 'What has made you so kind? How can I repay you?'

The good woman did not answer. She returned that evening bringing nothing for supper.

'Come with me,' she said, 'and not a word.'

She took him by the arm and walked with him for about a quarter of a mile into the country. They arrived at a house standing on its own, surrounded by gardens and waterways. The old woman knocked at a little door. Someone opened it. She led Candide up a secret staircase into a small gilded room, left him sitting on a brocaded couch, shut the door after her, and departed. Candide thought he was dreaming; his whole life seemed to him like a bad dream, and the present moment a sweet one.

The old woman soon reappeared. She was supporting with some difficulty the trembling figure of a majestic-looking woman, all sparkling with jewels and hidden by a veil.

'Remove this veil,' the old woman told Candide.

The young man drew near. With a timid hand he lifted the veil. What a moment! What a surprise! He thought he was looking at Miss Cunégonde. He was indeed looking at her, for it was she. His strength failed him, words failed him, and he fell at her feet. Cunégonde fell on the couch. The old woman showered them with various waters. They came to their senses. They spoke to each other. At first it was all half-finished sentences, and questions and answers getting crossed, and sighs, and tears, and exclamations. The old woman suggested they make less noise and left them to it.

'What! It is you!' said Candide. 'You're alive! To think that I should find you in Portugal! So you weren't raped? So you didn't have your stomach slit open as Pangloss the philosopher assured me you did?'

'I certainly was, and did,' said the fair Cunégonde. 'But those two particular misfortunes are not always fatal.'

'But were your father and mother killed?'

'That is only too true,' said Cunégonde tearfully.

'And your brother?'

'My brother was killed, too.'

'And why are you in Portugal? And how did you know that I was here? And how on earth did you arrange to have me brought to this house?'

'I will tell you all these things,' the young lady replied. 'But first you must tell me all that has happened to you since that innocent kiss you gave me and those kicks you got.'

With deep respect Candide obeyed her, and although he was at a loss for words, and his voice was weak and quavering, and his back still hurt a little, he gave her the most artless account of all that had happened to him since the moment of their separation. Cunégonde raised her eyes to heaven, and she shed tears at the deaths of the good Anabaptist and Pangloss; after which she spoke in these terms to Candide, who missed not a word and devoured her with his eyes.

CHAPTER 8

Cunégonde's story

'I was in bed fast asleep when it pleased heaven to send the Bulgars into our beautiful castle of Thunder-ten-tronckh. They slit the throats of my father and brother, and hacked my mother to pieces. A great big Bulgar, six feet tall, seeing that I had passed out at the sight of all this, began to rape me. That brought me round. I came to, screamed, struggled, bit him, scratched him. I wanted to tear that big Bulgar's eyes out, little realizing that what was taking place in my father's castle was standard practice. The brute knifed me in the left side, and I still have the scar.'

'Dear, oh dear! I hope I may see it,' said the guileless Candide.

'You shall,' said Cunégonde, 'but let me continue.'

'Go on,' said Candide.

She took up the thread of her story thus:

'A Bulgar captain came into the room and saw me all covered in blood. The soldier didn't take any notice. The captain became angry at this lack of respect being shown him by the brute and killed him where he lay on top of me. Then he had me bandaged up and took me to his quarters as a prisoner of war. I used to wash what few shirts he had, and I cooked for him. He found me very pretty, I must admit, and I won't deny he was a good-looking man himself, with skin that was white and soft. Apart from that, not much brain, not much of a thinker. You could tell he hadn't been educated by Dr Pangloss. Three months later, having lost all his money and grown tired of me, he sold me to a Jew called Don Issacar, who was a dealer in Holland and Portugal, and who was passionately fond of women. This Jew became much attached to my person, but he was unable to get the better of it. I resisted his advances more successfully than I had the Bulgar soldier's. A woman of honour may be raped once, but her virtue is all the stronger for it. In an attempt to win me over, the Jew brought me here to this country house. I had previously thought that there was nothing in the world as beautiful as the castle of Thunder-ten-tronckh. I have been proved wrong.

'The Grand Inquisitor noticed me one day during Mass. He kept eyeing me, and then sent word that he had to speak to me on a confidential matter. I was taken to his palace. I told him who I was. He pointed out how far beneath my station it was to belong to an Israelite. It was suggested on his behalf to Don Issacar that he should cede me to His Eminence. Don Issacar, who is the Court's banker and a man of some influence, would have none of it. The Inquisitor threatened him with an *auto-da-fé*. In the end, under intimidation, my Jew agreed to a deal whereby the house and I would belong to both of them jointly. The Jew would have Mondays, Wednesdays, and the sabbath, and the Inquisitor would have the other days of the week. This convention has been operating for six months now. It has not been without its quarrels, for it has often been a moot point which sabbath the period from Saturday night to Sunday morning belongs to, the Old Testament one or the New. For my own part I have resisted both men up till now, and I'm sure that's why they still love me.

'Anyway, in order to ward off the scourge of the earthquakes and to intimidate Don Issacar, it pleased my lord and master the Inquisitor to celebrate an *auto-da-fé*. He did me the honour of inviting me. I had a very good seat, and the ladies were served refreshments between the Mass and the execution. I was horrified, it must be said, to see those two Jews being burnt, as well as that nice man from Biscay who had married his fellow godparent. But how surprised, how shocked, how upset I was to see someone that looked like Pangloss in a *san-benito* and wearing a mitre! I rubbed my eyes, stared, saw him hanged, and fainted. I had hardly come to when I saw you standing there stark naked. That was my moment of greatest horror and consternation, the moment of greatest pain and despair. I can tell you truthfully, your skin is even fairer and more perfectly pink than my Bulgar captain's. The sight of it lent added force to all the feelings that were surging through me and devouring me. I screamed, I wanted to shout out: "Stop, you animals!", but nothing came out, and anyway my screaming and shouting would have done no good. "How is it," I said to myself, when you had been well and truly flogged, "that nice Candide and wise Pangloss come to be in Lisbon, and that one of them gets a hundred lashes, and the other is hanged by order of His Eminence the Inquisitor, who in turn is in love with me? So Pangloss deceived me cruelly when he told me that all was well with the world."

'Distressed, agitated, beside myself with anger one minute and ready to faint clean away the next, all I could think about was the massacre of my father and mother and brother, the insolence of my ugly Bulgar soldier, and the knife wound he gave me, my bondage, my menial work as a cook, my Bulgar captain, my ugly Don Issacar, my abominable Inquisitor, the hanging of Dr Pangloss, that great *Miserere* they sang in plainchant while you were being flogged, and above all that kiss I gave you behind a screen the day I last saw you. I praised God for bringing you back to me after so many trials and tribulations. I instructed my old servant to tend to you and to bring you here as soon as she could. She has carried out my commission most capably. I have had the indescribable pleasure of seeing you again, of hearing you and speaking to you. You must have a terrible hunger, and I have a large appetite. Let's begin with supper.'

With which they both sat down to eat. After supper they resumed their positions on the aforementioned beautiful couch. There they were when Señor Don Issacar, one of the masters of the house, arrived. It was the sabbath. He had come to enjoy his rights and press his suit.

CHAPTER 9

What became of Cunégonde, Candide, the Grand Inquisitor,
and a Jew

THIS Issacar was the most irascible Hebrew in the tribe of Israel since the time of the Captivity in Babylon.

'What!' he said, 'you whore of Galilee! So Mr Inquisitor isn't enough for you then? I've got to share you with this infidel too?'

With these words he drew a long dagger which he always carried with him and, not thinking his adversary would be armed, attacked Candide. But the old woman had given our good Westphalian a fine sword with his suit of clothes. Gentle though his disposition was, he drew his sword, and that was it: one Israelite stone dead on the floor at the feet of the fair Cunégonde.

'Holy Virgin!' cried she. 'What is to become of us? A man killed in my house! If the police come, we're lost!'

'If Pangloss had not been hanged,' said Candide, 'he would have given us some good advice in this predicament, for he was a great philosopher. Since he's not here, let's ask the old woman.'

She was a most prudent sort, and was just beginning to give her opinion when another little door opened. It was one hour after midnight: Sunday was beginning. This day belonged to His Eminence the Inquisitor. In he came to find Candide, who had been flogged, now standing sword in hand, with a corpse stretched out on the ground, Cunégonde in a fluster, and the old woman giving advice.

Here is what went through Candide's mind at that moment, and how he reasoned:

'If this holy man calls for help, he will certainly have me burned. He may well do the same to Cunégonde. He has already had me mercilessly whipped. He is my rival. I've already started killing. There's nothing else for it.'

This reasoning was clear and quick, and without giving the

Inquisitor the time to recover from his surprise, he ran him through and hurled him down beside the Jew.

'Well, here's a fine mess,' said Cunégonde. 'There's no going back now. That's us excommunicated. Our last hour has come. How is it that someone as soft-hearted as you can have ended up killing a Jew and a prelate in a matter of minutes?'

'My dear girl,' replied Candide, 'when a man's in love, jealous, and flogged by the Inquisition, there's no knowing what he may do.'

The old woman then broke in and said:

'There are three Andalusian horses in the stable, as well as saddles and bridles. Let brave Candide get them ready. Madam has moidores and diamonds. Let us mount quickly—though my seat is but one buttock—and ride to Cadiz. The weather is of the best, and it is always a great pleasure to travel in the cool of the night.'

At once Candide saddled up the three horses. Cunégonde, the old woman, and he covered thirty miles without stopping. While they were making their escape, the Holy Hermandad* reached the house. They buried His Eminence in a beautiful church, and threw Issacar on to the rubbish-heap.

Candide, Cunégonde, and the old woman had by this time reached the small town of Avacena, in the middle of the Sierra Morena mountains, where they had the following conversation in an inn.

CHAPTER 10

In what distress Candide, Cunégonde, and the old woman arrived in Cadiz, and of their embarkation

'BUT who can possibly have stolen my pistoles and diamonds?' sobbed Cunégonde. 'What shall we live on? How shall we manage? Where shall I find the Inquisitors and the Jews to replace them?'

'Alas!' said the old woman, 'I have a strong suspicion it was that Franciscan monk who spent yesterday night in the same inn as us in Badajoz. God preserve me from jumping to conclusions, but he did come into our room twice and he did leave long before us.'

'Oh dear!' said Candide. 'Good Pangloss often used to argue that the fruits of the earth are common to all and that everyone has an equal right to them. According to his principles, that Franciscan ought to have left us enough money behind to finish our journey. Have you really not got anything left, my fair Cunégonde?'

'Not a maravedi,' said she.

'What shall we do?' said Candide.

'Let's sell one of our horses,' said the old woman. 'I can ride behind Miss Cunégonde, even though I have only one buttock to sit on, and we'll make it to Cadiz.'

There was a Benedictine prior staying in the same hostelry. He bought the horse cheaply. Candide, Cunégonde, and the old woman passed through Lucena, Chillas, and Lebrija, and came at last to Cadiz. There a fleet was being fitted out and troops were being mustered to go and knock some sense into the Jesuit reverend fathers in Paraguay, who were accused of having incited one of their local native hordes to revolt against the Kings of Spain and Portugal near the town of San Sacramento.* Candide, having served with the Bulgars, performed the Bulgar drill for the general of this little army with so much grace, speed, skill, agility, and panache that he was given command of a company of foot. So there he was a captain. He boarded ship with Miss Cunégonde, the old woman, two valets, and the two Andalusian horses which had belonged to the Grand Inquisitor of Portugal.

During the crossing they discussed poor Pangloss's philosophy a great deal.

'We're going to another world,' Candide would say. 'I expect it must be there that all is well. For you have to admit, one could grumble rather at what goes on in our own one, both physically and morally.'

'I love you with all my heart,' Cunégonde would say, 'but my soul is still in something of a state, what with all I've seen and been through.'

'All will be well,' was Candide's reply. 'Already the sea in this new world is better than those we have in Europe. It's calmer, and the winds are more constant. It is assuredly the new world that is the best of all possible worlds.'

'God willing!' said Cunégonde. 'But I have been so horribly unfortunate in my own that my heart is almost closed to hope.'

'*You're* complaining!' said the old woman. 'Alas! You haven't had the misfortunes I have.'

Cunégonde almost burst out laughing and found it extremely droll of this little old woman to claim to be more unfortunate than she.

'I'm afraid, my good woman,' she said to her, 'that unless you have been raped by two Bulgars, stabbed twice in the stomach, had two of your castles demolished, seen two mothers' and two fathers' throats slit before your very eyes, and watched two of your lovers being flogged at an *auto-da-fé*, then I don't see you bettering me. Added to which, I was born a Baroness with seventy-two heraldic quarterings and yet I have been a cook.'

'My young lady,' replied the old woman, 'you do not know who I am by birth, and if I were to show you my bottom, you would not speak as you do, and you would reserve judgement.'

This declaration aroused the deepest curiosity in the minds of Cunégonde and Candide. The old woman had this to say to them.

CHAPTER 11

The old woman's story

'My eyes haven't always been bloodshot and red-rimmed, my nose hasn't always come down to my chin, and I haven't always been a servant. I am the daughter of Pope Urban X and the Princess of Palestrina. Until the age of fourteen I was brought up in a palace, next to which not one of your German barons' castles would even have done as a stable. And any single one of my dresses was worth more than all the treasures of Westphalia put together. As I grew older, so I grew in beauty, grace, and fine accomplishments. I took pleasure in life; I commanded respect; I had prospects. I was already able to inspire love, and my breasts were forming. And what breasts they were! White and firm, just like those of the Medici Venus. And what eyes! What eyelids! What black eyebrows! What fire burned in my pupils and outshone the sparkling of the stars, as the poets in that part of the world used to tell me. The women who dressed and undressed me would go into ecstasies when they saw me, back and front, and all the men would love to have changed places with them.

'I was engaged to be married to a sovereign prince of Massa-Carrara. What a prince! As handsome as I was beautiful, gentle and charming to a fault, brilliant in mind and ardent in love. I loved him as one does love for the first time, I worshipped him with passionate abandon. Arrangements were made for the wedding. The pomp and magnificence of it! No one had seen their like before. It was one continual round of entertainments, tournaments, opera buffa. And all Italy composed sonnets for me, though not one of them was any good. My moment of bliss was at hand when an old marchioness, who had been my prince's mistress, invited him to take chocolate with her. He died less than two hours later after appalling convulsions. But that was a trifle. My mother, being in despair and yet much less grief-stricken than I, wanted to absent herself for a time from so dreadful a scene. She had a very fine property near Gaeta. We took ship on a local galley, which was all covered in gilt like the altar of Saint Peter's in Rome. What happens but a corsair from Salé makes straight for us and boards us. Our soldiers defended themselves as if they were the Pope's own: they all knelt down, cast their weapons aside, and asked the corsair for absolution *in articulo mortis*.

'At once they were stripped as naked as monkeys, as were my mother, and our ladies-in-waiting, and I also. It is a remarkable thing, the eagerness of these gentlemen to undress everybody. But what surprised me more was that they put a finger up all of us in a place where we women ordinarily allow only enema nozzles to enter. This ritual struck me as being most odd. But that is how one judges everything when one has never been abroad. I soon gathered that this was to see if we'd hadn't hidden any diamonds up there. It has been established practice among civilized seafaring nations since time immemorial. I discovered that those religious gentlemen, the Knights of Malta, never fail to do it when they capture a Turk, man or woman. It is one article of the law of nations that has never been infringed.

'I needn't tell you how hard it is for a young princess to be taken to Morocco as a slave with her mother. You can well imagine all we had to suffer on the pirate ship. My mother was still very beautiful. Our ladies-in-waiting, even our maids, had more charms than are to be found in the whole of Africa. As for me, I was ravishing. I was beauty, grace itself, and I was a virgin. I did not remain one for long. The flower which had been kept for the handsome prince of Massa-Carrara was ravished by the pirate captain. He was a loathsome Negro, who even thought he was doing me a great honour. Yes indeed, the Princess of Palestrina and I had to be extremely tough to survive everything we went through up until our arrival in Morocco. But enough of this. Such things are so commonplace that they are barely worth mentioning.

'Morocco was bathed in blood when we arrived. The fifty sons of the Emperor Muley-Ismael each had his own followers, which in effect meant fifty civil wars—blacks against blacks, blacks against browns, browns against browns, mulattos against mulattos. It was one long bloodbath from one end of the empire to the other.

'We had scarcely disembarked when some blacks belonging to a faction opposed to that of my pirate appeared on the scene wanting to relieve him of his booty. After the diamonds and the gold, we were the most precious things he had. I was witness to a fight the like of which you in your European climates just never see. The Northern races are simply not hot-blooded enough. They don't have that thirst for women that they have in Africa. It's as if you Europeans had milk in your veins, whereas it is vitriol, fire, that flows in the veins of the inhabitants of Mount Atlas and that part of the world. They fought with the fury of the lions and tigers and serpents of their own country to decide which of them should have us. A Moor grabbed my mother by the right arm, my pirate's lieutenant held on to her left, a Moorish soldier took her by one leg, and one of our other pirates held her by the other. In an instant almost all our ladies-in-waiting found themselves being torn like this between four soldiers. My captain kept me hidden behind him. Scimitar in hand, he was killing anything that stood in the way of his own particular thirst. In the end I saw all our Italian women and my mother torn apart, cut to pieces, massacred by the monsters who were fighting over them. My fellow captives and their captors, soldiers, sailors, blacks, browns, whites, mulattos, and finally my captain, all were killed, and I lay dying on top of a pile of corpses. Similar scenes were taking place, as you know, over an area more than three hundred leagues across: and never once did they fail to say the five daily prayers ordered by Muhammad.

'I extricated myself with great difficulty from this pile of blood-soaked corpses, and dragged myself over to a tall orange-tree next to a nearby stream. There I collapsed in shock, exhaustion, horror, hunger, and despair. Soon afterwards my shattered senses gave themselves up to a sleep that was more like unconsciousness than rest. I was in this enfeebled and insensible state, halfway between life and death, when I felt myself being pressed down on by something squirming on my body. I opened my eyes and saw a white man with a friendly face sighing and muttering between his teeth: *O che sciagura d'essere senza c . . . !**

CHAPTER 12

The continuing story of the old woman's misfortunes

'ASTONISHED and delighted to hear my native tongue, and no less surprised at the words the man was uttering, I replied that there were greater misfortunes than that of which he complained. I informed him in a few words of the horrors to which I had been subjected, and passed out. He carried me to a house nearby, had me put to bed and given something to eat, waited on me, comforted me, flattered me, told me that he had never seen anything so beautiful, and that never had he so much regretted the loss of that which no one could restore to him.

' "I was born in Naples," he told me. "They castrate two or three thousand children every year there. Some die, some develop a voice more beautiful than any woman's, and some go off and govern the Papal States. They performed this operation on me most successfully and I sang in the chapel of the Princess of Palestrina."

' "My mother!" cried I.

' "Your mother!" cried he, with tears in his eyes. "What! Then you would be that young princess I taught till she was six, and who promised even then to be as beautiful as you are now?"

' "I am she. My mother lies not four hundred yards from here, in four pieces, beneath a pile of corpses . . ."

'I told him everything that had happened to me. He told me his adventures too, and about how one of the Christian powers had sent him as an envoy to sign a treaty with the King of Morocco, whereby this monarch would be supplied with powder, cannon, and ships to assist him in putting an end to the trading of the other Christian powers.

' "My mission is complete," the worthy eunuch told me. "I am on my way to board ship at Ceuta, and I shall take you back to Italy. *Ma che sciagura d'essere senza c . . . !*"

'I thanked him with tears of tender gratitude: instead of taking me to Italy, he took me to Algiers and sold me to the local dey. Hardly had I been sold than the plague which was going round Africa, Asia, and Europe broke out with a vengeance in Algiers. You have seen earthquakes; but you, my young lady, have you ever had the plague?'

'Never,' the Baron's daughter replied.

'If you had,' the old woman went on, 'you would agree that it comes well above an earthquake. It is extremely rife in Africa, and I caught it. Can you imagine? What a situation for the fifteen-year-old daughter of a pope to be in, and for one who in the space of three months had suffered poverty and enslavement, been raped almost daily, seen her mother torn limb from limb, survived starvation and war, and was now dying of the plague in Algiers. Die, however, I did not. But my eunuch and the dey and almost the entire seraglio at Algiers perished.

'When the first wave of this appalling plague had passed, they sold the dey's slaves. A merchant bought me and took me to Tunis. He sold me to another merchant who in turn sold me in Tripoli. After Tripoli I was resold in Alexandria, after Alexandria I was resold in Smyrna, and after Smyrna in Constantinople. In the end I became the property of an aga in the janissaries, who shortly afterwards received orders to go and defend Azov against the Russians, who were laying siege to it.

'This aga, who was quite a ladies' man, took his whole seraglio with him, and housed us in a little fort on the Palus-Meotides under the guard of two black eunuchs and twenty soldiers. An enormous number of Russians were killed, but they gave as good as they got. Azov was put to fire and sword, and no quarter was given either as to sex or to age. All that was left was our little fort. The enemy determined to starve us out. The twenty janissaries had sworn not to surrender. The extremes of hunger to which they were reduced forced them to eat our two eunuchs, for fear of breaking their oath. After a few days they decided to eat the women.

'We had a very pious and very understanding imam, who preached a fine sermon to persuade them not to kill us outright.

' "Cut off one buttock from each of these ladies," he said, "and you will eat well. If you have to come back for more in a few days' time, you'll still be able to have the same again. Heaven will be grateful to you for such a charitable deed, and you will be saved."

'He was very eloquent: he convinced them. They performed this dreadful operation on us. The imam rubbed us with the ointment they use on children who have just been circumcised. We were all at death's door.

'Hardly had the janissaries finished the meal with which we had provided them than the Russians turned up in flat-bottomed boats. Not one janissary got away. The Russians paid not a blind bit of notice to the state we were in. There are French surgeons all over the world, and a very skilful one took charge of us and made us better. And I shall never forget how, once my wounds were well and truly healed, he then propositioned me. Otherwise he told us all to cheer up and assured us that this sort of thing happened in lots of sieges, and that it was one of the laws of warfare.

'As soon as my companions could walk, they were sent to Moscow. I was part of a boyar's share of the spoils, and he put me to work in his garden and gave me twenty lashes a day. But after this nobleman was broken on the wheel two years later, along with thirty other boyars, because of some trouble or other at court, I took my chance and made my escape. I crossed the whole of Russia. For a long time I served in inns, first in Riga, then in Rostock, Weimar, Leipzig, Kassel, Utrecht, Leiden, The Hague, and Rotterdam. I grew old in poverty and dishonour, having but half a bottom, yet always mindful that I was the daughter of a pope. A hundred times I wanted to kill myself, but still I loved life. This ridiculous weakness for living is perhaps one of our most fatal tendencies. For can anything be sillier than to insist on carrying a burden one would continually much rather throw to the ground? Sillier than to feel disgust at one's own existence and yet cling to it? Sillier, in short, than to clasp to our bosom the serpent that devours us until it has gnawed away our heart? In the countries through which it has been my fate to travel and in the inns where I have served, I have seen a huge number of people who felt abhorrence for their own lives. But I've seen only a dozen voluntarily put an end to their wretchedness: three Negroes, four Englishmen, four Genevans, and a German professor called Robeck.*

'In the end I finished up as one of the servants in the household of Don Issacar the Jew. He gave me to you, my fair young lady, as your maid. I have become involved in your destiny and been more concerned with your adventures than with my own. Indeed I would never have mentioned my misfortunes if you hadn't provoked me to it a little, and if it were not the custom on board ship to tell stories to pass the time. So there you are, Miss. I have lived, and I know the world. Just for fun, why not get each passenger to tell you the story of his life, and if there is one single one of them who hasn't often cursed the day he was born and hasn't often said to himself that he was the most unfortunate man alive, then you can throw me into the sea head first.'

CHAPTER 13

How Candide was obliged to part from fair Cunégonde and the old woman

FAIR Cunégonde, having heard the old woman's story, treated her with all the civilities due to a person of her rank and quality. She accepted her suggestion and got all the passengers one after another to tell her their adventures. Candide and she conceded that the old woman was right.

'It's a great pity,' said Candide, 'that wise Pangloss was hanged, contrary to the usual custom, during an *auto-da-fé*. He would have some remarkable things to tell us about the physical and moral evil that prevails over land and sea—and I would feel able to venture a few respectful objections.'

While each person told his story, the ship continued on its way. They docked at Buenos Aires. Cunégonde, Captain Candide, and the old woman went to call on the Governor, Don Fernando d'Ibaraa y Figueora y Mascarenes y Lampourdos y Souza. This grandee had a pride to match his many names. He spoke to people with the most noble disdain, sticking his nose so far in the air, speaking in such a mercilessly loud voice, adopting so high and mighty a tone, and affecting so haughty a gait, that all who greeted him were also tempted to hit him. He loved women to distraction. Cunégonde seemed to him more beautiful than any he had ever seen. The first thing he did was to ask if she were not by any chance the Captain's wife. The air with which he put this question alarmed Candide. He did not dare say she was his wife, because in fact she was not. He did not dare say she was his sister, because she was not that either. And although this white lie had once been very fashionable among the Ancients, and could still come in very useful to the Moderns, his soul was too pure to be unfaithful to the truth.

'Miss Cunégonde', he said, 'is to do me the honour of marrying me, and we humbly beseech Your Excellency to condescend to offici-ate at our wedding.'

With a twirl of his moustache Don Fernando d'Ibaraa y Figueora y Mascarenes y Lampourdos y Souza smiled a bitter smile, and ordered Captain Candide to go and review his company. Candide obeyed. The Governor remained with Miss Cunégonde. He declared his love for her and made protestations that on the morrow he would marry her, in the eyes of the Church or anyone else's, just as it might please her lovely self. Cunégonde asked him for a quarter of an hour in which to collect herself, consult with the old woman, and come to a decision.

The old woman said to Cunégonde:

'Miss, you have seventy-two quarterings, and not a penny to your name. You can be the wife of the greatest nobleman in South America, who also has a very fine moustache. Are you in any position to make a point of unswerving fidelity? You have been raped by the Bulgars. A Jew and an Inquisitor have enjoyed your favours. Misfortune does give people some rights. Frankly, if I were in your position, I would have no scruples about marrying the Governor and making Captain Candide's fortune for him.'

While the old woman was speaking with all the prudence of age and experience, a small ship was seen entering the port. On board were an alcalde and some alguazils: what had happened was this.

The old woman had quite rightly guessed that it had been the Cordelier with the loose sleeves* who had stolen the money and jewels from Cunégonde in the town of Badajoz, when she was making her rapid escape with Candide. This monk tried to sell some of the stones to a jeweller. The merchant recognized them as belonging to the Grand Inquisitor. The Franciscan, before being hanged, con-fessed that he had stolen them. He gave a description of the people concerned and the route they were taking. Cunégonde and Candide were already known to have escaped. They were followed to Cadiz. No time was lost in sending a ship after them, and this ship was already in the port of Buenos Aires. Rumour spread that an alcalde was about to come ashore, and that they were after the Grand

Inquisitor's murderers. The prudent old woman saw at once what was to be done.

'You cannot run away,' she told Cunégonde, 'and you have nothing to fear. It wasn't you who killed His Eminence and, anyway, the Governor loves you and won't allow any harm to come to you. Stay here.'

Whereupon she rushed off to Candide: 'Quick, off you go,' she said, 'or in an hour you'll be burnt.'

There was not a moment to lose. But how could he leave Cunégonde, and where was he to hide?

CHAPTER 14

How Candide and Cacambo were received by the
Jesuits of Paraguay

CANDIDE had brought a manservant with him from Cadiz of the kind frequently found along the coasts of Spain and in the colonies. He was a quarter Spanish, the son of a half-breed in the Tucuman. He had been a choir-boy, sexton, sailor, monk, agent, soldier, and lackey. His name was Cacambo, and he loved his master very much, because his master was a very good man. He saddled up the two Andalusian horses as quickly as he could.

'Come on, master, let's do as the old woman says and be off. Let's ride away, and no looking back.'

Candide burst out crying.

'O my darling Cunégonde! Must I abandon you just when the Governor was going to marry us! Cunégonde, what will become of you so far from home?'

'She'll become what she can,' said Cacambo. 'Women are never at a loss. God sees to that. Let's go.'

'Where are you taking me? Where are we going? What will we do without Cunégonde?' said Candide.

'By Saint James of Compostela,' said Cacambo, 'you were going to fight against the Jesuits. Let's go and fight for them instead. I know the roads well enough. I'll take you to their kingdom. They'll be delighted to have a captain who can do drill the Bulgar way. You'll be all the rage. If one doesn't get what one wants in one world, one can always get it in another. It's always a great pleasure to see new places and do different things.'

'So you've already been to Paraguay then?' said Candide.

'I've been there all right!' said Cacambo. 'I used to be a servant at the College of the Assumption, and I know los Padres' way of running things like I know the streets of Cadiz. It's a wonderful way of governing they have. Their kingdom is already more than three hundred leagues wide, and it's been divided into thirty provinces. Los Padres own everything in it, and the people nothing—a masterpiece of reason and justice. If you ask me, nothing could be more divine than los Padres making war on the Kings of Spain and Portugal over here and being confessors to the very same Kings back in Europe, or than killing Spaniards here and speeding them on their way to heaven back in Madrid. It tickles me, that does. Come on, let's go. You're about to become the happiest man alive. How pleased los Padres are going to be when they discover there's a captain coming who knows the Bulgar drill!'

The moment they arrived at the first border post, Cacambo told the advance guard that a captain was asking to speak to His Eminence, the commanding officer. The main guard was notified. A Paraguayan officer made haste to go and kneel at the feet of the commanding officer and inform him of the news. Candide and Cacambo were first disarmed, and then their two Andalusian horses were taken from them. Both strangers were ushered between two lines of soldiers. The commanding officer was standing at the far end, with the three-cornered hat on his head, his cassock hitched up, a sword at his side, and a halberd in his hand. He made a sign. Instantly twenty-four soldiers surrounded the two newcomers. A sergeant told them they must wait, that the commanding officer could not speak to them, that the Reverend Father Provincial did not permit Spaniards to open their mouths unless he was present, or to remain in the country for more than three hours.

'And where is the Reverend Father Provincial?' asked Cacambo.

'He has said Mass, and now he's taking parade,' replied the sergeant. 'And you won't be able to kiss his spurs for another three hours yet.'

'But,' said Cacambo, 'the Captain—who incidentally is dying of hunger, as indeed I am—isn't Spanish. He's German. Couldn't we have lunch while we wait for His Reverence?'

With this the sergeant went off to tell the commanding officer what had been said.

'May God be praised!' said this reverend gentleman. 'Since he's German, I can speak to him. Show him to my arbour.'

At once Candide was led into a closet of greenery, embellished with a very pretty colonnade of green and gold marble, and trellis-work containing parrots, colibris, humming-birds, guinea-fowl, and all manner of rare birds. An excellent lunch had been laid out in vessels of gold, and while the Paraguayans ate maize from wooden bowls out in the open in the full glare of the sun, the reverend father-in-command entered the arbour.

He was a very handsome young man, rather pale-skinned, with a round, ruddy face, arched eyebrows, a keen gaze, red ears, vermilion lips, and a proud demeanour—though proud in a way quite unlike a Spaniard or a Jesuit. Candide and Cacambo were given back the weapons which had been taken from them, as well as their two Andalusian horses. Cacambo gave the latter their oats near the arbour and kept a watchful eye on them in case of surprise.

First Candide kissed the hem of the commanding officer's cassock, and then they all sat down to table.

'So you're German, you say?' said the Jesuit in that language.

'Yes, reverend father,' said Candide.

As they uttered these words, they looked at each other in absolute astonishment and with a degree of emotion which it was beyond them to control.

'And from which part of Germany do you come?' said the Jesuit.

'From the lousy province of Westphalia,' said Candide. 'I was born in the castle of Thunder-ten-tronckh.'

'Good heavens! It's not possible?' exclaimed the commanding officer.

'It's a miracle!' exclaimed Candide.

'Can it really be you?' said the commanding officer.

'It's impossible,' said Candide.

They both fell back in amazement, and kissed each other, and wept buckets of tears.

'What! Can it really be you, reverend father? You, the brother of the fair Cunégonde! You who were killed by the Bulgars! You the son of the Baron! You a Jesuit in Paraguay! The world really is a very strange place, I must say. O Pangloss! Pangloss! how pleased you would be now if you hadn't been hanged!'

The commanding officer dismissed the Negro slaves and the Paraguayans who were serving drinks in goblets of rock-crystal. He thanked God and Saint Ignatius a thousand times, and he hugged Candide. Their faces were bathed in tears.

'You will be even more astonished, even more moved, even more beside yourself,' said Candide, 'when I tell you that Miss Cunégonde, your sister whom you thought disembowelled, is in the best of health.'

'Where?'

'Not far from here, with the Governor of Buenos Aires. And I was coming over here to fight against you.'

Each word they uttered in this long conversation piled wonder upon wonder. The soul of each took wing upon his tongue, paid careful heed with either ear, and sparkled in his eyes. Being Germans, they sat on at table for a long time; and while they waited for the Reverend Father Provincial, the commanding officer spoke thus to his dear Candide.

CHAPTER 15

How Candide killed the brother of his dear Cunégonde

'For as long as I live I shall always remember that dreadful day when I saw my father and mother killed and my sister raped. When the Bulgars had gone, my adorable sister was nowhere to be found, and my mother and father and I, together with two servant girls and three little boys who'd had their throats slit, were placed on a cart to be taken for burial at a Jesuit chapel two leagues from our ancestral home. A Jesuit threw some holy water over us. It was horribly salty. A few drops of it went in my eyes. The reverend father saw my eyelids quiver. He put his hand on my heart and felt it beating. I was saved, and three weeks later you wouldn't have known there'd ever been anything the matter. You know how good-looking I was, my dear Candide. I became even more so, with the result that the reverend father Croust, who was Father Superior, developed the most tender affection for me. He initiated me as a novice. Some time later

I was sent to Rome. The Father General had need of a batch of young German Jesuit recruits. The rulers of Paraguay admit as few Spanish Jesuits as they can. They prefer foreign ones in the belief that they can control them better. The Father General thought I was just the right sort of person to go and toil in this particular vineyard. So off we went, a Pole, a Tyrolean, and myself. On arrival I had the honour of being made subdeacon and lieutenant. Today I am colonel and priest. We shall give the King of Spain's troops a warm reception. They will be excommunicated and beaten, I can promise you. Providence has sent you here to help us. But is it really true that my dear sister Cunégonde is not far away, at the Governor's in Buenos Aires?'

Candide swore to him that nothing could be more true. Their tears began once more to flow.

The Baron could not desist from embracing Candide. He called him his brother, his saviour.

'Ah, my dear Candide,' he said, 'perhaps we can enter the city as victors, the two of us together, and rescue my dear sister Cunégonde.'

'There's nothing I'd like better,' said Candide, 'for I was intending to marry her, and I still hope to.'

'You insolent man!' retorted the Baron. 'You would have the audacity to marry my sister who has seventy-two quarterings! I consider it great effrontery on your part to dare speak to me of so bold an intention!'

Candide's blood turned to stone at such a statement. He answered him:

'Reverend father, all the quarterings in the world have nothing to do with it. I have rescued your sister from the arms of a Jew and an Inquisitor. She owes me a number of debts, and she intends to marry me. Maître Pangloss always told me that men are equal, and marry her I most assuredly shall.'

'We'll see about that, you scoundrel!' said the Jesuit Baron of Thunder-ten-tronckh and, so saying, struck him a heavy blow across the face with the flat of his sword.

Candide, quick as a flash, drew his own and plunged it up to the hilt into the Jesuit Baron's gut. But as he withdrew it, all steaming, he began to cry.

'Dear God,' he said, 'I've killed my former master, my friend, my brother-in-law. I am the best fellow in the world, and already that makes three men I've killed, and two of them priests!'

Cacambo, who had been standing guard at the door of the arbour, came running.

'There's nothing for it but to sell our lives dearly,' his master said to him. 'They're bound to come into the arbour, so we'll have to die fighting.'

Cacambo, who had seen a thing or two, kept his head. He removed the Baron's Jesuit cassock, put it on Candide, handed him the dead man's biretta, and made him mount his horse. This was all done in a trice.

'Quickly, master, at the gallop. Everyone will take you for a Jesuit dashing off to give orders, and we'll have passed the frontier before they can give chase.'

He was already riding like the wind when he said this, shouting out in Spanish:

'Make way, make way for the reverend father colonel.'

CHAPTER 16

What became of the two travellers with two girls, two monkeys,
and the savages called the Lobeiros

CANDIDE and his manservant were past the frontier, and still no one in the camp knew that the German Jesuit was dead. The vigilant Cacambo had taken care to fill his bag with bread, chocolate, ham, fruit, and a quantity of wine. They rode their Andalusian horses deep into unknown country where they found no sign of a track. Eventually a beautiful stretch of grassland, criss-crossed with streams, opened up before them. Our two travellers halted to allow their mounts to graze. Cacambo suggested to his master that they eat something and duly set him an example.

'How do you expect me to eat ham,' said Candide, 'when I have killed the Baron's son and see myself doomed never to see fair Cunégonde again in my life? What's the use of prolonging my miserable existence if I must drag it out, far away from her, in remorse and despair? And what will the *Journal de Trévoux** say?'

So saying, he did not abstain from eating. The sun was setting.

The two lost travellers heard one or two faint cries which sounded as though they came from women. They could not tell if they were cries of joy or pain, but they quickly sprang to their feet, full of that apprehension and alarm which anything in a strange land can arouse. The clamour was emanating from two completely naked girls who were scampering along the edge of the meadow pursued by two monkeys who were nibbling at their bottoms. Candide was moved to pity. He had learnt to shoot with the Bulgars, and he could have downed a hazelnut in a thicket without so much as touching a single leaf. He raised his Spanish double-barrelled gun, fired, and killed the two monkeys.

'God be praised, my dear Cacambo! I have delivered those two poor creatures from great peril. If it was a sin to kill an Inquisitor and a Jesuit, I've certainly atoned for it by saving the lives of these two girls. Perhaps the two young ladies are well-to-do and this chance episode will prove to be of great advantage to us hereabouts.'

He was about to continue, but he was struck dumb when he saw the two girls throw loving arms around the two monkeys, dissolve into tears over their dead bodies, and rend the air with wails of utmost grief.

'I didn't expect the kindness of their hearts to go that far,' Candide said at last to Cacambo, who replied:

'A fine thing you've done there, master. You've just killed those two young ladies' lovers.'

'Their lovers! Impossible! You're joking, Cacambo. How can they possibly be?'

'My dear master,' continued Cacambo, 'you're always surprised by everything. Why do you find it so strange that in some countries monkeys should enjoy the favours of the ladies? They're a quarter human, just as I am a quarter Spanish.'

'Oh, dear!' replied Candide, 'I remember now Maître Pangloss saying that such accidents did use to happen once upon a time, and that these couplings produced centaurs, fauns, and satyrs, and that several of the great names of antiquity had seen them. But I used to think that it only happened in fables.'

'Well, you ought to be convinced now that it's true,' said Cacambo. 'You see how people behave when they haven't had a bit of education. All I hope is that these ladies don't cause us any trouble.'

These solid reflections persuaded Candide to leave the meadow and plunge into a wood. There he supped with Cacambo and, having cursed the Inquisitor of Portugal, the Governor of Buenos Aires, and the Baron, they both fell asleep on some moss. When they awoke, they felt unable to move. The reason was that during the night the Lobeiros,* who inhabit that country, and to whom the two ladies had denounced them, had pinioned them with rope made of bark. They were surrounded by some fifty naked Lobeiros armed with arrows, cudgels, and hatchets made of flint. Some of them were warming a large cauldron, others were preparing skewers, and they were all chanting:

'It's a Jesuit! It's a Jesuit! We shall be avenged, our stomachs will be full. Let's eat Jesuit! Let's eat Jesuit!'

'I told you so, my dear master,' cried Cacambo sadly. 'I told you those two girls would play us false.'

Candide, seeing the cauldron and the skewers, exclaimed:

'We're going to be roasted or boiled, that's for certain. Ah! what would Maître Pangloss say if he could see how human nature is in its pure state? All is well. So it may be. But I must say it's pretty rotten to have lost Miss Cunégonde and be spit-roasted by Lobeiros.'

Cacambo was not one to lose his head.

'Don't despair,' he said to the disconsolate Candide. 'I know these people's lingo a bit. I'll have a word with them.'

'Make sure you point out to them,' said Candide, 'how frightfully inhuman it is to cook people, and how unchristian it is too.'

'So, gentlemen,' said Cacambo, 'you think you're going to have Jesuit today. That's fine by me. Nothing could be fairer than to treat your enemies this way. The laws of nature do indeed tell us to kill our neighbour, and that is the way people behave throughout the world. If we ourselves do not exercise our right to eat our neighbour, that's because we've got better things to eat. But you haven't the same resources as we have. Certainly it is better to eat one's enemies than to leave the fruits of one's victory for the rooks and the crows. But, gentlemen, you would not want to eat your friends. You think you're about to skewer a Jesuit, while in fact it's your defender, the enemy of your enemies, that you'll be roasting. Me, I was born in these parts. This gentleman here is my master and, far from being a Jesuit, he has just killed a Jesuit and is wearing the spoils of combat. That's how you came to be mistaken. If you want to check the truth of what I say, take his cassock to the nearest frontier post of the kingdom of los Padres. Ask them if my master didn't kill a Jesuit officer. It won't take you long, and you'll always be able to eat us anyway if you discover I've lied to you. But if I've told you the truth, you are too well acquainted with the principles, articles, and procedures of international law not to pardon us.'

The Lobeiros found this speech very reasonable. They deputed two eminent persons to proceed post-haste to find out the truth. The two deputies carried out their commission like intelligent men and soon returned bearing good tidings. The Lobeiros untied their two prisoners, did them all kinds of honour, offered them girls, gave them refreshments, and escorted them back to the boundary of their lands merrily chanting: 'He isn't a Jesuit, he isn't a Jesuit!'

Candide could not get over the manner of his deliverance.

'What a people!' he was saying. 'What men! What manners! If I hadn't had the good fortune to run Miss Cunégonde's brother through with a hefty thrust of my sword, I would have been eaten, and without remission of sentence. But human nature in its pure state is good after all, since these people, instead of eating me, were all sweetness and light the minute they knew I wasn't a Jesuit.'

CHAPTER 17

The arrival of Candide and his manservant in Eldorado, and what they saw there

WHEN they reached the Lobeiro frontier, Cacambo said to Candide:

'You see, this half of the world is no better than the other. Take my advice, let's head back to Europe by the shortest route possible.'

'But how?' said Candide, 'and where to? If I go back to my own country, I'll find the Bulgars and Abars busy cutting everyone's throats. If I return to Portugal, I'll be burnt at the stake. And if we stay here, we may end up on a spit at any moment. But how can I bring myself to leave the part of the world that contains Miss Cunégonde?'

'Let's make for Cayenne,' said Cacambo. 'We'll find the French there. They travel all over the place. They'll be able to help us. Perhaps God will have pity on us.'

Getting to Cayenne was no simple matter. They knew roughly

which direction to take, but what with the mountains and the rivers and the precipices and the brigands and the savages, terrible obstacles presented themselves at every turn. Their horses died of exhaustion, they ran out of provisions, and for a whole month they survived on wild fruits, before they eventually found themselves by a small river lined with coconut palms, which kept both them and their hopes alive.

Cacambo, whose advice was always as good as the old woman's had been, said to Candide:

'We've had it, we've walked as far as we can. I see an empty canoe on the bank. Let's fill it with coconuts, get in and let the current take us. A river always leads to some kind of habitation. If we don't find anything nice, at least we'll find something new.'

'All right,' said Candide. 'Let's trust in Providence.'

They drifted downstream for a few leagues between river-banks now covered in flowers, now bare of vegetation, now flat, now steep. The river grew wider and wider. At length it ran under a vault of fearsome-looking rocks that reached high into the sky. The two travellers had the pluck to let the water carry them under this vault. The river, which narrowed at this point, swept them along with horrifying speed and made a terrifying din. Twenty-four hours later they saw the light of day once more, but their boat was dashed to pieces in the rapids. They had to drag themselves from rock to rock for a whole league. Eventually they came to a vast open space surrounded by impassable peaks. The land had been cultivated as much to give pleasure as to serve a need. Everywhere whatever was useful was also agreeable. The roads were covered, or rather adorned, with conveyances of the most lustrous form and substance, bearing men and women of singular beauty, and drawn at great speed by large red sheep who could outpace the finest horses in Andalusia, Tetuan, or Mequinez.

'This, on the other hand,' said Candide, 'is something of an improvement on Westphalia.'

He and Cacambo stepped ashore at the first village they came to. A few village children, covered in tattered gold brocade, were playing quoits at the entrance to the settlement. Our two men from the other world stopped to watch them. Their quoits were fairly large, round objects, some of them yellow, some red, some green, and they gleamed in an odd way. The travellers were prompted to pick some of them up. They were pieces of gold, emerald, and ruby, and the smallest of them would have been the greatest ornament on the Mogul's throne.

'No doubt,' said Candide, 'these children playing quoits are the sons of the King of this country.'

The village schoolmaster appeared at that moment to call them back to the classroom.

'That', said Candide, 'must be the royal family's private tutor.'

The little urchins stopped their game at once, leaving their quoits and everything else they had been playing with lying on the ground. Candide picked them up, ran to the tutor, and humbly presented him with them, explaining in sign language that their Royal Highnesses had forgotten their gold and their precious stones. The village schoolmaster threw them on the ground with a smile, stared at Candide for a moment in great surprise, and walked off.

The travellers did not fail to gather up the gold, rubies, and emeralds.

'Where can we be?' exclaimed Candide. 'The royal children here must be very well brought up if they're taught to turn their noses up at gold and precious stones.'

Cacambo was just as surprised as Candide. At length they drew near to the first house in the village. It was built like a European palace. There was a crowd of people at the door, and an even bigger one inside. Some very pleasant music could be heard, and there was a mouth-watering smell of cooking. Cacambo went up to the door and heard Peruvian being spoken. This was his native tongue: for, as everyone knows, Cacambo was born in the Tucuman in a village where this was the only language they knew.

'I'll interpret for you,' he told Candide. 'Let's go inside. This is an inn.'

At once two waiters and two waitresses, dressed in cloth of gold and wearing ribbons in their hair, showed them to a table and offered them the set menu. The meal consisted of four different soups, each garnished with a couple of parrots, then a boiled condor weighing two hundred pounds, two excellent roast monkeys, one platter of three hundred colibris, and another of six hundred humming-birds, some delicious casseroles, and mouth-watering pastries. Everything was served on dishes made of a kind of rock-crystal. The waiters and waitresses poured out a variety of liquors distilled from sugar-cane.

The guests were tradesmen and waggoners for the most part, all of them extremely polite. They asked Cacambo one or two questions with the most scrupulous discretion, and returned full answers to those he put to them.

When the meal was over, Cacambo thought, as Candide did, that he could more than cover the cost of their meal by tossing two of the large pieces of gold he had picked up on to the table. The innkeeper and his wife burst out laughing and held their sides for a long time. Finally they recovered themselves:

'Gentlemen,' said the innkeeper, 'we can see you're strangers. We're not used to them here. Forgive us if we started laughing when you offered to pay with the stones off our roads. Presumably you don't have any of the local currency, but you don't need any to dine here. All inns set up for the convenience of those engaged in commerce are paid for by the government. The meal wasn't very good here because this is a poor village, but anywhere else you'll get the kind of reception you deserve.'

Cacambo interpreted for Candide all that the innkeeper had said, and Candide was as amazed and bewildered to hear it as Cacambo was to tell it.

'What is this place,' said one to the other, 'which is unknown to the rest of the world and where the whole nature of things is so different from ours? It's probably the place where all goes well, for there absolutely must be such a place. And whatever Maître Pangloss might have said, I often observed that everything went rather badly in Westphalia.'

CHAPTER 18

What they saw in the land of Eldorado

CACAMBO gave the innkeeper to understand how curious he was to know more. The innkeeper said:

'I know very little about things, and that suits me well enough. But we have an old man living in the village who used to be at court and who is the most knowledgeable man in the kingdom, as well as the most communicative.'

Thereupon he took Cacambo to see the old man. Candide was

playing second fiddle now, and it was he who accompanied his servant. They entered a house of a very modest sort, for its front door was only of silver and the panelling of its room merely gold, though the workmanship was in such good taste that more opulent panelling could not have outshone it. It has to be said that the antechamber was studded only with rubies and emeralds, but the pattern in which they had all been arranged more than made up for this extreme simplicity.

The old man received the two strangers on a sofa stuffed with colibri feathers and gave orders for them to be served various liquors in diamond goblets. After which he satisfied their curiosity in the following fashion:

'I am one hundred and seventy-two years old, and I learnt from my late father, who was a crown equerry, of the extraordinary upheavals that he had witnessed in Peru. This kingdom we are in now is the former homeland of the Incas, who most imprudently left it to go and conquer another part of the world and ended up being wiped out by the Spanish.

'The princes of their race who remained behind in their native country were wiser. They ordained, with the consent of the nation, that no inhabitant was ever to leave our little kingdom. And that's how we've managed to remain innocent and happy. The Spanish knew vaguely about the place and called it Eldorado, and an English knight called Raleigh even came fairly near it about a hundred years ago. But since we are surrounded by unclimbable rocks and cliffs, we have always hitherto been safe from the rapacity of European nations with their unaccountable fondness for the pebbles and dirt off our land, and who would kill us to the very last man just to lay their hands on the stuff.'

Their conversation was a long one and touched on the form of government there, on local customs, on women, public entertainment, and the arts. Eventually Candide, ever one for metaphysics, asked through Cacambo if there was a religion in this country.

The old man flushed a little.

'But how could you suppose there might not be?' he said. 'What do you take us for? Ungrateful wretches?'

Cacambo humbly asked what the religion of Eldorado was. The old man flushed again.

'Can there be more than one religion?' he asked. 'As far as I know, we have the same religion as everyone else. We worship God from dusk till dawn.'

'Do you worship only one God?' asked Cacambo, who was still acting as interpreter to the doubting Candide.

'Obviously,' said the old man. 'There aren't two Gods, or three, or four. I must say people from your part of the world do ask some very strange questions.'

Candide persisted in having further questions put to this genial old man. He wanted to know how they prayed to God in Eldorado.

'We don't pray to God,' said the good and worthy sage. 'We have nothing to ask him for. He has given us all we need, and we never cease to thank him.'

Candide was curious to see the priests. He had Cacambo ask where they were. The kindly old man smiled.

'My friends,' he said, 'we are all priests. The King and the head of each family sing hymns of thanksgiving solemnly every morning, to the accompaniment of five or six thousand musicians.'

'What! You mean you don't have any monks to teach and dispute and govern and intrigue and burn people to death who don't agree with them?'

'We'd be mad to,' said the old man. 'We're all of like mind here, and we can't see the point of your monks.'

Each of these remarks left Candide in raptures, and he kept thinking to himself:

'This is all rather different from Westphalia and His Lordship's castle. If our friend Pangloss had seen Eldorado, he would no longer have said that the castle of Thunder-ten-tronckh was the best place on earth. It just goes to show: travel's the thing.'

After this long conversation the kind old man had six sheep harnessed to a carriage and lent the two travellers twelve of his servants to take them to the court.

'Forgive me,' he said to them, 'if my advancing years deprive me of the honour of accompanying you. You will not be dissatisfied with the way the King receives you, and I am sure you will be tolerant of our customs if any are not to your liking.'

Candide and Cacambo stepped into the carriage. The six sheep went like the wind, and in less than four hours they had arrived at the palace of the King, situated at one end of the capital. The main entrance was two hundred and twenty feet high and one hundred wide. There are no words to describe what it was made of, which in itself gives some idea of just how prodigiously superior it was to the sand and pebbles we call 'gold' and 'precious stones'.

Twenty beautiful guardswomen received Candide and Cacambo upon arrival, escorted them to the baths, and dressed them in robes of humming-bird down, after which the Grand Officers and the Grand Dames of the Crown led them to His Majesty's apartments between two lines of musicians each a thousand strong, in accordance with normal protocol. As they approached the throne-room, Cacambo asked one of the Grand Officers what to do when being presented to His Majesty. Should one fall on one's knees or flat on the ground; should one put one's hands on one's head or over one's backside; should one lick the dust off the floor? In a word, what was the done thing?

'It is customary', said the Grand Officer, 'to embrace the King and kiss him on both cheeks.'

Candide and Cacambo fell upon His Majesty's neck. He welcomed them with all imaginable graciousness and politely asked them to supper.

Before then they were shown round the city, with its public buildings raised (and praised) to the skies, its market-places decorated with a thousand columns, its fountains of spring-water and rose-water and sugar-cane liquors, all playing ceaselessly in the middle of large squares paved with special stones which gave off an aroma similar to that of clove and cinnamon. Candide asked to see the law courts.* He was told there weren't any, and that there were never any cases to hear. He asked if there were any prisons, and he was told there weren't. What surprised him most and gave him the greatest pleasure was the Palace of Science, in which he saw a gallery two thousand feet long all full of instruments for the study of mathematics and physics.

Having seen about a thousandth part of the city in the course of the entire afternoon, they were then brought back to the King. Candide sat down to table next to His Majesty, his servant Cacambo, and several ladies. Never did anyone dine better, and never was anyone wittier at supper than His Majesty. Cacambo interpreted the King's 'bons mots' for Candide, and even in translation they still seemed 'bons'. Of all the things that surprised Candide, this was not what surprised him the least.

They spent a month in this hospice. Candide never stopped saying to Cacambo:

'It's true, my friend, and I'll say it again. The castle where I was born is nothing compared to this place. But still, Miss Cunégonde isn't here, and doubtless you have some sweetheart back in Europe. If we stay on here, we'll simply be the same as everyone else, whereas if we return to Europe with even a mere dozen sheep loaded up with Eldorado pebbles, then we'll be richer than all the kings put together, we'll have no more inquisitors to worry about, and we'll easily be able to get Miss Cunégonde back.'

Cacambo liked what he heard. Such is the desire to be always on the move, to be somebody, and to show off about what you've seen on your travels, that the two happy men resolved to be happy no longer and to ask leave of His Majesty to depart.

'You're making a great mistake,' the King told them. 'I know my country isn't up to much, but when one is reasonably content in a place, one ought to stay there. But I certainly have no right to stop strangers from leaving. That is a piece of tyranny which has no part in our customs or our laws. All men are free. Leave when you wish, though getting out is difficult. It is impossible to return up the rapids which, by a miracle, you managed to come down: the river runs under vault after vault of rock. The mountains that surround my kingdom are ten thousand feet high and as sheer as a city wall. Each one is about ten leagues thick, and the only way down the other side is one long cliff-face. However, since you are absolutely determined to leave, I shall give orders for the machine intendants to make one which will transport you in comfort. When they've got you to the other side of the mountains, no one will be able to accompany you any further, for my subjects have vowed never to set foot outside these boundaries, and they are too sensible to break their vow. Apart from that you can ask me for whatever you want.'

'All we ask of Your Majesty,' said Cacambo, 'is a few sheep laden with provisions and pebbles and some of the local dirt.'

The King laughed.

'I really don't understand this passion you Europeans have for our yellow dirt,' said the King, 'but take all you want, and much good may it do you.'

He immediately ordered his engineers to make a machine to winch these two extraordinary men out of his kingdom. Three thousand of the best scientists worked on it. It was ready in a fort-night and cost no more than the equivalent of twenty thousand pounds sterling in local currency. Candide and Cacambo were installed on the machine, together with two large red sheep saddled up for them to ride when they had crossed the mountains, twenty pack-sheep laden with provisions, thirty carrying a selection of the best local curios and gifts the country could offer, and fifty loaded up with gold, diamonds, and other precious stones. The King embraced the two wanderers and bid them a fond farewell.

They presented quite a sight as they departed, as did the ingeni-ous way in which they were hoisted, men and sheep together, to the top of the mountains. The scientists took their leave of them once they were safely across, and Candide was left with no other desire or object but to go and present Miss Cunégonde with his sheep.

'We have the wherewithal to pay the Governor of Buenos Aires now,' he said, 'if a price can be put on Miss Cunégonde, that is. Let's head for Cayenne and take ship there, and then we'll see what kingdom we're going to buy.'

CHAPTER 19

What happened to them in Surinam and how Candide met Martin

FOR our two travellers the first day's journey passed pleasantly enough. They were spurred on by the prospect of being themselves the owners of more treasures than Asia, Europe, and Africa can muster between them. Candide, quite carried away, carved the name of Cunégonde on trees as he passed. On the second day two of their sheep became bogged down in a swamp and were swallowed up with their entire load. A few days afterwards two more sheep died of exhaustion. Seven or eight then starved to death in a desert. Others fell down some mountainsides a day or two later. In the end, after a hundred days of journeying, they had only two sheep left.

Said Candide to Cacambo:

'My friend, you see how perishable are the riches of this world. The only sure thing is virtue and the happiness of seeing Miss Cunégonde again.'

'I'm sure,' said Cacambo. 'But we do still have two sheep left and more treasure than the King of Spain will ever have, and in the distance I can see a town which, I suspect, is Surinam, where the Dutch are. Our troubles are over and the good times are just beginning.'

As they drew near to the town, they came on a Negro lying on the ground half-naked, which in his case meant in half a pair of short denim breeches. The poor man was missing his left leg and his right hand.

'My God!' said Candide in Dutch, 'what are you doing lying here, my friend, in this dreadful state?'

'I'm waiting for my master, Mr Van der Hartbargin, the well-known trader,' replied the Negro.

'And is it Mr Van der Hartbargin', said Candide, 'who has treated you like this?'

'Yes, sir,' said the Negro, 'it is the custom. We are given one pair of short denim breeches twice a year, and that's all we have to wear. When we're working at the sugar-mill and catch our finger in the grinding-wheel, they cut off our hand. When we try to run away, they cut off a leg. I have been in both these situations. This is the price you pay for the sugar you eat in Europe. However, when my mother sold me for ten Patagonian crowns on the coast of Guinea, she said to me: "My dear child, bless our fetishes, worship them always, they will bring you a happy life. You have the honour of being a slave to our lords and masters the Whites and, by so being, you are making your father's and mother's fortune." Alas! I don't know if I made their fortune, but they didn't make mine. Dogs, monkeys, parrots, they're all a thousand times less wretched than we are. The Dutch fetishes who converted me tell me every Sunday that we are all the sons of Adam, Whites and Blacks alike. I'm no genealogist, but if these preachers are right, we are all cousins born of first-cousins. Well, you will grant me that you can't treat a relative much worse than this.'

'O Pangloss!' cried Candide, 'this is one abomination you never thought of. That does it. I shall finally have to renounce your Optimism.'

'What's Optimism?' asked Cacambo.

'I'm afraid to say,' said Candide, 'that it's a mania for insisting that all is well when things are going badly.'

And he began to weep as he gazed at his Negro, and he entered Surinam in tears.

The first thing they enquired about was whether there were a ship in the port that could be sent to Buenos Aires. The person they approached happened to be a Spanish skipper, who offered to name them a fair price himself. He arranged to meet them in an inn. Candide and the faithful Cacambo went to wait for him there along with their two sheep.

Candide, whose heart was always on his lips, told the Spaniard all about his adventures and confessed that he wished to carry off Miss Cunégonde.

'I'm not taking you to Buenos Aires, that's for sure,' said the skipper. 'I'd be hanged, and so would you. The fair Cunégonde is His Excellency's favourite mistress.'

This came as a bolt from the blue to Candide. He wept for a long time. Eventually he took Cacambo to one side:

'Look, my dear friend,' he said to him, 'this is what you must do. We've each got about five or six million in diamonds in our pockets. You're cleverer than I am. Go and fetch Miss Cunégonde from Buenos Aires. If the Governor makes difficulties about it, give him a million. If he won't budge, give him two. You haven't killed any inquisitors, they won't be suspicious of you. I'll have another ship made ready. I'll go and wait for you in Venice. Theirs is a free country where one has nothing to fear from Bulgars or Abars or Jews or Inquisitors.'

Cacambo applauded this wise decision. He was in despair at the thought of parting from so good a master, who had become his close friend. But the pleasure of being of use to him outweighed the pain of leaving him. They tearfully embraced each other. Candide told him to make sure and not forget the kind old woman. Cacambo left the same day. He was a very fine fellow, Cacambo.

Candide stayed some while longer in Surinam, waiting to find another skipper who would be prepared to take him and his two remaining sheep to Italy. He engaged servants and bought everything he needed for a long voyage. At last Mr Van der Hartbargin, the master of a large ship, came and introduced himself.

'How much will you charge,' he asked this man, 'to take myself, my servants, my baggage, and these two sheep directly to Venice?'

The master asked ten thousand piastres. Candide did not hesitate.

'Hallo,' the careful Van der Hartbargin said to himself, 'this stranger parts with ten thousand piastres just like that! He must be pretty rich.'

He came back at him a moment later and indicated that he could not sail for less than twenty thousand.

'Very well, then, you shall have them,' said Candide.

'Blow me!' said the merchant under his breath. 'This man parts with twenty thousand piastres as easily as ten.'

He came back at him once more and said that he could not take him to Venice for less than thirty thousand piastres.

'Then thirty thousand it is,' replied Candide.

'Hallo, indeed!' the Dutch merchant said to himself again. 'Thirty thousand piastres are nothing to this man. Those two sheep must be carrying immense treasures. Better not press things any further. Let's get paid the thirty thousand piastres first, and then we'll see.'

Candide sold two little diamonds, the smaller of which was worth more than all the money the shipmaster was asking. He paid him in advance. The two sheep were loaded on board. Candide was following behind in a small boat to join the ship moored out in the roads, when the master calmly set his sails and weighed anchor. The wind favoured him. Candide, helpless and quite flabbergasted, soon lost sight of him.

'Alas!' he lamented, 'that's just the kind of dirty trick you'd expect from the old world.'

He returned to the shore deep in misery, for, after all, he had lost what would have been enough to make the fortune of twenty monarchs.

He took himself off to the Dutch Resident Magistrate and, as he was a little upset, knocked rather peremptorily on the door. In he went, explained what had happened to him, and shouted rather more loudly than was proper. The magistrate began by fining him ten thousand piastres for the noise he had made. Then he listened to him patiently, promised to look into his case as soon as the merchant returned, and charged a further ten thousand piastres for the cost of the hearing.

This treatment was the last straw for Candide in his despair. To be sure, he had suffered misfortunes a thousand times more grievous, but the sang-froid of the magistrate, and of that ship-master who had robbed him, stirred his bile and plunged him into a black melancholy. The wickedness of men struck him in all its ugliness, and his mind fed on images of gloom. Finally, there being a French vessel all ready to sail for Bordeaux, and as he had no more sheep laden with diamonds to place aboard, he paid for a cabin on the ship at the standard price, and made it known in the town that he would pay passage and board for, and give two thousand piastres to, any respectable person who would make the journey with him, on condition that this person was the most disgusted with his lot and the unhappiest man in the province.

A crowd of applicants came forward such as an entire fleet could not have carried. Wanting to choose among the most likely candidates, Candide selected twenty who seemed to him fairly companionable and who all claimed to deserve preference. He got them together in his inn and gave them supper on condition that each would swear to give a faithful version of his story. He undertook to choose the one who would seem to him most to be pitied and to have the greatest reason for being the most dissatisfied with his lot. To the others he promised a small consideration.

The session lasted until four o'clock in the morning. Candide, as he listened to all their adventures, recalled what the old woman had said to him on their way to Buenos Aires and how she had wagered that not a single person on board would not have suffered very great misfortunes. He thought of Pangloss with every story he was told.

'Pangloss', he said, 'would be hard put to it to prove his system. I wish he were here. One thing's certain: if all is going well, it's happening in Eldorado and not in the rest of the world.'

In the end he decided in favour of a poor scholar who had spent ten years working for the publishing houses of Amsterdam. He took the view that there was no form of employment in the world with which one could possibly be more disgusted.

This man of learning, who was a perfectly decent fellow moreover, had been robbed by his wife, assaulted by his son, and abandoned by his daughter, who had eloped with a Portuguese. He had just been removed from a small post which had provided him with a living, and the preachers of Surinam were persecuting him because they took him for a Socinian.* It must be admitted that the other applicants were at least as unhappy as him, but Candide hoped that the scholar would keep him amused on the voyage. All his rivals

considered that Candide was doing them a great injustice, but he
pacified them by giving them a hundred piastres each.

CHAPTER 20

What happened to Candide and Martin at sea

So the old scholar, who was called Martin, took ship for Bordeaux
with Candide. Both had seen much and suffered much, and even if
the ship had had to sail all the way from Surinam to Japan via the
Cape of Good Hope, they would still have had matter enough to
sustain their discussion of physical and moral evil throughout the
entire voyage.

However, Candide had one great advantage over Martin, which
was that he was still hoping to see Miss Cunégonde again, while
Martin had nothing to hope for. Moreover, he had gold and diamonds, and although he had lost a hundred large sheep laden with
the greatest treasure on earth, and although the Dutch master's
villainy still rankled, nevertheless when he thought about what he
had left in his pockets, and when he talked about Cunégonde, especially at the end of a meal, then he would be inclined to favour the
philosophical system of Pangloss.

'But you, Mr Martin,' he said to the scholar, 'what are your
thoughts on all this? How do you see physical and moral evil?'

'Sir,' replied Martin, 'my priests accused me of being a Socinian,
but the fact of the matter is that I am a Manichaean.'*

'You're pulling my leg,' said Candide. 'There aren't any Man-
ichaeans left any more.'

'There's me,' said Martin. 'I can't help it. I just can't see things
any other way.'

'It's the devil in you,' said Candide.

'He's mixed up in the affairs of this world to such an extent', said
Martin, 'that he may well be in me, just as he's in everything else.
But to be frank, when I look about me on this globe, or rather this
globule, I begin to think God has abandoned it to some malign
being—apart from Eldorado, that is. I've scarcely seen one town that
did not wish the ruination of its neighbour, or one family that did
not want to see the end of another. Everywhere you look, the weak

execrate the strong while they grovel at their feet, and the strong treat them like so many sheep, providing wool and meat to be sold. One million regimented assassins, rushing from one end of Europe to the other, commit murder and brigandage by the rule book in order to earn their daily bread, because there is no more respectable profession; and in the cities, where people appear to live in peace and the arts flourish, men are devoured by more envy, worry, and dissatisfaction than all the scourges of a city under siege. Secret sorrows are more cruel even than public tribulations. In short, I have seen so many of them, and suffered so many, that I am a Manichaean.'

'Yet there is good,' Candide would answer.

'That's as may be,' Martin would say, 'but I've never met it.'

In the middle of this debate, they heard the sound of cannon fire. The noise increased by the moment. Each of them grabbed his telescope. Two ships were to be seen engaging at a distance of about three miles. The wind brought both of these ships so close to the French vessel that they had the pleasure of seeing the engagement in perfect comfort. Eventually one ship let fly a broadside at the other that was so low and so accurate that it sank it. Candide and Martin could distinctly see a hundred men on the deck of the ship that was going down. They were all raising their hands heavenwards and letting out the most appalling screams. In an instant everything disappeared beneath the waves.

'Well, there you are,' said Martin. 'That's how men treat each other.'

'It is true,' said Candide. 'The devil has had a hand in this business.'

So saying, he noticed something bright red swimming near their ship. The ship's launch was lowered to go and see what it could be. It was one of his sheep. There was more joy in Candide at finding this one sheep* than there had been sorrow at losing an hundredfold all laden with large Eldorado diamonds.

The French captain soon observed that the captain of the sinker was Spanish, while the captain of the sunk was a Dutch pirate. It was the very man who had robbed Candide. The immense riches with which this villain had absconded had gone down with him, and all that had been saved was one sheep.

'You see,' Candide said to Martin, 'crime is sometimes punished. That scoundrel of a Dutch skipper got the fate he deserved.'

'Yes,' said Martin, 'but did the passengers on his ship have to perish also? God punished the rogue: the devil drowned the rest.'

Meanwhile the French and Spanish ships resumed their voyages, and Candide and Martin their conversations. They argued for a solid fortnight, and at the end of the fortnight they were as far forward as the day they began. But, well, they talked, and exchanged ideas, and consoled each other. Candide would stroke his sheep and say:

'I have found you, so I may well be able to find Cunégonde.'

CHAPTER 21

Candide and Martin approach the French coast and reason together

AT last they came in sight of the French coast.

'Have you ever been to France, Mr Martin?' said Candide.

'Yes,' said Martin, 'I've travelled through several of its provinces. There are some where half the inhabitants are mad, one or two where they're too clever by half, some where they're generally quite gentle and rather stupid, and others where they try to be witty. And in all of them the principal occupation is love. Next comes slander and gossip, and third comes talking nonsense.'

'But, Mr Martin, have you been to Paris?'

'Yes, I've been to Paris. There they have all of these types. It's a chaotic place, a throng in which everyone seeks pleasure and where practically no one finds it, at least not as far as I could see. I haven't spent much time there. When I arrived, I was robbed of everything I had by pickpockets at the Saint-Germain fair. I myself was taken for a thief and spent a week in prison, after which I did some proof-reading to earn enough to be able to return to Holland on foot. I got to know the pen-pushing brigade, and the political intriguers, and the religious convulsions crowd.* They say there are some very well-mannered people in that city. I dare say there are.'

'Personally I have no desire to see France,' said Candide. 'As I'm sure you can imagine, when one's spent a month in Eldorado, there's nothing in the world one much wants to see other than Miss Cunégonde. I'm on my way to wait for her in Venice. We will be going through France to get to Italy. Why don't you come with me?'

'Delighted to,' said Martin. 'They say Venice is only fit to live in if you're a Venetian nobleman, but that foreigners are well looked after none the less, providing they have a lot of money. I haven't, you have; I'll follow you anywhere.'

'Incidentally,' said Candide, 'do you believe the Earth was originally a sea, as they say it was in that big book the captain has?'

'I don't believe anything of the sort,' said Martin, 'no more than I believe any of the other rubbish they've been coming out with recently.'

'But for what purpose was this world created then?' said Candide.

'To drive us mad,' replied Martin.

'Don't you find it absolutely amazing,' Candide went on, 'the way the two girls I told you about, the ones who lived in the land of the Lobeiros, loved those two monkeys?'

'Not at all,' said Martin. 'I don't see what's odd about that particular passion. I've seen so many extraordinary things that nothing's extraordinary any more.'

'Do you think', said Candide, 'that men have always massacred each other the way they do now? that they've always been liars, cheats, traitors, ingrates, brigands? that they've always been feeble, fickle, envious, gluttonous, drunken, avaricious, ambitious, bloodthirsty, slanderous, debauched, fanatical, hypocritical, and stupid?'

'Do you think', said Martin, 'that hawks have always eaten pigeons when they find them?'

'Yes, no doubt,' said Candide.

'Well, then,' said Martin, 'if hawks have always had the same character, why do you expect men to have changed theirs?'

'Oh!' said Candide, 'there's a big difference, because free will . . .' Arguing thus the while, they arrived in Bordeaux.

CHAPTER 22

What happened to Candide and Martin in France

CANDIDE broke his journey in Bordeaux just long enough to sell a few Eldorado pebbles and to procure a good post-chaise with two seats, for he could no longer be without Martin, his philosopher. He was only very sorry to be parted from his sheep, which he left with the Academy of Science at Bordeaux. They set as the subject of that year's prize the question why the wool of this sheep was red, and the prize was awarded to a scientist from the North who proved by A plus B minus C divided by Z that the sheep had necessarily to be red, and to die of sheep-pox.

Meanwhile all the travellers Candide met in the inns along the way told him: 'We're off to Paris.' In the end this universal eagerness made him want to see that capital city. It would not take him much out of his way on his journey to Venice.

He entered by the Faubourg Saint-Marceau and thought he was in the ugliest village in Westphalia.

Scarce had Candide put up at his inn than he was laid low by a minor indisposition brought on by his exertions. As he had an enormous diamond on his finger, and as an extremely heavy strong box had been noticed among his luggage, he soon had by him two doctors whom he had not sent for, a number of bosom companions who never left his side, and two ladies of good works who were heating up his broth.

Martin said:

'I remember being ill on my first trip to Paris too. I was very poor, so I had no friends or do-gooders or doctors, and I got better.'

Meanwhile, by dint of many potions and bloodlettings, Candide's illness became serious. A local priest came and kindly asked him for a confessional note payable to bearer in the other world.* Candide would have none of it. The ladies of good works assured him that it was the new fashion. Candide replied that he was not a one for fashion. Martin was for throwing the priest out of the window. The cleric swore that Candide would not be granted burial. Martin swore that he would bury the cleric if he continued to bother them. The quarrel grew more heated. Martin took him by the shoulders and unceremoniously ejected him. This caused a great scandal, which was the subject of an official enquiry.

Candide recovered, and during his convalescence he had some very fine company to supper with him. There was gambling for high stakes. Candide was most surprised never to get a single ace, and Martin was not surprised.

Among those who did him the honours of the city was a little abbé from Périgord,* one of those busy little, pushy, fawning, frightfully accommodating types, always on the make, always ready to please, who lie in wait for strangers passing through and give them all the local gossip and scandal and offer them entertainments at all sorts of prices. This one took Candide and Martin to the theatre first. A new tragedy was on. Candide found himself sitting next to some of the intellectual smart set. This did not prevent him from crying at scenes that were played to perfection.

One of these arbiters of taste sitting nearby said to him during an interval:

'You are quite wrong to cry. That actress is very bad. The actor playing opposite her is still worse. The play is even worse than the actors. The author doesn't know a word of Arabic, and yet the play is set in Arabia. And what's more, the man doesn't believe in innate ideas. Tomorrow I can bring you twenty pamphlets criticizing him.'

'Sir, how many plays do you have in France?' Candide asked the abbé, who replied:

'Five or six thousand.'

'That's a lot,' said Candide. 'How many of them are any good?'

'Fifteen or sixteen,' was the answer.

'That's a lot,' said Martin.

Candide was much taken with an actress who was playing Queen Elizabeth in a rather dull tragedy which is sometimes put on.

'I do like that actress,' he said to Martin. 'She looks a bit like Miss Cunégonde. I should be rather pleased to call on her.'

The abbé from Périgord offered to effect an introduction. Candide, brought up in Germany, asked what the form was and how queens of England were treated in France.

'We must distinguish,' said the abbé. 'In the provinces you take them to an inn. In Paris you respect them when they're beautiful, and you throw them on to the rubbish-heap when they're dead.'

'Queens on the rubbish-heap!' said Candide.

'Yes, really,' said Martin. 'The abbé is right. I was in Paris when Mlle Monime passed, as they say, from this life to the next. She was refused what people here call "the honours of the grave", that is to say of rotting in a filthy cemetery with all the beggars of the neighbourhood. Unlike the rest of her troupe she was buried alone at the corner of the rue de Bourgogne, which must have pained her exceedingly, for she thought very nobly.'*

'That's not a very nice way to treat people,' said Candide.

'What can you expect?' said Martin. 'That's the way they are round here. Take any contradiction or inconsistency you can think of, and you will find it in the government, the courts, the churches, or the theatres of this strange nation.'

'Is it true that people in Paris are always laughing?' enquired Candide.

'Yes,' said the abbé, 'but through gritted teeth. For they complain about everything with great gales of laughter, and they laugh even when doing the most detestable things.'

'Who', asked Candide, 'was the fat pig who was telling me so many bad things about that play I cried such a lot at, and about those actors I liked so much?'

'He is evil incarnate,' replied the abbé. 'He earns his living by decrying all new plays and books. He hates the up-and-coming writer, just as eunuchs hate the up-and-coming lover. He's one of those vipers of literature that feeds off filth and venom. He's a hack.'

'What do you mean by "hack"?' said Candide.

'I mean', said the abbé, 'someone who churns out articles by the dozen, a Fréron.'*

Such was the discussion between Candide, Martin, and the man from Périgord as they stood on the staircase, watching people pass by on their way out after the play.

'Although I can't wait to see Miss Cunégonde again,' said Candide, 'nevertheless I would like to have supper with Mlle Clairon, for she did seem quite admirable to me.'

The abbé was not the right man for an approach to Mlle Clairon, who moved only in the best circles.

'She has a prior engagement this evening,' he said, 'but if you will allow me the honour of taking you to a lady of quality, there you will get to meet Paris society as if you'd already been living here for years.'

Candide, who was curious by nature, allowed himself to be taken to the lady, at the bottom end of the Faubourg Saint-Honoré. There they were busy playing faro. Twelve sad punters each held a small hand of cards, the dog-eared register of their misfortunes. A profound silence reigned; pallor was upon the punters' brows, anxiety upon that of the banker; and the lady of the house, seated beside this implacable banker, noted with the eyes of a lynx all the doubling up and any illegal antes whenever each player turned down the corner of his card. She would make them turn the corners back with firm but polite insistence, and never lost her temper for fear of losing her clients. This lady called herself the Marchioness of Dubelauchwitz. Her daughter, aged fifteen, was one of the punters and would indicate with a wink any cheating on the part of these poor people endeavouring to repair the cruel blows of fate. The abbé from Périgord, Candide, and Martin walked in. No one got up, or greeted them, or looked at them; they were all deeply engrossed in their cards.

'The Baroness of Thunder-ten-tronckh was more civil,' said Candide.

Meanwhile the abbé had a word in the ear of the Marchioness, who half rose and honoured Candide with a gracious smile and Martin with a thoroughly grand tilt of the head. She had Candide given a seat and dealt a hand: he lost fifty thousand francs in two rounds. Afterwards they supped merrily, and everyone was surprised that Candide was not more upset about his losses. The lackeys said to each other in their own lackey language:

'He must be one of your English lords.'

The supper was like most suppers in Paris. First, silence; then a cacophonous welter of words that no one can make out; and then jokes, which mostly fall flat, false rumours, false arguments, a smattering of politics, and a quantity of slander. They even talked about the latest books.

'Have you read', said the abbé from Périgord, 'that nonsense by Master Gauchat, doctor of theology?'

'Yes,' replied one of the party, 'but I couldn't finish it. There's enough irrelevant rubbish in print as it is, but the whole lot put together doesn't come anywhere near the irrelevance of Master Gauchat, doctor of theology. I'm so sick of this great flood of detestable books that I've taken to punting at faro.'

'And the *Miscellany* of Archdeacon T . . . ?* What do you think of that?' said the abbé.

'Oh,' said the Marchioness of Dubelauchwitz, 'that crashing bore! The way he tells you with great interest what everybody knows already! The ponderous discussion of points that aren't even worth a passing reference! The witless way he borrows other people's wit! How he ruins what he filches! How he disgusts me! But he won't disgust me any further. One or two pages of the archdeacon are quite enough.'

At table there was a man of taste and learning, who agreed with what the Marchioness was saying. Conversation then moved on to tragedies. The lady asked why it was that some tragedies were staged from time to time but were totally unreadable. The man of taste explained very well how a play could be of some interest but of almost no merit. He showed in a few words how it was not enough to contrive one or two of the stock situations which can be found in any novel, and which always captivate the audience, but that one had to be original without being far-fetched; often sublime and always natural; to know the human heart and to make it speak; to be a great poet without any of the characters in the play appearing to be poets themselves; to have perfect command of one's own language, and to use it with fluent euphony, without forcing it, and without ever sacrificing the sense to the rhyme.

'Whoever fails to follow every one of these rules,' he added, 'may produce one or two tragedies that are applauded in the theatre, but he will never be counted a good writer. There are very few good tragedies. Some are simply idylls in a dialogue that happens to be well-written and well-rhymed; some have political messages, and send you to sleep, while others are so overdone they fail to move; and some are the fantasies of fanatics, written in a barbarous style with broken-off sentences and long speeches to the gods—because they don't know how to communicate with human beings—and full of false maxims and pompous platitudes.'

Candide listened attentively to these remarks and formed a high opinion of the speaker. As the Marchioness had taken good care to place Candide next to her, he took the liberty of asking, by means of a whisper in her ear, who this man was who spoke so well.

'He's a man of learning', said the lady, 'who doesn't gamble and whom the abbé brings to supper sometimes. He knows all about tragedies and books, and he has himself written a tragedy, which was whistled off the stage, and a book, of which but one copy has ever been seen outside a bookshop, and that was the one he presented to me with a dedication.'

'A great man!' said Candide. 'He's another Pangloss.'

Then, turning to him, he said:

'Sir, doubtless you think that everything is for the best in the physical and moral worlds, and that things could not be other than as they are?'

'I, sir?' replied the man of learning. 'I don't think anything of the sort. I find that everything in our world is amiss, that nobody knows his place or his responsibility, or what he's doing or what he should do, and that, except for supper parties, which are quite jolly and where people seem to get on reasonably well, the rest of the time is spent in pointless quarrelling: Jansenists with Molinists,* lawyers with churchmen, men of letters with men of letters, courtiers with courtiers, financiers with the general public, wives with husbands, relatives with relatives. It's one battle after another.'

Candide answered him:

'I've seen worse ones. But a wise man, who has since had the misfortune to be hanged, told me that that's all fine. Those are just the shadows in a beautiful painting.'

'Your hanged man was having people on,' said Martin. 'What you call shadows are horrible stains.'

'It's human beings who make the stains,' said Candide. 'They can't help it.'

'So it's not their fault,' said Martin.

The majority of the punters, who did not understand a word of all this, were drinking. Martin had a discussion with the man of learning; and Candide recounted some of his adventures to the lady of the house.

After supper the Marchioness took Candide to her room and bid him be seated on a couch.

'Well, then,' she said to him, 'so you're still madly in love with Miss Cunégonde de Thunder-ten-tronckh?'

'Yes, madame.'

The Marchioness returned a tender smile:

'You answer like the young man from Westphalia you are. A Frenchman would have said to me: "It is true that I did once love Miss Cunégonde, but on seeing you, madame, I fear that I love her no longer." '

'Oh, dear,' said Candide. 'Madame, I shall answer as you please.'

'Your passion for her began', said the Marchioness, 'when you picked up her handkerchief. I want you to pick up my garter.'

'With all my heart,' said Candide, and he picked it up.

'But I want you to put it back for me,' said the lady, and Candide put it back for her.

'You see,' she said, 'you are a foreigner. Sometimes I make my Parisian lovers wait a whole fortnight, but here I am giving myself to you on the very first night, because one must do the honours of one's country to a young man from Westphalia.'

The fair lady, having noticed two enormous diamonds on the hands of her young foreigner, enthused about them with such sincerity that from Candide's fingers they passed on to the fingers of the Marchioness.

Candide, as he returned home with his abbé from Périgord, felt some remorse at having been unfaithful to Miss Cunégonde. The abbé commiserated with him; he was only slightly responsible for the fifty thousand francs Candide had lost at cards and the value of the two brilliants which had been half given and half extorted. His object was to profit as much as he possibly could from the advantages that knowing Candide might bring him. He asked him all about Cunégonde, and Candide told him that he would certainly beg that fair lady's pardon for his infidelity when he saw her in Venice.

The man from Périgord became even more courteous and attentive and took a touching interest in everything that Candide said, or did, or wanted to do.

'So you have arranged to meet in Venice then, sir?' he said.

'Yes, Monsieur l'abbé,' said Candide. 'I really must go and find Miss Cunégonde.'

Then, drawn on by the pleasure of talking about the one he loved, he recounted, as was his wont, a part of his adventures with this illustrious Westphalian lady.

'I expect Miss Cunégonde is witty and clever,' said the abbé, 'and that she writes charming letters?'

'I've never had any from her,' said Candide. 'The thing is, you see, having been kicked out of the castle for loving her, I couldn't write to her, and then I learnt soon afterwards that she was dead, and then I found her again, and then I lost her, and then I sent an express messenger two thousand five hundred leagues to her, and I am still awaiting a reply.'

The abbé listened attentively and seemed somewhat lost in thought. Soon he took his leave of the two strangers, after embracing them warmly. The next day, upon waking, Candide received the following letter:

My very dear and beloved sir, I have been lying ill in this city for the past week. I discover that you are here too. I would fly to your arms if I could move. I heard in Bordeaux that you had passed through. I left the faithful

Cacambo there and the old woman, and they are soon to follow on after me. The Governor of Buenos Aires took everything, but I still have your heart. Come to me. Your presence will restore me to life, or make me die of pleasure.

This charming, this unexpected letter sent Candide into transports of inexpressible joy, while the illness of his dear Cunégonde weighed him down with grief. Torn between these two emotions, he grabbed his gold and diamonds and had himself and Martin escorted to the hotel where Miss Cunégonde was staying. He entered the room trembling with emotion, his heart aflutter, his voice choked. He made to open the curtains round the bed and was about to send for a lamp.

'Do no such thing,' said the maid, 'the light will kill her.' And at once she shut the curtains.

'My dear Cunégonde,' wept Candide. 'How are you? If you cannot look at me, at least speak to me.'

'She cannot speak,' said the maid. The lady then drew from the bedclothes a chubby little hand, which Candide bathed with his tears for a long time and subsequently filled with diamonds, leaving a pouch full of gold on the chair.

In the midst of his transports an officer of the watch arrived, followed by the abbé from Périgord and a squad of men.

'Are these the two suspicious foreigners then?' he said.

He had them arrested on the spot and ordered his lads to haul them off to prison.

'This is not how they treat travellers in Eldorado,' said Candide.

'I feel more Manichaean than ever,' said Martin.

'But, sir, where are you taking us?' said Candide.

'To the deepest of dark dungeons,' said the officer.

Martin, having recovered his sang-froid, judged that the lady claiming to be Cunégonde was a fraud, the abbé from Périgord a scoundrel who had taken advantage of Candide's innocence at the earliest opportunity, and the officer another scoundrel, whom it would be easy to be rid of.

Rather than be exposed to the process of law, Candide, enlightened by Martin's counsel and, more especially, ever impatient to see the real Miss Cunégonde again, offered the officer three little diamonds worth about three thousand pistoles each.

'Ah, sir,' the man with the ivory baton said to him, 'had you committed every crime in the book, you'd still be the most honest man alive. Three diamonds! And each worth three thousand pistoles! Sir, I'd sooner die for you than take you to a dungeon. There are orders to arrest all foreigners, but leave it to me. I have a brother in Normandy, in Dieppe, I'll take you there. And if you have a diamond or two to give him, he'll take care of you as if it were myself he was looking after.'

'And why are they arresting all foreigners?' says Candide.

The abbé from Périgord intervened:

'It's because a wretch from Atrabatia listened to some silly talk, which was all it took to make him commit parricide—not like the one in May 1610 but like the one in December 1594, and like several others committed in other months and other years by other wretches who had listened to similar silly talk.'

The officer then explained what this was all about.*

'Ah, the monsters!' exclaimed Candide. 'What! Such horrors, and from a people that loves singing and dancing! Can't I leave this very minute? Let me out of this country where monkeys provoke tigers. I have seen bears in my own country; I have seen men only in Eldorado. In the name of God, officer, take me to Venice, where I am to wait for Miss Cunégonde.'

'Lower Normandy is the best I can do,' said the right arm of the law.

Thereupon he had his irons removed, said he must have made a mistake, dismissed his men, and took Candide and Martin to Dieppe and left them in the hands of his brother. There was a small Dutch ship out in the roads. The Norman, who with the help of three more diamonds had now become the most obliging of men, put Candide and his servants aboard the ship, which was about to set sail for Portsmouth in England. It was not the way to Venice, but Candide felt as though he were being delivered from hell, and he fully intended to rejoin the route to Venice at the first opportunity.

CHAPTER 23

Candide and Martin proceed to the shores of England;
what they see there

'Ah, Pangloss! Pangloss! Ah, Martin! Martin! Ah, my dear Cunégonde! What sort of a world is this?' Candide was asking on board the Dutch ship.

'A rather mad and rather awful one,' answered Martin.

'You know England. Are they as mad there as they are in France?'

'It's a different kind of madness,' said Martin. 'As you know, the two countries are at war over a few acres of snow across in Canada, and they're spending more on this war than the whole of Canada is worth. To tell you exactly if there are more people who should be locked up in one country than in the other is something my feeble lights do not permit. All I know is that, by and large, the people we are going to see are extremely glum.'

Thus conversing, they landed at Portsmouth. A multitude of people covered the shore, all gazing intently at a rather stout man who was kneeling blindfold on the deck of one of the naval ships. Four soldiers, posted opposite this man, each fired three shots into his skull, as calmly as you please, and the assembled multitude then dispersed, thoroughly satisfied.

'What is all this?' said Candide. 'And what evil spirit is it that holds such universal sway?'

He asked who this stout man was who had just been ceremonially killed.

'He's an admiral,' came the answer.

'And why kill this admiral?'

'Because he didn't kill enough people,' Candide was told. 'He gave battle to a French admiral, and it has been found that he wasn't close enough.'

'But', said Candide, 'the French admiral was just as far away from the English admiral as he was from him!'

'Unquestionably,' came the reply. 'But in this country it is considered a good thing to kill an admiral from time to time so as to encourage the others.'*

Candide was so dumbfounded and so shocked by what he was

seeing and hearing that he refused even to set foot ashore, and he negotiated with the Dutch master of the ship (it was just too bad if he fleeced him like the one in Surinam) to take him to Venice as soon as possible.

The master was ready in two days. They sailed down the French coast. They passed within sight of Lisbon, and Candide shuddered. They entered the straits and the Mediterranean. At last they put in at Venice.

'God be praised!' said Candide, embracing Martin. 'This is where I shall see fair Cunégonde again. I trust Cacambo as I would myself. All is well, all is going well, all is going as well as it possibly can.'

CHAPTER 24

Of Paquette and Brother Giroflée

As soon as he reached Venice, he instigated a search for Cacambo in every inn and coffee house, and in all the brothels. He was nowhere to be found. Each day he had enquiries made of every new ship or boat that came in. No sign of Cacambo.

'I don't know,' he was saying to Martin. 'I have had time to cross from Surinam to Bordeaux, to go from Bordeaux to Paris, from Paris to Dieppe, from Dieppe to Portsmouth, to sail the length of Portugal and Spain, to cross the entire Mediterranean, to spend several months in Venice, and fair Cunégonde has still not got here! All I've encountered instead is some hussy and an abbé from Périgord. Cunégonde is probably dead, so I may as well die too. Ah! it would have been better to remain in the paradise of Eldorado than come back to this accursed Europe. How right you are, my dear Martin! All is but illusion and calamity.'

He sank into a dark melancholy and took no part in the opera *alla moda* or in any of the other carnival entertainments. Not a single lady caused him a moment's temptation.

Martin said to him:

'You really are rather simple to imagine that a half-caste man-servant with five or six millions in his pocket will go and look for your lady-love on the other side of the world and bring her to you in Venice. He'll take her for himself if he finds her. If he doesn't find her, he'll take somebody else. My advice to you is to forget your manservant Cacambo and your beloved Cunégonde.'

Martin was not consoling. Candide's melancholy deepened, and Martin kept on proving to him that there was little virtue and little happiness in this world—except perhaps in Eldorado, where no one could ever go.

While they disputed this important subject and waited for Cunégonde, Candide noticed a young Theatine monk* in Saint Mark's Square, who was walking with a girl on his arm. The Theatine had a fresh, chubby, robust appearance. His eyes shone, and there was an air of assurance about him. His expression was haughty, his gait proud. The girl, who was very pretty, was singing. She gazed lovingly at her Theatine, and tweaked his podgy cheeks from time to time.

'You'll grant me at least', Candide said to Martin, 'that those two are happy. So far, throughout the inhabited world, I have encountered only unfortunates—except in Eldorado, that is. But as for that girl and her Theatine, I bet they are very happy creatures.'

'I bet they're not,' said Martin.

'All we have to do is to invite them to dinner,' said Candide, 'and you'll see if I'm wrong.'

Thereupon he went up to them, presented his compliments, and invited them back to his hostelry for some macaroni, Lombardy partridge, and caviar, washed down with Montepulciano, Lachryma Christi, and some of the wines of Cyprus and Samos. The young lady blushed, the Theatine accepted the invitation, and the girl followed him, glancing at Candide with eyes wide in surprise and embarrassment and clouded with tears.

Scarcely had she entered Candide's room than she said to him:

'Well? Doesn't Master Candide recognize Paquette any more?'

At these words Candide, who had not looked at her closely until then (because he had thoughts only for Cunégonde), said to her:

'Oh dear, my poor girl, so you are the one who got Dr Pangloss into the fine state I saw him in?'

'Alas, sir, I am indeed,' said Paquette. 'I see you know all about it. I heard about the dreadful misfortunes that befell Her Ladyship's household and the fair Miss Cunégonde. I swear to you, my own fate has hardly been less wretched. I was utterly innocent when last you saw me. A Franciscan monk who was my confessor had no difficulty in seducing me. The consequences were terrible. I was obliged to leave the castle not long after His Lordship kicked you up the backside and sent you packing. If a famous doctor had not taken pity on me, I'd have had it. For a time I became the doctor's mistress, as a way of showing my gratitude. His wife, who was madly jealous, beat me every day without mercy. She was a fury. This doctor was the ugliest of men, and I the unhappiest of creatures to be continually beaten for a man I did not love. As you know, sir, it's very dangerous for a shrewish woman to have a doctor for a husband. One day, sick and tired of the way his wife was behaving, he treated her for a slight cold by giving her some medicine, which proved so effective that within two hours she was dead, having had some horrible convulsions. The mistress's family brought an action against the master. He upped and fled, and I was put in prison. My innocence would not have saved me had I not been reasonably pretty. The judge let me go on condition that he would succeed the doctor. I was soon supplanted by a rival, dismissed without a penny, and obliged to continue in this unspeakable profession which seems so harmless to you men, and which for us is nothing but a vale of tears. I chose Venice to practise my profession in. Oh, sir, if you could imagine what it's like having to caress just anybody, an old merchant, a lawyer, a monk, a gondolier, an abbé; to be exposed to all manner of insult and degradation; to be reduced often to having to borrow a skirt, only then to go and have it lifted up by some disgusting man or other; to be robbed by one of what one's earned with another; to be held to ransom by officers of the law, and to have nothing to look forward to but a gruesome old age, the workhouse, and the rubbish-heap; then you would agree that I am one of the unhappiest and most unfortunate creatures alive.'

This was how, in a private room in the hostelry, Paquette opened her heart to good Candide in the presence of Martin, who said to Candide:

'You see, I've already won half my bet.'

Brother Giroflée had remained in the dining-room, and was having a drink as he waited for dinner.

'But,' Candide said to Paquette, 'you were looking so gay, so happy, when I ran into you. You were singing, you were fondling the Theatine quite naturally and willingly. You seemed to me every bit as happy as you say you are unhappy.'

'Ah, sir,' replied Paquette, 'that's another of the awful things about our profession. Yesterday I was robbed and beaten by an officer, and today I have to appear to be in a good mood just to please a monk.'

That was enough for Candide; he admitted that Martin was right. They sat down to dinner with Paquette and the Theatine. The meal was quite good-humoured, and at the end they were all talking to each other with some degree of freedom.

'Father,' Candide said to the monk, 'you seem to me to be enjoying the kind of life everyone must envy. You are the picture of health, you have a happy face, you have a very pretty girl to keep you amused, and you seem perfectly content with your monastic condition.'

'By my faith, sir,' said Brother Giroflée, 'I wish all Theatines were at the bottom of the sea. I've been tempted a hundred times to set fire to the monastery and to go and turn Turk. My parents forced me to don this detestable habit at the age of fifteen so that I would leave a bigger fortune for my damned elder brother, may God confound him! The monastery is rife with jealousy, and backbiting, and bad feeling. It's true that I have preached a few miserable sermons that have brought me in some money, half of which the Prior steals—the rest I use for keeping girls. But when I get back to the monastery in the evening, I'm ready to beat my head in on the dormitory walls. And all the brothers feel the same way.'

Martin turned to Candide with his usual sang-froid:

'Well?' he said. 'Have I not won the whole bet?'

Candide gave Paquette two thousand piastres, and Brother Giroflée a thousand.

'I guarantee you', he said, 'that with this money they'll be happy.'

'I shouldn't think so for a minute,' said Martin. 'With these piastres you may make them even more unhappy still.'

'Whatever shall be, shall be,' said Candide. 'But one thing consoles me. I see that people one never thought to see again often do turn up. It may well turn out that, having run into my red sheep and Paquette, I will also run into Cunégonde.'

'I wish', said Martin, 'that she may one day make you happy. But I very much doubt she will.'

'You are a bit hard,' said Candide.

'That's because I've lived,' said Martin.

'But look at those gondoliers,' said Candide. 'They're always singing, aren't they?'

'You don't see them at home with their wives and screaming children,' said Martin. 'The doge has his problems, the gondoliers have theirs. It is true that, all things considered, the life of a gondolier is preferable to that of a doge, but I think there's so little in it that it's not worth arguing about.'

'I've heard people talk', said Candide, 'about a Senator Pococurante who lives in that beautiful palace on the Brenta, and who's very hospitable to visiting foreigners. They say he's a man who's never had any troubles.'

'I'd like to meet such a rare breed,' said Martin.

Candide at once sent someone to ask the noble Signor Pococurante's permission to call on him the following day.

CHAPTER 25

The visit to Signor Pococurante, a Venetian nobleman

CANDIDE and Martin proceeded down the Brenta by gondola and came to the palace of the noble Pococurante. The gardens were well laid out and embellished with beautiful marble statues, while the palace itself was a fine piece of architecture. The master of the house, a man of sixty, and very rich, received the two curious visitors most politely but with very little fuss, which disconcerted Candide and did not displease Martin.

First, two pretty and neatly dressed girls poured out some chocolate, managing to give it a good frothy top. Candide could not help but compliment them on their beauty, their kindness, and their skill.

'They're not bad creatures,' said Senator Pococurante. 'I have them sleep with me sometimes, because I'm rather tired of the society ladies here with all their flirting, and their jealousy, and their quarrelling, and their moods, and their petty-mindedness, and their arrogance, and their silliness, not to mention the sonnets you have to compose, or have composed, for them. But, well, in the end I'm beginning to find these two girls exceedingly boring too.'

Candide, walking in a long gallery after lunch, was surprised at the beauty of the paintings. He asked which master had painted the first two.

'They're by Raphael,' said the Senator. 'I bought them out of vanity some years ago for a considerable amount of money. They are said to be the finest in Italy, but I don't like them at all. The colouring is very dark, the faces aren't sufficiently rounded and don't stand out enough, and the draperies don't bear the slightest resemblance to any real cloth. Basically, whatever anyone may say, I don't consider they're a true imitation of nature. You'll only get me to like a picture when I think I'm looking at nature itself—and there aren't any like that. I have lots of paintings, but I don't look at them any more.'

As they waited for dinner, Pococurante gave orders for a concerto to be played. Candide found the music delightful.

'This sort of noise helps pass the odd half-hour,' said Pococurante, 'but if it goes on any longer, everybody finds it tedious, though no one dares say so. Nowadays music is simply nothing more than the art of playing difficult pieces, and that which is merely difficult gives no pleasure in the end.

'Perhaps I'd prefer opera, if they hadn't found a way of turning it into a monstrous hybrid that I find quite repugnant. Let anyone who wishes go and see bad tragedies set to music, with all those scenes that have been put together simply as pretexts—and pretty poor ones at that—for two or three ridiculous songs which allow an actress to show off her vocal cords. Let anyone that wants to—and that can—go and swoon away with ecstasy at the sight of a *castrato* humming the roles of Caesar and Cato and strutting about the stage in that ungainly fashion. For my part I have long since given up going to these paltry affairs, even though nowadays they are the glory of Italy and put its ruling princes to so much expense.'

Candide demurred somewhat, though with tact. Martin was entirely of the Senator's opinion.

They sat down to eat, and after an excellent dinner, they went into the library. Candide, on seeing a magnificently bound edition of Homer, complimented his most illustrious host on his good taste.

'This book', he said, 'used to delight the great Pangloss, the finest philosopher in Germany.'

'It doesn't delight me,' said Pococurante coolly. 'They did once have me believe that I took pleasure in reading it. But that endless repetition of combats which all seem the same, those gods who are always doing things but never getting anywhere, that Helen who causes the war and then plays scarcely any part in the thing, that Troy they besiege and never take, I found all that deadly boring. I've sometimes asked men of learning if they found reading it as boring as I did. The honest ones admitted that the book used to drop from their hands, but said that you had to have it in your library, like an ancient monument, or like those rusty medals that have no commercial value.'

'Your Excellency doesn't think the same about Virgil?' said Candide.

'I agree that the second, fourth, and sixth books of the *Aeneid* are excellent,' said Pococurante. 'But as for his pious Aeneas, and valiant Cloanthus, and faithful Achates, and little Ascanius, not to mention half-witted King Latinus, and parochial Amata, and insipid Lavinia, I can think of nothing more disagreeable or more likely to leave one absolutely cold. I prefer Tasso and those improbable tales of Ariosto.'

'Dare I ask, sir,' said Candide, 'whether Horace does not afford you considerable pleasure?'

'There are one or two maxims', said Pococurante, 'which a man of the world may profit by, and which fix themselves more readily in the memory for being compressed in powerful verse. But I care very little for his journey to Brindisi, or the description of that poor dinner he had, or that foul-mouthed quarrel between someone or other called Pupilus, whose language, he says, "was full of pus", and someone else whose language "was like vinegar". It was only with extreme distaste that I read his crude verses against old women and witches, and I cannot see what merit there can be in telling his friend Maecenas that if he were to place him among the ranks of the lyric poets, he would bang his sublime forehead on the stars in the heavens.* Fools admire everything in a respected author. I read only for myself. I like only what may be of use to me.'

Candide, who had been brought up never to judge things for himself, was much astonished by what he heard; and Martin found Pococurante's way of thinking rather sensible.

'Oh, look! Here's a copy of Cicero,' said Candide. 'I'm sure when it comes to this great man, you never tire of reading him?'

'I never read him,' replied the Venetian. 'What does it matter to me whether he defended Rabirius or Cluentius? What with the cases

I try myself, I have quite enough of all that as it is. I might have got on better with his philosophical works, but when I saw that he doubted everything, I decided that I knew as much as he did, and that I didn't need anyone else's help if I was going to be ignorant.'

'Ah, look, eighty volumes of the proceedings of an Academy of Science,' exclaimed Martin. 'There may be something worthwhile there.'

'There would be', said Pococurante, 'if but one of the authors of all that rubbish had so much as invented the art of making pins. But in every one of those books there's nothing but pointless theorizing, and not a single thing that's useful.'

'What a lot of plays there are!' said Candide; 'in Italian, in Spanish, in French!'

'Yes,' said the Senator, 'there are three thousand of them, and not three dozen good ones. As for the collected sermons, which between them aren't worth one page of Seneca, and all those fat tomes on theology, well, you can be sure I never open them, not I, not anyone.'

Martin noticed some shelves full of English books.

'I imagine', he said, 'that a republican must find most of these enjoyable to read, given how free the authors were to write them?'

'Yes,' answered Pococurante, 'it is a fine thing to write what one thinks. It is man's privilege. Throughout this Italy of ours, people write only what they do not think. Those who live in the land of the Caesars and the Antonines dare not have an idea without obtaining permission from a Dominican friar. I would be content with the freedom which inspires these English men of genius if their passion for the party interest didn't spoil all the estimable things that would otherwise flow from this precious freedom.'

Candide, catching sight of a copy of Milton, asked him if he did not regard this author as a great man.

'Who?' said Pococurante, 'that barbarian with his long commentary on the first book of *Genesis* in ten books of difficult verse? That crude imitator of the Greeks who gives such a distorted view of the Creation and, where Moses shows the Eternal Being producing the world with the spoken word, has the Messiah take a great big compass out of a toolchest in heaven and start drawing a plan? Me, admire the man who ruined Tasso's vision of hell and the devil; who has Lucifer appear disguised variously as a toad or a pygmy; who makes him say the same things over and over again; who makes him discuss theological points; who takes Ariosto's bit of comic invention about the firearms seriously and has the devils firing the cannon into heaven? Neither I nor anyone else in Italy has ever been able to enjoy all these extravagant absurdities. The marriage of Sin and Death, and the adders to which Sin gives birth, are enough to make anyone with a delicate stomach vomit. And his long description of a hospital is fit only for a gravedigger. That obscure, bizarre, disgusting poem was spurned at birth. Now I treat it the way it was treated in its own time by the readers in its own country. Anyway, I say what I think, and I couldn't care less whether anyone thinks the way I do or not.'

Candide was distressed to hear all this. He admired Homer, and he had a sneaking fondness for Milton.

'Oh, dear!' he said to Martin under his breath, 'I'm very much afraid that this man may have a sovereign disregard for our German poets.'

'There would be no great harm in that,' said Martin.

'Oh, what a great man!' Candide continued to mutter to himself. 'What a great genius this Pococurante is! There is no pleasing him.'

Having thus inspected all the books, they went down into the garden. Candide praised all its finer features.

'I know of nothing that could be in worse possible taste,' said the master of the house. 'All you see here are just pretty bits and pieces. But, as from tomorrow, I'm going to have a new one planted along much nobler lines.'

When the two curious visitors had taken their leave of His Excellency, Candide turned to Martin:

'Well, there you are,' he said. 'You will agree that there is the happiest of men, for he is above all that he owns.'

'Don't you see', said Martin, 'that he's sated on everything he owns? Plato said a long time ago that the best stomachs are not those which reject all foods.'

'But', said Candide, 'isn't there pleasure in criticizing everything, in finding fault where other men think they find beauty?'

'Which is to say,' rejoined Martin, 'that there's pleasure in not having pleasure?'

'Oh, all right. Have it your way then,' said Candide. 'So the only one who's happy is me, when I see Miss Cunégonde again.'

'One does well to hope,' said Martin.

Meanwhile the days, the weeks went by. Still Cacambo did not return, and Candide was so sunk in misery that it did not even occur to him that Paquette and Brother Giroflée had not so much as come to thank him.

CHAPTER 26

Of a supper that Candide and Martin ate in the company of
six strangers, and who they were

ONE evening as Candide, accompanied by Martin, was about to sit down to table with the other passing strangers staying in the same hostelry, a man with a face the colour of soot came up behind him and, taking him by the arm, said:

'Be ready to leave when we do, and do not fail.'

He turned round: it was Cacambo. Only the sight of Cunégonde could have surprised and pleased him more. He went nearly mad with joy. He embraced his dear friend.

'Cunégonde must be here, then. Where is she? Take me to her. Let me die of joy with her.'

'Cunégonde is not here,' said Cacambo. 'She's in Constantinople.'

'Ah, heavens! In Constantinople! But were she in China, I should fly to her! Let's go!'

'We will leave after supper,' replied Cacambo. 'I can't say any more. I'm a slave and my master's waiting for me. I've got to go and wait on him at table. Don't breathe a word. Have supper, and then be ready and waiting.'

Candide, torn between joy and pain, absolutely delighted to have seen his faithful agent again, surprised to see him now a slave, full of the idea of being reunited with his beloved, his heart in tumult and his mind in a spin, sat down to eat in the company of Martin, who was watching all these goings-on with equanimity, and of the six strangers who had come to spend carnival in Venice.

Cacambo, who was filling the glass of one of these strangers, drew near to his master's ear at the end of the meal and said to him:

'Sire, Your Majesty may depart when he wishes. The ship is ready.'

Having said this, he left the room. Astonished, the supper guests were exchanging silent glances, when another servant came up to his master and said:

'Sire, Your Majesty's carriage is at Padua, and the boat is ready.'

His master made a sign, and the servant left. All the guests stared at each other again, and the general amazement increased. A third servant, coming up to a third stranger, said to him:

'Believe me, Sire, Your Majesty must not stay here a moment longer. I shall go and get everything ready.'

And he disappeared at once.

Candide and Martin now had no doubt that this was some masquerade to do with the carnival. A fourth servant said to a fourth master:

'Your Majesty may depart at his convenience,' and left the room like the others.

The fifth servant said the same to the fifth master. But the sixth servant spoke differently to the sixth stranger, who was sitting next to Candide.

He said to him:

'Lor me, Sire, they're refusing to let Your Majesty have any more credit, nor me neither, and the pair of us'll as like be carted off to clink this very night. I'm off to look after number one, thank you very much. Good-bye.'

The servants having all vanished, the six strangers, Candide and Martin remained deep in silence. Finally Candide broke it:

'Gentlemen,' he said, 'this is some strange joke. How is it that you are all kings? For my part I must tell you that neither I nor Martin are anything of the sort.'

Cacambo's master then intervened gravely and said in Italian:

'I am no joke, my name is Achmed III. I was Grand Sultan for several years; I dethroned my brother; my nephew has dethroned me; my viziers have had their heads cut off; I am spending the rest of my days in the old seraglio; my nephew the Grand Sultan Mahmood occasionally allows me to travel for my health, and I have come to spend carnival in Venice.'

A young man who was next to Achmed spoke after him and said:

'My name is Ivan, I was Emperor of all the Russias. I was dethroned in my cradle; my father and mother were locked up; I was brought up in prison; I occasionally get permission to travel, accompanied by my guards, and I have come to spend carnival in Venice.'

The third said:

'I am Charles Edward, King of England. My father renounced his claim to the throne in my favour; I have fought many battles to make good my claim; eight hundred of my supporters had their hearts ripped out and their cheeks slapped with them; I was put in prison; I am on my way to Rome to visit my father the King, dethroned like me and my grandfather, and I have come to spend carnival in Venice.'

The fourth then spoke up and said:

'I am the King of Poland. The fortunes of war have dispossessed me of my ancestral domains; my father suffered the same reverses; I am resigned to Providence like Sultan Achmed, Emperor Ivan, and King Charles Edward, whom God preserve, and I have come to spend carnival in Venice.'

The fifth said: 'I too am the King of Poland. I have lost my kingdom twice; but Providence has given me another domain, in which I have done more good than all the Kings of Sarmatia put together have ever been able to manage on the banks of the Vistula. I too am resigned to Providence, and I have come to spend carnival in Venice.'

It remained for the sixth monarch to speak.

'Gentlemen,' he said, 'I am not so great a lord as any of you but, well, I have been a King just like everyone else. I am Theodore; I was elected King in Corsica; they called me "Your Majesty", and now they hardly call me "Sir"; once I minted money, and now I haven't a penny; once I had two secretaries of state, and now I have scarcely a valet; I once sat on a throne, and I have spent a long time in prison in London, with straw for a bed. I am much afraid I shall be treated in the same way here, although I came like Your Majesties to spend carnival in Venice.'*

The other five kings listened to this speech with a noble compassion. Each of them gave King Theodore twenty sequins to buy coats and shirts, and Candide made him a present of a diamond worth two thousand sequins.

'Who can this be then,' said the five kings, 'a mere private individual who is in a position to give a hundred times as much as each of us, and who gives it?'

Just as they were leaving the table, there arrived in the same hostelry four Serene Highnesses who had also lost their domains through the fortunes of war, and who were coming to spend what was left of the carnival in Venice. But Candide did not even notice these new arrivals. All he could think about was going to find his dear Cunégonde in Constantinople.

CHAPTER 27

Candide's journey to Constantinople

FAITHFUL Cacambo had already obtained permission from the Turkish captain who was to take Sultan Achmed back to Constantinople for Candide and Martin to join them on board. Together they made their way to the ship, having prostrated themselves before His unhappy Highness.

On the way Candide was saying to Martin:

'There you are, you see. That was six dethroned kings we had supper with. And that's not all. Among those six kings there was one I could give alms to. Perhaps there are lots more princes who are even more unfortunate. Whereas me, all I've lost is a hundred sheep, and I'm flying to the arms of Cunégonde. My dear Martin, once more, Pangloss was right: all is well.'

'I certainly hope so,' said Martin.

'But', said Candide, 'that was a pretty unlikely adventure we had in Venice. Who ever saw or heard tell of six dethroned kings having supper together in a tavern.'

'It's no more extraordinary', said Martin, 'than most of the things that have happened to us. It's very common for kings to be dethroned, and as for the honour of having supper with them, there's nothing special about that.'

Scarce was Candide aboard than he fell upon the neck of his former manservant, his friend Cacambo.

'Well, then,' said Candide, 'what's Cunégonde doing? Is she still a paragon of beauty? Does she still love me? How is she? Presumably you bought her a palace in Constantinople?'

'My dear master,' replied Cacambo, 'Cunégonde is washing dishes on the shores of the Sea of Marmara for a prince who has very few dishes. She's a slave in the household of an ex-ruler called Ragotsky,* to whom in his exile the Grand Turk gives three crowns a day. But, worse than that, she has lost her beauty and become horribly ugly.'

'Ah, beautiful or ugly,' said Candide, 'I'm a man of honour, and my duty is to love her always. But how can she possibly have fallen so low with the five or six millions you took her?'

'Look here,' said Cacambo. 'Didn't I have to give two million to Señor don Fernando d'Ibaraa y Figueora y Mascarenes y Lampourdos y Souza, Governor of Buenos Aires, for permission to take Miss Cunégonde back? And didn't a pirate very kindly relieve us of the rest? And didn't the same pirate take us to Cape Matapan, Milo, Nicaria, Samos, Petra, the Dardanelles, Marmora, and Scutari? Cunégonde and the old woman are now working as servants to the prince I told you about, and I am a slave of the dethroned sultan.'

'What a chain of appalling calamities one after another,' said Candide. 'But after all, I do still have some diamonds left. I shall easily secure Cunégonde's release. It really is a pity that she has become so ugly.'

Then, turning to Martin:

'Who do you think one should feel most sorry for,' he said, 'Emperor Achmed, Emperor Ivan, King Charles Edward, or me?'

'I've no idea,' said Martin. 'I'd have to see inside all your hearts to know the answer to that.'

'Ah!' said Candide, 'if Pangloss were here, he would know, he would tell us the answer.'

'I don't know what sort of scales your Pangloss could have used to weigh the misfortunes of men and calculate their sufferings,' said Martin. 'All I presume is that there are millions of people on this earth one might feel a hundred times sorrier for than King Charles Edward, Emperor Ivan, and Sultan Achmed.'

'That may well be so,' said Candide.

In a few days they reached the channel leading to the Black Sea. The first thing Candide did was to buy Cacambo back at a very high price, and then without delay he and his companions quickly boarded a galley and made for the shores of the Sea of Marmara in search of Cunégonde, ugly though she might be.

Amongst the galley-slaves were two prisoners who rowed extremely badly, and to whose naked shoulders the Levantine captain would periodically apply a few lashes of his bull's pizzle. Candide's natural reaction was to pay more attention to them than to the other galley-slaves, and he drew near them with compassion. One or two features on their disfigured faces seemed to him to bear some resemblance to those of Pangloss and that unfortunate Jesuit, Miss Cunégonde's brother, the Baron. The thought touched and saddened him. He watched them even more closely.

'Quite honestly,' he said to Cacambo, 'if I hadn't seen Maître Pangloss hanged and if I hadn't had the misfortune to kill the Baron, I could swear it was them rowing on this galley.'

On hearing the names of the Baron and Pangloss, the two galley-slaves gave a great shout, stopped still on their bench, and dropped their oars. The Levantine captain rushed up to them, and the lashes from his bull's pizzle rained down anew.

'Stop, stop, good sir,' screamed Candide. 'I will give you all the money you want.'

'Why, it's Candide!' said one of the two galley-slaves.

'Why, it's Candide!' said the other.

'Am I dreaming all this?' said Candide. 'Am I awake? Am I really here on this galley? Is that the Baron I killed? Is that the Maître Pangloss I saw hanged?'

'It is we, it is we,' they replied.

'What, so that's the great philosopher?' said Martin.

'Look here, Mr Levantine captain,' said Candide, 'how much ransom do you want for Mr von Thunder-ten-tronckh, one of the foremost barons of the Empire, and for Mr Pangloss, the profoundest metaphysician in Germany?'

'You Christian cur,' replied the Levantine slave-driver. 'Since these two Christian slave dogs are barons and metaphysicians, which is no doubt a great honour where they come from, you can give me fifty thousand sequins.'

'You shall have them, sir. Get me to Constantinople as fast as you possibly can, and you will be paid on the spot. On second thoughts, take me to Miss Cunégonde.'

The Levantine captain, at Candide's first offer, had already altered course for the city, and he bid the crew row faster than a bird may cleave the air.

Candide embraced the Baron and Pangloss a hundred times.

'And how did I not kill you, my dear Baron? And you, my dear Pangloss, how is it that you are alive after being hanged? And what are you both doing on a galley in Turkey?'

'Is it really true that my dear sister is here in this country?' said the Baron.

'Yes,' replied Cacambo.

'So here is my dear Candide again,' exclaimed Pangloss.

Candide introduced them to Martin and Cacambo. They all embraced; everybody talked at once. The galley was flying along; they were already in port. A Jew was summoned, to whom Candide sold a diamond worth a hundred thousand sequins for fifty thousand, and who swore by Abraham that he could offer not a sequin more. Thereupon Candide paid the ransom for the Baron and Pangloss. The latter threw himself at the feet of his liberator and bathed them in tears; the other thanked him with a nod of his head and promised to reimburse him at the earliest opportunity.

'But can it really be that my sister is in Turkey?' he said.

'It really can,' retorted Cacambo, 'seeing as how she's washing dishes for a Prince of Transylvania.'

At once two Jews were sent for. Candide sold some more diamonds, and they all left by another galley to go and deliver Cunégonde from bondage.

CHAPTER 28

What happened to Candide, Cunégonde, Pangloss, Martin, and co.

'ONCE more, forgive me,' Candide said to the Baron. 'Forgive me, reverend father, for running you through with my sword like that.'

'We'll say no more about it,' said the Baron. 'I did speak rather sharply, I admit. But since you want to know how you came to find me on a galley, I will tell you that after being cured of my wounds by the college's apothecary monk, I was set upon and abducted by a group of Spaniard . I was put in prison in Buenos Aires just after my sister left there. I asked to be allowed to return to Rome to be with the Father General: I was appointed almoner to His Excellency the ambassador of France in Constantinople. I hadn't been in post more than a week when one evening I ran into a young icoglan,* who was very good-looking. It was extremely hot: the young man wanted to go for a swim; I took the opportunity to go swimming too. I did not know that it was a capital offence for a Christian to be found stark naked with a young Muslim. A cadi had me birched a hundred times on the soles of the feet and sent me to the galleys. I don't believe there's ever been a more ghastly miscarriage of justice. But what I'd like to know is why my sister is working in the kitchens of a Transylvanian ruler in exile among the Turks.'

'But you, my dear Pangloss,' said Candide, 'how is it that we meet again?'

'It is true that you did see me hanged,' said Pangloss. 'I was, of course, to have been burned but, as you will remember, it poured with rain just as they were about to roast me. The storm was so violent that they gave up trying to light the fire, and I was hanged for want of a better alternative. A surgeon bought my body, took me home with him, and dissected me. First he made a cruciform incision in me from my navel to my collarbone. One can't have a worse hanging than I'd had. The executive arm of the high works of the Holy Inquisition, namely a sub-deacon, certainly did a splendid job when it came to burning people, but he wasn't used to hanging. The rope was wet and wouldn't slip through properly, and it got caught. So I was still breathing. The crucial incision made me give such an enormous shriek that my surgeon fell over backwards and, thinking it was the devil himself he was dissecting, rushed away, nearly dying of fright, and then, to cap it all, fell down the stairs in his flight. His wife came running from the next room at the noise, saw me stretched out on the table with my crucial incision, took even greater fright than her husband, fled, and fell over him.

'When they had collected their wits a little, I heard the surgeon's wife say to her husband: "My dear, what on earth were you thinking of dissecting a heretic like that? Don't you know those sort of people always have the devil in them? I'm going to fetch a priest this minute to exorcize him." I shuddered to hear this, and I mustered what little strength I had left and cried out: "Have mercy on me!" In the end the Portuguese barber plucked up courage. He sewed me up again, and his wife even nursed me. I was up and about in a fortnight. The barber found me a position and made me lackey to a Knight of Malta who was going to Venice. But since my master had not the means to pay me, I entered service with a merchant of Venice and followed him to Constantinople.

'One day I happened to enter a mosque. There was no one in there apart from an old imam and a very pretty young worshipper, who was saying her paternosters. Her bosom was uncovered for all to see, and in her cleavage was a lovely posy of tulips, roses, anemones, buttercups, hyacinths, and auriculas. She dropped her posy; I picked it up and replaced it for her with respectful zeal. I took so long about replacing it that the imam became angry and, seeing I was a Christian, called for help. I was taken to the cadi, who sentenced me to a hundred strokes of the lath on the soles of my feet and sent me to the galleys. I was chained up in precisely the same galley and on precisely the same bench as His Lordship the Baron. On the galley were four young men from Marseilles, five Neapolitan priests, and two monks from Corfu, who all told us that this sort of thing happened every day. His Lordship claimed he'd been more unjustly treated then I had. I maintained for my part that it was much more permissible putting a posy back on a woman's bosom than being stark naked with an icoglan. We used to argue the whole time, and were getting twenty lashes a day with the bull's pizzle when, by a turn in the chain of events that governs this universe, you were led to our galley and bought us back.'

'Now then, my dear Pangloss!' Candide said to him. 'When you were being hanged, and dissected, and beaten, and made to row in a galley, did you continue to think that things were turning out for the best?'

'I still feel now as I did at the outset,' replied Pangloss. 'I am a philosopher after all. It wouldn't do for me to go back on what I said before, what with Leibniz not being able to be wrong, and pre-established harmony being the finest thing in the world, not to mention the *plenum* and *materia subtilis*.'*

CHAPTER 29

How Candide was reunited with Cunégonde and the old woman

WHILE Candide, the Baron, Pangloss, Martin, and Cacambo were recounting their adventures, and philosophizing about which events in the universe are contingent and which not contingent, and arguing about effects and causes, moral and physical evil, freedom and necessity, and about what consolations are to be had on board a Turkish galley, they landed on the shores of the Sea of Marmara at the house of the Prince of Transylvania. The first thing they saw was Cunégonde and the old woman hanging towels out on a line to dry.

The Baron went pale at the sight. Candide, the tender-hearted lover, on seeing his fair Cunégonde all brown, with her eyes bloodshot, her bosom shrivelled, her cheeks wrinkled, and her arms red and peeling, recoiled three paces in horror, and then stepped forward out of sheer good manners. She embraced Candide and her brother. They embraced the old woman. Candide bought them both free.

There was a small farm in the vicinity. The old woman suggested to Candide that it would do them nicely while they waited for the whole company to fall on better times. Cunégonde did not know that she had become ugly; no one had told her. She reminded Candide of his promises in such a firm tone that good Candide did not dare refuse her. He intimated to the Baron, therefore, that he was going to marry his sister.

'I will not tolerate such a demeaning act on her part,' he said, 'nor such insolence from you. Never shall it be said that I allowed such infamy: my wife's children would never be able to mix in Germany's noble chapters. No, my sister will marry no one but a baron of the Empire.'

Cunégonde threw herself at his feet and bathed them with her tears; he was inflexible.

'You great numskull,' said Candide, 'I've saved you from the galleys, I've paid your ransom, and I've paid your sister's. She was washing dishes here, she's ugly, I have the goodness to make her my wife, and you still think you're going to stand in our way! I'd kill you all over again if I let my anger have its way.'

'You can kill me all over again if you want,' said the Baron, 'but you won't marry my sister so long as I live.'

CHAPTER 30

Conclusion

CANDIDE, in his heart of hearts, had no desire to marry Cunégonde. But the extreme impertinence of the Baron made him decide to go through with the marriage, and Cunégonde was pressing him so keenly that he could not go back on his word. He consulted Pangloss,

Martin, and the faithful Cacambo. Pangloss wrote a fine dissertation in which he proved that the Baron had no rights over his sister, and that it was open to her, under all the laws of the Empire, to marry Candide with the left hand. Martin was for throwing the Baron into the sea. Cacambo decided that they should return him to the Levantine captain and have him put back in the galleys, after which he was to be packed off to the Father General in Rome on the first available ship. This view of the matter was thought to be very sound. The old woman approved, nothing was said to his sister, the thing was done with the help of a little money, and they had the pleasure of bettering a Jesuit and punishing the arrogance of a German baron.

It was quite natural to imagine that, after so many disasters, Candide, now married to his sweetheart and living with the philosophical Pangloss, the philosophical Martin, the prudent Cacambo and the old woman and, moreover, having brought back so many diamonds from the land of the ancient Incas, would be leading the most agreeable of all possible lives. But he was swindled so many times by the Jews that all he had left in the end was his little farm; his wife, who grew uglier with every day that passed, became shrewish and impossible to live with; the old woman was infirm and even more bad-tempered than Cunégonde; Cacambo, who worked in the garden and travelled to Constantinople to sell vegetables, was worn out with work and cursed his fate; Pangloss was in despair at not being a luminary in some German university. As for Martin, he was firmly persuaded that one is just as badly off wherever one is; he put up with things as they were. Candide, Martin, and Pangloss would argue sometimes about metaphysics and ethics. They would often see boats passing beneath the windows of the farmhouse laden with effendis, pashas, and cadis, who were being exiled to Lemnos or Mytilene or Erzerum. They would see more cadis, more pashas, and more effendis coming to take the place of those who had been expelled, and being themselves in their turn expelled. They would see heads duly stuffed with straw being taken for display before the Sublime Porte.* Such sights would give rise to yet further disquisitions, and when they were not arguing, the boredom was so excessive that the old woman made bold to say to them one day:

'I would like to know which is worse: being raped a hundred times by negro pirates, having a buttock chopped off, running the gauntlet of the Bulgars, being flogged and hanged in an *auto-da-fé*, being dissected, rowing in a galley, in short, suffering all the misfortunes we've all suffered, or simply being stuck here doing nothing?'

'That is a good question,' said Candide.

This speech gave rise to renewed speculation, and Martin in particular came to the conclusion that man was born to spend his life alternately a prey to the throes of anxiety and the lethargy of boredom. Candide did not agree, but asserted nothing. Pangloss admitted that he had always suffered horribly; but having once maintained that everything was going marvellously, he still maintained it, and believed nothing of the sort.

One thing finally confirmed Martin in his detestable principles, gave Candide more than ever pause, and embarrassed Pangloss. This was the sight one day of Paquette and Brother Giroflée arriving at their farm in a state of extreme wretchedness. They had very quickly gone through their three thousand piastres, left each other, patched things up, quarrelled again, been put in prison, escaped; and in the end Brother Giroflée had turned Turk. Paquette still pursued her profession, and no longer earned any money at it.

'I told you so,' Martin said to Candide. 'I knew what you gave them would soon be gone and would only make them even more wretched. You had more piastres than you knew what to do with, you and Cacambo, and you are no happier than Brother Giroflée and Paquette.'

'Aha!' said Pangloss to Paquette, 'so heaven brings you back here among us, my poor child! Do you know, you've cost me the tip of my nose, an eye and an ear? And you, just look at the state you're in! What a world we live in!'

This new turn of events led them to philosophize more than ever.

There lived in the neighbourhood a very famous dervish, who passed for the greatest philosopher in Turkey. They went to consult him. Pangloss acted as their spokesman and said to him:

'Master, we have come to ask you to tell us why such a strange animal as man was created.'

'What's that to you?' said the dervish. 'Is it any of your business?'

'But, reverend father,' said Candide, 'there's an awful lot of evil in the world.'

'What does it matter whether there's evil or there's good,' said the dervish. 'When His Highness sends a ship to Egypt, does he worry whether the mice on board are comfortable or not?'

'So what must we do then?' said Pangloss.

'Be silent,' said the dervish.

'I had flattered myself', said Pangloss, 'that we might have a talk about effects and causes, the best of all possible worlds, the origin of evil, the nature of the soul, and pre-established harmony.'

The dervish, at these words, slammed the door in their faces.

During this conversation news had spread that two viziers of the bench and the mufti had been strangled in Constantinople, and several of their friends impaled. This catastrophe made a great stir everywhere for some hours. On their way back to the farm Pangloss, Candide, and Martin met a kindly old man who was taking the air at his door beneath an arbour of orange-trees. Pangloss, who was as curious as he was prone to philosophizing, asked him the name of the mufti who had just been strangled.

'I have no idea,' replied the fellow, 'and I never have known what any mufti or vizier was called. What you have just told me means absolutely nothing to me. I have no doubt that in general those who get involved in public affairs do sometimes come to a sad end and that they deserve it. But I never enquire what's going on in Constantinople. I am content to send my fruit for sale there from the garden I cultivate.'

Having said this, he invited the strangers into his house. His two daughters and two sons offered them several kinds of sorbet which they made themselves, some *kaïmak* sharpened with the zest of candied citron, some oranges, lemons, limes, pineapple, and pistachio nuts, and some Mocha coffee which had not been blended with that awful coffee from Batavia and the islands. After which the two daughters of this good Muslim perfumed the beards of Candide, Pangloss, and Martin.

'You must have a vast and magnificent property,' said Candide to the Turk.

'I have but twenty acres,' replied the Turk. 'I cultivate them with my children. Work keeps us from three great evils: boredom, vice, and need.'

Candide, on his way back to his farm, thought long and hard about what the Turk had said, and commented to Pangloss and Martin:

'That kind old man seems to me to have made a life for himself which is much preferable to that of those six kings with whom we had the honour of having supper.'

'High rank can be very dangerous,' said Pangloss; 'all the philosophers say so. For the fact is, Eglon, King of the Moabites, was slain by Ehud; Absalom was hanged by the hair on his head and had three darts thrust through his heart; King Nadab, son of Jeroboam, was smitten by Baasha; King Elah by Zimri; Joram by Jehu; Athaliah by Jehoiada; and Kings Jehoiakim, Jehoiachin, and Zedekiah entered into captivity. You know what sort of deaths befell Croesus, Astyages, Darius, Dionysius of Syracuse, Pyrrhus, Perseus, Hannibal, Jugurtha, Ariovistus, Caesar, Pompey, Nero, Otho, Vitellius, Domitian, Richard II of England, Edward II, Henry VI, Richard III, Mary Stuart, Charles I, France's three Henris, and the Emperor Henri IV? You know . . .'

'I also know', said Candide, 'that we must cultivate our garden.'

'You're right,' said Pangloss; 'for when man was placed in the garden of Eden, he was placed there *ut operaretur eum*—that he might work—which proves that man was not born to rest.'

'Let's get down to work and stop all this philosophizing,' said Martin. 'It's the only way to make life bearable.'

The little society all fell in with this laudable plan. Each began to exercise his talents. Their small amount of land produced a great deal. Cunégonde was in truth very ugly, but she became an excellent pastry-cook. Paquette embroidered. The old woman took care of the linen. Everyone made themselves useful, including Brother Giroflée; he was a very fine carpenter, and even became quite the gentleman. And sometimes Pangloss would say to Candide:

'All events form a chain in the best of all possible worlds. For in the end, if you had not been given a good kick up the backside and chased out of a beautiful castle for loving Miss Cunégonde, and if you hadn't been subjected to the Inquisition, and if you hadn't wandered about America on foot, and if you hadn't dealt the Baron a good blow with your sword, and if you hadn't lost all your sheep from that fine country of Eldorado, you wouldn't be here now eating candied citron and pistachio nuts.'

'That is well put,' replied Candide, 'but we must cultivate our garden.'

MICROMEGAS

A Philosophical Story

CHAPTER 1

*The journey of a worldly inhabitant of the star Sirius
to the planet Saturn*

On one of the planets which orbit the star named Sirius there once
was a young man of great intelligence, whom I had the honour of
meeting when last he journeyed to our little anthill. He was called
Micromegas, a most suitable name for all men of stature. He was
eight leagues tall, and by eight leagues I mean twenty-four thousand
geometrical paces each measuring five feet.

Certain algebraists, persons ever useful to the public, will at once
reach for their pen and find that since Mr Micromegas, inhabitant of
the land of Sirius, measures twenty-four thousand paces from head
to toe, which is the equivalent of one hundred and twenty thousand
French feet,* and since we, the citizens of the earth, measure barely
five, and since our globe has a circumference of nine thousand
leagues, will find, I say, that it necessarily follows that the globe
which produced him must be exactly twenty-one million, six hundred thousand times greater in circumference than our little Earth.
In nature nothing could be simpler or more commonplace. Compar-
ing the domains of some German or Italian sovereign, which may be
compassed in half an hour, with the empires of Turkey, or Muscovy,
or China, gives but a very inadequate picture of the prodigious
differences which nature has established between all beings.

His Excellency's height being of the dimension stated, all our
sculptors and painters will readily agree that he can measure fifty
thousand French feet around the waist, which makes for a very
pretty proportion. As for his mind, it is one of our most cultivated.
He knows many things, and some of them he discovered himself.
When not yet two hundred and fifty years old, and still a pupil, in the
usual way, at the Jesuit college on his planet, he worked out more

than fifty of the propositions of Euclid for himself. That is eighteen more than Blaise Pascal who, having worked out thirty-two of them just for fun (or so his sister says),* subsequently became a rather mediocre geometer and a very bad metaphysician. At about the age of four hundred and fifty, towards the end of his childhood, he dissected lots of those little insects which are no more than a hundred feet in diameter and which cannot be seen through ordinary microscopes. He wrote a most interesting book on the subject, but it landed him in some trouble. The local mufti, who was a great pedant and extremely ignorant, found some of the arguments in his book to be suspect, offensive, foolhardy, and heretical, indeed to be steeped in heresy; and he proceeded energetically against it. The case turned on whether the substantial form of the fleas on Sirius was of the same nature as that of the snails. Micromegas defended himself with wit and won the ladies over to his side. The trial lasted two hundred and twenty years. In the end the mufti had the book condemned by legal experts who had not read it, and the author was ordered not to appear at court for the next eight hundred years.

He was only moderately grieved to be banished from a court full of nothing but needless fuss and pettiness. He wrote a very funny song about the mufti, whom it little troubled, and set out to travel from planet to planet in order to complete the education of his 'heart and mind', as they say. Those who travel only by post-chaise or berlin will doubtless be surprised at the carriages they have up there, for down here on our little clod of earth we can conceive of nothing beyond our own ways of doing things. Our traveller had a marvellous grasp of the laws of gravity and of all the forces of attraction and repulsion. He put this to such good use that he and his retinue managed, sometimes with the help of a sunbeam, sometimes by means of a convenient comet, to proceed from globe to globe like a bird flitting from branch to branch. He covered the Milky Way in almost no time, and I am obliged to confess that never once did he glimpse, through the stars with which it is strewn, that fair empyreal heaven which the celebrated Reverend Derham boasts of having seen at the end of his telescope.* Not that I am claiming that Mr Derham was mistaken in what he saw. God forbid! But Micromegas was on the spot, he is a good observer, and I do not wish to contradict anyone.

After a satisfactory spin Micromegas arrived on the globe of

Saturn. Accustomed though he was to the sight of new things, he found it impossible at first, on seeing the smallness of this globe and its inhabitants, to suppress that smile of superiority which sometimes comes over even the most wise. For indeed Saturn is scarcely nine hundred times bigger than the Earth, and the citizens of the place are dwarfs a mere thousand fathoms or so tall. At first he and his men had something of a joke at their expense, rather as an Italian musician starts laughing at Lully's music* when first he comes to France. But as the Sirian was no fool, he very soon realized that a thinking being may perfectly well not be ridiculous just because he is only six thousand feet tall. He got to know the Saturnians, having at first caused them some measure of surprise. He struck up a close friendship with the Secretary of the Saturnian Academy, a most intelligent man who had not, it is true, discovered anything of his own, but who could give a very good account of the discoveries of others, and who was moderately adept at producing light verse and long calculations.* I shall here relate for the satisfaction of my readers a singular conversation which Micromegas had one day with Mr Secretary.

CHAPTER 2

*The conversation between the inhabitant of Sirius
and that of Saturn*

ONCE His Excellency had lain down and the Secretary had drawn close to his face, Micromegas began:

'One has to admit,' he said, 'that nature is very varied.'

'Yes,' said the Saturnian. 'Nature is like a flower-bed in which the flowers . . .'

'Pah,' said the other. 'Enough of your flower-bed.'

'It is like', the Secretary continued, 'a collection of blondes and brunettes whose dresses . . .'

'And what are your brunettes to me?' said the other.

'Well, then, it is like a gallery of paintings where the individual features . . .'

'But no,' said the traveller. 'I will say it again: nature is like nature. Why cast about for comparisons?'

'To please you.'

'I don't want to be pleased,' the traveller rejoined. 'I want to be instructed. You can start by telling me how many senses the people on your globe have.'

'We have seventy-two,' said the academician, 'and daily we complain how few that is. Our imagination exceeds our needs. We find that with our seventy-two senses, our ring, and our five moons, we really are much too limited, and despite all our curiosity and the quite considerable number of passions which derive from our seventy-two senses, we still have plenty of time to get bored.'

'I can well believe it,' said Micromegas, 'for on our globe we have nearly a thousand senses, and we are still left with a kind of vague longing, a sort of uneasiness, which constantly reminds us how insignificant we are and that far more accomplished beings exist. I have travelled a little. I have seen mortals who are considerably inferior to us, and I have seen some who are considerably superior. But I have never seen any who did not have more desires than they had real needs, and more needs than they had possibilities of satisfaction. Perhaps one day I shall find the place where nothing is lacking, but so far no one has been able to give me firm news of such a place.'

The Saturnian and the Sirian then engaged in exhaustive conjecture, but after much highly ingenious and highly speculative reasoning, they had to come back to the facts.

'How long do you live for?' said the Sirian.

'Ah, a very short time,' replied the little man from Saturn.

'It's just the same with us,' said the Sirian. 'We're always complaining that life is too short. It must be a universal law of nature.'

'Alas,' said the Saturnian, 'we live only five hundred complete revolutions of the sun. (This is the equivalent, by our reckoning, of fifteen thousand years, or thereabouts.) So you see, it's like dying practically the instant you're born. Our existence is but a point, our lifespan a moment, our globe an atom. One has scarcely begun to learn from instruction, and then death comes before we can learn from experience. For my own part I dare not plan ahead. I feel like a drop of water in an immense ocean. I am ashamed, especially in front of you, of how ridiculous I must look in this world.'

Micromegas answered him:

'If you were not a philosopher, I would be afraid of upsetting you when I tell you that our life is seven times longer than yours. But, as you know only too well, when the moment comes to return one's body to the elements and to reanimate nature in a different form— what they call dying—, when this moment of metamorphosis comes, it makes absolutely no difference whether you have lived an eternity or one single day. I have been in places where they live a thousand times longer than we do, and I found that still they grumbled. But wherever one goes, there are always some people with the good sense to accept their lot and give thanks to the author of nature. He has bestowed a profusion of varieties on the universe, but with a kind of marvellous uniformity. For example, all thinking beings are different, and yet all resemble each other fundamentally in possessing the natural gift of thought and having desires. Matter everywhere has extension, but on each globe it has different properties. How many different properties have you established for your matter?'

'If you mean', said the Saturnian, 'those properties without which we think this globe could not exist in its present state, we make it three hundred, including ones like extension, impenetrability, motion, gravitation, divisibility, and so on.'

'It would seem then', replied the traveller, 'that this small number is sufficient for what the Creator had in mind for your little abode. I marvel at his wisdom in everything. Everywhere I see differences, but everywhere, too, I see proportion. Your globe is small, so are your inhabitants. You have few sensations. Your matter has few properties. That is all the work of Providence. What colour is your sun when examined closely?'

'A very yellowy white,' said the Saturnian. 'And when we divide up one of its rays, we find seven colours in it.'

'Our sun is a bit on the red side,' said the Sirian, 'and we have thirty-nine primary colours. There is not one sun, amongst all those I have been near, which looks like any other, just as with you there is not one face which isn't different from all the others.'

After several questions of this nature he enquired how many essentially different substances there were on Saturn. He learnt that there were only thirty, such as God, space, matter, beings with extension that sense, beings with extension that sense and think, thinking beings that do not extend themselves, ones that interpenetrate, ones that do not interpenetrate, and so on. The Sirian, who came from where there were three hundred and had discovered three thousand others in the course of his travels, caused the philosopher from

Saturn some considerable astonishment. In the end, having shared with each other a little of what they knew and much of what they didn't, and having spent one revolution of the sun in discussion, they resolved to make a little philosophical journey together.

CHAPTER 3

The journey of two inhabitants of Sirius and Saturn

OUR two philosophers were ready to sail off into the atmosphere of Saturn with a very fine supply of mathematical instruments, when the Saturnian's mistress got to hear of it and came to make tearful remonstration. She was a pretty little brunette, a mere six hundred and sixty fathoms tall but with many charms to make up for her diminutive stature.

'Ah, you cruel man!' she burst out. 'I've resisted you for fifteen hundred years, and just as I was finally beginning to yield, just when I've been in your arms a bare two hundred years, now you go and leave me, off travelling with some giant from another world. Go on, it was just idle curiosity, you never really loved me. If you were a real Saturnian, you would be faithful. Where do you think you're going? What do you think you're up to? You're more of a rover than any of our five moons and more fickle than our ring. Well, that's it then. I shall never love another.'

The philosopher embraced her and wept with her, for all that he was a philosopher; and the woman, having duly swooned, went off and found consolation with some local fop.

Meanwhile our two inquiring minds departed. First they hopped on to the ring, which they found to be rather flat, just as a celebrated inhabitant of our own little globe quite rightly predicted it would be.* From there they proceeded easily from moon to moon. A comet was passing very close to the last of these, and they hurled themselves upon it together with their servants and their instruments. When they had covered about a hundred and fifty million leagues, they came to the satellites of Jupiter. They continued on to Jupiter itself and spent a year there, during which time they discovered many fine secrets. These would currently be at the printer's, were it not for those good gentlemen, the Inquisitors, who have found one or two of the propositions a trifle hard to swallow. But I have read the manuscript in the library of the illustrious Archbishop of . . . who, with a kindness and generosity that can never sufficiently be praised, granted me permission to consult his books.

But let us return to our travellers. On leaving Jupiter they crossed a space of about a hundred million leagues and passed close to the planet Mars which, as everyone knows, is five times smaller than our own little globe. They observed two moons which serve that planet and which have escaped the gaze of our astronomers. I am well aware that Father Castel will write—and quite entertainingly too—arguing against the existence of these two moons.* But I appeal to those who reason by analogy. These good philosophers know how difficult it would be for Mars, which is so far from the sun, to manage with less than two moons. Be that as it may, our two fellows found the planet so small that they were afraid they would not find room enough to lie down and sleep, and they continued on their way, like two travellers turning their noses up at a paltry village inn and pressing on to the next town. But the Sirian and his companion soon regretted their decision. They carried on for a long time and found nothing. At last they made out a small gleam of light. It was Earth. For people coming from Jupiter it was a sorry sight. However, in case they should have cause for regret a second time, they resolved to disembark. They passed on to the tail of the comet and, finding an aurora borealis close to hand, boarded it, and arrived on Earth on the northern shore of the Baltic Sea, on the fifth day of July, in the year seventeen hundred and thirty-seven, new style.

CHAPTER 4

What happens to them on the globe of Earth

AFTER resting for some time, they breakfasted off two mountains which their servants had prepared for them moderately well. Then they decided to reconnoitre the little place in which they found themselves. First they went from north to south. The average steps of the Sirian and his servants covered about thirty thousand French feet. The dwarf from Saturn panted along far behind: the trouble was that he had to take about twelve paces to the other's one. Picture (if such comparisons be permitted) a tiny lapdog following a captain in the King of Prussia's guards.

As these particular foreigners were rather fast walkers, one circuit of the globe took them thirty-six hours. A similar journey, it is true, takes the sun, or rather the Earth, one day, but one must bear in mind that it is much easier to turn on one's axis than to walk on one's feet. So there they were, back where they started, having seen the pond called the 'Mediterranean'—which was almost imperceptible to them—and that other little pool which, bearing the name of 'Great Ocean', surrounds this molehill. In the dwarf's case the water had never come above mid-calf, and the other had scarcely got his heel wet. On the way down under, and on the way back over, they made every effort to discover whether this globe was inhabited or not. They stooped low, they lay down, they groped in every corner, but their eyes and their hands not being in proportion to the little beings crawling about here, they felt not the slightest sensation which might have led them to suspect that we and our fellow inhabitants on this globe have the honour to exist.

The dwarf, who was sometimes a little too hasty in his judgement, decided at first that there was no one on Earth. His primary reason was that he had not seen anyone. Micromegas intimated to him politely that this was rather a poor way to reason.

'For', he said, 'with your small eyes you are unable to see certain stars of the fifth magnitude which I can make out quite distinctly. Do you conclude from this that these stars do not exist?'

'But', said the dwarf, 'I had a good feel.'

'But', replied the other, 'you must have felt badly.'

'But', said the dwarf, 'this globe is so badly constructed. It's so irregular, and the shape of it looks absolutely ridiculous to me! Everything here seems chaotic. Do you see those little streams? Not one of them runs in a straight line. And those ponds, which are neither round, nor square, nor oval, nor regular in any shape or form? And all these little pointed particles sticking up like bristles all over the globe and which have torn the skin off my feet? (He meant the mountains.) And just look at the shape of the whole thing, how flat it is at the poles, how it moves round the sun in that awkward way, and how this means that the climates at the poles are inevitably barren? Frankly, what makes me thing there is no one here is that, as I see it, no one with any sense would want to live here.'

'Or perhaps', said Micromegas, 'the people who do live here are not people with sense. But, well, it does seem a little as though this hasn't all been put here for no reason. Everything seems to you irregular, as you call it, because everything on Saturn and Jupiter is laid out all neat and tidy. But then perhaps that's the very reason why there's a measure of confusion here. Haven't I told you how, in the course of my travels, I have always found variety?'

The Saturnian replied to all these arguments. The debate would have gone on for ever had not Micromegas fortunately broken the string of his diamond necklace in the heat of the discussion. The diamonds fell. They were pretty little stones of slightly different sizes, with the largest ones weighing four hundred pounds and the smallest fifty. The dwarf picked up one or two. He noticed on holding them up to his eyes that, thanks to the way they had been cut, these diamonds made excellent microscopes. So he took a little microscope with a diameter of a hundred and sixty feet and applied it to his eyeball, and Micromegas chose one with a diameter of two thousand five hundred feet. They were excellent, but to begin with they could see nothing through them. Some adjustment was necessary. At length the inhabitant of Saturn saw something imperceptible moving about just beneath the surface of the Baltic Sea. It was a whale. He picked it up very deftly with his little finger and, placing it on his thumbnail, showed it to the Sirian who, for the second time, began to laugh at the excessively small size of the inhabitants of our globe. The Saturnian, now persuaded that our world is inhabited, at once thought that it was so only by whales, and as he was much given to rational analysis, he wanted to work out from whence so small an atom derived its movement, and whether it had ideas, and a will, and was free. Micromegas was much perplexed by all this. He examined the animal most patiently, and concluded from his examination that it was impossible to believe that a soul was lodged therein. The two travellers were therefore inclined to think that there is no intelligent life in this abode of ours when, with the aid of the microscope, they saw something bigger than a whale floating on the Baltic Sea. As everyone knows, a flock of philosophers was at that very moment on its way back from the Arctic Circle, where they had gone in order to make observations which it had not hitherto occurred to anyone else to make.* The gazettes said that their vessel ran aground on the coast of Bothnia and that they escaped with their lives only by the skin of their teeth. But in this world people never know the half of it. I shall relate quite simply how things happened and without adding anything of my own, which is no small feat for an historian.

CHAPTER 5

What the two travellers observed and how they reasoned

MICROMEGAS very gently stretched out his hand to where the object seemed to be and, moving two fingers forward and then drawing them back in case he should make a false move, then opening and shutting them, very adroitly took hold of the vessel bearing these gentlemen and placed it likewise on his nail as before, without squeezing too hard for fear of crushing it.

'Here's a very different sort of animal from the first,' said the dwarf from Saturn. The Sirian placed the alleged animal in the palm of his hand. The passengers and crew, who had thought they were being swept away by a hurricane and now believed they were on some sort of rock, started rushing all over the place; sailors were seizing hold of casks of wine, throwing them on to Micromegas's hand and hurling themselves after them, and geometers were grabbing their quadrants, their sectors, and the odd Lapp girl, and climbing down on to the Sirian's fingers. So much action was there that the latter finally felt something moving and tickling his fingers. It was the iron tip of a walking stick being driven a foot deep into his index finger. He concluded from the pricking sensation that something had protruded from the little animal he was holding. But at first his suspicions went no further than this. The microscope, which only just allowed them to make out a whale and a ship, was useless when it came to a being as imperceptible as man. It is not my intention to injure anyone's pride in this matter, but I must ask those who take themselves seriously to observe one small fact with me: which is, that if we take a man's height as being about five feet, then we cut no greater figure on this Earth than would an animal approximately one six-hundred-thousandth of an inch tall standing upon a ball with a circumference of ten feet. Imagine a form of matter which could hold the Earth in its hand and which had organs in proportion to ours (and it may well be that there are many such forms of matter).

Now kindly consider what they would think of those battles we fought which won us two villages which we then had to give back. (I have no doubt that if some captain in the great Grenadiers ever reads this work, he will increase the height of his company's bearskins by a good two feet at least. But I can tell him now that it will do him no good: he and his men will always be infinitesimally small.)

What marvellous skill it took on the part of our philosopher from Sirius to perceive the atoms I have just been talking about! When Leeuwenhoek and Hartsoeker were the first to see—or to think they saw—the seed from which we grow, they were making nowhere near so astonishing a discovery.* What pleasure it gave Micromegas to see these little machines in motion, to examine them as they went round and round, and to follow all their operations! How he exclaimed! With what joy he handed one of the microscopes to his travelling-companion!

'I can see them,' they both said at once. 'Look how they're carrying things round, and bending down, and straightening up.'

As they said this, their hands trembled with excitement at seeing such novel objects and with fear of losing them. The Saturnian, passing from the one extreme of scepticism to the other of credulity, thought he could observe them engaged upon propagation.

'Aha,' he said, 'I have caught nature in the act.'*

But he was deceived by appearances, which is an all-too-frequent occurrence, whether one uses microscopes or not.

CHAPTER 6

How they fare with humans

MICROMEGAS, a much better observer than his dwarf, saw clearly that the atoms were talking to each other; and he pointed this out to his companion, who, being ashamed at his mistake on the subject of generation, refused to believe that species like this could communicate ideas to each other. He had the gift of tongues just as much as the Sirian had: he could not hear our atoms talking; and he supposed that they were not talking. Besides, how could these imperceptible beings have speech organs, and what could they possibly have to say to each other? To speak one has first to think, or more or less. But if they could think, they would then have the equivalent of a soul. Well, to attribute the equivalent of a soul to this species, that seemed to him absurd.

'But,' said the Sirian, 'a moment ago you thought they were making love. Do you think one can make love without thinking and without saying a word or two, or without at least making oneself understood? Besides, do you suppose it's more difficult to produce an argument than a child? To my mind it is a great mystery how one does either.'

'I don't dare believe or deny anything any more,' said the dwarf. 'I have no opinions left. We must try to examine these insects, and then we can reason afterwards.'

'Very well said,' Micromegas replied, and at once he took out a pair of scissors and proceeded to cut his nails. With one thumbnail clipping he promptly made a kind of large speaking-trumpet, like an enormous funnel, and placed the pipe-end in his ear. The rim of the funnel went round the ship and its whole company. The faintest voice registered in the circular fibres of the nail so that, thanks to his industry, the philosopher up above could hear perfectly the droning of the insects below. Within a few hours he managed to make out individual words and eventually to understand French. The dwarf managed this too, although with more difficulty. The astonishment of our travellers increased with each moment that passed. They were hearing tiny mites talking really rather good sense: this trick of nature seemed to them quite inexplicable. As you can imagine, the Sirian and his dwarf were burning with impatience to strike up a conversation with the atoms. The latter was afraid that his thundering voice, and even more so that of Micromegas, might simply deafen the mites without their understanding what was being said. They would have to lower the volume. Each placed in his mouth a kind of small toothpick, the finely sharpened end of which reached down by the side of the ship. The Sirian held the dwarf on his knees, and the ship and its company on one nail. He bent his head down and spoke softly. Finally, taking all these precautions and more, he began to address them thus:

'Invisible insects, whom it has pleased the hand of the Creator to bring into being in the abyss of the infinitesimally small, I give thanks that he has deigned to reveal secrets to me which had seemed impenetrable. Perhaps nobody at my court would condescend to look at you, but I despise no one and I offer you my protection.'

If ever anyone was surprised, it was the people who heard these words. They could not work out where they were coming from. The ship's chaplain said the prayers of exorcism, the sailors swore, and the philosophers on board devised a system: but whatever system they devised, they could not work out who was speaking to them. The dwarf from Saturn, who was more soft-spoken than Micromegas, then briefly explained to them with what class of person they were dealing. He recounted the story of their journey from Saturn, put them in the picture as to who Mr Micromegas was and, after commiserating with them for being so small, asked them if they had always been in this abject state bordering on extinction, what on earth they were doing on a globe which seemed to belong to whales, whether they were happy, whether they multiplied, whether they had a soul, and a hundred other questions of this nature.

One quibbler in the party, bolder than the others and shocked at the doubt cast upon his soul, observed his interlocutor through sights mounted on a quadrant, took two bearings and, on the third, said this:

'So you believe, sir, that just because you measure a thousand fathoms from head to foot, and just because you are a . . .'

'A thousand fathoms!' cried the dwarf. 'Good heavens! How can he possibly know my height? A thousand fathoms! He is not an inch out. What! Measured by an atom! He is a geometer, and he knows my size: while I have only a microscope to observe him with, and I do not yet know his!'

'Yes, I have taken your measure,' said the physicist, 'and I shall even measure your tall companion.'

The proposal was accepted. His Excellency stretched out full length on the ground, for, if he had remained standing, his head would have been too far above the clouds. Our philosophers stuck a tall tree in a place which Dr Swift would name, but which I will certainly refrain from calling by its name out of my great respect for the ladies. Then, from a series of interlocking triangles, they concluded that what they were looking at was indeed a young man, and that he was about a hundred and twenty thousand French feet tall.

Then Micromegas spoke these words:

'I see more than ever that one must not judge anything by its apparent size. O God, who has given intelligence to forms of matter which seem so negligible, the infinitesimally small costs you as little effort as the infinitely large. And if it is possible that there are beings yet smaller than these, then they may even have greater intelligence than those magnificent animals I have seen in the heavens, whose foot alone would cover this globe on to which I have stepped.'

One of the philosophers replied that he could rest assured in his belief that there were intelligent beings much smaller than man. He told him, not all that fable nonsense of Virgil's about the bees, but about what Swammerdam had discovered and Réaumur* had dissected. Lastly he informed him that there are animals which are to bees as bees are to human beings, as the Sirian himself was to those enormous animals of which he spoke, and as those large animals are to other substances beside which they look like mere atoms. Gradually the conversation became interesting, and Micromegas had this to say.

CHAPTER 7

Conversation with the humans

'O intelligent atoms, in whom it has pleased the Eternal Being to manifest his skill and his power, the joys which you experience on your globe must doubtless be very pure. For, having so little material substance and being apparently all mind and spirit, you must spend your lives loving and thinking—the true life of the spirit. Nowhere have I seen real happiness, but no doubt it exists here.'

At these words the philosophers all shook their heads, and one of them, being franker than the others, admitted honestly that, except for a small number of inhabitants of little consequence, the rest were a collection of the mad, the malevolent, and the miserable.

'We have more than enough matter', he said, 'to do a lot of evil, if evil comes from matter, and more than enough spirit, if evil comes from the spirit. Are you aware, for example, that at this very minute there are a hundred thousand lunatics of our species in hats busy massacring—or being massacred by—a hundred thousand other animals in turbans,* and that almost everywhere on Earth that is how we have gone on since time immemorial?'

The Sirian shuddered and asked what could possibly be the cause of such dreadful quarrels between such puny animals.

'It's all about a few lumps of earth,' replied the philosopher, 'no bigger than your heel. Not that a single person among the millions getting slaughtered has the slightest claim to these lumps of earth. The question is simply whether they will belong to one man called "Sultan" or to another man who, for some reason, is called "Caesar". Neither one nor the other has ever seen, or ever will, the little bit of land in question, and almost none of the animals engaged in this mutual slaughter have ever seen the animal for whom they're doing all the slaughtering.'

'Oh, you wretched people,' cried the Sirian in indignation. 'How can one conceive of such mad fury, such pointless violence? I feel like taking three steps forward and crushing this whole anthill of ridiculous assassins just like that, one, two, three.'

'Don't trouble yourself,' came the reply. 'They're doing enough to destroy themselves as it is. The fact is that after ten years there's never a hundredth of the wretches left, and even if they never draw a sword, starvation or exhaustion or intemperance carry most of them off. Besides, they aren't the ones who need punishing, it's those barbarians sitting on their backsides in offices, who give orders for the massacre of a million men while they digest their meal, and then solemnly thank God for it.'

The traveller felt moved to pity for the little human race in which he was discovering such surprising contrasts.

'Since you are among the small number of wise men,' he said to these gentlemen, 'and since apparently you don't kill people for money, tell me, I pray, what do you do?'

'We dissect flies,' said the philosopher, 'we measure lines, we combine numbers, we agree about two or three things which we do understand, and we disagree about two or three thousand which we don't.'

At once the Sirian and the Saturnian were of a mind to find out from these thinking atoms what it was that they did agree about.

'How far do you think it is', the Sirian asked, 'from the dog-star to the great star in Gemini?'

They all replied at once:

'Thirty-two and a half degrees.'

'How far do you think it is from here to the moon?'

'Sixty times the radius of the Earth, in round figures.'

'How heavy is your air?'

He thought this would catch them out, but they all told him that air weighs approximately nine hundred times less than the same volume of the lightest water, and nineteen hundred times less than the gold in a ducat. The little dwarf from Saturn, amazed at their replies, was tempted to regard as sorcerers these selfsame people to whom he had refused a soul a quarter of an hour previously.

Finally Micromegas said to them:

'Since you know so much about what is outside you, doubtless you know even more about what is inside you. Tell me what your soul is, and how you form your ideas.'

The philosophers all spoke at once as before, but were each of a different opinion. The oldest quoted Aristotle, one mentioned the name of Descartes, another Malebranche, another Leibniz, and another Locke.

An old peripatetic confidently declared in a loud voice:

'The soul is an "entelechy", and a reason whereby it has the power to be what it is. This is what Aristotle specifically says, on page 633 of the Louvre edition: Εντελέχεια έστι, etc.'*

'I don't understand Greek too well,' said the giant.

'Neither do I,' said the mite-sized philosopher.

'So why then', the Sirian went on, 'do you quote this Aristotle person in Greek?'

'Because', replied the learned man, 'it is best one should quote what one doesn't understand at all in the language one knows the least.'

The Cartesian intervened and said:

'The soul is a pure spirit which has been imbued with all metaphysical ideas in its mother's womb and which, on leaving there, is obliged to go to school and learn all over again what it once knew so well and will never know again.'*

'So there was no point then', replied the eight-league-tall animal, 'in your soul being so clever inside your mother's womb, if it was then going to be so ignorant when you got some hair on your chin. But what do you mean by spirit?'

'What a question,' said the disputant. 'I haven't the slightest idea. They say is is not matter.'

'But do you at least know what matter is?'

'Certainly,' the man answered. 'This stone, for example, is grey and of a given shape, it has its three dimensions, it has weight, and it is divisible.'

'All right,' said the Sirian. 'This thing which seems to you to be divisible, weighable, and grey, would you mind telling me what it is? You can see some of its attributes, but what about the nature of the thing? Do you understand that?'

'No,' said the other.

'In which case you don't know what matter is.'

Then Mr Micromegas spoke to one of the other sages he was holding on his thumb and asked him what his soul was and what it did.

'Not a thing,' replied the Malebranchist. 'It is God who does everything for me. I see everything in him, and I do everything in him. It is he who does everything, and I have nothing to do with it.'*

'One might as well not exist,' retorted the sage from Sirius. 'And you, my friend,' he said to a Leibnizian who was present, 'what is your soul?'

'It is the hand of a clock,' came the Leibnizian's reply, 'and it points to the time while my body chimes. Or, if you prefer, it is my soul which chimes while my body points to the time. Or else my soul is the mirror of the universe, and my body is the mirror-frame. That much is clear.'*

A tiny follower of Locke was standing nearby, and when it was finally his turn to speak, he said:

'I do not know how I think, but I do know that I have never thought except with the aid of my senses. That there are immaterial and intelligent substances is something I do not doubt, but that it is impossible for God to endow matter with the power of thought is something I do strongly doubt. I revere the eternal power and it is not for me to set limits on it. I affirm nothing and I am content to believe that more things are possible than people think.'*

The animal from Sirius smiled. He did not find this one the least wise, and the dwarf from Saturn would have embraced the follower of Locke but for their extreme disproportion. Unfortunately, however, a little animalcule in academic dress* was present, who interrupted all the philosopher animalcules. He said he knew the answer, and that it was all in the *Summa* of Saint Thomas. He looked the two celestial inhabitants up and down and told them that everything, their persons, their worlds, their suns, their stars, had been made uniquely for man. On hearing this, our two travellers fell about, choking with that irrepressible laughter which, according to Homer, is the portion of the gods. Their shoulders and their bellies heaved and sank, and during these convulsions the ship, which the Sirian had been balancing on his nail, fell into the Saturnian's trouser-pocket. The two good people spent a long time looking for it. Eventually they found the ship's company and gave them a thorough dusting. The Sirian took hold of the little mites again. He still spoke to them with much kindness, although deep down he was a trifle vexed to see that beings so infinitesimally small should have a degree of pride that was almost infinitely great. He promised to write them a nice book of philosophy, in very small script just for them, and that in this book they would discover what was what. Sure enough, he gave them this volume before he left. It was taken to Paris to the Academy of Sciences. But when the secretary opened it, he found nothing but blank pages.

'Aha', he said, 'just as I thought.'

ZADIG
or
Destiny

A Tale of the Orient

THE SEAL OF APPROVAL

I, the undersigned, being one who has succeeded in passing himself off as a man of learning, and even as a wit, have read this manuscript and found it, despite myself, to be interesting, amusing, moral, philosophical, and worthy to give pleasure even to those who hate romances. I have therefore disparaged it and assured His Honour the Cadi that it is a detestable piece of work.

An Epistle Dedicatory
from Sadi
to Sultana Sheraa

This 18th day of the month of Schewal,
in the 837th year of the Hegira

O thou enchantment of the eye, thou torment of the heart, thou light of the mind! I shall not kiss the dust from thy feet, for thou walkest but rarely, and then thou walkest only upon the carpets of Iran or upon roses. Rather I here present thee with this translation of a book written by a sage of yore who, having the good fortune to have nothing to do, had the further good fortune to pass his time in writing the story of Zadig—a work which sayeth more than it may appear to say. I beg thee to read it and to decide of this for thyself: for though thou art in the springtime of thy life, though all manner of pleasure seeketh thee out, though thou art beautiful, and thy accomplishments complement thy beauty, though thy praises be sung from dusk to dawn, and though for all these reasons thou art fully entitled to be quite devoid of common sense, yet hast thou a mind most wise and taste most subtle, and I have heard thee reason better than any old dervish with a long beard and a pointed cap. Thou art discreet and hast not a suspicious mind. Thou art gentle, and yet thou art not weak. Thou dost good but with discernment. Thou lovest thy friends, and thou makest not enemies. Thy wit looks not to the borrowed barbs of gossip and scandal for its adornment. Thou speakest no evil nor dost thou commit any, notwithstanding the prodigious opportunities thou hast to do both. In short, thy soul hath always seemed to me as unblemished as thy beauty. Thou hast even the rudiments of philosophy, which hath led me to think that thou wouldst find more pleasure in this sage's work than others of thy sex.

It was originally written in the Ancient Chaldee, which language neither thou nor I understand. It was translated into Arabic for the amusement of the celebrated Sultan Ouloug-Beg. This was about the time that the Arabs and the Persians were beginning to write the Thousand and One Nights, *the* Thousand and One Days, *etc. Ouloug preferred* Zadig; *but the sultanas were fonder of the* Thousand and One Nights. *'How can thee possibly,' wise Ouloug would say to them, 'prefer stories that make no sense and have no point?—'That is precisely why we do like them,' would come the sultanas' reply.*

I flatter myself that thou wilt not be as they, and that thou wilt be a real Ouloug. I venture even to hope that when thou tirest of general conversation, which is rather like the Thousand and One Nights *except that it is less amusing, I shall find a minute in which to have the honour of a serious word with thee myself. Hadst thou been Thalestris in the days of Alexander, son of Philip, or the Queen of Sheba in the days of Solomon, it would have been the Kings who made the journey.**

I pray the heavenly powers that thy pleasures be unalloyed, thy beauty everlasting, and thy happiness without end.

Sadi*

ZADIG

or

Destiny

A Tale of the Orient

CHAPTER 1

The man with one eye

ONCE upon a time in Babylon, in the days of King Moabdar, there lived a young man called Zadig,* whom nature had endowed with a fine disposition upon which education had improved. Although both rich and young, he had the ability to moderate his passions; he was without affectation; he did not always wish to be right; and he was tolerant of weakness in others. People were surprised to find that, though a considerable wit, he never poked fun at all the vague, incoherent, strident statements, the heedless gossip, the ill-informed pronouncements, the crude jokes, in short, at the whole vain tumult of words that people in Babylon called 'conversation'. He had learnt from the first book of Zoroaster that self-esteem is a balloon filled with wind, from which great tempests surge when it is pricked. Above all, Zadig did not regard it as a matter of pride to despise and subjugate women. He was generous; and he was not afraid to oblige the ungrateful, thereby observing Zoroaster's great precept: 'When thou eatest, givest also unto the dogs, even should they bite thee.' He was as wise as can be, seeing that he sought to live among wise men. Though versed in the learning of the ancient Chaldeans, he was not unacquainted with the principles of natural philosophy as they were then understood, and he knew as much about metaphysics as men in any age have ever known—which is to say, precious little. He was firmly persuaded, despite the latest philosophical notions of his day, that the year consisted of three hundred and sixty-five and a quarter days, and that the sun was at the centre of the universe. And when the senior magi looked down their noses at him and told him that he had unsound views, and that only enemies of the State thought that the sun turned on its own axis and that there were twelve months in a year, he kept his peace without anger or disdain.

Zadig, possessed as he was of great wealth and hence of many friends, and having also a healthy constitution, a genial air, a fair mind, a level head, and a sincere and noble heart, believed that he could be happy. He was to marry Semira, who was by beauty, birth, and fortune the finest match in Babylon. He held a firm and virtuous attachment for her, while Semira was passionately fond of him. The happy day which was to unite them was drawing near when, out walking together near one of the gates of Babylon, beneath the palm-trees which used to grace the banks of the Euphrates, they saw some men coming towards them, armed with sabres and bows and arrows. They were henchmen belonging to young Orcan, the nephew of a minister, who had been led to believe by his uncles' minions that he might behave just as he pleased. He had none of the virtues and graces of Zadig but, thinking himself much the better man, despaired at never being preferred to him. This jealousy, which derived entirely from his vanity, made him think that he was madly in love with Semira. He had resolved upon her abduction. Her assailants seized her and, in the heat of their violence, wounded her, so shedding the blood of one the sight of whom would have melted the hearts of the very tigers on Mount Imaus. She rent the heavens with her laments. She cried out:

'My dear husband! They are taking me from the man I love!'

She had no care for her own danger; she thought only of her dear Zadig. He, meanwhile, was rallying to her defence with all the might that valour and love may inspire. Assisted only by two slaves, he put the abductors to flight and bore Semira home, unconscious and bleeding from her wounds. On opening her eyes she beheld her deliverer, and said to him:

'O Zadig! Once I loved you as my future husband. Now I love you as the man to whom I owe my honour and my life.'

Never was there a heart more profoundly moved than that of Semira. Never did a mouth more ravishing express sentiments more touching, and all in those words of fire that spring from a sense of gratitude for the greatest gift of all and from the tenderest transport of the most lawful passion. Her wound was slight: she soon recovered. Zadig's wound was more serious: an arrow had struck him near one eye and left a deep gash. Semira asked of the gods only that they might cure her lover. Her eyes were bathed in tears, night and day. She waited for the moment when Zadig's own might once more enjoy her gaze; but an abscess which had developed in the wounded eye gave every cause for concern. The great doctor Hermes was summoned all the way from Memphis, and he arrived with his numerous attendants. He visited the patient and declared that he would lose the eye. He even predicted the day and the hour when this fateful event would occur.

'If it had been the right eye,' he said, 'I could have cured it. But wounds in the left eye are incurable.'

All Babylon, while lamenting Zadig's fate, marvelled at the depth of Hermes' knowledge. Two days later the abscess burst of its own accord. Zadig was completely cured. Hermes wrote a book, proving to him that he should not have got better. Zadig did not read it. But, as soon as he was well enough to go out, he made ready to visit the person who was his one hope of future happiness, and for whom alone he wished to have eyes.

Semira had spent the previous three days in the country. On his way to her he learnt that this fine lady, having loudly proclaimed an insurmountable aversion to men with one eye, had just married Orcan that very night. On hearing this news he swooned. The pain which he suffered brought him to the very brink of death. He was ill for a long time. But in the end reason prevailed over his affliction, and the sheer awfulness of the experience served even as a kind of consolation.

'Since I have been the victim of such a cruel whim on the part of a young lady brought up at court,' he said, 'I must marry a commoner's daughter.' He chose Azora, the best behaved and the best born in the city. He married her and lived with her for a month, enjoying the delights of the most tender union. Only, he then began to notice a certain flightiness in her, and a marked tendency to find the best-looking young men to be also the wittiest and the most sterling.

CHAPTER 2

The nose

ONE day Azora returned from a walk much angered and expostulating loudly.

'My dear wife, whatever is the matter?' asked Zadig. 'Who can have upset you like this?'

'Alas, you would be just as indignant', she said, 'if you had seen the spectacle I have just witnessed. I went to comfort that young widow Cosrou who, just two days ago, saw her husband buried by the stream that runs alongside the meadow. In her grief she vowed to the gods that she would remain at his tomb for as long as the waters of the stream should flow beside it.'

'Well!' said Zadig, 'there's an estimable woman for you. She must really have loved her husband!'

'Ah,' said Azora, 'if you only but knew what she was doing when I visited her!'

'What then, fair Azora?'

'She was having the stream diverted.'

Azora launched forth into such a torrent of abuse and delivered herself of such violent reproaches against the young widow that Zadig took exception to this extravaganza of righteousness.

He had a friend called Cador, who was one of the young people in whom his wife found more integrity and worth than in others. He took him into his confidence and sought to ensure his loyalty, as best he could, by making him a handsome present. Azora, having spent two days in the country at the house of one of her friends, returned home on the third. Weeping servants informed her that her husband had died suddenly that very night, that they had not dared bring her such terrible news, and that they had just buried Zadig in the tomb of his forefathers at the bottom of the garden. She wept, pulled her hair out, and vowed that she would die. That evening Cador begged leave to speak with her, and they wept together. Next day they wept less and had dinner together. Cador confided in her that his friend had left him the greater part of his estate and gave her to understand that it would make him very happy if she would share his fortune with him. The lady burst into tears; took offence; was mollified.

Supper lasted longer than dinner. They talked together more freely. Azora sang the praises of the deceased; but she owned that he had had faults from which he, Cador, was quite free.

In the middle of this supper Cador complained of a violent pain in his spleen. The lady, most concerned and eager to help, sent for all the oils with which she was wont to perfume herself in order to essay them and see if there were not one which was good for pains in the spleen. She was most sorry that the great Hermes was not still in Babylon. She was even kind enough to touch Cador on the side where he felt such griping pains.

'Are you particularly prone to this cruel complaint?' she asked him with compassion.

'Sometimes it has me at death's door,' Cador replied, 'and there is only one remedy that can relieve it for me. That is to rub on my side the nose of a man who has died the day before.'

'That's a strange remedy,' said Azora.

'No more strange', he replied, 'than Dr Arnou's sachets[1] against apoplexy.'

This argument, added to the exceptional qualities of the young man, finally decided the lady.

'After all,' she said, 'when my husband passes across the bridge of Chinivar from the world of yesterday into the world of tomorrow, is the angel Asraël going to be any less ready to let him through just because his nose may be a little shorter in his second life than in his first?'

So she took a razor, went to her husband's tomb, wet it with a few tears, and drew near to remove the nose from off Zadig, whom she found stretched out in the tomb. Up sat Zadig, holding his nose in one hand and fending off the razor with the other.

'And now, madam,' he said, 'you can stop all your ranting against that young Cosrou woman. Wanting to cut my nose off is just as bad as wanting to divert a stream.'

---

[1] There was at that time a Babylonian called Arnou who could, according to the advertisements in the gazettes, cure and prevent all forms of apoplexy with a sachet hung around the neck.*

CHAPTER 3

The dog and the horse

IN Zadig's experience the first month of marriage was, as it says in the *Zend Avesta*, the moon of honey, and the second the moon of bitter wormwood. Shortly afterwards he was obliged to disown Azora, who had become quite impossible to live with, and he sought happiness instead in the study of nature.

'There is no greater happiness,' he would say, 'than that of a philosopher reading in the great book which God has placed before us. He discovers its truths for himself and makes them his own. He nurtures and elevates his mind. He enjoys a quiet life. He has nothing to fear from other men, and his dear wife does not come cutting off his nose.'

Full of such ideas, he retired to a country house on the banks of the Euphrates. There he did not spend his time calculating how many inches of water per second flowed beneath the arches of a bridge, nor whether, in the month of the mouse, there fell one cubic rod of rain more than in the month of the sheep. He thought not how to make silk from spiders' webs, nor porcelain out of broken bottles.* But he did make a special study of the properties of animals and plants, and soon developed an acuteness of perception which revealed to him a thousand differences where other men see only uniformity.

One day, out walking near a little wood, he saw one of the Queen's eunuchs running towards him, followed by several officers of the royal household, who appeared to be in a considerable state of concern and were running hither and thither, like men gone mad in search of some most precious missing object.

'Young man,' said the chief eunuch, 'you haven't seen the Queen's dog, have you?'

'It is a bitch, not a dog,' Zadig modestly replied.

'So it is,' replied the chief eunuch.

'She's a very small spaniel,' added Zadig. 'She has recently had a litter. She limps with her left front paw, and she has very long ears.'

'So you have seen her then?' said the chief eunuch, quite out of breath.

'No,' replied Zadig, 'I have never set eyes on her, and I never even knew the Queen had a dog or a bitch.'

At that precise moment, by a perfectly common twist of fate, the finest horse in the King's stable had slipped his groom and was loose on the plains of Babylon. The Master of the Royal Hunt and all the other officers were rushing after it with as much concern as the chief eunuch was in pursuit of his bitch. The Master approached Zadig and asked if he had seen the King's horse go past.

'That horse', said Zadig, 'has a very fine action when he gallops. He stands fifteen hands high and has very small hoofs. His tail is three and a half feet long. The bosses on the ends of his bit are in twenty-three carat gold. His shoes are made of solid silver.'

'Which way did he go? Where is he?' asked the Master Huntsman.

'I haven't seen him,' answered Zadig, 'and I've never heard of him before.'

The Master Huntsman and the chief eunuch were in no doubt that Zadig had stolen the King's horse and the Queen's bitch. They had him brought before the Assembly of the Grand Defterdar, where he was sentenced to the knout and condemned to spend the rest of his days in Siberia. Scarcely had the judgement been pronounced than the horse and the bitch were found. The judges found themselves under the painful obligation to reverse their judgement; but they fined Zadig four hundred ounces of gold for having said that he had not seen what he had seen. Zadig was required to pay the fine first; only then was he allowed to plead his case before the Council of the Grand Defterdar. He spoke in these terms:

'O ye luminaries of justice, ye founts of knowledge, ye mirrors of truth, whose deliberations are as weighty as lead, who possess the hardness of iron, whose brilliance glitters like diamonds, and who have such a considerable affinity with gold! Since I have been permitted to speak before this august assembly, I swear to you by Ormuzd that I have never seen the Queen's most estimable bitch nor the blessed horse of the King of Kings. What happened was this. I was out walking near the little wood where I subsequently met the venerable eunuch and the most illustrious Master of the Hunt. I saw some animal tracks in the sand, and I could easily tell that they were those of a small dog. Long, shallow grooves drawn across tiny heaps of sand between the paw-marks told me that it was a bitch whose teats were hanging down, which meant that she had whelped a few days previously. Other traces going in a different direction, and apparently made by something brushing constantly over the surface of the sand beside the front paws, told me that she had very long ears. And as I noticed that the sand was always less indented by one paw than by the other three, I realized that the bitch belonging to our most august Queen had, if I may dare say so, a slight limp.

'As to the horse belonging to the King of Kings, you must know that, as I was walking along the woodland paths, I noticed some horseshoe tracks. They were all the same distance apart. "That horse", I said to myself, "has a perfect action." Along a narrow path, which was only seven feet wide, some of the dust had been knocked off the trees on either side at a distance of three and a half feet from the centre of the path. "That horse", I told myself, "has a tail three and a half feet long which brushed the dust off the trees when he swished it from side to side." Beneath the trees, which formed a bower some five feet high, I saw some leaves which had recently fallen from the branches, and I deduced that the horse must have touched them, and therefore that he stood fifteen hands high. As for his bit, it must be made of twenty-three carat gold: for he had rubbed its bossed ends against a stone which I recognized as a touch-stone and which I assayed myself. Finally I judged from the marks which his shoes had left on some small stones of a different kind that he was shod in finest silver.'

The judges all marvelled at Zadig's penetrating and subtle powers of discernment. News of this reached the King and Queen. Zadig was the sole topic of conversation in antechamber, council chamber, and cabinet alike; and although several magi expressed the opinion that he should be burnt as a sorcerer, the King ordered that he be reimbursed for the fine of four hundred ounces of gold to which he had been sentenced. The clerk of the court, the bailiffs, and the public prosecutors arrived at his house with much pomp and cir- cumstance to resto e to him his four hundred ounces. They retained a mere three hundred and ninety-eight ounces to cover legal expenses, and their valets each demanded an honorarium.

Zadig saw how dangerous it sometimes was to be too clever, and promised himself that, when the occasion next presented itself, he would not divulge what he had seen.

This occasion soon did present itself. A state prisoner escaped: he passed beneath the windows of his house. Zadig was questioned. He said nothing, but they proved to him that he had been looking out of the window. For this crime he was fined five hundred ounces of gold and, following the Babylonian custom, he thanked the judges for their leniency.

'Good God!' he said to himself. 'How wretched can one be, just for walking in a wood where the Queen's bitch and the King's horse have been! How dangerous it is to stand looking out of the window! And how difficult it is to be happy in this life!'

CHAPTER 4

The Man of Envy

ZADIG resolved to seek consolation in philosophy and friendship for the blows that fortune had dealt him. He owned a house in a suburb of Babylon, which was decorated in good taste and provided opportunity for the pursuit of every art and pastime worthy of a gentleman. In the morning his library was open to all men of learning: in the evening his table was open to good company. But he soon discovered how dangerous men of learning can be. A great argument arose concerning one of the laws of Zoroaster, which forbids the eating of griffin.

'How can you forbid the eating of griffin,' said some, 'when the animal itself does not exist?'

'It must exist,' said the others, 'since Zoroaster wants us not to eat it.'

Zadig tried to reconcile them by saying:

'If there are any griffins, then let's not eat them. If there aren't any, then we will eat even less of them. That way we shall all be obeying Zoroaster.'

One scholar, who had written thirteen volumes on the properties of the griffin and was a great theurgist to boot, rushed off and denounced Zadig to an archimagus called Yebor, the least intelligent of all Chaldeans and hence the most fanatical. This man would have had Zadig impaled for the greater glory of the sun, and then recited the breviary of Zoroaster in an even more self-satisfied tone. Friend Cador (one friend is worth a hundred priests) went off to find Yebor and said to him:

'Long live the sun and all griffins! Beware of punishing Zadig. He is a saint. He has griffins in his poultry-yard, and yet he does not eat them. And his accuser is a heretic who dares to maintain that rabbits have cloven feet and are not unclean.'

'In that case,' said Yebor, shaking his bald head, 'Zadig must be impaled for thinking ill of griffins, and the other man for speaking ill of rabbits.'

Cador hushed up the affair with the help of a maid of honour whom he had once got with child and who had much influence with the College of Magi. No one was impaled; which raised a few eyebrows among the learned doctors, who foretold the fall of Babylon. Zadig exclaimed:

'On what does happiness depend! Everything in the world is against me, even the things that don't exist.'

He cursed all men of learning and decided to mix only in the better circles.

He collected around him the most cultivated men in Babylon and the most delightful ladies. He gave exquisite supper parties, which were often preceded by a concert and always enlivened by charming conversation, from which he had succeeded in banishing that eagerness to show off one's wit which is the surest way to be in want of it, as it is to spoil the most brilliant gathering. Neither the choice of his friends nor that of the menu was dictated by vanity. For in everything he preferred reality to appearance; and thereby commanded genuine respect, though he had not sought it.

Opposite his house lived one Arimazes, whose wicked soul was stamped upon the coarse features of his face. He was consumed with bitterness and puffed up with pride, and to cap it all he was a tedious, would-be wit. Never having managed to get on in society, he took his revenge by decrying it. Rich as he was, he had difficulty in gathering even sycophants around him. Hearing the chariots arriving at Zadig's every evening irked him: hearing his praises sung irritated him even more. Sometimes he would go to Zadig's house and sit down to table unbidden. He spoilt everyone's enjoyment, as harpies are said to taint the meat they touch. On one occasion he decided that he was going to give a party for a certain lady who, instead of accepting, went and supped with Zadig. On another, as he was talking with Zadig at the palace, they met a minister, who asked Zadig to supper but did not invite Arimazes. The most implacable enmities are not built on firmer foundations. This man, who was known in Babylon as the Man of Envy, wanted to do Zadig down because he was called Zadig the Happy.

As Zoroaster says: Occasion for harm cometh with every hour of the day, but occasion for good but once a year. The Man of Envy called on Zadig and found him walking in his gardens together with two friends and a certain lady to whom he was in the habit of saying things of an amorous nature without meaning anything by them. The conversation had turned to a war which the King had just waged successfully against the Prince of Hyrcania, his vassal. Zadig, who had distinguished himself by his courage during this brief war, was heaping praises upon the King, and even more upon the lady. He took his tablets and wrote down four lines of verse, which he had composed there and then, and handed them to this fair person for her to read. His friends begged to see them too. Modesty, or rather a shrewd self-regard, prevented him: he knew that impromptu verses seem good only to the person in whose honour they have been composed. He broke the tablet on which he had written in two and threw both halves into a rose-bush, where his friends looked for them in vain. A light shower fell, and they returned indoors. The Man of Envy remained behind in the garden and searched everywhere till he found a piece of the tablet. It had been broken in such a way that each half-line made sense and even scanned in a shorter metre. But, by an even stranger coincidence, these short lines of verse turned out to make sense as containing the most terrible insults against the King. They read:

> By crimes most real
> On throne is set
> Midst public weal
> This single threat.

For the first time in his life the Man of Envy was happy. In his hands he held the means to ruin a good and decent man. Filled with this cruel joy, he saw to it that this piece of satirical verse written in Zadig's hand found its way to the King. Zadig was put in prison, together with his two friends and the lady. He was soon brought to trial, though no one deigned to hear him give evidence. As he arrived to be sentenced, the Man of Envy stood close by and told him loudly that his verses were not up to much. Zadig had no pretensions to be a good poet; but he was in despair at being found guilty of *lèse-majesté* and at seeing a beautiful lady and two friends held in prison for a crime which he had not committed. He was not allowed to speak, because his tablet had spoken: such was the law of Babylon. And so he was led to his execution through a crowd of curious onlookers, not one of whom dared express any sympathy for him, and who all pressed forward to examine the expression on his face to see whether he was going to die with a good grace. Only his relatives were upset, for they would not inherit. Three quarters of his estate was forfeit to the King, and the other quarter was to go to the Man of Envy.

While Zadig was preparing to die, the King's parrot flew down from his balcony and landed on a rose-bush in Zadig's garden. A peach had been blown down there from a nearby tree. It had fallen on a piece of writing-tablet and was stuck to it. The bird picked up the peach and the tablet and bore them to the monarch's lap. The King, intrigued, read some words on it which made no sense and seemed to be the ends of some lines of verse. He was fond of poetry, and when a ruler likes verse, there is still hope. His parrot's adventure set him musing. The Queen, who remembered what had been written on the other piece of Zadig's tablet, ordered it to be fetched. The two pieces were placed together, and they fitted perfectly. The verses were then read out as Zadig had written them:

> By crimes most real have I seen many nations rocked.
> On throne is set our King a steady course to steer.
> Midst public weal, love alone in war is locked;
> This single threat, love alone is what we fear.

The King at once gave orders for Zadig to be brought before him and for his two friends and the beautiful lady to be released from prison. Zadig prostrated himself at the feet of the King and Queen: he most humbly begged their pardon for having composed such poor verse. He spoke with so much grace, wit, and good sense that the King and Queen wished to meet him again. He returned, and they liked him even more. He was given the entire estate of the Man of Envy who had falsely accused him, but Zadig returned it all to him, and the only emotion this caused the Man of Envy was one of relief at not losing everything he owned. The King's respect for Zadig grew with each day that passed. He bid him share in all his amusements and consulted him in all his affairs. Henceforth the Queen began to look on him with a degree of favour which might one day prove dangerous for her, for her noble husband the King, for Zadig, and for the whole kingdom. Zadig began to think that being happy was not so difficult after all.

CHAPTER 5

Generosity

THE season was upon them for the celebration of a great festival which came round every five years. It was the custom in Babylon, at the end of every fifth year, to declare with solemn ceremony which citizen had performed the greatest act of generosity. The nobles and the magi acted as judges. The chief satrap, who had overall responsibility for the city, would give an account of the most notable good deeds to have been performed during his period of office. A vote would be taken, and the King would announce the result. People came from the ends of the earth to attend this ceremony. The winner was presented by the monarch with a gold cup set with jewels, and the King would say these few words: 'Take thee this prize for thy generosity, and may the gods grant me many subjects like thee!'

When this memorable day arrived, the King mounted his throne, surrounded by the nobles, the magi, and the representatives of all the nations attending these games in which glory was won, not by the agility of a horse, nor by the strength of a man's body, but by virtue. The chief satrap publicly related such deeds as might win their authors this inestimable prize. He did not mention the magnanimity which Zadig had shown in returning the Man of Envy's estates: it was not a sufficiently meritorious deed to contend for the prize.

First he presented a judge who, having caused a member of the public to lose an important case because of a mistake for which he, the judge, was not himself responsible, had then given him everything he possessed, which was equal in value to what the other man had lost.

Then he produced a young man who, though madly in love with the girl he was going to marry, had given her up for the sake of a friend who was himself dying of love for her, and then even paid the dowry as he did so.

Next he introduced a soldier who, during the war against Hyrcania, had set an even greater example of generosity. Some enemy soldiers were abducting his lady-love, and he was trying to save her from them. He was told that, not far away, another party of Hyrcanians was abducting his mother. Tearfully he left his sweetheart and ran to save his mother. Then he returned to the woman he loved and found her dying. He wanted to kill himself. His mother remonstrated that he was all she had left in the world to protect her, and he found the courage to suffer life.

The judges were inclined towards the young soldier. The King intervened and said:

'His deed and the deeds of the others are very fine. But they do not surprise me. Yesterday Zadig performed one which did surprise me. A few days previously, I had banished my minister and favourite, Coreb, in disgrace. I was complaining about him vociferously, and all my courtiers were assuring me that I was too lenient, and they tried to outdo each other in speaking ill of Coreb. I asked Zadig what he thought, and he dared speak well of him. I must confess that whereas I have seen other examples in our history-books of people paying for an error with their entire fortune, or giving up the woman they love, or putting their mother before the object of their affection, I have never read of a courtier speaking up for a disgraced minister who has incurred the wrath of his sovereign. I shall give twenty thousand pieces of gold to each of those whose generous deeds have here been described, but the cup I award to Zadig.'

'Sire,' said he, 'it is Your Majesty alone who deserves the cup. It is Your Majesty who has performed the most unprecedented deed of all since, though King, you were not angry with your servant when he stood up to you in your wrath.'

There was widespread admiration for the King and for Zadig. The judge who had made over his estate, the lover who had given his sweetheart in marriage to his friend, and the soldier who had chosen to save his mother rather than his beloved, all received their gifts from the monarch, and saw their names inscribed on the roll of generosity. Zadig accepted the cup. The King acquired the reputation of a good prince, though he was not to keep it for long. The day was given over to celebrations which lasted much longer than was enjoined by statute. The memory of it still lives on throughout Asia. Said Zadig:

'So at last I am happy!'
But he was wrong.

CHAPTER 6

The minister

THE King had lost his Prime Minister. He chose Zadig to replace him. Every beautiful woman in Babylon applauded the choice; for there had never been, since the Empire was founded, a younger minister. All the courtiers were angry: the Man of Envy spat blood, and his nose became prodigiously swollen. Zadig, having thanked the King and Queen, went to thank the parrot also.

'O beautiful bird,' he said, 'it is you that have saved my life and made me Prime Minister. Their Majesties' bitch and horse brought me a lot of harm, but you have done me yet more good. To think that the destiny of mortal men should depend on such as these!'

'But perhaps', he added, 'good fortune so strangely come by will not last long.'

'Aye,' answered the parrot.

This word gave Zadig pause. Nevertheless, as he knew his natural philosophy and did not believe that parrots were prophets, he soon took heart and set about discharging his ministerial duties to the best of his ability.

He sought to impress on everyone the inviolate nature of the law, whereas the dignity of his office he sought to impress on no one. He did not try to influence the voting of the Divan, and each vizier could express an opinion without fear of incurring his displeasure. When he ruled in a particular case, it was not he who was judging, it was the law. But when the law was too harsh, he exercised discretion, and when no relevant laws existed, his sense of fairness devised ones which could have been drawn up by Zoroaster himself.

It is to Zadig that nations owe the great principle that it is better to risk sparing a guilty man than it is to condemn an innocent one. He believed that laws were made as much to protect citizens as to deter them. His principal talent lay in uncovering the truth, which all men endeavour to conceal.

From the very first days of his administration he put this great

talent to use. A famous Babylonian merchant had died in the Indies.
He had divided his estate equally between his two sons, having made
due provision for marrying off their sister, and he had left a further
sum of thirty thousand gold pieces to that son who would be judged
to love him the more. The elder son built a tomb for him: the
younger added part of his legacy to his sister's dowry. Everyone said:
'It's the elder son who loves his father more. The younger prefers his
sister. The thirty thousand gold pieces should go to the elder of the
two.'

Zadig summoned each of them in turn. He told the elder son:

'Your father is not dead. He has recovered from his recent illness,
and he is on his way back to Babylon.'

'God be praised,' the young man replied. 'But that tomb cost me a
tidy sum!'

Zadig then told the younger son the same thing.

'God be praised,' he replied. 'I shall give my father back everything I have. But I would like him to let my sister keep what I have
given her.'

'You will not give anything back,' said Zadig, 'and you will have
the thirty thousand gold pieces. It is you who loves your father more.'

A very rich young woman had promised her hand in marriage to
two magi and, having received premarital religious instruction from
both of them for a number of months, discovered that she was with
child. They each wanted to marry her.

'I shall take as my husband', she said, 'the one who has thus put
me in the position of furnishing the Empire with a citizen.'

'It is I who did this good work,' said one of them.

'It is I who had this good fortune,' said the other.

'Well then,' she replied, 'I shall recognize as the child's father the
one who can give it the better education.'

She gave birth to a son. Each of the magi wanted to bring him up.
The case was brought before Zadig. He summoned the two magi.

'What will you teach your pupil?' he asked the first of them.

'I', said the learned doctor, 'will teach him the eight parts of
speech, dialectics, astrology, and demonology, and about what is
meant by matter and contingency, the abstract and the concrete,
monads, and pre-established harmony.'

'I', said the second, 'will try and make of him a just and fair-minded
person, someone fit to have friends.'

Zadig pronounced judgement:

'Whether or not you are his real father, it is you who shall marry his mother.'

CHAPTER 7

Disputes and audiences

THUS did he daily demonstrate the subtlety of his mind and the goodness of his soul. He was admired, and yet he was loved also. He was thought to be the most fortunate of men. Throughout the Empire his name was on everyone's lips. The ladies had eyes only for him. The men all praised him for his sense of justice. The learned looked on him as their oracle. Even the priests conceded that he knew a good deal more about things than Yebor, the old archimagus. There was no question now of taking him to court over any griffins: people lent credence only to what seemed credible to him.

There was a great controversy which had been going on in Babylon for fifteen hundred years and which had split the Empire into two implacably opposed sects. The one claimed that the only correct way to enter the temple of Mithra was with the left foot: the other regarded this custom as an abomination and never entered other than with the right foot. Everyone was waiting for the solemn feast-day of the Sacred Fire to see which sect Zadig would favour. The eyes of the entire world were on Zadig's two feet, and the whole city was in a state of great excitement and suspense. Zadig entered the temple by jumping in with his feet together, and then proceeded to argue, in an eloquent speech, that the God of heaven and earth, being even-handed in all things, attaches no more importance to the left leg than he does to the right.

The Man of Envy and his wife alleged that his speech lacked for figurative expression, and that there had not been enough about mountains being moved or hills coming alive.

'He's dull. He has no flair,' they were saying. 'No seas being put to flight, no stars falling to earth, no suns melting like wax. He doesn't have the proper Oriental style.'

Zadig was content to have the style of reason. Everyone took his side—not because he was right, not because he was reasonable, not because he was a decent man, but because he was the grand vizier.

He put an equally happy end to the great legal battle between the white magi and the black magi. The white ones maintained that it was the height of impiety to pray facing east, from where the winter comes. The black ones asserted that God had an absolute horror of prayers made facing west, towards the setting sun that betokens summer's end. Zadig ordained that people could face whichever way they liked.

In this way he found the secret of dispatching both private business and affairs of state in a morning's work. During the rest of the day he busied himself with bringing beauty to Babylon. He had tragedies performed that people might weep at them, and comedies that people might laugh, both of which had long gone out of fashion and which he revived because he was a man of taste. He did not claim to know more about art than the artists themselves. He rewarded them with honours and material benefits and was not secretly jealous of their talents. In the evening he himself provided most entertaining company for the King, and especially for the Queen. The King would say: 'What a great minister!', and the Queen would say: 'What a delightful minister!'; and both would add: 'It would have been a great shame if he had been hanged.'

Never was one in high office obliged to give more audiences to the ladies. The majority came to speak to him about affairs they did not have, in order to have one with him. The wife of the Man of Envy was one of the first to appear. She swore to him by Mithra, by the *Zend Avesta*, and by the Sacred Fire, that she had found her husband's conduct towards him quite detestable. She then confided to him that her husband was a jealous, indeed a brutal man. She gave him to understand that the gods were punishing him by withholding from him those precious effects of the Sacred Fire by which alone man may rival the gods. She ended by letting fall her garter. Zadig picked it up with his usual politeness, but he did not replace it above the lady's knee; and this little oversight, if oversight it were, was to cause the most fearful calamities. Zadig did not give the matter a thought, but the wife of the Man of Envy gave it several.

Other ladies presented themselves every day. The secret annals of Babylon have it that he did once succumb, but that he was surprised to experience no pleasure in the act and that his mind was on other things as he embraced his mistress. The young woman upon whom he had thus, almost without noticing, bestowed the marks of his favour was one of Queen Astarte's personal maids. This amorous Babylonian consoled herself by reflecting:

'That man must have an awful lot of things on his mind, seeing that he still thinks about them even when he's making love.'

Zadig had happened, at that point in proceedings when several people say nothing at all and others utter only words of a sacred kind, to cry out suddenly: 'the Queen!' The young woman of Babylon thought that he had finally come to his senses at this operative moment and that he was saying 'my Queen' to her. But Zadig, his thoughts still very far away, then spoke the name of Astarte. The young lady, who was, in this happy position, construing everything to her own advantage, imagined that this meant: 'You are more beautiful than Queen Astarte!' She departed from Zadig's seraglio with many fine presents. She went to call on the wife of the Man of Envy, who was her best friend, and related what had happened. This lady was sorely put out at being thus passed over.

'He didn't even deign to replace this garter,' she said. 'I shall never wear it again.'

'Oh look, just fancy,' said the woman of good fortune to her envious friend, 'you wear the same sort of garters as the Queen! Do you get them from the same woman?'

This gave the woman of envy considerable pause for thought. She made no reply, and went to consult her husband, the Man of Envy.

Meanwhile Zadig noticed that he was unable to concentrate when he was giving audiences or hearing a case. To what he should attribute this, he did not know: it was the one and only thing that troubled him.

He had a dream. In it he imagined first that he was lying on some dry grass in which were some rather prickly stalks that were sticking into him, and then that he was lying back comfortably on a soft bed of roses, from which a serpent emerged and bit him in the heart with its sharp and venomous fang.

'Alas,' he said, 'I spent a long time lying on that dry and prickly grass, and now I am on the bed of roses. But what shall the serpent be?'

CHAPTER 8

Jealousy

ZADIG's downfall stemmed from his very good fortune, and in particular from his own exceptional qualities. Each day he would call on the King and Astarte, his noble consort. The delightful nature of his conversation was further enhanced by that desire to please which is to wit what ornament is to beauty. By insensible degrees his youth and charm began to make an impression on Astarte, an impression of which she was not at first aware. Her love grew within the bosom of innocence. Astarte gave herself up, without a moment's thought or apprehension, to the pleasure of seeing and hearing a man who was dear to her husband and to the nation. She did not cease to sing his praises to the King. She would talk about him to her women, who would add yet further words of approbation. Everything served, without her noticing, to drive the dart ever deeper into her heart. She gave Zadig presents of a more suggestive kind than she realized. She thought to speak to him merely as a Queen well-pleased with his services, but sometimes her turns of phrase were those of a woman of feeling.

Astarte was much more beautiful than that Semira who had such an aversion to one-eyed men, or that other woman who had wanted to cut her husband's nose off. Astarte's confiding tone, her tender remarks (which were beginning to bring a blush to her face), and those glances which she tried to direct elsewhere but which kept meeting his, all combined to light a fire in Zadig's heart, a fire which surprised him. He fought against it. He summoned the aid of philosophy, which had always helped him in the past: it simply shone further light, and offered no comfort. Duty, gratitude, and the thought of sovereign majesty besmirched rose up before his eyes as so many vengeful deities. He fought on, and he triumphed; but this victory, which had to be won and rewon with every moment, cost him many a groan and many a tear. He no longer dared to speak to the Queen with that sweet freedom which they had both found so captivating. His eyes would cloud over; his speech became forced and incoherent; he would lower his gaze, and when, in spite of himself, his eyes would turn towards Astarte, they would find the Queen's eyes all moist with tears and darting looks of fire. Each of them seemed to be saying to the other: 'We adore each other, and yet we dare not love. Each of us burns with a flame, yet this flame we repudiate.'

Zadig would leave her presence thoroughly bewildered and distraught, his heart weighed down by a burden he could no longer bear. In the violence of his agitation he let slip his secret to his friend Cador, rather as a man who, having long suffered the repeated stabbing of a sharp pain, finally betrays his ailment by a cry wrenched from him by a new and sharper spasm, and by the cold sweat dripping from his forehead.

'I had already suspected', Cador told him, 'these feelings which you have sought to conceal even from yourself. The symptoms of passion are unmistakeable. You must realize, my dear Zadig, that if I have read your heart, then so also will the King discover sentiments there of a kind that do him injury. His one failing is to be the most jealous of men. You are fighting against your passion with more strength than the Queen is able to combat hers because you are a philosopher and because you are Zadig. Astarte is a woman. She allows her eyes to speak the more incautiously because she does not yet believe herself guilty. Reassured, unfortunately, by her own innocence, she neglects to keep up the necessary outward appearances. I shall fear for her reputation for just so long as she has nothing with which to reproach herself. If you were in league with each other, you could deceive the eyes of all. Incipient and reluctant passion is plain for all to see; a love that's satisfied knows how to hide itself away.'

Zadig shuddered at the suggestion of betraying the King, his benefactor; and never did he feel more loyal to his prince than now that he was guilty of an involuntary crime against him. However, the Queen mentioned Zadig's name so often—her brow colouring deeply every time she did so—, she was alternately so animated and so tongue-tied when she spoke to him in the King's presence, and such profound reverie came over her when he had gone, that the King grew troubled in his mind. He believed the evidence of everything he saw, and imagined everything he did not. He noticed especially that his wife's babouches were blue, and that Zadig's babouches were blue, that his wife's ribbons were yellow, and that Zadig's cap was yellow. For a prince so susceptible, these were sure and terrible signs. Suspicion turned to certainty in his poisoned mind.

In the slave of every king and queen lurks a willing spy upon the royal heart. It was soon perceived that Astarte was in love and that Moabdar was jealous. The Man of Envy bid his envious wife send the King her garter which was like the Queen's. Just to make matters worse, the garter was blue. The monarch now thought only of how to exact his revenge. One night he resolved to poison the Queen and have Zadig garrotted at daybreak. The order was given to a ruthless eunuch, the instrument of all his acts of vengeance. There was at that time in the King's chamber a little dwarf, who was mute but not deaf. His presence was always tolerated: he was witness to the most secret events, like a domestic pet. This little mute was very attached to the Queen and Zadig. He was as astonished as he was horrified to hear the order given for their death. But how to forestall this dreadful order which was to be carried out in a matter of hours? He could not write; but he had learnt to paint and was particularly good at achieving a likeness. He spent part of the night drawing what he wanted to communicate to the Queen. His drawing showed the King in one corner, beside himself with rage and giving orders to his eunuch; on the table, a blue garrotte and a vase, together with some blue garters and yellow ribbons; in the middle of the picture, the Queen, dying in the arms of her women, and Zadig strangled at her feet. On the horizon was a rising sun, to indicate that this fearful execution was to take place at first light. As soon as he had finished his work, he hurried to one of Astarte's women, roused her, and conveyed to her that she should take this picture to the Queen that very instant.

Next, at dead of night, there came a knock at Zadig's door. He was woken and given a note from the Queen: he wondered if this were all a dream. He opened the letter with a trembling hand. Imagine his surprise! What words could express the consternation and despair which overcame him when he read the following:

'Flee this very moment, or they will come and take your life. Flee, Zadig, I command you in the name of our love and of my yellow ribbons. I have done no wrong, but I sense that I may die a criminal.'

Zadig was scarcely able to speak. He sent for Cador and, without a word, handed him the note. Cador compelled him to obey and to leave at once for Memphis.

'If you dare go and seek out the Queen,' he told him, 'you will simply hasten her death. If you speak to the King, again you will be her ruin. I shall be responsible for her fate: you look to your own. I shall spread the rumour that you have left for the Indies. I'll come and find you soon to let you know what's happened in Babylon.'

Cador immediately had two of the fastest racing dromedaries brought round to a secret palace-gate. He bid Zadig mount, but the latter had to be lifted on as he was almost insensible. Just one servant went with him. And soon, lost in sorrow and disbelief, Cador watched his friend slowly pass from view.

This illustrious fugitive, on reaching the brow of a hill from which it was possible to look down on Babylon, turned his gaze upon the Queen's palace and swooned. He recovered consciousness only to shed more tears and to wish himself dead. In the end, having thought only of the grievous fate that had befallen the most adorable of women and the foremost Queen in all the world, he began to reflect on himself and cried out:

'What, then, is human life? O virtue, what good have you done me? Two women have basely deceived me, and the third, to whom no blame attaches, and who is more beautiful than the others, is going to die. Any good thing I have ever done has been a source of calamity to me, and I have been raised to the pinnacle of greatness only to be cast down into the most dreadful chasm of misfortune. If I had been wicked like so many others, I should be happy like them too.'

Overwhelmed by these dire reflections, his eyes veiled with anguish, the pallor of death upon his face, and his soul sunk deep in the abysmal excess of darkest despair, he continued on his journey towards Egypt.

CHAPTER 9

The battered woman

ZADIG steered his course by the stars. The constellation of Orion and the bright star of Sirius guided him, with the help of Canopus, southwards. He stared in wonder at these vast globes of light which seem to us mere feeble sparks, while the Earth, which is in reality but an imperceptible point in the scheme of things, appears to our covet-ous eyes something so noble and grand. He saw men then for what they really are, insects devouring each other upon a tiny speck of dirt. This telling image seemed to blot out his misfortunes by reminding him of the nullity of his own being and of that of Babylon. His soul soared up into the infinite and, unencumbered by his senses, beheld the immutable order of the universe. But when afterwards he considered, on coming down to earth again and reflecting once more upon his own heart, that Astarte was perhaps dead on his account, the universe ceased to exist in his eyes, and he could see nothing in the whole of nature but a dying Astarte and a hapless Zadig.

While he thus gave himself up to the ebb and flow of being sublimely philosophical one minute and overwhelmed by pain and sorrow the next, he drew near to the frontiers of Egypt; and his faithful servant was already in the first village finding him lodgings. Zadig, meanwhile, was riding in the vicinity of the gardens which lay on the outskirts of the village. He saw, not far from the main track, a woman in tears summoning heaven and earth to her aid, and a furious man pursuing her. He had already caught up with her, and she was clinging to his knees. The man was belabouring her with reproach and fist alike. Zadig judged by the Egyptian's violence and the lady's repeated calls for his forgiveness that here was a jealous man and an unfaithful wife. But when he had looked more closely at this woman, whose beauty was enhanced by her plight, and who even bore some slight resemblance to the unfortunate Astarte, he was filled with compassion for her and with revulsion against the Egyptian.

'Help me,' she shouted to Zadig between her sobs. 'Save me from this vile barbarian. He's going to kill me. Save me.'

In response to these cries Zadig flung himself between her and the barbarian. He knew some Egyptian and addressed him in that language:

'If you have any humanity, I beg you to show some respect for beauty and weakness. How can you commit such an outrage against this masterpiece of nature? Here she is lying at your feet with only tears to defend her.'

'Aha,' said the man in a rage, 'so you love her too, then! Well, I can take my revenge on you.'

So saying, he let go of the lady, whom he had been holding with one hand by the hair and, taking up his lance, he made to run the stranger through. The latter, remaining cool, had no difficulty in avoiding the madman's thrust. He grabbed the lance just beyond its iron point. The one tried to pull it back, the other to wrest it away: it came apart in their hands. The Egyptian drew his sword; Zadig took up his. They set upon each other. The one made a hundred hasty slashes; the other deftly parried them. The lady, sitting on a patch of grass, tidied her hair and watched. The Egyptian was stronger than his opponent, Zadig the more adroit. The latter fought as one whose arm was governed by his head; and the other like a man possessed whose movements were directed by blind anger and random chance. Zadig made a pass and disarmed him; and as the Egyptian, who was even more furious now, tried to jump on him, he grabbed hold of him, held him tight, wrestled him to the ground and, with his sword pointing at his chest, then offered to spare him. The Egyptian, quite beside himself with rage, drew his dagger and wounded Zadig with it just as the victor was offering mercy. Zadig, outraged, plunged his sword into him. The Egyptian let out a bloodcurdling cry, and died amidst thrashing limbs.

Zadig then went up to the lady and said in a respectful voice:

'He forced me to kill him. I have avenged you. You are delivered from the most violent man I have ever seen. May I be of further service, madam?'

'May you die, villain,' she replied. 'Yes, die. You have killed my lover. If only I could tear your heart out.'

'I must say, madam, you had rather a strange man for a lover,' said Zadig. 'He was beating you for all he was worth, and he wanted to kill me because you had begged me to rescue you.'

'I wish he were beating me still,' screamed the lady. 'I deserved what I got. I had made him jealous. Would to God he might beat me again, and that you were in his place.'

Zadig, more surprised and more angry than he had ever been in his life before, said:

'Madam, beautiful as you are, you deserve a good thrashing from me, too. Your behaviour's quite outrageous. But I shan't give myself the trouble.'

Thereupon he remounted his camel and proceeded towards the village. Scarcely had he gone a few paces than the sound of four despatch-riders from Babylon made him turn round. They were riding at full tilt. One of them, seeing the woman, cried:

'That's her. She looks like the woman they described to us.'

They did not pay the slightest attention to the dead man and promptly grabbed the lady. She kept calling out to Zadig:

'Help me one more time, o generous stranger! Forgive me for complaining about what you did. Help me, and I am yours unto the grave.'

Zadig no longer felt quite the same desire to fight on her behalf.

'Try someone else!' he replied. 'You won't catch me doing that again.'

Anyway, he was wounded. He was bleeding, and he needed assistance; and the sight of the four Babylonians, who had probably been sent by King Moabdar, filled him with disquiet. He hurried on towards the village, having no idea why four riders from Babylon should have come and taken this Egyptian woman, but even more astonished still by the lady's character.

CHAPTER 10

Slavery

As he entered the Egyptian village, he found himself surrounded by the populace. They were all shouting:

'That's the man who ran off with fair Missouf and murdered Cletofis!'

'Good sirs,' he said, 'God forbid that I should ever run off with your fair Missouf! She is much too capricious. And as for Cletofis, I didn't murder him. It was self-defence. He wanted to kill me because I had very humbly asked him to spare the fair Missouf, whom he was beating mercilessly. I am a stranger come to seek asylum in Egypt, and it is hardly likely that in coming to seek your protection I would begin by abducting a woman and murdering a man.'

Egyptians at that time were just and humane. The crowd escorted Zadig to the village hall. First they dressed his wound, and then they questioned him and his servant, separately, in order to discover the truth. They acknowledged that Zadig was not a murderer; but he was guilty of manslaughter, for which the legal penalty was slavery. His two camels were sold, and the proceeds donated to the village. All the gold which he had brought with him was distributed among the inhabitants. His person was displayed for sale in the public square, together with that of his travelling-companion. An Arab merchant named Setoc was the highest bidder, though the servant, being more used to hard work, fetched a much higher price than his master. There was simply no comparison between the two men. So Zadig entered slavery as the subordinate of his valet. They were chained together by the ankle, and in this state they followed the Arab merchant to his house. On the way Zadig comforted his servant and bid him be patient; but, as was his wont, he also reflected on the lives of men.

'I can see', he said, 'that the misfortunes of my own destiny have rather impinged on yours. In my case, things have been turning out very strangely so far. I have been fined for seeing a bitch go by. I thought I would be impaled on account of a griffin. I have been sent to the scaffold for writing some verses in praise of the King. I was nearly garrotted because the Queen had yellow ribbons. And here I am in slavery with you because some brute was beating up his mistress. Ah well, let us not lose heart. Perhaps there will be an end to all this. Arab merchants have to have their slaves, and why should I not be one just like anyone else? I am a human being just like anyone else, am I not? This merchant won't be too harsh. He has to treat his slaves well if he wants any work out of them.'

This was how he talked, but deep down in his heart of hearts his sole concern was for what might have happened to the Queen of Babylon.

Setoc the merchant set out two days later for the Arabian Desert, taking his slaves and camels with him. His tribe lived near the Horeb Desert. The journey was long and arduous. On the way Setoc was much more impressed with the servant than the master because the former was much better at loading the camels; and so all the little marks of favour were for him.

A camel died some two days' journey short of Horeb: his load was distributed on to the backs of the servants. Zadig had his share. Setoc started to laugh at the sight of all his slaves bent over double as they walked. Zadig took the liberty of explaining to him the reason for this, and told him about the laws of equilibrium. The merchant, astounded, began to regard Zadig in a different light. Zadig, seeing that he had aroused his curiosity, whetted it still further by telling him many things which might be of relevance to the merchant's trading practices—such as the specific gravity per volume of different metals and other commodities, the peculiar qualities and uses of certain animals, and the way to make useless ones useful. In short, he seemed quite the sage. Setoc now preferred him to his companion whom he had previously held in such esteem. He treated him well, and had no cause to regret it.

Having reached his tribe, Setoc began by asking a Hebrew to give him back the five hundred ounces of silver he had lent him in the presence of two witnesses. But these two witnesses were dead, and the Hebrew, who was not to be persuaded, appropriated the merchant's money and thanked God for having given him the means to cheat an Arab. Setoc confided his problem to Zadig, who had become his adviser.

'Where was it', Zadig enquired, 'that you lent the infidel these five hundred ounces of yours?'

'On top of a large stone', the merchant replied, 'near Mount Horeb.'

'What sort of a man is he, your debtor?' asked Zadig.

'A swindler,' rejoined Setoc.

'No, I mean is he impulsive or phlegmatic? Is he a cautious man, or is he reckless?'

'Of all the bad payers I know,' said Setoc, 'he is the most impulsive.'

'In that case,' Zadig persisted, 'allow me to plead your cause before the judge.'

And so indeed he brought a suit against the Hebrew, and spoke thus to the judge:

'O pillow upon the throne of equity, I appear before you on behalf of my master to demand back from this man five hundred ounces of silver which he has refused to return.'

'Do you have witnesses?' said the judge.

'No, they are dead. But the stone on which the money was counted out is still there, and if it please Your Greatness to give orders for the stone to be fetched, I hope that it may bear witness. The Hebrew and I will remain behind here while the stone is brought. I will see to it that the stone is fetched at my master Setoc's own expense.'

'Very well,' said the judge. And he began to deal with other business.

'Well then,' he said to Zadig at the end of the sitting, 'is there still no sign of your stone?'

The Hebrew answered with a laugh:

'Your Greatness could sit here till tomorrow, and there still wouldn't be any stone. It lies more than six miles from here, and it would take fifteen men to move it.'

'There you are,' cried Zadig, 'I told you the stone would bear witness. Since this man knows where it is, he has as good as admitted that it was the stone on which the silver was counted out.'

The Hebrew, nonplussed, was soon obliged to admit everything. The judge ordered him to be bound to the stone, without food or water, until he had returned the five hundred ounces, which he soon did.

Zadig the slave and his stone became the talk of Arabia.

CHAPTER 11

The funeral-pyre

SETOC, absolutely delighted, now looked on his slave as his best friend. He could no more do without him than the King of Babylon had been able to; and Zadig was glad that Setoc did not have a wife. He discovered in his master a natural inclination to the good, together with much integrity and good sense. He was sorry to find that, in accordance with ancient Arab custom, he worshipped the heavenly host, namely the sun, the moon, and the stars. Sometimes, very tactfully, he would broach the subject with him. He eventually told him that they were bodies like any other, and no more deserved his homage than did a tree or a rock.

'But', said Setoc, 'they are eternal beings from whom all good things come down to us. They breathe life into nature. They regulate the seasons. And, besides, they are so far away from us that we cannot help but revere them.'

'More good things come to you from the waters of the Red Sea,' said Zadig. 'They carry your merchandise to the Indies. Why shouldn't they be as old as the stars? And if you worship what is far away, you ought to worship the land of the Gangarides,* which lies at the edge of the world.'

'No,' said Setoc, 'the stars are too bright for me not to worship them.'

That evening Zadig lit a large number of candles in the tent where he was to have supper with Setoc; and as soon as his master appeared, he fell to his knees in front of these lighted tapers and said:

'O everlasting, shining brightnesses, look thou upon me with thy favour always.'

Having proffered these words, he sat down to table without even a glance at Setoc.

'What on earth are you doing?' asked Setoc in amazement.

'I am doing what you do,' replied Zadig. 'I am worshipping the candles and neglecting their master and mine.'

Setoc took the point of this apologue. He allowed the wisdom of his slave to enter his soul: he stopped wasting his incense on what had been created, and began to worship the Eternal Being who had made them.

There was an appalling custom in Arabia at that time, which had originally come from Scythia and which, having become established in the Indies through the influence of the Brahmans, threatened to spread throughout the entire Orient. When a married man died and his beloved wife wanted to be holy, she publicly burnt herself to death on top of her husband's corpse. This was a solemn ceremony known as 'the Widow's Pyre'.* The tribe which could count the greatest number of its women to have burnt themselves was the most respected. An Arab in Setoc's tribe having died, his widow, who was called Almona and who was very devout, announced the day and the hour when she would cast herself into the fire to the sound of drums and trumpets. Zadig put it to Setoc how contrary this horrible custom was to the better interests of the human race; namely, letting young widows go burning themselves every day when they could be providing the nation with children, or at least bringing up their own. And he secured his consent that such a barbaric practice should, if at all possible, be abolished.

Setoc countered:

'Women have been free to burn themselves for more than a thousand years. Which of us shall dare to change a law which has been hallowed by the passage of time? Is there anything more respectable than a time-honoured abuse?'

'Reason is more time-honoured still,' Zadig retorted. 'Speak to the tribal chiefs, and I shall go and find the young widow.'

He had himself shown in; and having ingratiated himself by

extolling her beauty, and having told her what a shame it was to put so many charms on the fire, he praised her further for her constancy and her courage.

'You must have loved your husband very much indeed, then?' he enquired.

'Me? Not in the slightest. He was a brute, always jealous, an intolerable man. But I am firmly resolved to cast myself on to his funeral-pyre.'

'It would seem then', said Zadig, 'that being burnt alive must be a particularly exquisite pleasure.'

'Oh, it's a crime against nature,' said the lady. 'But one has to do the done thing. I am a religious woman. My reputation would be ruined and everyone would laugh me to scorn if I didn't burn myself.'

Zadig, having got her to acknowledge that she would be burning herself to death for the sake of other people, out of vanity, then talked to her for a long time in a manner intended to restore to her some small taste for living; and managed even to inspire in her a certain benevolence towards the man who was talking to her.

'What would you in fact do,' he asked her, 'if it were not for this need to burn yourself for vanity's sake?'

'Oh dear,' said the lady, 'I think I should ask you to marry me.'

Zadig's head was too full of Astarte for him not to meet this declaration with evasion. But he went at once to find the tribal chiefs, told them what had happened, and advised them to make a law whereby widows would be allowed to burn themselves only after they had spent one whole hour alone in the company of a young man. Since that time no lady has ever burnt herself in Arabia. They owed it to Zadig, and Zadig alone, to have put an end in one single day to so cruel a custom, and which had persisted for so many centuries. And thus did he become the benefactor of Arabia.

CHAPTER 12

The supper party

SETOC, no longer able to be parted from this man in whom all wisdom dwelt, took him to the great fair at Balzora, which was to be attended by all the most important traders in the known world. It gladdened Zadig's heart to see so many men from different countries brought together in one place. It was as if the world were one great family and they were all getting together in Balzora. Already on the second day he found himself at table with an Egyptian, an Indian from the Gangarides, an inhabitant of Cathay, a Greek, a Celt, and several other foreigners who, on their frequent journeys to the Arabian Gulf, had learnt enough Arabic to make themselves understood. The Egyptian seemed to be very angry about something.

'What a frightful place Balzora is,' he was saying. 'They've refused to lend me a thousand ounces of gold against the best security in the world!'

'How can that be?' said Setoc. 'What sort of security is it that they won't lend an amount like that against it?'

'The body of my aunt,' replied the Egyptian. 'She was the finest woman in Egypt. She used to go everywhere with me. She died on the way here. I've had her made into one of the most beautiful mummies in the world. And I could borrow all I wanted back in my own country if I were to put her up as collateral. It's most odd that here they won't let me have even a thousand ounces of gold against such a tangible asset.'

While he fumed away, he was just going to eat a piece of excellent boiled chicken, when the Indian grabbed him by the hand and cried out in distress:

'What are you doing?'

'Eating this chicken,' said the man with the mummy.

'You must do no such thing,' said the man from the Gangarides. 'It is quite possible that the soul of the departed lady may have passed into the body of this chicken, and surely you would not want to run the risk of eating your aunt. Cooking chickens is a manifest outrage against nature.'

'What are you on about with your nature and your chickens?' the choleric Egyptian rejoined. 'We all worship a bull, but that doesn't stop us eating the stuff.'

'You worship a bull! Can that be possible?' said the man from the Ganges.

'It most certainly can,' the other went on. 'We've been doing it for a hundred and thirty-five thousand years, and not one of us has ever had reason to complain.'

'Oh, one hundred and thirty-five thousand years!' said the Indian.

'That's rather an exaggeration. It is only eighty thousand since people first lived in India, and most assuredly we are the older race. And Brahma forbade us to eat beef long before you even thought of putting it on your altars or your spits.'

'He's a fine one, your Brahma, to be compared with Apis!' said the Egyptian. 'What's he done that's so clever, then?'

The Brahman answered him:

'It was he who taught men to read and write, and it is to him that we owe the game of chess.'

'You're wrong,' said a Chaldean sitting near him. 'It is Oannes the fish that we must thank for these great boons, and it is meet that we should do homage only unto him. Anyone will tell you that he was a divine being, that he had a golden tail and the handsome head of a man, and that he used to come out of the water and preach on dry land for three hours every day. He had several children who all became kings, as everyone knows. I have his portrait at home, which I venerate as I ought. You can eat all the beef you want, but it is unquestionably a very great act of impiety to cook a fish. Besides, your origins are far too base and recent for either of you to be able to argue the point with me. The Egyptian nation goes back only a hundred and thirty-five thousand years, and the Indians boast of a mere eighty, whereas we have almanacs going back four thousand centuries. Take my word for it. Give up these silly notions of yours, and I will let each of you have a nice portrait of Oannes.'

The man from Cambalu* broke in and said:

'I have great respect for the Egyptians, the Chaldeans, the Greeks, the Celts, Brahma, the Bull Apis, and Oannes the handsome fish. But it is possible that Li—or Tien,[1] if you prefer—is worth any beef or fish. I shall say nothing of my own country. It is as big as Egypt, Chaldea, and the Indies put together. I shall not argue about antiquity because what matters is being happy, and being ancient is of very little consequence. But if we're going to talk about almanacs, I would point out that ours are used all over Asia, and that we had some very good ones before they even knew about arithmetic in Chaldea.'

---

[1] Chinese words meaning literally: *Li*, natural light, reason; and *Tien*, the sky: and which both also mean God.

'You don't know a blind thing about anything, the whole lot of you,' cried the Greek. 'Don't you know that Chaos is the father of all, and that form and matter have made the world the way it is?'

The Greek spoke for a long time. But he was eventually interrupted by the Celt, who, having drunk rather a lot while they were all arguing, now thought that he knew more than the rest of them, and declared with an oath that the only things worth talking about were Teutates* and the mistletoe off an oak-tree; that, as far as he was concerned, he always carried mistletoe in his pocket; that his ancestors the Scythians were the only decent people ever to walk the earth; that, to be sure, they had occasionally eaten people, but that that didn't mean one shouldn't have the greatest respect for his nation; and, finally, that if anyone said a bad word against Teutates, he would teach them a thing or two.

The quarrel now grew heated, and Setoc could see the table becoming a scene of bloodshed. Zadig, who had remained silent throughout the discussion, at length rose to his feet. First he addressed the Celt, as being the one with the worst temper. He told him he was quite right and asked him for a piece of mistletoe. He praised the Greek for his eloquence, and thus proceeded to bring calm to all these fevered spirits. He said very little to the man from Cathay because he had been the most reasonable. Then he addressed the company at large:

'My friends, you were just about to have a fight over nothing, for you are each and every one of you of the same opinion.'

At this they all remonstrated at once.

'It is true, is it not,' he said to the Celt, 'that it is not this mistletoe you worship but Him who made the mistletoe and the oak?'

'Surely,' replied the Celt.

'And you, Mr Egyptian, presumably you revere in one particular bull Him that gave you all bulls?'

'Yes,' said the Egyptian.

'Oannes the fish', he continued, 'must be subordinate to Him who made the sea and the fish.'

'True,' said the Chaldean.

'The Indian and the man from Cathay', he added, 'recognize, as you do, a first principle. I didn't quite understand the wonderful things the Greek was saying, but I am sure that he too allows for a higher Being upon whom form and matter depend.'

The Greek, who was the object of this wonder, said that Zadig had caught his drift most excellently.

'So there you are. You are all of the same opinion,' Zadig concluded, 'and you have no reason to be quarrelling.'

Everyone embraced him. Setoc, having sold his wares for a very good price, returned to his tribe with his friend Zadig. On arriving back, Zadig learnt that he had been tried in his absence and that he was to be burnt to death over a low flame.

CHAPTER 13

Assignations

DURING his journey to Balzora the Priests of the Stars had decided to punish him. The jewels and other ornaments on the young widows they used to send to the funeral-pyre belonged by right to them. The least they could do was to burn Zadig for the dirty trick he had played on them. So they accused Zadig of having unsound views about the heavenly host. They brought charges against him and swore that they had heard him say that the stars did not set in the sea. The judges shuddered to hear this fearful piece of blasphemy; they were ready to rend their garments at such impious words, and would doubtless have done so had Zadig possessed the means to pay for their replacement. But, despite the enormity of their distress, they made do with condemning him to be burnt to death over a low flame. Setoc, in despair, vainly tried to use his influence to save his friend: he was soon reduced to silence. The young widow Almona, who had developed a considerable taste for living and owed it to Zadig, resolved to save him from the pyre, that selfsame evil practice to which he had opened her eyes. She hatched a plan, which she kept to herself. Zadig was to be executed the next day: she had but that one night left in which to save him. This is how she set about it, charitable and prudent woman that she was.

She put on some perfume, displayed her own natural beauty to best advantage in the most opulent and suggestive attire, and went to request a private audience with the High Priest of the Stars. When she came before this venerable old man, she addressed him in the following terms:

'O eldest son of the Great Bear, brother of Taurus, and cousin of the Great Dog (such were the titles of this pontiff), I have come to share my scruples with you. I am very much afraid that I may have committed an enormous sin in not burning myself to death on my husband's funeral-pyre. For in fact what business had I to preserve mere mortal flesh, and flesh that has long since lost its bloom?'

So saying, she drew forth from her long silk sleeves two bare arms of admirable shape and dazzling whiteness.

'As you can see,' she said, 'they're nothing special.'

The pontiff felt in his heart that they were very special. His eyes said as much, and his mouth confirmed it: he swore he had never in his life seen such beautiful arms.

'Oh dear,' said the widow, 'well perhaps my arms are not quite as bad as the rest of me. But you will grant me that my bosom was hardly worth all the fuss.'

She then revealed the most charming breast that ever nature formed. Compared to it, a rosebud upon an ivory apple would have looked like madder upon boxwood, and lambs emerging from a cleansing dip a sort of yellowy brown. That bosom; her great black eyes, in whose languorous gaze there glowed a soft and tender fire; her cheeks, suffused with finest purple mixed with purest milky white; her nose, which bore no resemblance whatsoever to the tower upon Mount Lebanon;* her lips, like two rims of coral round the prettiest pearls in the Arabian Sea; all combined to make the old man feel he was twenty again. He stammered out a declaration of love. Almona, on seeing his ardour, asked for Zadig's pardon.

'Alas, my fair lady,' he said, 'even if I did grant you his pardon, my indulgence would be of no use. It has to be signed by three of my colleagues.'

'Sign anyway,' said Almona.

'Willingly,' said the priest, 'on condition that your favours shall be the price of my compliance.'

'You do me too much honour,' said Almona. 'But if it be your pleasure, come to my chamber when the sun has set and as soon as the bright star Sheat appears above the horizon. You shall find me on a pink sofa, and I shall be your servant for you to do with as you can.'

She then departed, bearing his signature and leaving the old man alone, full of love and in some doubt of his own capacities. He spent the rest of the day bathing. He drank a liquor made from the cinnamon of Ceylon and precious spices from Tidor and Ternate, and he waited impatiently for Sheat to rise.

Meanwhile the fair Almona went in search of the second pontiff. This one assured her that the sun, the moon, and all the fires in the firmament were but will-o'-the-wisps in comparison with her charms. She asked him for the same pardon, and the same price was proposed. She allowed herself to be persuaded, and arranged to meet this second pontiff when the star Algenib should rise. From thence she proceeded to the third and the fourth priests, each time departing with a signature and arranging an assignation for star after star. Then she bid the judges call on her concerning a matter of some importance. They came. She showed them the four names and informed them of the price for which the priests had sold Zadig's pardon to her. Each of the priests arrived at the appointed hour; each was most surprised to find his colleagues there, and even more surprised to find the judges there too, before whom their disgrace became public. Zadig was saved. Setoc was so entranced by Almona's ingenuity that he made her his wife. Zadig departed, having prostrated himself at the feet of his fair liberator. Setoc and he parted in tears, swearing undying friendship to one another and promising that whichever of them should make a fortune first would share it with the other.

Zadig proceeded in the direction of Syria, ever mindful of the unfortunate Astarte, and ever given to reflection upon the nature of the fate which persisted in persecuting him and treating him as a plaything.

'Just to think,' he said, 'four hundred ounces of gold for seeing a bitch go by! Sentenced to execution for four lines of bad verse in praise of the King! Nearly garrotted because the Queen's babouches were the same colour as my cap! Reduced to slavery for coming to the rescue of a woman being beaten! And about to be burned to death for saving the lives of all the young widows of Arabia!'

CHAPTER 14

The brigand

UPON his arrival at the frontier between Arabia Petraea and Syria, and as he was passing near a fortified, or at least fairly fortified, castle, a group of armed Arabs issued forth. He found himself surrounded, and someone shouted at him:

'Everything you own is ours, and you now belong to our master.'

By way of reply Zadig drew his sword: his servant, who was a man of courage, did likewise. They slew the first of the Arabs who tried to lay a hand on them, but they were increasingly outnumbered. They remained undaunted and resolved to die fighting. It was two against a multitude: such a combat could not last for long. The master of the castle, whose name was Arbogad, had been observing Zadig's prodigious feats of valour from a window, and was most impressed. He rushed down and went in person to call off his men and deliver the two wayfarers.

'Everything that passes over my land belongs to me,' he said, 'as well as everything I find on other people's lands. But you seem to me such a stout fellow that I shall make an exception in your case.'

He then escorted him into his castle, giving orders to his men that he was to be well treated; and that evening Arbogad desired to sup with Zadig.

The lord of the castle was one of those Arabs commonly known as 'robbers', but once or twice he did some good things amongst a score of bad. He thieved with furious rapacity, and bestowed with great liberality. He was intrepid in action, yet rather gentle in his dealings with others; intemperate at table, but merry in his intemperance; and, above all, a man to speak his mind. He took a great liking to Zadig, whose increasingly animated conversation prolonged the meal. At length Arbogad said to him:

'If you take my advice, you'll join up with us. You couldn't do better. It's not a bad living, and who knows, one day you may end up like me.'

'May I ask you', Zadig enquired, 'how long you've been following this noble profession?'

'Since I was a tender youth,' replied the master. 'I was the servant of a moderately successful Arab; but I found my situation in life intolerable. I despaired to see that, in a world which belongs equally to all men, destiny had reserved no portion for me. I confided my troubles to an old Arab, who said to me: 'Do not despair, my son. There once was a grain of sand which complained that it was no more than an insignificant little speck in the midst of a desert. In a few years it turned into a diamond, and it is now the brightest jewel in the crown of the King of the Indies." What he said made an impression on me. I was the grain of sand, and I was determined to become a diamond. I began by stealing two horses. I gathered a band of men round me. I developed the capacity to rob small caravans. In this way I gradually put an end to the disparity which had at first set me apart from other men.* I had my share of the world's wealth, and I had even been repaid with interest. I was greatly respected. I became a robber baron. I acquired, *de facto*, the freehold on this castle. The satrap of Syria tried to take it off me, but I was too rich to have anything to fear. I gave the satrap some money, thanks to which I kept the castle and enlarged my estates. He even appointed me treasurer in charge of the tributes that Arabia Petraea pays to the King of Kings. I discharged my responsibility as a collector, if not as a forwarder.

'The Grand Defterdar in Babylon sent some minor satrap or other, in the name of King Moabdar, to have me garrotted. The man duly arrived with his orders. I knew all about it. I had the four men he had brought with him to twist the cord garrotted in front of him; after which I asked him what the going rate was for garrotting me. He told me that his fees sometimes came to as much as three hundred gold pieces. I made it clear to him that he could earn more working for me. I appointed him a sub-brigand. Today he is one of my best officers, and one of the richest. Believe me, you can go as far as him. There never was a better time for thieving, what with Moabdar being killed and everything in Babylon being in such a turmoil.'

'Moabdar's been killed!' exclaimed Zadig. 'And what has become of Queen Astarte?'

'I've no idea,' replied Arbogad. 'All I know is that Moabdar went mad, that he's been killed, that Babylon is now a den of cutthroats, that the whole Empire is in disarray, that there are still some rich pickings to be had, and that, speaking personally, I've already done rather nicely.'

'But the Queen?' said Zadig. 'I beg you, don't you know anything at all of what may have happened to her?'

'I did hear about some Prince of Hyrcania,' he replied. 'She's probably one of his concubines by now, if she wasn't killed in the fray, that is. But loot's what interests me, not news. I've captured several women on my sorties, but I never hang on to any of them. I sell them for a high price if they're beautiful, and I never trouble to find out who they are. Rank is not something people buy; a queen who was ugly simply wouldn't sell. Perhaps I may have sold Queen Astarte myself, perhaps she's dead. But it doesn't concern me much, and if you ask me, it shouldn't bother you either.'

As he was talking, he drank so heartily and became so muddled in his mind that Zadig could get no further sense out of him in the matter.

He sat there speechless, overwhelmed, quite stunned. Arbogad kept on drinking, and telling stories, and repeating endlessly that he was the happiest man alive, and urging Zadig to be happy like him. In the end, nicely drowsy from the fumes of the wine, he departed to bed and fell sound asleep. Zadig spent the night in a state of the most violent agitation.

'What!' he said to himself. 'The King gone mad! Killed! I cannot help but feel sorry for him. The Empire is torn with strife, and this brigand is happy. O fortune! O destiny! A thief is happy, and nature's loveliest creation may have died a most dreadful death, or met a fate yet worse than death. O Astarte! What has become of you?'

At daybreak he questioned everyone he came across in the castle, but they were all too busy to reply. Further booty had been taken during the night, and they were dividing the spoils. All he managed to obtain in the midst of this chaos and confusion was permission to leave. He took advantage of this without delay and departed, more deeply absorbed than ever in his painful thoughts.

Zadig went on his disturbed and fretful way, his mind full of the unfortunate Astarte, of the King of Babylon, of Cador his faithful friend, of Arbogad the happy brigand, and of that most capricious woman whom the Babylonians had abducted on the borders of Egypt; full, in short, of all the reverses and misfortunes which he had undergone.

CHAPTER 15

The fisherman

SOME leagues hence from Arbogad's castle he came to the banks of a small river, still bemoaning his fate and thinking himself the very epitome of misery. He noticed a fisherman lying on the river-bank, his limp hand barely holding on to his net, which he seemed to be about to let go, and his eyes raised to heaven.

'I must assuredly be the unhappiest man alive,' the fisherman was saying. 'I used generally to be considered the greatest cream-cheese monger in Babylon, and now I am ruined. I had the prettiest wife someone like me could possibly hope to have, and she has played me false. I still had a modest little house, and I have seen even that looted and destroyed. With a mere hut for shelter my only resource is my fishing, and I cannot catch a single fish. O net of mine! I shall cast you into the water no more. It is I who should cast myself.'

With these words, he stood up and moved forward in the manner of someone who is about to throw himself in and end his life.

'So,' thought Zadig, 'there are people just as unhappy as I am!'

Eagerness to save the fisherman's life came as quickly as did this thought. He ran up to him, stopped him, and questioned him with an air of sympathetic concern. It is said that one is less unhappy when one is not alone in one's unhappiness. But, according to Zoro-aster, this is not because one wishes people ill but because one senses a need. On such occasions one feels oneself drawn to another unfortunate as to one of one's own sort. The joy of a happy man would seem offensive; whereas two unhappy people are like two tender saplings which, by leaning one upon the other, stiffen themselves against the storm.

'Why do you let your misfortunes bear you down like this?' Zadig asked the fisherman.

'Because', he replied, 'I can see no way out. I was once the most respected man in the village of Derlback near Babylon and, with my wife's help, I used to make the finest cream cheeses in the Empire. Queen Astarte and Zadig, the famous minister, had a passion for them. I had supplied their households with some six hundred cheeses, and one day I went up to the city to collect my payment. On arriving in Babylon I was told that the Queen and Zadig had disappeared. I ran to the house of Lord Zadig, whom I had never met. I found the constables of the Grand Defterdar, equipped with a royal warrant, dutifully and methodically looting his house. I flew to the Queen's kitchens. Some Gentlemen of the Royal Mouth told me she was dead; others said she was in prison; and others claimed that she had run away. But all of them assured me that no one would pay me for my cheese. My wife and I then went to Lord Orcan's. He was one of my clients. We asked for his protection in our hour of need: he granted it to my wife, and refused it to me. She had a skin even whiter than the cream cheese she made and which had been the cause of my misfortunes; and the rosy tints that bloomed in its whiteness were no less vivid than the radiance of a Tyrian hue. Which is what made Orcan detain her and turn me out. I wrote my dear wife the letter of a desperate man. "Ah yes, of course," she said to the messenger, "I know who this is from. They say he makes excellent cream cheese. Kindly have some delivered, and see that he is paid."

'In my wretchedness I resolved to try the courts. I still had six ounces of gold left. I had to give two to the lawyer whom I consulted, two to the advocate who took on my case, and two to the senior judge's secretary. When I had done all this, my trial had still not yet begun, and I had already spent more money than my cheeses or my wife were worth. I returned to my village, intending to sell my house in order to get my wife back.

'My house was easily worth sixty ounces of gold, but people could see I was hard pressed and in a hurry to sell. The first person I approached offered me thirty ounces for it, the second twenty, and the third ten. In the end, in sheer desperation, I was on the point of selling, when a certain Prince of Hyrcania marched on Babylon and laid waste everything that stood in his way. They ransacked my house first and then burnt it to the ground.

'Having thus lost my money, my wife, and my house, I withdrew to this place where you now find me. I have tried to eke out a subsistence as a fisherman, but the fish just laugh at me, people too. I don't catch anything, and I'm starving to death. And but for you, most worthy comforter, I should have perished in this river.'

The fisherman did not relate this story all at once, for at every juncture Zadig would ask him in heartfelt excitement:

'What! You mean you know absolutely nothing of the Queen's fate?'

'No, my lord,' the fisherman would reply. 'But I do know that the Queen and Zadig never paid me for my cream cheeses, that my wife has been taken from me, and that I am in despair.'

'I flatter myself to think', said Zadig, 'that you will not lose all your money. I have heard of this Zadig. He is an honourable man, and if he does return to Babylon, as he hopes to do, he will give you more money than he owes you. But as for your wife, who is not quite so honourable, I advise you not to try and get her back. Take my advice, return to Babylon. I shall be there before you, because I am riding and you are on foot. Call on the worthy Cador. Tell him that you have met his friend, and wait for me at his house. Go on, off you go. Perhaps you won't always be so unhappy.'

'O mighty Ormuzd!' he continued, 'you have made me your servant to bring comfort to this man. Who then will you send to bring comfort to me?'

So saying, he gave the fisherman half the money he had brought with him from Arabia, and the fisherman, embarrassed and delighted, kissed the feet of Cador's friend, and said:

'You are an angel of mercy.'

Zadig, meanwhile, was still weeping and wanting news.

'Why, my lord!' cried the fisherman, 'are you unhappy too, then, you who are able to do good?'

'A hundred times unhappier than you,' replied Zadig.

'But how can it be', the fellow said, 'that he who gives is more to be pitied than he who receives?'

'It can be', Zadig rejoined, 'because your greatest misfortune was need, whereas my misfortune is of the heart.'

'Would Orcan by any chance have run off with your wife too?' enquired the fisherman.

This remark reminded Zadig of all that had befallen him: he recited his catalogue of woe, beginning with the Queen's bitch and ending with his arrival at Arbogad the brigand's.

'Ah!' he said to the fisherman, 'Orcan deserves to be punished. But he's just the sort of person fate generally seems to favour. Oh well, be that as it may, off you go to Lord Cador's and wait for me there.'

They parted company. The fisherman journeyed on foot and thanked his lucky stars, while Zadig galloped along and continued to curse his lot.

CHAPTER 16

The basilisk

ON coming to a fine stretch of meadowland, he saw several women busy looking for something. He took the liberty of going up to one of them and asking her if he might have the honour of assisting them in their search.

'You'll do no such thing,' replied the lady, who was from Syria. 'Only women may touch what we're looking for.'

'How very peculiar,' said Zadig. 'Might I make so bold as to beg you to tell me what it is that only women may touch?'

'A basilisk,'* said she.

'A basilisk, madam? And for what reason, pray, are you searching for a basilisk?'

'It's for Ogul, our lord and master, whose castle you can see there beside the river at the far end of the meadow. We are his humble slaves. Lord Ogul* is ill. His doctor has ordered him to eat a basilisk cooked in rose-water, and as it's a very rare animal, which allows itself to be captured only by women, Lord Ogul has promised to take as his beloved wife whichever one of us brings him a basilisk. Permit me to continue my search, I pray you, for you can see what it would cost me if my companions were to succeed before me.'

Zadig let the Syrian woman and the others carry on searching for their basilisk, and continued on across the meadow. On coming to the edge of a little stream, he found another lady, who was lying on the grass and not searching for anything. She was of noble bearing, but her face was covered by a veil. She was bending over by the stream: deep sighs were to be heard coming from her. In her hand she held a small stick with which she was tracing letters in some fine sand that lay between the grass and the stream. Zadig was curious to see what the woman was writing. He drew near and saw the letter Z, then an A. He was surprised. Then came a D. He gave a start. No one was ever more astonished in his life when he saw the last two letters of his name. He stood there motionless for a while. Then, breaking the silence in a voice faltering with emotion:

'O bountiful lady! Forgive a stranger, a poor unfortunate, for daring to ask you by what amazing coincidence I find the name ZADIG traced here by your divine hand.'

At the sound of this voice, at these words, the lady lifted her veil with a trembling hand, looked at Zadig, uttered a tender cry of startled joy, and then, succumbing to the many conflicting emotions by which her soul was simultaneously assailed, fell senseless into his arms. It was Astarte herself, the Queen of Babylon, she whom Zadig adored, and whom he blamed himself for adoring. It was she for whom he had wept so much and feared so much. For a moment he was deprived of the use of his own senses; but when his eyes fell upon those of Astarte, which were now opening anew in an expression of languor both shy and tender, he cried out:

'O ye immortal powers! Ye who preside over the destinies of us frail mortals, are you then restoring Astarte to me? To find her here, now, like this!'

He fell to his knees in front of Astarte and pressed his forehead to the dust at her feet. The Queen of Babylon bid him rise and sit by her at the water's edge. Repeatedly she brushed away the tears which kept on falling. Again and again she began to speak, only to be interrupted by a sigh or a moan. She enquired of him how they had thus chanced to be reunited, and would suddenly anticipate his replies with yet further questions. She would begin an account of her own misfortunes and then want to hear about Zadig's. In the end, when they had both a little eased the tumult of their souls, Zadig told her in a few words how he came to be in the meadow.

'But, o unhappy and most worthy Queen, how do I come to find you here in this solitary place, dressed as a slave and in the company of other slaves, all searching for a basilisk to cook in rose-water under a doctor's prescription?'

'While they're searching for their basilisk,' said the fair Astarte, 'I shall tell you of all I have suffered, or rather of all I pardon heaven for, now I see you again. As you know, my husband took it amiss that you should be the most agreeable of men, and so resolved one night to have you garrotted and me poisoned. As you also know, heaven permitted that little mute of mine to warn me of His Sublime Majesty's order. Well, scarcely had faithful Cador compelled you to obey me and leave, than he made bold to come to my room at dead of night by a secret passage. He took me away and brought me to the temple of Ormuzd where the magus, his brother, put me inside that colossal statue, the base of which goes down as far as the foundations of the temple, while its head touches the vaults of the ceiling. It was as if I had been buried there, except that the magus served me and that I lacked for none of the necessities of life. Meanwhile, at day-break, His Majesty's apothecary entered my room with a potion of henbane, opium, hemlock, black hellebore, and aconite, and another officer went to your room with a noose of blue silk. They found neither of us. Cador, the better to deceive the King, went and made a show of denouncing us both to him. He said you had taken off for the Indies, and I for Memphis. Minions were dispatched in pursuit of us.

'The riders who were chasing me had no idea what I looked like. I had hardly ever shown my face to anyone but you, and then only in the presence of the King and by his express order. They came after me in hot pursuit, relying on a description of me which they had been given. At the Egyptian border they came across a woman who was of the same height as I, though her charms were possibly greater. She was in tears and seemed to have nowhere to go. They had no doubt that this was the Queen of Babylon and took her back to Moabdar. At first their mistake sent the King into a violent rage. But presently, on closer inspection of the woman, he found she was very beautiful, and this was a comfort to him. She was called Missouf. I have since been told that in Egyptian her name means "fair capri-cious one". And so she was. But she was as artful as she was capri-cious. Moabdar found her attractive, and she acquired such a hold over him that she was eventually proclaimed his wife. Then her character showed itself in its true colours. Brazenly she indulged every mad whim that occurred to her. She took it into her head to have the Chief Magus, who was old and gout-ridden, dance before her; and when the magus refused, she persecuted him mercilessly. She ordered her chief equerry to make her a jam tart. It was no use the equerry pointing out to her that he was no pastry cook: he had to make the tart. And then she dismissed him because it was overbaked. She gave the post of chief equerry to her dwarf, and made her page chancellor. That was the way she governed things in Babylon. Everyone wanted me back. The King, who had been a reasonably honourable man until he decided to poison me and garrotte you, seemed to have allowed his better nature to be overruled by his immoderate fondness for the fair capricious one. He came to the temple on the feast-day of the Sacred Fire. I watched him praying to the gods for Missouf at the feet of the statue in which I was confined. So I lifted up my voice and cried out unto him: "The gods shall not answer the prayers of a King who hath become a tyrant, and who hath desired the death of a sensible wife that he might marry an extravagant hussy."

'Moabdar was so staggered by these words that his mind began to go. The oracle I had pronounced and the tyranny of Missouf were enough to deprive him of his reason. He went mad in a matter of days.

'His madness, which seemed to be a punishment from on high, served as the signal for revolt. People rose up in arms. Babylon, for so long sunk in slothful ease, became the theatre of a ghastly civil war. I was taken from the empty shell of my statue and made leader of a party. Cador hurried off to Memphis to bring you back to Babylon. The Prince of Hyrcania, on hearing the dire tidings, returned with his army to be a third force in the politics of Chaldea. He declared war on the King, who rode out to meet him with his Egyptian jade. Moabdar was mortally wounded: Missouf fell into the victors' clutches. As fate would have it, I too met my match at Hyrcanian hands, and was brought before the Prince at the very same instant as Missouf. You will doubtless be flattered to learn that the Prince found me more beautiful than the Egyptian, but you may be sorry to hear that he intended me for his seraglio. He made it quite plain to me that, as soon as he had returned from a military expedition upon which he was embarking, he would come and see me. Imagine my misery. The bonds which had united me with Moabdar had been broken. I was free to be Zadig's. And here I was now, caught in the shackles of a barbarian. I answered him with the full weight of my rank and feelings. I had always heard it said that heaven bestows upon persons of my condition an air of natural authority which, by a quelling word or look, redraws the bounds of humble respect about those who have had the temerity to overstep them. I spoke like a queen. But I was treated like a handmaid. The Hyrcanian, without even deigning to speak to me directly, remarked to his black eunuch that I was a pert one, though he did find me pretty. He instructed him to take special care of me, and to subject me to the favourites' regimen in order to freshen up my complexion and render me worthier of his favours come the day when he should find it convenient to honour me with them. I told him I would sooner kill myself. He replied with a laugh that people didn't kill themselves and that he was used to this sort of behaviour; and then left, like someone who has just added a parrot to his menagerie. What a situation for the most noble Queen on earth to find herself in and, more especially, for a heart that belonged to Zadig!'

At these words the latter threw himself to the ground at her knees and bathed them in tears. Astarte gently helped him to his feet and continued:

'So there I was, in the hands of a barbarian and rival to the mad-woman I was locked up with. She told me all about what had happened to her in Egypt. I could tell by the way she described you, by the date, by the dromedary you were riding, by all the attendant circumstances, that it was Zadig who had fought on her behalf. I was sure you were in Memphis, so I resolved to hide away there. "Fair Missouf," I said to her, "you're much more entertaining than I am, you'll be far better company for the Prince of Hyrcania than I will. Help me to escape. Then you'll be able to have him all to yourself, and you'll be making me happy at the same time as getting rid of a rival." Together Missouf and I made plans for my escape. And so I left, undetected, with an Egyptian slave.

'I had almost reached the Arabian frontier when a notorious robber called Arbogad captured me and sold me to some merchants, who brought me to this castle where Lord Ogul lives. He bought me without knowing who I was. He is a voluptuary, and his one ambition in life is to eat well, as if he believed God had put him on this earth for no other purpose but to sit at table. He is so excessively fat that he can hardly breathe. His doctor, who has very little influence when his digestion is working well, rules him with a rod of iron when he has over-indulged. He has convinced him that a basilisk cooked in rose-water would cure him. Lord Ogul has promised his hand to which-ever of his slaves brings him a basilisk. As you can see, I'm leaving them to vie for this honour on their own. And I have never wanted less to find a basilisk now that heaven has restored you to my sight.'

Then Astarte and Zadig said to each other every possible thing that their love, their misfortunes, and their feelings long suppressed now called forth in these most noble and most passionate hearts; and the genii that preside over love bore their words away, up into the realm of Venus.

The women returned to Ogul empty-handed. Zadig had himself announced and said to him:

'May everlasting good health descend from heaven and keep you all your days! I am a doctor. I hastened here the moment I heard of your illness, and I have brought you a basilisk cooked in rose-water. Not that I want to marry you. All I ask is that you free a young Babylonian slave whom you acquired a few days ago. And I agree to remain behind as your slave in her place if I am not fortunate enough to cure the mighty Lord Ogul.'

The proposal was accepted. Astarte left for Babylon, accompanied by Zadig's servant, and promised to send word of herself as soon as she possibly could. Their farewells were no less tender than their scene of recognition had been. The times of parting and of being reunited are the two greatest moments that life has to offer, as it says in the great *Zend Avesta*. Zadig loved the Queen as much as he protested that he did, and the Queen loved Zadig more than she acknowledged that she did.

Next, Zadig told Ogul:

'My Lord, the basilisk I brought is not for eating. Its beneficial qualities have all to be absorbed through the pores. I have placed it in a little bladder which has been fully inflated and covered with fine leather. What you have to do is to punch this bladder away from you as hard as you can, and I'll keep returning it. After a few days of this you will soon see what my skills can do.'

On the first day Ogul felt completely out of breath and thought he would die of exhaustion. On the second he was less tired and slept better. In a week he had recovered all the strength, vitality, suppleness, and high spirits of his prime.

'You have played with a ball and been moderate in your habits,' Zadig said to him. 'Learn, then, that there is no such thing as a basilisk. With moderation and regular exercise one will always be healthy, and the possibility of being able successfully to combine intemperance with good health is as illusory as the philosopher's stone, horoscopical predictions, and the theology of the magi.'

Ogul's chief doctor, sensing what a danger to the medical profession this man was, plotted with Ogul's personal apothecary to send Zadig off on a hunt for basilisks in the world to come. Thus, having consistently been punished for doing good, he was now ready to perish for curing a gluttonous lord. They invited Zadig to a sumptuous dinner. He was to be poisoned by the second course, but during the first a message came from Astarte. He left the table, and departed.

'When one has the love of a beautiful woman,' said the great Zoroaster, 'in this world one can survive anything.'

CHAPTER 17

The tournament

THE Queen had been welcomed back to Babylon with that warmth of reception that people always reserve for a beautiful princess who has met with misfortune. Things were now a little calmer in Babylon. The Prince of Hyrcania had been killed in battle. The victorious Babylonians declared that Astarte would marry whomever they chose as their ruler. No one wanted the filling of the world's highest position, that of being husband to Astarte and King of Babylon, to be decided by intrigues and cabals. They undertook to take as their King him who was most valiant and most wise. A large arena surrounded by gorgeously decorated amphitheatres was created for the lists a few leagues outside the city. Here the combatants were to present themselves in full armour. Each of them was given separate quarters behind the amphitheatres, where they were to remain incommunicado. Each combatant would have to make four runs with the lance. Those fortunate enough to defeat four knights were then to joust with each other, so that the one who was left master of the field at the end would be proclaimed champion of the games. He would then have to return four days later, bearing the same arms, and solve some riddles, which the magi would propound. If he did not solve the riddles, he did not become King, and it would be necessary to repeat the jousting until such time as they found a man who won both contests. For it was absolutely their wish to have as King both the wisest and the most valiant of men. The Queen, meanwhile, was to be kept under close guard. She was allowed simply to be present at the games, covered in a veil; but she was not permitted to speak to any of the contestants, so that there should be no favouritism or unfairness.

All this Astarte communicated to her lover, hoping that he would display more valour and intelligence for her than anyone else. He set off, and he prayed to Venus to stiffen his courage and sharpen his wits. He came to the banks of the Euphrates on the eve of the great day. He had his heraldic emblem added to the roll along with those of the other combatants, taking care to conceal his face and name as the rules required, and went off to rest in the quarters which had been allocated to him by lot. His friend Cador, who had returned to Babylon after looking for him in vain in Egypt, saw that a full suit of armour, which the Queen had sent, was delivered to his lodgings; and he had a most handsome Persian horse, likewise from the Queen, led round there also. Zadig recognized Astarte's hand in these gifts: from them his courage and his love drew renewed strength and renewed hope.

On the following day, the Queen having taken her place beneath a jewelled canopy, and the amphitheatres having filled with every lady in Babylon and people from every other section of society, the combatants entered the arena. Each of them came and laid his heraldic device at the feet of the Grand Magus. The devices were drawn by lot: Zadig's was drawn last. The first to take up position was a very wealthy nobleman called Itobad, who was a man of great vanity, not much courage, little dexterity, and no intelligence. His servants had persuaded him that a man in his position ought to be King. He had agreed with them: 'Yes, a man in my position must rule.' And so they had armed him from head to foot. He wore a suit of armour made of gold and decorated with green enamel and a green plume; and his lance was decked with green ribbons. It became immediately obvious from the way Itobad rode his horse that it was not a man in his position that heaven had in mind to wield the sceptre of Babylon. The first horseman to ride against him unseated him: the second knocked him backwards on to his horse's hindquarters, where he lay with his arms and legs in the air. Itobad recovered his seat in the saddle but in such an ungainly manner that the whole crowd began to laugh. A third horseman disdained even to use his lance. Instead, as he was making his pass, he grabbed him by the right leg and swung him round full circle in the saddle before depositing him on the sand. The tournament officials ran up to him laughing and hoisted him back into the saddle. The fourth combatant took hold of him by the left leg and made him fall off the other side. He was booed and whistled all the way back to his quarters where, as the rules required, he was to spend the night. Scarcely able to walk, he kept saying to himself: 'What a thing to happen to a man in my position!'

The other knights acquitted themselves rather better. There were some who overcame two combatants in succession, and a few even managed three. Only Prince Otames vanquished all four. At length it was Zadig's turn to compete: he unseated four horsemen in a row with the greatest of ease. So it was between Otames and Zadig. The former wore blue and gold armour with a matching plume: Zadig was in white. Everyone took sides, whether for the blue rider or the white. The Queen, whose heart was pounding, prayed to heaven for the white.

The two champions made such agile runs and turns, exchanged such expert blows of the lance, and were so secure in the saddle, that everyone, apart from the Queen, wished Babylon could have two Kings. Finally, when their horses had tired and their lances were broken, Zadig did a clever thing: he passed behind the prince in blue, jumped on to the back of his horse, seized him round the waist, threw him to the ground, took his place in the saddle, and made the horse prance around Otames, who was lying prostrate on the ground. The whole crowd shouted: 'White has won.' Otames indignantly rose to his feet and drew his sword: Zadig leapt off the horse, sabre in hand. So there they were, down on the ground, engaged in further combat, with brute strength or quick-footedness alternately winning the day. Fragments of plume from off their helmets, studs from off their brassards, and links of chain mail flew in all directions, as they rained a hundred blows down, the one upon the other. They thrust with point and blade, to right and left, to head and chest; they retreated, they advanced, they crossed swords, they closed, they grappled, they coiled back like snakes, they fell upon each other like lions. Sparks flew with every hit they made. Finally Zadig, having collected his thoughts for a moment, stopped, feinted, made a pass over Otames' sword, toppled him to the ground, and disarmed him. And Otames cried out:

'O knight in white armour! It is you who shall reign over Babylon.'

The Queen was overjoyed. The blue knight and the white knight were each escorted back to their quarters like all the others, as the rules required. Mutes came to wait on them and bring them food. It may be guessed whether the Queen's little mute was the one to serve Zadig! Then they were left alone to sleep till morning, at which point the victor was to take his device before the Grand Magus to have it compared with the one with which he had enrolled and to be declared champion.

Zadig slept, so tired was he, and despite the fact that he was in love. Itobad, whose quarters were next to his, did not sleep. He got up in the middle of the night, entered Zadig's room, took his white armour and heraldic emblem, and substituted his own green ones. At daybreak, off he went proudly to the Grand Magus to announce that a man in his position had won. This came as something of a surprise; but he was declared the winner while Zadig slept on. Astarte, astonished and sick at heart, returned to Babylon. The whole place was almost deserted by the time Zadig woke up. He looked for his armour and found only the green: he was obliged to wear it, having nothing else to hand. Caught unawares and full of indignation, he donned it in a fury and emerged thus attired.

The few people remaining in and around the arena greeted him with jeers. A crowd gathered round him, and he was insulted to his face. Never was a man more mortified or humiliated. He lost his patience: with a few blows of his sabre he cleaved a way through this crowd that dared to insult him. But he was at a loss to know what to do next. He could not go and see the Queen; and he could not go and demand back the suit of white armour which she had sent him, for that would have been to compromise her. Thus, while she was plunged in misery, he was filled with anger and disquiet.

He walked along the banks of the Euphrates, persuaded that his stars had destined him to be irremediably unhappy, and going over in his mind all the reverses with which he had met, from the business with the woman who hated one-eyed men to the problem of his armour.

'That's what comes of getting up late,' he told himself. 'If I had not overslept, I should now be King of Babylon, and Astarte would be mine. But there it is. Education, virtue, courage: they've brought me nothing but disaster.'

In the end he even began to grumble at the ways of Providence; and he was tempted to believe that the world was governed by a cruel destiny that did down decent men and favoured knights in green. One source of his distress was having to wear this green armour which had exposed him to such ridicule. He sold it to a passing merchant for a pittance and bought from him a robe and a deep hood. In this garb he proceeded on his way along the banks of the Euphrates, deep in despair, and inwardly blaming Providence for thus continuing to persecute him.

CHAPTER 18

The hermit

ALONG the way he met a hermit, who wore a white and venerable beard that came down to his waist. In his hand he held a book, which he was reading intently. Zadig stopped and bowed low. The hermit greeted him with such a gentle, cordial air that Zadig felt the urge to speak with him. He asked him what he was reading.

'It is the Book of Destiny,' said the hermit. 'Would you like to have a look?'

He handed the book to Zadig who, though familiar with several languages, was unable to decipher one single character in the book. This made him all the more curious.

'You seem rather miserable,' said the kindly monk.

'Alas, yes,' said Zadig, 'and with what good reason!'

'If you will allow me to accompany you,' the old man went on, 'perhaps I may be of service to you. I have sometimes been able to bring a measure of comfort to troubled souls.'

Zadig was filled with respect for the hermit's manner, for his beard and his book. In the course of their conversation he found him to be a man of superior lights. The hermit spoke to him of destiny, justice, morality, the general good, human frailty, the virtues and the vices, all with such lively and affecting eloquence that Zadig felt drawn to him as if by an irresistible spell. He begged him earnestly not to leave him until they should arrive in Babylon.

'It is I who ask this very favour of you,' said the old man. 'Swear to me by Ormuzd that you will not leave my side for the next few days, whatever I do.'

Zadig swore it, and they set off together.

The two travellers arrived that evening at an imposing castle. The hermit begged hospitality for himself and for the young man who was with him. The porter, who could have been mistaken for some great nobleman, ushered them in with a kind of disdainful courtesy.

They were introduced to one of the head servants, who showed them round his master's magnificent apartments. They were admitted to the master's table at the lower end, without the lord of the castle so much as acknowledging them with a glance. But they were served, like everyone else, with discretion and liberality. They were then handed a gold basin, decorated with emeralds and rubies, for them to wash in. They were taken to a fine apartment where they might rest, and in the morning a servant brought each of them a gold coin, after which they were shown the door.

'The master of that household seemed a generous man to me,' said Zadig, as they went on their way, 'if somewhat stand-offish. He has a noble idea of hospitality.'

As he was saying this, he noticed that a kind of large pouch which the hermit carried seemed to be all stretched and bulging. In it he saw the gold basin set with precious stones: the hermit had stolen it. For the moment he did not dare say anything; but he was most uncommonly surprised.

Towards midday the hermit knocked on the door of a tiny little house where there lived a rich miser. Here he asked to be extended hospitality for an hour or two. A scruffy old servant answered him in a gruff tone and showed them both into the stable, where they were given a few rotten olives, some stale bread, and some beer that had turned sour. The hermit ate and drank with as much seeming satisfaction as he had on the previous evening. Then, turning to the old servant, who was keeping an eye on the pair of them to make sure they did not steal anything and was chivvying them to depart, the hermit gave him the two gold coins they had been given that morning, and thanked him for all his kindness.

'And I wonder, I beg you,' added the hermit, 'if I might have a word with your master.'

In his astonishment the manservant showed the two travellers in.

'My most munificent Lord,' said the hermit, 'I can offer you only but the most humble thanks for the noble manner in which you have received us. Be so good as to accept this gold basin as a small token of my gratitude.'

The miser nearly fell over backwards. The hermit gave him no time to recover his composure but left at once with his young travelling-companion.

'Father,' said Zadig, 'what is the meaning of all this? You don't seem to be quite like other men. You steal a gold basin covered in jewels from a nobleman who entertains you lavishly, and you give it to a miser who treats you shabbily.'

'My son,' replied the old man, 'the generous gentleman, who keeps open house only out of vanity and so that he can show off his wealth, will be the wiser for it. The miser will have been taught to be more hospitable. Don't be so surprised at things, and follow me.'

Zadig was still not sure whether he was dealing with the wisest or the most foolish of men; but the hermit spoke with such natural and higher authority that Zadig, bound anyway by his oath, could but follow him.

They arrived that evening at a pleasant but unpretentious house, in which there was not the least suggestion either of prodigality or of avarice. The master of the house was a philosopher: retired from the world, he devoted himself to the quiet cultivation of wisdom and virtue, and yet was not bored. It had given him pleasure to build this retreat, to which he welcomed strangers in a noble and cordial manner which was quite devoid of ostentation. He greeted the two travellers, and bid them rest a while in a comfortable apartment. Some time later he came in person to invite them to what was a perfectly adequate, well-balanced meal, during which he talked unemphatically about the latest unheavals in Babylon. He seemed sincerely attached to the Queen, and wished that Zadig had appeared in the lists to compete for the crown.

'But well,' he added, 'people don't deserve a king like Zadig.'

The latter blushed and felt his sorrows still more keenly. It was agreed in the course of conversation that in this world things did not always turn out the way wise men wanted. The hermit continued to maintain that no one knows the ways of Providence, and that men are wrong to judge of a whole when they see only the smallest part of it.

They talked of the passions.

'Ah, how dangerous they are!' said Zadig.

'They are the winds that fill the vessel's sails,' retorted the hermit. 'Sometimes they sink her, but without them she would not sail at all. Bile makes us choleric and ill; but without bile we could not live. Everything in this life has its dangers, and everything has to be the way it is.'

They talked of pleasure, and the hermit argued that it is a gift from the Deity.

'For,' he said, 'man cannot independently cause himself to have sensations or ideas. These come to him. Pain and pleasure come from outside himself, as does his very existence.'

Zadig marvelled that a man who had behaved so oddly could reason so well. Eventually, after a discussion which had been as instructive as it had been pleasurable, their host escorted the two travellers to their room, duly acknowledging heaven's blessing in sending him two such wise and virtuous men. He offered them some money in a natural and courteous way that could not possibly offend. The hermit refused it, and told him that he would take his leave of him now as he intended to set out for Babylon before it was light. They all bid each other a fond farewell. Zadig, especially, felt full of esteem and liking for such a thoroughly decent man. Once the hermit and he were alone in their apartment, they did not stop from singing the praises of their host.

At daybreak the old man roused his companion.

'It's time to leave,' he said. 'But while everyone is still asleep, I want to leave this man a token of my esteem and affection.'

So saying, he took hold of a torch and set fire to the house. Zadig, appalled, screamed at him and tried to prevent him from doing this dreadful thing. The hermit, being of superior strength, dragged him away. The house was engulfed in flames. The hermit, who had already gone some distance with his companion, calmly looked back to see it burn.

'Thank God,' he said. 'There goes my dear host's house, destroyed from top to bottom! O happy man!'

At these words Zadig was tempted simultaneously to laugh at the reverend father and to hurl abuse at him, to hit him and to run away from him. But he did none of these things and, with the hermit still in the ascendant, followed him despite himself to the last of their nightly sojourns.

This was at the house of a charitable and virtuous widow who had a fourteen-year-old nephew, a most accomplished youth and her one hope for the future. She did the honours of the house to the best of her ability. The following day she told her nephew to accompany the travellers as far as a bridge which, being lately damaged, had become dangerous to cross. The young man, all eager, led the way. Once they were on the bridge, the hermit said to the young man:

'Come, I must show your aunt how grateful I am.'

Whereupon he grabbed him by the hair and threw him into the river. The lad sank to the bottom, surfaced briefly, and was then swept away by the current.

'You monster!' screamed Zadig. 'You wicked, evil man!'

'You promised you'd be more patient,' the hermit interjected. 'It may interest you to know that, beneath the ruins of that house which Providence set on fire, its master has discovered a huge hoard of treasure. It may also interest you to know that that young man, who's just had his neck wrung by Providence, would have murdered his aunt within a year, and you within two.'

'Who says so, you barbarian?' cried Zadig. 'And even if you did read about it in your Book of Destiny, does that mean you have the right to drown a child who never did you any harm?'

As the Babylonian was talking he noticed that the old man had lost his beard and that his face was assuming a youthful appearance. His hermit's habit vanished: four beautiful wings overlaid a majestic body that was radiant with light.

'O heavenly envoy! O angel divine!' exclaimed Zadig, prostrating himself on the ground. 'Are you then come down to earth from empyreal heaven to teach a feeble mortal to submit to the eternal decrees?'

'Men', said the angel Jesrad, 'have an opinion on everything and know nothing. You were the one human being who most deserved to be enlightened.'

Zadig asked permission to speak.

'I hesitate to say this,' he said, 'but may I venture to ask if you would clear up one point for me? Wouldn't it have been better to teach that young man a lesson and make him virtuous rather than drown him?'

Jesrad answered him:

'Had he been virtuous, and had he lived, it was his destiny to be murdered himself, together with the wife he would have married and the son they would have had.'

'But that means, doesn't it,' said Zadig, 'that disasters and crimes have to exist, and that disasters will happen to innocent people?'

'The wicked are always unhappy,' replied Jesrad. 'Their function is to be a trial to the small number of the just that are scattered throughout the world. There is no evil from which no good comes.'

'But,' said Zadig, 'what if there were only good, and no evil at all?'

'Then,' replied Jesrad, 'this world would be a different world. The logic of its events would belong to a different order of wisdom; and such an order, which would be a perfect order, can exist only in the eternal abode of the Supreme Being, whom no evil may touch. He has created millions of worlds, not one of which can be like any other. This immense variety is an attribute of His immense power. There are no two leaves on all the trees of the Earth nor any two globes in all the infinite reaches of the heavens which are alike. And everything you see down here, on this little speck of dust where you have been born, necessarily occupies its own appointed place and time in accordance with the immutable laws of Him who embraces all things. Men think that this child who has just perished fell into the water by chance, and that it was likewise by chance that the house burnt down. But there is no such thing as chance. Everything is either a test or a punishment, a reward or a precaution. Remember that fisherman who thought he was the unhappiest man alive. Ormuzd sent you to change the course of his destiny. Feeble mortal, cease to argue against that which rather you should worship and adore.'

'But . . .', said Zadig.

As he said 'But . . .', the angel was already winging his way towards the tenth heaven. Zadig, kneeling, worshipped and adored Providence; and he bowed down. The angel cried out to him from on high:

'Go you unto Babylon.'

CHAPTER 19

The riddles

ZADIG, thoroughly shaken and feeling rather like someone who has almost been hit by a thunderbolt, let chance direct his steps. He entered Babylon on the very day that those who had fought in the lists were assembled in the great hall of the palace to solve the riddles and to answer the questions which were to be put by the Grand Magus. All the knights had arrived, except for the knight in green. As soon as Zadig appeared in the city, the people flocked round him: all eyes were upon him, blessings poured from every lip, and every heart wished him the Empire. The Man of Envy saw him go past, shuddered, and turned away. The crowd swept him along as far as the place where the assembly was being held. The Queen, who had been informed of his arrival, fell prey to the alternate agitation of fond hope and fearful apprehension. She was consumed with anxiety. She could understand neither why Zadig was without armour, nor how Itobad came to be wearing white. There was a murmuring of voices as Zadig appeared. People were surprised and delighted to see him again; but only the knights who had taken part in the tournament were allowed to appear in the assembly.

'I fought in the lists like everyone else,' he said, 'but someone else here is bearing my arms. And while I wait to have the honour of proving it, I ask permission to present myself for the solving of the riddles.'

A vote was taken. His reputation for honesty was still so firmly fixed in people's minds that they did not hesitate to let him take part.

The first question put by the Grand Magus was this:

'Which of all things in the world is at once the longest and the shortest, the quickest and the slowest, the most divisible and the most continuous, the most squandered and the most regretted, something without which nothing can be done, which obliterates what is small and gives life to what is great?'

It was Itobad's turn to speak. He replied that a man in his position did not understand the first thing about riddles, and that it was quite enough for him to have prevailed by his prowess with the lance. Some said the answer to the riddle was fortune, some said the earth, and others light. Zadig said that it was time.

'Nothing is longer,' he elaborated, 'since it is the measure of eternity; nothing is shorter, since we never have enough in which to carry through what we will. Nothing is slower for him who waits; nothing is quicker for him who enjoys. It stretches, continuous and unbroken, into infinity; it can be divided into the infinitely small. All men waste it, all regret its loss. Nothing can be done without it. It consigns everything unworthy of posterity to oblivion, and it immortalizes that which is great.'

The assembly acknowledged that Zadig was right. The next question was this:

'What is it that we receive without thanks, that we enjoy without knowing how or why, that we give to others when we're having the time of our own, and that we lose without being aware of it?'

Each of them had his say. Only Zadig guessed that it was life. He solved all the other riddles with the same facility. Itobad was still saying that nothing could be simpler, and that he could have solved them just as easily if he had tried. There were questions on justice, the general good, the art of being a ruler. Zadig's replies were adjudged the most sound.

'It really is a pity', people said, 'that such a fine mind should have such a poor seat.'

'Most noble Lords,' said Zadig, 'I did have the honour to be victorious in the lists. The white armour is mine. Lord Itobad stole it while I was asleep. Evidently he must have thought it would suit him better than the green. I am ready to prove to him here and now in front of you, with this sword and dressed only in this robe, against all this fine white armour which he took from me, that it was I who had the honour of defeating brave Otames.'

Itobad accepted the challenge with the greatest confidence. He had no doubt that, what with his helmet, his cuirass, and his brassard, he would easily get the better of a champion in gown and nightcap. Zadig drew his sword and saluted the Queen, who watched him full of joy and apprehension. Itobad drew his and saluted no one. He advanced on Zadig like a man in the position of having nothing to fear: he made to cleave his head in two. Zadig was able to parry this blow by presenting what is called the forte of his blade to the faible of his adversary's, so that Itobad's broke in two. Then Zadig, seizing his enemy round the waist, toppled him backwards on to the ground and, holding the point of his sword to the chink in his armour, said:

'Let me take your armour off or I'll kill you.'

Itobad, ever surprised that such calamities could befall a man in his position, let Zadig have his way, and the latter calmly removed the resplendent helmet and the proud cuirass, the fine brassards and the gleaming cuisses, put them on, and hastened, thus accoutred, to throw himself at Astarte's feet. Cador had no difficulty proving that the armour belonged to Zadig. He was proclaimed King by unanimous consent, and not least by that of Astarte who, after so many adversities, was savouring the sweet pleasure of seeing her lover deemed worthy, in the eyes of the whole world, to be her husband. Itobad went off home to be addressed as 'my noble Lord' by his own household. Zadig became King, and was happy. He was constantly mindful of what the angel Jesrad had said to him. He even remembered about the grain of sand becoming a diamond. The Queen and he worshipped and adored Providence. Zadig left Missouf, the fair capricious one, to her own devices. He sent for Arbogad the brigand and appointed him to a respectable rank in his army with the promise to promote him to the very highest positions if he conducted himself like a real warrior, and to have him hanged if he went in for more brigandage.

Setoc was summoned from deepest Arabia, along with fair Almona, to preside over the commercial life of Babylon. To Cador went position and affection to match his services: he was the King's friend, and the King was thus the only monarch in the world to have a friend. The little mute was not forgotten. The fisherman was given a fine house. Orcan was required by the courts to pay him a large sum of money and to give him back his wife; but the fisherman, now an older and wiser man, took just the money.

The fair Semira never got over having once thought that Zadig might end up one-eyed, nor did Azora for a moment cease to lament that she had once tried to cut his nose off. He tempered their grief with gifts. The Man of Envy died of shame and frustration. The Empire knew a time of peace, a time of glory, a time of plenty: it was the finest age the world had ever known. Justice and love ruled the Empire. The people glorified Zadig, and Zadig glorified heaven.

APPENDIX

The dance

SETOC had to go to the Island of Serendib on business. But, it being the first moon of his marriage which, as everyone knows, is the moon of honey, this meant that he could not leave his wife, nor even think that he ever could. He asked Zadig to undertake the journey for him.

'Oh dear,' said Zadig, 'must I set an even greater distance between fair Astarte and myself? Still, patrons are there to be served.'

He had his say: he wept: he departed.

He was not on the Island of Serendib long before he came to be regarded as rather an exceptional person. He became the arbitrator of all mercantile disputes, a friend to the wise, and a counsellor to the small number of people ready to take counsel. The King wanted to meet him and hear him for himself. He soon discovered the full extent of Zadig's worth: he trusted to his wisdom and made him his friend. The King's friendship and esteem made Zadig fear the worst. At each hour of the day and night he kept thinking about the misfortune which Moabdar's favour had brought upon him.

'The King has taken a liking to me,' he would say. 'Shall I not be ruined?'

However, he was unable to elude the marks of His Majesty's affection. For it must be said that Nabussan, King of Serendib, son of Nussanab, son of Sabusna, was one of the finest princes in Asia, and that when one talked to him, it was difficult not to like him.

This good prince was continually being fawned upon, and cheated, and robbed: anyone who wanted could plunder his treasury. The Collector-General of the Island of Serendib steadfastly set an example in this respect, and it was faithfully followed by everyone else. The King knew it: he had changed treasurers several times. But he had not been able to change the established practice of dividing the King's revenues into two unequal halves, the smaller of which would go to His Majesty, and the larger to his administrators.

The King confided his problem to Zadig.

'You know so many splendid things,' he said. 'Would you know a way of finding me a treasurer who won't rob me?'

'Certainly,' Zadig replied. 'I know a foolproof way of finding you a man with a clean pair of hands.'

The King, delighted, threw his arms round him and asked him how he should proceed.

'All you need to do,' said Zadig, 'is require all those who apply for the office of treasurer to dance, and the one who dances with the lightest foot will without fail be the most honest man amongst them.'

'You're pulling my leg,' said the King. 'That's a fine way of choosing someone to collect my taxes. What? You mean to say that the one who does the nicest entrechat will be the financier with the most integrity and the most acumen?'

'I can't promise you that he'll have the most acumen,' returned Zadig, 'but I can assure you that he will indubitably have the most integrity.'

Zadig spoke with such conviction that the King thought he must have some magic secret for reading the financial mind.

'I don't like magic,' said Zadig. 'I've always hated prodigies, both the human ones and the ones you read about in books. If Your Majesty will let me carry out the test I propose, he will soon see for himself that my secret is the simplest and most straightforward affair.'

Nabussan, King of Serendib, was even more astonished to hear that the secret was this simple than he would have been to be told it was a miracle.

'Very well, then,' he said, 'do as you please.'

'Leave it to me,' said Zadig. 'You will gain more by this test than you think.'

That very day he had it publicly announced, in the name of the King, that all who sought the position of Collector-General of Taxes to His Gracious Majesty Nabussan, son of Nussanab, should present themselves in the royal antechamber on the first day of the month of the Crocodile dressed in garments of light silk.

There presented themselves sixty-four such persons. Fiddlers had been installed in an adjacent room, and everything had been got ready for the ball. But the door of the ballroom itself had been locked so that the only means of entry was along a small, rather poorly-lit gallery. An usher came to fetch each candidate in turn and to show him in along this corridor, leaving each one unattended there for a few minutes. The King, who had been made privy to the secret, had laid out the entire contents of his treasury in the gallery. When all the candidates had arrived in the ballroom, His Majesty gave orders for them to begin dancing. Never was there dancing so heavy-footed and graceless as theirs: every head was bowed, every back bent, every hand glued to its side.

'The scoundrels,' Zadig said to himself.

Just one of them was executing the steps of the dance in a sprightly fashion, with his head up, his eyes fixed straight ahead of him, his arms out, his body upright, and his calf firm.

'Ah, an honest man! What a splendid fellow!' commented Zadig.

The King embraced the good dancer and appointed him treasurer, while all the rest were punished and taxed, and with every possible justification: for each one of them had filled his pockets while he was in the gallery and was scarce able to move. The King felt angry on behalf of human nature that out of these sixty-four dancers sixty-three were thieves. The badly-lit gallery was dubbed the Corridor of Temptation. In Persia these sixty-three gentlemen would have been impaled. In some countries a Court of Enquiry would have been instituted, which would have run up costs to three times the amount that had been stolen, and without putting a single penny back in the royal coffers. In another kingdom they would have exonerated themselves completely and impugned the dancer for some rather fancy footwork. In Serendib they were simply sentenced to replenish the public coffers, for Nabussan was a most indulgent man.

He was also most grateful. He gave Zadig a sum of money which was considerably larger than any treasurer had ever stolen from his master the King. Zadig used some of it to dispatch express messengers to Babylon to find out what had happened to Astarte. His voice trembled as he gave them his orders, the blood rushed to his head, his eyes glazed over, and his soul was ready to depart his body. The courier set off, and Zadig saw him take ship. He returned to the palace, oblivious of everyone around him and, thinking himself alone in his own room, muttered to himself about love.

'Ah, love!' said the King. 'You're absolutely right. You have guessed what ails me. What a great man you are! I hope you will find me a good woman the same way you found me a reliable treasurer.'

Zadig, having remembered where he was, promised to serve him in love as he had in finance, although the task appeared altogether more difficult.

Blue eyes

'My heart and body . . .', said the King to Zadig.

At these words the Babylonian could not help interrupting His Majesty.

'How grateful I am to you', he said, 'for not saying "my heart and mind"! Because people in Babylon seem to talk about nothing else these days. Every single book one comes across seems to be about hearts and minds, and they're all written by people with neither. But please, I beg you, Sire, do go on.'

Nabussan went on like this:

'My heart and body were made for love. The second of these two masters has every reason to feel that its dictates have been satisfied. I have a hundred wives here at my service, all of them beautiful, compliant, attentive, responsive even, or at least ready to appear so when they are with me. My heart is far from being as contented. I know only too well from experience that they are most ready to caress the King but that they care very little for Nabussan. Not that I think my wives are unfaithful to me, but I would like to find one who would give me her soul. For a treasure like that I would exchange all hundred wives whose charms I own. See if among these hundred sultanas you can't find one of whose love I can be sure.'

Zadig answered him as he had done on the subject of financiers:

'You may rely on me, Sire. But, first, may I have permission to use everything you put on display in the Corridor of Temptation? I will keep a careful account of everything, and you may rest assured that you have nothing to lose.'

The King gave him a free hand. Zadig selected thirty-three of the ugliest hunchbacks he could find on Serendib, thirty-three of the handsomest pages, and thirty-three bonzes of the most eloquent and robust kind. He gave them all permission to come and go as they pleased among the cells in which the sultanas lived. Each little hunchback had four thousand gold coins to lavish as he wished, and from the very first day every single hunchback found happiness. It took the pages, who had naught to lavish but themselves, two or three days to make their conquests. The bonzes had a little more trouble, but eventually thirty-three of the more pious sultanas duly gave themselves. The King, who could see into all the cells at once through some blinds, observed all these trials of virtue, and was lost in wonder. Of his hundred wives, ninety-nine succumbed before his very eyes.

There remained one, all young and untouched, whom His Majesty had never approached. One, two, three hunchbacks were dispatched to deal with her, and they offered her up to twenty thousand gold coins. She was not to be bought, and indeed she could not help laughing at the very idea that these hunchbacks should think that money would improve their looks. She was introduced to the two most handsome pages: she said she found the King even more handsome. They set the most eloquent of the bonzes on her, and then the boldest: she declared the first a windbag, and the second she did not even bother to consider.

'The heart is all,' she would say, 'and I shall never yield to a hunchback's gold, nor to a young man's looks, nor to the blandishments of a bonze. I shall love only Nabussan, son of Nussanab, and I shall wait until he deigns to honour me with his love.'

The King was transported with joy, surprise, and tenderness. He took back all the money with which the hunchbacks had secured their success, and presented it to the fair Falide (for such was the name of this young person). He gave her his heart, and well she deserved it. Never was the flower of youth more radiant; never did the charms of beauty weave such a spell of enchantment. The demands of historical accuracy permit no concealment of the fact that her curtseys were rather poor; but she danced like a fairy, sang like a siren, and spoke like one of the Graces. She was replete with talents and virtues.

Nabussan, being loved, adored her; but she had blue eyes, and this was to be the source of the greatest misfortunes. There was an ancient law which forbade Kings to love any woman of the sort the Greeks have since termed 'boopis'.* The High Bonze had brought in this law more than five thousand years previously: it had been in order to appropriate to himself the mistress of the first King of the Island of Serendib that the High Bonze had thus caused this ban on blue eyes to be incorporated into the constitution. All sections of society throughout the land came to remonstrate with Nabussan. People declared openly that the last days of the kingdom were at hand, that new depths of depravity had been plumbed, that nature itself was threatened with imminent catastrophe; in short, that Nabussan, son of Nussanab, was in love with a pair of big blue eyes. The hunchbacks, the financiers, and the bonzes, as well as all brunettes, protested till the kingdom rang to the sound of their laments.

The wild people who inhabit the north of Serendib took advantage of the general unrest. They invaded good King Nabussan's territory. He tried to levy his subjects: the bonzes, who controlled half of the state revenue, simply threw their hands in the air rather than put them in their coffers to help the King. They offered up some fine prayers set to music, and left the nation prey to the barbarians.

'Oh, my dear Zadig, can you save me from this terrible predicament too?' exclaimed Nabussan in his misery.

'Certainly,' replied Zadig. 'You shall have as much money from the bonzes as you want. Simply leave the areas round their castles unprotected, and defend only your own strongholds.'

Nabussan duly did so. The bonzes came and threw themselves at the King's feet and begged for his help. The King's response was a fine piece of choral music, the words to which were prayers beseeching heaven to preserve their lands for them. So the bonzes finally paid up, and the King brought the war to a successful conclusion. Thus did Zadig, by his wise and fitting counsel and his great service to the King, make implacable enemies of the most powerful men in the land. Bonze and brunette alike pledged themselves to his ruin. The financiers and the hunchbacks did not spare him either; they sought to discredit him in the eyes of the good Nabussan. As Zoroaster says: news of service rendered oft remains in the antechamber, while the door of the council chamber is ever open to suspicion. Every day brought fresh allegations: the first can be denied, but the second begins to hurt, the third is damaging, and the fourth is fatal.

Zadig, in some alarm, and having conducted his friend Setoc's business successfully and despatched his money to him, thought only of leaving the island, and so resolved to go himself and seek word of Astarte.

'For,' he said, 'if I remain in Serendib, the bonzes will have me impaled. But where shall I go? In Egypt they'll only take me into slavery. In Arabia I'll most likely be burnt to death. And in Babylon I'll be strangled. Still, I must find out what has become of Astarte. Let us depart, and we shall see what my sorry destiny still has in store for me.'

This is where the manuscript which was discovered containing the story of Zadig comes to an end. These two chapters should clearly come after the twelfth and before Zadig's arrival in Syria. It is said that he had many other adventures which have also been faithfully recorded. Gentlemen engaged in the interpretation of Oriental Languages are requested to communicate them, should any come into their hands.

WHAT PLEASES THE LADIES

Now that the God of long fine days
Has circled south to scorch the African plain,
Leaving us his meagre arc of rays,
And winter's eve draws in again,
Listen, my friends, and take delight
In a charming and postprandial tale.
It tells of a poor and noble knight
And an adventure worthy to regale.
His name it was Sir John Roebear,
And he lived in the reign of good King Dagobert.*   10

He had journeyed to that holy city, Rome,
A Rome so much finer than the Caesars',
And from that august precinct was returning home,
Laden not with laurels from the Field of Mars,
But with pardons and some lovely dispensations,
Indulgences that answered all vocations,
And sundry agnus dei* his pack to fill.
Though of richer pickings he went in constant search,
Times were hard, and paladins* fared ill;
 For somehow all the money seemed to end up with the
    Church.   20
A horse and dog were all that he possessed,
And an ancient suit of armour for his vest.
But the brilliant gifts of radiant youth
Had been showered on this knight so couth,
The might of Hercules and Adonis' grace—
Advantages, you'll grant, in every time and place.

As he approached Lutetia,* there—
Beside a wood near Charenton—
He spied the blonde and frisky Marton,
Who wore a pretty ribbon in her hair;   30
A figure trim, a step so sprightly,

A petticoat short and a leg so sightly . . .
Sir John draws near, and meets such eyes
As would tempt the very saints in paradise.
A posy of lilies and roses lies
Prettily nestling 'twixt alabaster
Globes, which surely spell disaster;
But these floral hues, though near perfection,
Pale beside the charms of her complexion.
If truth be told, this young vision   40
Was off to market to sell provision,
To offer choice delights—but oh so utter!—
From her basket full of eggs and butter.
Sir John, his passions now quite stirred,
Dismounted fast and said lest she demurred:
'Twenty crowns I've got.' 'Here in my bag', he purred:
'Take all twenty, and my heart beside,
For they are yours.' 'No, no,' she cried.
'You do me too much honour.' Thereupon
She's brought to ground, and good Sir John   50
Does fall on top—and break her eggs.
By this noble sight of flailing legs
The steed is spooked and promptly flees,
Racing off to vanish 'neath the trees.
A monk comes by, from Saint Denis,*
And rides him back to his monastery.

Marton anon sits tidying her hair
And says to John: 'So where's the money?'
Our startled knight now thinks: 'That's funny.
No sign of horse nor purse. Not anywhere.'   60
'I'm so sorry,' he says. But sorry won't do.
Marton decides it just isn't fair,
And runs to the King without further ado.
'I've been raped and pillaged,' says she, 'by a knight.
But worse than that, he won't pay me a mite.'
Dagobert, wise ruler, to Marton replied:
'Since rape is the issue, I cannot decide:
Your case you shall plead to Bertha, my wife,*
For the queen is conversant with these facts of life.

She'll receive you kindly, in her own sweet way,   70
And justice will be done without further delay.'

Marton bows low, and goes straight to the Queen.
Now Bertha was kind, all calm and serene,
Humane, if in one regard severe:
On maidens and their modesty she was absolutely clear.
So she summoned her pious ladies to a moot.
The knight appeared, *sans* spur, *sans* boot,
Bare of head and eyes downcast,
And duly told them what had passed:
How at Charenton, by the devil tempted,   80
He had succumbed, nay not attempted
To resist: he expressed remorse with every breath.
Whereupon the ladies sentenced him to death.

But Sir John he was handsome, and had such charm,
So fine a figure, so fresh a face,
That Queen and Council in their judges' lace
Gazed and wept: That he should come to harm!
In her humble corner Marton sighed.
All hearts were moved to pity by his plight.
So Bertha told her counsellors who cried   90
That they could pardon him, a knight,
That he might live had he but the wit:
'For, as you know, and so our laws are writ,
We must pardon him who can the means acquire
To tell us what it is that women most desire;
And of course he must take care and show good sense,
Speak true and yet not cause offence.'

The matter thus in Council posed,
They told Sir John what was proposed.
And Bertha then, to save his face,   100
Accorded him a full week's grace.
On bended knee he gave his word
To return upon the date deferred;
He thanked her for such leniency
And departed hence most pensively.

'How shall I plainly say, without offence,
What ladies like for preference?'
He wondered loud: 'for Queen and court
Have simply made my plight more fraught.
I rather wish, since death's my lot,   110
That they had hanged me, right there on the spot.'
As he travelled on his way, our knight enquired
Of every maid and matron that he passed
Quite what it was she most desired.
But no reply was ever like the last:
All of them lied; not one to truth aspired.
Sir John began to wish himself in hell, and fired.

Full seven times the star that turns our day to night
Had rimmed the world with golden light,
When in a meadow far he saw, 'neath leafy shade,   120
Twenty of the fairest beauties dancing
In a circle, their flimsy garb enhancing,
Barely veiling, their charms' parade.
Lustrous tresses swirled like braid
In the wafts of playful Zephyr's prancing;
O'er the soft grass they danced their round,
Skimming, hovering, ne'er touching ground.
Sir John draws near and does his best
To seek their counsel in his sorry quest.
But all have fled, vanished, out of sight.   130

The day was ending, 'twas already night,
When his gaze fell upon a toothless crone,
Black with grime, all skin and bone,
Shrunk with age, and leaning on a stick.
A pointed nose hooked down to prick
A shrivelled chin, 'neath scab-lined eyes;
White hairs straggled midst the dirt
Of unwashed scalp; in place of skirt
An old mat, half-draped o'er wrinkled thighs.
All in all, she frightened our brave knight.   140

Up she sidles, pert and bright,
And says to him, without a 'by your leave':
'I see, young man, your heart does grieve.
So come now, tell me of your tribulations.
It's good to talk: so unburden and assuage.
We each have woes, but there are always consolations.
In my time I've seen a lot, and wisdom comes with age.
One or two unfortunates have done as I advised:
And they've been glad they thus my counsel prized.'
The knight cried out: 'Alas! Alack!   150
I seek for counsel, too, but all in vain.
Good woman, it is time I lack,
For on the morrow I must surely hang,
If I do not tell the Queen and Co.,
Without offence, what pleases ladies so.'

The crone then said: 'Fear not, forsooth,
Since God's design has sent you hither;
'Tis for your better good, my son, and that's the truth.
Go gladly to the court, and cease your dither,
For I shall tell you, as along the road we go,   160
This great secret that you long to know.
But promise first, when once your life I've saved,
That you will fairly give me what you owe,
What pleases *me*, and what I long have craved.
Ingratitude is hateful, a debt deferred,
So swear it for my sake, upon your sacred word,
That anything I ask of you, you thereupon will do.'
Sir John so promised, and laughed a little too.
'Laugh not,' the crone admonished, 'and beware:
This is no laughing matter.' And so the pair   170
Made haste towards the palace to report
Before Queen Bertha and her royal court.
The Council met without delay:
The Queen presided, and heard John say:
'I know your secret, ladies. Yes, I do.
What pleases you in every age and nation,
Even when the flames of love may warm you,
Is not the number of your gallants, nor their adoration.

But rather, be she widow, wife, or maid,
Rich or poor, fright or jade,   180
Or soul most kind with tender way,
Every woman wants to wield a sovereign's sway.
For she must be obeyed, morning, noon, and night.
That is her pleasure: hang me, but I'm right.'

Thus spoke Sir John: the Council was convinced.
He'd hit the mark, and not a word was minced.
As the absolvèd knight stooped to kiss
The royal hand, our toothless and most ancient miss,
All rags and filth, bustled through the throng
Demanding justice, loud and strong,   190
And to the throne addressed her oratory:

'O beauteous queen, whose lips are free
Of vile untruth and base deceit,
Whose mind knows only what is just and meet,
Whose generous heart is e'er to others turned,
This knight from me your secret learned
And therefore owes his life to me alone.
So swore he on his honour and my own
That he would grant me what I have in mind.
And here I claim my due, for you are fair and kind.'   200

''Tis true,' said John, 'and nor do I refuse.
I remember favours and always pay my dues.
My fortune was my armour, horse, and pack,
And a score of crowns, which now I sadly lack;
They were stolen by a monk of virtuous intention
Whilst I was paying Marton my most firm attention.
I own nothing in this world and can see no way
My good, kind benefactress ever to repay.'

To which the Queen replied: 'We'll see that all's recovered,
And this monk we'll punish once he's been discovered.   210
But so that now your fortune best be used,
We propose that you divide it into three;
Give twenty crowns to Marton, whom you abused:

Her due for broken eggs and your satiety.
The crone shall have your mount, for he'll not harm her,
And you, Sir John, can keep your suit of armour.'

Said the old woman: 'I shouldn't ask for more,
But it's really not his horse I'm longing for.
Sir John himself is all I really relish,
His grace and valour fond I cherish.   220
I wish to rule his heart and bind
Him to me, now and for the rest of life.
My bed Sir John must share, his bliss there find;
From this night forth I wish to be his wife.'
On hearing words so wholly unexpected
Sir John in horror froze and quick reflected,
Gaping at each noisome feature,
At the rags and tatters of this ghastly creature.
Appalled, distraught, most thoroughly dejected,
He crossed himself and, groaning, said: 230
'Do I really merit such indignity?
Such ridicule, such rank absurdity?
I'd rather that your noble majesty
Bid me now the devil's mother wed.
The hag is mad, her mind is blown.'

Now cried our toothless, lovelorn crone:
'See, noble Queen, how he turns away.
Like all men, I fear, he is ungrateful,
Since I deserve not he should find my looks so hateful.
But he is handsome, and I shall find a way.   240
I love him dearly, and he must love me back.
It's the heart that matters most; and though today
The bloom of youth I may slightly lack,
That makes me kinder, readier to care,
A better person, with a sounder mind.
One starts to think more, and, as Solomon opined:
'Tis better woman wise than woman fair.
I'm poor, it's true, but where's the blame,
Since poverty's no proper cause for shame.
Knows one bliss but on a bed of lace?   250

And you, Madame, in this sumptuous place,
When next the King you wifely lie,
Sleep you—hug you—any better than I?
Remember Philemon, in his hovel, who yet with grace
Did serve and love his loving Baucis*
Till his hundredth year, and never spared a kiss?
Dark thoughts, the aged's remnant brood,
In humble cottage find no room nor board,
For vice dwells not where life is rude.
Like kings and queens we also serve Our Lord;   260
Our country's honour is our own desire,
We give you soldiers to defend the nation.
And believe me, in the cause of population,
A pauper not a prince is much the surer sire.
Should heaven refuse my prayers chaste
That motherhood may be my happy lot,
There are always other nuptial joys to taste,
For flowers please even when they fruit not.
And I intend to pick, from now until I'm dead,
Every bloom and petal upon my marriage bed.'   270

As the hag delivered this charming disquisition
The ladies slowly yielded to its verbal grace,
And John was sentenced to her long embrace.
For a promise is a promise, and his disposition
Counted for naught. So the dame persisted:
They must ride at once, together on one horse,
To her modest shack, where she'd then enforce
Her nuptial rights e'er day had run its course.
And all turned out just as she had insisted.

Our sorry knight bestrides his steed   280
And hoists his bride o'er pommel high;
Horror-struck and shamed in deed,
His dearest wish that she might die.
A fall perhaps, a drowning? Nay, and fie!
For by the ancient laws of chivalry a knight
Knew well that murder simply wasn't right.
And as they trotted home his loving wife

Tried hard to take his mind off all this strife.
She told him of brave Frenchmen, by destiny appointed:
How great Clovis to achieve his ends   290
Did slay three kings who'd been his friends,
And was by heaven pardoned and anointed!
She said she'd seen that blessèd dove
On Rheims descend from skies above,
With the sacred chrism in its phial glistening,
Just what Clovis needed for his christening.*
She lent her tales the personal touch,
With maxim, comment, and opinion much,
Delighting him even when instructing,
And never once the story's flow obstructing.   300
She gave her listener food for thought,
Teaching him, though he knew not he was taught.
Our good Sir John did listen rapt,
And up her wondrous stories lapped,
Pleased as Punch to hear her speak,
Sick at heart to smell her reek.

And thus this oddest couple rode
To our wanton harridan's abode.
Here at once she preens and prinks,
And feast prepares with hand that stinks,   310
The simple repast of an earlier age,
Less aped than lauded by the wiser sage.
Two rotten planks, three legs unequal,
Comprised the table where they now partook,
On tiny trestles seated, thinking of the sequel:
Our hapless groom could hardly bear to look.
The crippled crone, e'en though she scarce could sit,
Regaled them with her subtle and amusing wit;
So naturally they came, her mots upon bon mots,
Well judged, unforced, and apropos,   320
It was just as if you'd thought of them yourself.
Sir John in fond delight began to pinch himself:
She really was less ugly in this light.
But then at supper's end the new bride said
'Twas time her husband came to bed;

And how our desperate and most furious knight
Wanted to escape! He even wished for death!
But down he lay and held his breath:
He'd made his promise. It was simply not his night.

It was not so much the dirty and exiguous bedding,   330
Holèd victim of a rodent's shredding,
Rough-draped in wrinkles o'er a mattress torn,
Whose errant straw had long since parted from its corn,
That turned the stomach of our noble warrior.
No, what made him feel distinctly sorrier
Were the standing duties of an upright groom;
'Does heaven ask th' impossible?' he anguished in the gloom.
'In Rome they say it is God's grace
That fires the will and makes one active;
Alas, I fear this may not be his time or place.   340
By her wit my wife is most attractive,
And her heart is kind; but midst love's ferment
What matter these when comes the crucial moment?'
And so our good Sir John turned over on his side,
And lay as cold and still as if indeed he'd died;
Clinging to the edge, his reluctance to conceal,
He beckoned sleep, but sleep came not to heel.
The crone now snuggles close and whispers softly,
With a loving pinch: 'Are you asleep, John dear?
My lovely and ungrateful man, see here: 350
I am all yours, all mine you now must be.
The chaste and timid voice of modesty
Is silenced by my want of some carnality.
Rule over my senses as you rule within my soul!
Oh, how I yearn! Heavens, John, what have you done?
I find my better self by nature quite undone.
I melt, I burn, I've lost all self-control.
Ah, the pleasure of it quite outstrips my virtue.
Come quick, or must I swoon away without you?
Can I prick your conscience? Do now what you ought!'   360

Our good Sir John, a most obliging sort—
No godless, selfish heathen he—

Took pity on his wife and said quite evenly:
'Alas, Madame, I could not now wish harder
To answer you with all mine equal ardour.
But what can I do?' A plea that met with outrage.
'What? In your prime? Why, almost anything!
The sky's the limit for a man with courage:
A touch of knowing art, and you'll soon find you're managing.
Then think what the ladies of the court will say!   370
How they'll praise your prowess in some amorous lay!
So you find me just a tad malodorous,
A trifle raddled even, and your duty onerous;
But what are such obstacles to well-born heroes?
Just shut your eyes and hold your nose.'

Our noble knight, on glory bent,
Resolved at length to act the gent,
And to occasion rose. In chivalrous submission,
Imagining he rode on some intrepid mission,
Enlisting heaven's aid and a youthful vigour,   380
For want of love and beauty, to negotiate this rigour,
He boldly shut his eyes and went about his duty.

'Enough, enough', his loving wife now shouted:
'I've seen of you what I did wish to see.
Now I know that I can make you please me:
That I could sway your heart was what I'd doubted.
And I was right, young man, as you can see:
A woman will be mistress of her destiny.
Henceforth Sir John—'tis all I demand—
You must let me be your guide;   390
So obey me now, and by my command
Open your eyes, and cast them on your bride.'
Sir John obeyed, and there in the dazzling light
Of a hundred torches in some twenty candelabra,
'Neath pearl-encrusted curtains he caught sight—
For the hovel was a palace, abracadabra!—
Of a beauty such as no mere painted figment,
From Apelles' brush or Van Loo's pigment,
Nor any sculpted likeness by Phidias sought,

Not Pigalle, not Lemoine,* ever could have caught.   400
Not just Venus, but a Venus deep in love,
Recumbent, her golden hair untied,
Gazing mistily towards the skies above
In languorous longing as for Mars she sighed.
'What you see is yours: myself, the palace too.
For your pleasure,' she told her conqueror.
'Of an ugly countenance you despisèd not the wearer,
And henceforth merit that beauty love thee true.'

And now I hear my listeners asking
Who on earth she was, this dame so belle,   410
As in her loving arms we leave Sir John a-basking.
My friends, she was the fairy called Urgele,
Who in her day protected soldiers all,
And sometimes helped distressèd knights withal.
O happy times of fairy deed,
Of elves and sprites and stories tall,
And kindly spirits tending mortal need.
People heard these marvellous tales and believed,
Seated round the hearth in every castle hall:
The chaplain was the teller, and father, mother,   420
Friend and daughter, neighbour, brother,
Listened rapt: for how could interest pall?
No matter what the fable, it held them in its thrall.

And now they've banished spirits, fairies too;
Reason rules, a story must be true.
But the heart grows dull in a world of grey,
Where sense and logic may not brook demur,
And correctness is the order of the day.
Believe me when I say: it can be right to err.

THE INGENU

*A True Story
taken from the manuscripts of Father Quesnel**

CHAPTER 1

*How the Prior of Our Lady of the Mountain and his
good sister met a Huron*

ONE day St Dunstan,* an Irishman by nationality and by profession a saint, left Ireland aboard a little mountain, which proceeded under sail towards the shores of France. By this conveyance did he arrive in Saint-Malo Bay. On stepping ashore he blessed the mountain, which made him some low bows and returned to Ireland the way it had come.

Dunstan founded a small priory in those parts and named it the 'Priory of the Mountain', which name, as everybody knows, it still bears to this day.

In the year 1689, on the evening of 15 July, the Abbé de Kerkabon, Prior of Our Lady of the Mountain, was strolling along the sea-shore with Mlle de Kerkabon, his sister, taking the air. The Prior, who was already getting on somewhat in years, was a most excellent cleric, beloved by his neighbours as once he had been by his neighbours' wives. What had led him above all to be held in high regard was that he was the only local incumbent who did not have to be carried to bed when he had supped with his colleagues. He had a reasonable grasp of theology, and when he was tired of reading St Augustine, he would read Rabelais for fun. Consequently everyone had a good word to say for him.

Mlle de Kerkabon had never married, though she much wanted to, and was well preserved for someone of forty-five. She was of good and sensible character: she liked enjoying herself, and she went to church.

'Alas!' the Prior was saying to his sister, as he gazed out to sea, 'this is the very spot where our poor brother took ship on the frigate

Swallow in 1669 with Mme de Kerkabon, his wife and our dear sister-in-law, to go and serve in Canada. Had he not been killed, we might be looking forward to seeing him again.'

'Do you think', Mlle de Kerkabon replied, 'that our sister-in-law really was eaten by the Iroquois, as we were told she was? Certainly, had she not been eaten, she would have come back home. I shall mourn her to the end of my days. She was a charming woman. And our brother was very clever. He would surely have made a large fortune.'

Just as their hearts were growing fonder at the memory of this, they saw a small ship entering the Bay of Rance on the tide. It was Englishmen coming to sell some of their country's wares. They sprang ashore without so much as a glance at the Prior or his good sister, who was most shocked at the lack of consideration shown to her.

Such was not the case when it came to a very handsome young man who leapt right over the heads of his companions in a single bound and landed straight in front of Mademoiselle. Unaccustomed as he was to bowing, he gave her a nod. His physical appearance and manner of dress drew the gaze of brother and sister alike. He was hatless, and hoseless, and wore little sandals; his head was graced with long plaits of hair; and a short doublet clung to a trim and supple figure. He had a look about him that was at once martial and gentle. In one hand he held a small bottle of Barbados water* and, in the other, a sort of pouch containing a goblet and some very fine ship's biscuit. He spoke French most intelligibly. He offered some of his Barbados water to Mlle de Kerkabon and her good brother, drank some with them, and pressed them to have some more, all with such a simple, natural air that brother and sister both were charmed. They put themselves at his service and asked him who he was and where he was going. The young man replied that he had no idea, that he was curious, that he had wanted to see what the French coast was like, that he had come, and that he would be going back.

The good Prior, guessing by his accent that he was not English, took the liberty of asking him what country he was from.

'I am a Huron,' the young man replied.

Mlle de Kerkabon, amazed and delighted to have seen a Huron show her such civility, asked the young man to supper. He did not wait to be asked a second time, and all three went off together to the Priory of Our Lady of the Mountain.

The diminutive and rotund good lady could not take her little eyes off him, and would periodically say to the Prior: 'What a complexion he has, this big lad! Like lilies and roses! And what beautiful skin he's got for a Huron!'

'Yes, dear,' said the Prior.

She asked hundreds of questions, one after another, and each time the traveller's answer would be very much to the point.

Word soon spread that there was a Huron at the priory. Local society hastened to sup there. The Abbé de Saint-Yves came with Mademoiselle his sister, a young girl of Lower Breton pedigree, who was extremely pretty and very well bred. The magistrate and the tax-collector, and their wives, were also among the guests.* The visitor was placed between Mlle de Kerkabon and Mlle de Saint-Yves. Everyone looked at him in astonishment, and they all spoke and questioned him at once. The Huron did not turn a hair. It was as if he had taken Lord Bolingbroke's motto for his own: 'nihil admirari'.*

But eventually, worn out by so much noise, he said to them quite gently but firmly:

'Gentlemen, where I come from, people take it in turns to speak. How do you expect me to reply when you won't let me hear what you say?'

The voice of reason always gives people pause for a moment or two. There was a long silence.

His Honour the magistrate, who always buttonholed strangers no matter whose house he was in, and who was the greatest interrogator in the province, opened his mouth some six inches wide and said:

'What is your name, sir?'

'I always used to be called "the Ingenu",' replied the Huron, 'and I was confirmed in the name when I was in England because I always ingenuously say what I think, just as I always do exactly as I please.'

'How, sir, if you were born a Huron, were you able to come to England?'

'Because someone took me there. I was captured in battle by the English, after putting up rather a good fight, and the English, who like bravery—because they are brave too and just as honourable as we are—offered me the choice between being sent back to my family or coming to England. And I chose the latter because I am by nature passionately fond of travel.'

'But, sir,' said the magistrate in his important voice, 'how could you possibly abandon your father and mother like that?'

'Because I never knew my father and mother,' said the visitor.

This moved the company, and they all kept repeating: 'Never knew his father and mother!'

'We'll be his father and mother,' said the lady of the house to her brother the Prior. 'What an interesting person this Huron gentleman is!'

The Ingenu thanked her with proud and noble cordiality and gave her to understand that he lacked for nothing.

'I perceive, Mr Ingenu,' said the solemn magistrate, 'that you speak French better than a Huron ought.'

'There was this Frenchman we captured,' he said, 'back in Huronia when I was a young boy. We became good friends, and he taught me his language. I'm very quick at learning what I want to learn. When I arrived in Plymouth, I came across one of those French refugees of yours, the ones you call "Huguenots"* for some reason. He helped me to get to know your language better, and as soon as I could make myself understood, I came to have a look at your country, because I quite like the French—when they don't ask too many questions.'

The Abbé de Saint-Yves, despite this little admonishment, asked him which of the three languages he liked best: Huron, English, or French.

'Huron, without question,' replied the Ingenu.

'Well, would you believe it?' exclaimed Mlle de Kerkabon. 'I'd always thought that, after Lower Breton, French was the most beautiful language.'

Whereupon it was a matter of who could get in first to ask the Ingenu the Huron for 'tobacco', and he answered 'taya', and the Huron for 'to eat', and he answered 'essenten'. Mlle de Kerkabon simply had to know the Huron for 'to make love'. He told her it was 'trovander',[1] and maintained, not unreasonably on the face of it, that these words were just as good as their French and English equivalents. 'Trovander' struck all the guests as being particularly pretty.

The good Prior, who had in his library the Huron grammar given to him by the Reverend Father Sagard Théodat, the famous Recollect

---

[1] These are in fact all Huron words.

missionary,* left the table for a moment to go and consult it. He returned quite breathless with fond emotion and delight. He recognized the Ingenu as a true Huron. There was a brief discussion about the multiplicity of tongues, and it was agreed that, but for that business with the Tower of Babel, the whole world would have spoken French.

The interrogating magistrate, who until then had been somewhat wary of this personage, was filled with new and deep respect. He now spoke to him with more civility than before, a fact which quite escaped the Ingenu's notice.

Mlle de Saint-Yves was most curious to know how they made love in the land of the Hurons.

'By doing good deeds', he replied, 'to please people like you.'

All the guests applauded in amazement. Mlle de Saint-Yves flushed, and was most obliged. Mlle de Kerkabon flushed too, but she was rather less obliged. She was a little piqued that this compliment had not been paid to her, but she was such a good soul that her affection for the Huron was not in the least diminished. She asked him, in a very well-meaning way, how many sweethearts he had had in Huronia.

'I have only ever had the one,' said the Ingenu. 'That was Mlle Abacaba, the good friend of my dear wet-nurse. Rushes are not straighter, and ermine is not whiter, sheep are less gentle, eagles less proud, and deer less nimble, than Abacaba. One day she was out hunting a hare near where we lived, about fifty leagues away. An ill-mannered Algonquin, who lived a hundred leagues beyond that, came and stole her hare. I got to hear of it, rushed off, laid the Algonquin out with a single blow of my club, and brought him to the feet of my sweetheart bound hand and foot. Abacaba's family wanted to eat him, but I was never much of a one for that sort of feast, so I set him free, and we became friends. Abacaba was so touched by what I had done that she preferred me to all her other lovers. She would love me still if she hadn't been eaten by a bear. I punished the bear and wore its skin for ages, but it was no consolation.'

Mlle de Saint-Yves, on hearing this tale, felt secretly pleased to learn that the Ingenu had had only one sweetheart, and that Abacaba was no longer alive, but she did not understand quite why she was pleased. All eyes were on the Ingenu, and he was much praised for having prevented his friends from eating an Algonquin.

The relentless magistrate, who could not control his mania for asking questions, eventually indulged his curiosity to the point of enquiring what the Huron gentleman's religion was, and whether he had chosen the Anglican religion, the Gallican, or the Huguenot.

'I have my own religion,' he said, 'as you have yours.'

'Oh, dear!' cried la Kerkabon. 'Clearly it didn't even occur to those wretched English to baptize him.'

'But my God,' said Mlle de Saint-Yves, 'how can it be that the Hurons are not Catholic? Haven't the Jesuit fathers converted them all?'

The Ingenu assured her that no converting went on in his country, that no true Huron had ever changed his mind, and that his language did not even have a word for 'inconstancy'.

This last remark pleased Mlle de Saint-Yves exceedingly.

'We will baptize him, we will baptize him,' la Kerkabon was saying to the good Prior. 'The honour will be yours, my dear brother. I absolutely insist on being his godmother, and the good Abbé de Saint-Yves can be his godfather, and we shall have a jolly splendid service, and it will be the talk of Lower Brittany and do us immense credit.'

The whole company supported the lady of the house, and they were all shouting: 'We will baptize him!'

The Ingenu replied that in England they let people live as they pleased. He indicated that their proposal was not at all to his liking, and that the religious laws of the Hurons were at least as good as those of Lower Brittany. He ended by saying that he would be leaving the next day. They finished off the bottle of Barbados water, and everyone went to bed.

When the Ingenu had been shown to his room, Mlle de Kerkabon and her friend, Mlle de Saint-Yves, could not refrain from looking through a large keyhole to see how a Huron slept. They saw that he had spread the bedcover on the floor and was lying there in the most beautiful posture one could imagine.

CHAPTER 2

The Huron, known as the Ingenu, is recognized by his family

THE Ingenu, as was his wont, awoke with the sun at cock-crow, which in England and Huronia is called the 'crack of dawn'. He was not like society people who languish in an idle bed until the sun has run half its course, who can neither sleep nor rise, and who lose so many precious hours in this intermediate state between life and death and then complain that life is too short.

He had already covered two or three leagues and bagged thirty head of game in as many shots, when he returned to find the good Prior of Our Lady of the Mountain and that soul of discretion, his sister, taking a stroll round their little garden still in their nightcaps. He presented them with his entire bag and, taking from inside his shirt a sort of small talisman which he always wore around his neck, begged them to accept it as a token of his gratitude for their kind hospitality.

'It is the most precious thing I have,' he informed them. 'I was told I would always be happy as long as I wore this little trinket about me, and I am giving it to you so that you shall always be happy.'

The Prior and Mademoiselle smiled fondly at the naïvety of the Ingenu. The present consisted of two rather poorly drawn little portraits tied together with an extremely greasy strap.

Mlle de Kerkabon asked him if there were any painters in Huronia.

'No,' said the Ingenu, 'this rarity came from my wet-nurse. Her husband acquired it as part of the spoils of war when he was stripping the bodies of some Frenchmen from Canada who had attacked us. That's all I know about it.'

The Prior looked carefully at the portraits. His colour changed. He was overcome by emotion, and his hands began to tremble.

'By Our Lady of the Mountain,' he exclaimed, 'I do believe that these are the faces of my brother, the captain, and his wife!'

Mademoiselle, having inspected them with the same emotion, came to the same conclusion. Both were filled with astonishment, and with a joy tinged with sorrow. They became agitated: they wept, their hearts pounded, they cried out, they tore the portraits from each other's hands, they grabbed them and handed them back twenty times a second. They scrutinized the portraits intently, and the Huron too. They asked him, each in turn and both at once, where, when, and how these miniatures had fallen into the hands of his wet-nurse. They compared dates. They counted the days since the captain's departure. They remembered receiving word that he had got as far as the land of the Hurons and how they had heard nothing more since then.

The Ingenu had told them that he had known neither father nor mother. The Prior, who was a man of sense, noticed that the Huron had the beginnings of a beard. He was well aware that Hurons cannot grow one.

'There is fluff on his chin, so he must be the son of a European. My brother and sister-in-law were never seen again after the expedition against the Hurons in 1669. My nephew must then have been at the breast. The Huron wet-nurse saved his life and became a mother to him.'

Eventually, after hundreds of questions and answers, the Prior and his sister concluded that the Huron was their own nephew. They embraced him in tears, and the Huron laughed, finding it inconceivable that a Huron could be the nephew of a Prior in Lower Brittany.

The rest of the company arrived downstairs. M. de Saint-Yves, who was a great student of physiognomy, compared the two portraits with the Ingenu's face. He pointed out most expertly that the Ingenu had his mother's eyes, the forehead and nose of the late Captain de Kerkabon, and the cheeks of both.

Mlle de Saint-Yves, who had never seen the father or the mother, was firmly of the opinion that the Ingenu looked just like them. They all marvelled at Providence and at the way things turn out in this world. In the end they were all so persuaded, so convinced, of the Ingenu's parentage that he himself consented to be the good Prior's nephew, saying that he was just as happy to have him for an uncle as anyone else.

They all went to give thanks to God in the church of Our Lady of the Mountain, while the Huron, with unconcerned expression, remained behind and was content to drink.

The Englishmen who had brought him, and who were ready to set sail, came to tell him that it was time to leave.

'It is quite evident that you', he said, 'have not just been reunited with your uncles and aunts. I'm staying here. Off you go back to Plymouth. You can have my old clothes. I don't need anything any more, now I'm the nephew of a prior.'

The English set sail, caring very little whether the Ingenu had family in Lower Brittany or not.

Once the uncle and aunt and their guests had sung the *Te Deum*, once the magistrate had again badgered the Ingenu with questions, and once they had all exhausted everything that amazement, joy, and warmth of feeling can prompt one to say, the Prior of the Mountain and the Abbé de Saint-Yves decided to have the Ingenu baptized at the earliest opportunity. But a grown Huron of twenty-two was rather different from a baby being spiritually reborn without knowing a thing about it. He would have to be prepared, and that seemed a tall order, for the Abbé de Saint-Yves supposed that someone who had not been born in France would be quite devoid of common sense.

The Prior pointed out to the company that even though Mr Ingenu, his nephew, had not had the good fortune to be raised in Lower Brittany, that did not make him any the less intelligent; that this was evident from all the answers he had given; and that nature had most definitely smiled on him, as much on the paternal side as on the maternal.

First they asked him if he had ever read a book. He said he had read an English translation of Rabelais and a few passages from Shakespeare, which he knew by heart; that he had found these books in the captain's cabin on the ship which had brought him from America to Plymouth, and that he was very pleased he had. The magistrate did not fail to question him about these books.

'I must confess', said the Ingenu, 'that while I think I understood some of it, the rest was beyond me.'

The Abbé de Saint-Yves, on hearing this, reflected that this was just how he had always read, and that most people read in much the same way.

'No doubt you have read the Bible?' he said to the Huron.

'Not a word of it, sir. It was not one of my captain's books. I've never heard of it.'

'There you are, that's typical of the damned English,' cried Mlle de Kerkabon. 'They care more about Shakespeare's plays, and plum puddings, and bottles of rum, than they do about the Pentateuch.

Which is why they have never converted a soul in America. They really are God's accursed race. And we'll have Jamaica and Virginia off them before too long.'

Be that as it may, the most skilful tailor in Saint-Malo was summoned to come and dress the Ingenu from head to foot. The company took their leave: the magistrate took his questions elsewhere. Mlle de Saint-Yves turned round several times as she was departing to look at the Ingenu, and he bowed lower to her than he had ever bowed to anyone in his life before.

The magistrate, before taking his leave, introduced Mlle de Saint-Yves to his great booby of a son who was just out of college, but she scarcely glanced at him, so absorbed was she by the good manners of the Huron.

CHAPTER 3

The Huron, known as the Ingenu, is converted

THE good Prior, in view of the fact that he was getting on in years and that here was God sending him a nephew to comfort him in his old age, took it into his head that he could resign his living in this nephew's favour if he succeeded in baptizing him and getting him to enter holy orders.

The Ingenu had an excellent memory. The soundness of Lower Breton organs, further fortified by the Canadian climate, had given him a head so strong that when it got banged, he hardly felt it, and when something registered within it, not a trace would fade. He had never forgotten a thing. His understanding was all the quicker and sharper for the fact that his childhood had not been burdened with all the useless nonsense that encumbers ours, and things entered his brain as clear as daylight. The Prior resolved at length to make him read the New Testament. The Ingenu devoured it with much enjoyment but, not knowing when or where all the adventures related in the book had taken place, did not for a moment doubt that the scene of the action was Lower Brittany; and he swore that he would cut Caiaphas's and Pilate's ears and noses off for them if he ever came across those scoundrels. His uncle, delighted that he should be so well disposed, explained the position. He praised his

zeal but told him that the zeal was misplaced, given that these particular individuals had died approximately sixteen hundred and
ninety years earlier.

Soon the Ingenu knew almost the entire book by heart. Sometimes
he raised one or two difficulties which considerably embarrassed the
Prior. Often he had to go and consult the Abbé de Saint-Yves who, at
a loss for a reply, called in a Lower Breton Jesuit to complete the
Huron's conversion.

At last grace wrought its effect: the Ingenu promised to become a
Christian. He was in no doubt that he should begin by being
circumcised.

'For', he said, 'I cannot think of one person in that book you made
me read who wasn't. It is therefore evident that I must sacrifice my
foreskin. The sooner the better.'

He did not think twice. He sent for the village surgeon and asked
him to perform the operation, thinking to delight Mlle de Kerkabon
and the whole company exceedingly with the news once the deed was
done. The barber, who had not performed this type of operation
before, notified the family, and they kicked up a terrible fuss. Good
Kerkabon was afraid that her nephew, who seemed a determined,
no-nonsense sort, might perform the operation on himself, and
clumsily at that, and that this might have sorry consequences of the
kind in which the ladies, out of the goodness of their hearts, always
take such an interest.

The Prior set the Huron straight. He pointed out that circumci-
sion was no longer the done thing, that baptism was altogether gent-
ler and better for one's health, and that the law of grace was not the
same as the law of self-denial. The Ingenu, who had a lot of common
sense and decency, argued his case but recognized his error, which is
rather a rare thing in Europe among people who debate. In the end
he promised to be baptized whenever they wished.

First he would have to say confession, and this was the most
difficult part. The Ingenu always carried with him in his pocket the
book which his uncle had given him. In it he could find not one
single apostle who had said confession, and that made him very
uncooperative. The Prior silenced him by showing him the words
from the Epistle of Saint James the Less which are such a problem
for heretics: 'Confess your faults one to another.'* The Huron
held his peace and said his confession to a Recollect. When he had

finished, he hauled the Recollect out of the confessional and, with a firm hold on his man, took his place and made him kneel down before him.

'Now then, my friend. It says: "Confess your faults one to another". I've told you my sins, and you're not getting out of here till you've told me yours.'

So saying, he kept his ample knee pressed against the chest of the opposing party. The Recollect screamed and howled, and the whole church echoed. People came running at the noise to find the catechumen now laying into the monk in the name of Saint James the Less.

The joy at baptizing a Lower Breton Anglo-Huron was so great that they were prepared to overlook this strange behaviour. There was even quite a number of theologians who thought that confession was not necessary, since baptism took the place of everything else. A date was fixed with the Bishop of Saint-Malo, and he, flattered, as well he might be, at having a Huron to baptize, arrived with much pomp and circumstance and a retinue of clergy. Mlle de Saint-Yves, thanking God, put on her best frock and had a hairdresser come from Saint-Malo that she might be the belle of the baptism. The magistrate with all the questions came, as did the whole of local society. The church was magnificently decorated. But when the moment arrived to lead the Huron to the baptismal font, he was nowhere to be found.

Uncle and aunt looked for him everywhere. They thought he might be out hunting, as was his wont. All the guests scoured the nearby woods and villages: not a trace of the Huron.

They began to worry that he might have gone back to England. They remembered hearing him say how much he liked that country. The good Prior and his sister were convinced that no one was ever baptized over there and feared for their nephew's soul. The Bishop was nonplussed and all set to go home, the Prior and the Abbé de Saint-Yves were in despair, and the magistrate interrogated every passer-by with his usual gravity. Mlle de Kerkabon was crying. Mlle de Saint-Yves was not crying, but she was heaving deep sighs which seemed to suggest a certain fondness for the sacraments. They were walking disconsolately beside the willows and reeds which grow along the banks of the little river Rance when, in the middle of the river, they caught sight of a tall, rather white figure, with its two hands crossed over its chest. They shrieked and turned away. But, with curiosity soon overcoming all other considerations, they slipped quietly in amongst the reeds and, when they were quite sure they could not be seen, determined to find out what all this was about.

CHAPTER 4

The Ingenu is baptized

THE Prior and the Abbé came running up and asked the Ingenu what he was doing there.

'For goodness sake, gentlemen, I'm waiting to be baptized. I've been standing up to my neck in this water for an hour now. It's just not right leaving me to freeze to death like this.'

'My dear nephew,' said the Prior affectionately, 'this isn't the way we baptize people in Lower Brittany. Put your clothes back on and come with us.'

Mlle de Saint-Yves, on hearing this, whispered to her companion:

'Mademoiselle, do you think he's going to put his clothes back on this minute?'

The Huron, however, answered the Prior back:

'You're not going to pull the wool over my eyes this time the way you did the last. I've gone into things a lot since then, and I am quite certain that there is no other way of being baptized. Queen Candace's eunuch was baptized in a stream.* I defy you to show me in that book you gave me any other way of going about it. I will be baptized in a river or not at all.'

It was no use telling him that customs had changed. The Ingenu was stubborn, for he was a Breton and a Huron. He kept coming back to Queen Candace's eunuch, and although his maiden aunt and Mlle de Saint-Yves, who had observed him through the willows, had just cause to tell him that he was in no position to quote a man of that water, they nevertheless did no such thing, so great was their discretion. The Bishop himself came to speak to him, which was quite something, but he had no success. The Huron argued his case with the Bishop.

'Show me,' he said, 'in that book my uncle gave me, one single person who was not baptized in a river, and I will do anything you want.'

Aunt, now desperate, had noticed that the first time her nephew had bowed, he had made a deeper bow to Mlle de Saint-Yves than to anyone else in the company, and that he had greeted not even the Bishop with the same mixture of respect and cordiality that he had shown the beautiful young lady. She decided to turn to her at this very ticklish moment. She asked her to use her influence to get the Huron to agree to be baptized the Breton way, not believing that her nephew could ever become a Christian if he persisted in wanting to be baptized in running water.

Mlle de Saint-Yves blushed with secret pleasure at being charged with such an important commission. She approached the Huron modestly and, shaking his hand in a thoroughly noble fashion, said to him:

'Would you do something for me?'

And as she uttered these words, she lowered her eyes and lifted them again with a grace that warmed the heart.

'Oh, anything you wish, mademoiselle, anything you command: baptism by water, by fire, by blood. There is nothing I would not do for you.'

Mlle de Saint-Yves had the honour and glory of effecting in a few words what neither the entreaties of the Prior nor the repeated questioning of the magistrate nor the arguments even of the Bishop had been able to achieve. She was sensible of her triumph: but she was not yet sensible of its extent.

The baptism was administered and received with all possible decency, magnificence, and enjoyment. Uncle and aunt ceded to M. l'Abbé de Saint-Yves and his sister the honour of holding the Ingenu over the font. Mlle de Saint-Yves beamed with joy to find herself a godmother. She was ignorant of what obligations this great title laid her under, and she accepted the honour without knowing its fatal consequences.

As there never was ceremony that was not followed by a grand dinner, they all sat down to eat after the baptism. The wags of Lower Brittany said how one should never baptize one's wine. The Prior was saying that, according to Solomon, wine rejoices the heart of man.* The Lord Bishop added that Judah the Patriarch had had to bind his ass's colt unto the vine and wash his coat in the blood of grapes,* and that he personally was very sad one couldn't do the same in Lower Brittany, to which God had denied the vine. Everyone tried to produce some witticism about the Ingenu's baptism and some compliments for the godmother. The magistrate, ever full of questions, asked the Huron if he would be faithful to his promises.

'How could I possibly break my promises,' replied the Huron, 'since Mademoiselle de Saint-Yves was holding me when I made them?'

The Huron warmed to the occasion. He drank a great deal to the health of his godmother.

'If I had been baptized by your hand,' he said, 'I feel as though the cold water poured upon the nape of my neck would have scalded me.'

The magistrate found this all far too poetical, not knowing how common allegory is in Canada. But godmother was extremely happy about it.

They had given the baptized the name of Hercules.* The Bishop of Saint-Malo kept asking who this patron saint was of whom he had never heard. The Jesuit, who was most learned, told him that he was a saint who had worked twelve miracles. There was a thirteenth which was worth more than the other twelve put together, but which it ill became a Jesuit to mention. That was the one of transforming fifty maidens into women in the course of a single night. One of those present, who was something of a humorist, energetically elaborated on the merits of this miracle. The ladies all lowered their gaze and considered that, to judge by his face, the Ingenu was worthy of the saint whose name he bore.

CHAPTER 5

The Ingenu in love

It must be admitted that after this baptism and dinner Mlle de Saint-Yves wished passionately that the Lord Bishop would once more make her a participant in some fine sacrament with Mr Hercules, the Ingenu. However, as she was well brought up and very modest, she did not dare admit to herself the full extent of her fondness. But if a look, a word, a gesture, or a thought, did escape her, she covered it up completely beneath an infinitely delightful veil of maidenly modesty. She was lively, and affectionate, and a good girl.

As soon as the Lord Bishop had left, the Ingenu and Mlle de Saint-Yves met, without realizing they had sought each other out, and talked together, without having thought in advance what they would say. The Ingenu told her first that he loved her with all his heart, and that the fair Abacaba, whom he had been mad about back home, was not a patch on her. Mademoiselle answered him with her usual modesty that he ought to talk this over at once with his uncle the Prior and with Mademoiselle his aunt, and that on her side she would have a word or two with her dear brother the Abbé de Saint-Yves, and that she had every confidence that they would all consent.

The Ingenu retorted that he had no need of anyone's consent, that he found it quite ridiculous to go asking other people what one should do, and that when two parties are agreed, one does not require a third to bring them together.

'I don't ask anyone's opinion', he said, 'when I feel like having breakfast, or going hunting, or having a sleep. I know that with love it's not a bad idea to have the consent of the person one has in mind, but since it's neither my uncle nor my aunt I'm in love with, it's not them I need to ask in this case. And if you want my advice, you can give the good Abbé de Saint-Yves a miss as well.'

As one might imagine, the fair Breton used all her subtlety to get the Huron to abide by the rules of polite society. She even lost and then quickly recovered her temper. In the end there is no knowing how this conversation would have ended if at dusk the good Abbé de Saint-Yves had not taken his sister back home to his abbey. The Ingenu allowed his uncle and aunt, who were a trifle tired after the ceremony and their long dinner, to go to bed. He spent part of the night composing verses in Huron for his beloved. It is a fact that there is no country in the world where love does not turn lovers into poets.

Next day, after breakfast, his uncle said this to him in the presence of Mlle de Kerkabon, who was in a very emotional state:

'Heaven be praised that you have the honour, my dear nephew, to be both a Christian and a Lower Breton! But that alone is not enough. I am getting on in years, and my brother left me only a small piece of land of little consequence, but I do have a good priory. If you will only agree to be a sub-deacon, as I hope you will, then I shall resign my living in your favour, and you will be able to live very comfortably, having been a comfort to me in my old age.'

The Ingenu replied:

'Uncle, really, what good would that do you? You go on living just as long as you can. I have no idea what it means to be a sub-deacon or to resign one's living, but everything will be fine by me as long as I can have Mlle de Saint-Yves to myself.'

'Oh, my God! Dear nephew, what are you saying? Has your love for that beautiful young lady made you mad?'

'Yes, uncle.'

'Alas, nephew, it is impossible for you to marry her.'

'It is distinctly possible, uncle, for not only did she squeeze my hand when she left me, but she also promised she would ask for my hand in marriage, and I shall most assuredly give it.'

'That is impossible, I tell you. She is your godmother. It is an appalling sin for a godmother to squeeze the hand of her godson. Marrying one's godmother is not allowed.* All laws, both God's and man's, are against it.'

'Come now, uncle, you must be joking. Why should it be forbidden to marry one's godmother when she's young and pretty? I didn't see anywhere in that book you gave me where it said it was wrong to marry girls who've helped out at baptisms. I notice every day how you all do a whole host of things which are not in that book of yours, and how you don't do the things it does say. I will tell you honestly: I find that surprising, and infuriating. If anyone tries to come between us on the pretext of my baptism, I'm warning you, I'll run away with her and unbaptize myself.'

The Prior was at a loss. His sister wept.

'My dear brother,' she said, 'our nephew must not damn himself. Our Holy Father the Pope may grant him dispensation, and then he can live in Christian happiness with the one he loves.'

The Ingenu gave his aunt a hug.

'Who's this, then,' he said, 'this charming man who so kindly helps out boys and girls with their love affairs? I shall go and speak to him at once.'

They explained to him who the Pope was, and the Ingenu was even more astonished than before.

'There isn't a single word about all this in your book, my dear uncle. I have travelled a little, I know the sea, and here we are on the shores of the Ocean. But you expect me to leave Mlle de Saint-Yves and go and get permission to love her from a man who lives four hundred leagues away somewhere near the Mediterranean, and whose language I don't even understand! That is quite incomprehensibly ridiculous! I'm going straight this minute to the Abbé de Saint-Yves. He lives only one league away. And I can promise you, I'll be married to my sweetheart before the day is out.'

As he was still talking, in came the magistrate who, in his usual manner, asked him where he was going.

'I'm off to get married,' said the Ingenu, as he rushed away, and in a quarter of an hour he was already at the house of his beloved Breton beauty, who was still asleep.

'Ah, brother,' said Mlle de Kerkabon to the Prior, 'you will never make a sub-deacon of our nephew.'

The magistrate was not at all pleased at this journey. For he intended that his son should marry the Saint-Yves girl, and this son was even more stupid and disagreeable than his father.

CHAPTER 6

The Ingenu flies to the arms of his sweetheart and into a rage

No sooner had the Ingenu arrived than, having asked an old servant where the mistress's room was, he had flung open the door, which had not been securely shut, and sprung towards the bed. Mlle de Saint-Yves, awaking with a start, had cried out:

'What, you here! Ah, it's you! Stop, what are you doing?'

He had replied:

'I'm marrying you.'

And indeed he would have done if she had not resisted with all the decency of one who has had a good education.

The Ingenu was in no mood for jokes. He found all this standing on ceremony quite beside the point.

'Miss Abacaba, my first sweetheart, didn't use to carry on like this. You're not being straight with me. You promised me marriage, and you will not marry. That is against the basic rules of the code of honour. I'll teach you to keep your word, I'll return you to the paths of virtue.'

The Ingenu's virtue was an intrepid masculinity worthy of Hercules his patron, with whose name he had been christened. He was about to exercise it to its fullest extent when the piercing cries of the young lady whose virtue was of a more discreet kind brought the wise Abbé de Saint-Yves, his housekeeper, a God-fearing old servant, and a local parish priest all running to the scene. The sight of these people moderated the courage of the assailant.

'Oh, my God!' said the Abbé. 'My dear fellow, what on earth are you doing?'

'My duty,' replied the young man. 'I am keeping my vows, which are sacred.'

Mlle de Saint-Yves blushed and straightened her clothing. The Ingenu was taken to another room. The Abbé pointed out to him the enormity of his action. The Ingenu defended himself on the basis of the privileges allowed under the laws of nature, with which laws he was entirely conversant. The Abbé tried to prove that real laws took precedence, and that without the conventions established between men the laws of nature would scarcely amount to much more than natural skulduggery.

'We have need', he was saying, 'of notaries, and priests, and witnesses, and contracts, and dispensations.'

The Ingenu answered him with the observation that savages have always made:

'You must be a pretty dishonest lot then, if you have to take so many precautions with each other.'

The Abbé had some trouble in meeting this objection.

'There are, I admit,' he said, 'a lot of rogues and shady characters among us, and there would be just as many among the Hurons if they were all gathered together in a large town. But there are also some wise, honest, enlightened souls, and it is they who have made the laws. The more upright one is, the more one must submit to these laws. One sets an example to the men of vice, who respect a curb which virtue has placed upon itself.'

The Ingenu was struck by this reply. (It has already been noted how sound his judgement was.) They soothed him with words of flattery, and they gave him hope—the two traps into which people the world over will always fall. They even brought Mlle de Saint-Yves to him, when she had got dressed. Everything was conducted with the utmost propriety. But, despite this decorum, the sparkling eyes of the ingenuous Hercules still made his sweetheart lower hers, and still gave the company cause for alarm.

They had considerable difficulty sending him back to his family. Once again it was necessary to call on the influence of the fair Saint-Yves; and the more she felt her power over him, the more she loved him. She made him leave, and was most upset to do so. Finally, when he had gone, the Abbé, who was not only Mlle de Saint-Yves's considerably older brother but also her guardian, decided to shield his ward from the eager attentions of this redoubtable lover. He went and consulted the magistrate who, still intending his son for the Abbé's sister, advised him to hand the poor girl over to a religious community. This was a drastic step. Put a girl who is not in love into a convent, and she will scream and shout; but do it to a girl who is in love, and whose sense of what is right is as strong as her feelings, and it is enough to drive her to despair.

The Ingenu, on his return to the Prior's house, related everything with his customary naivety. He came in for the same remonstrations, which had some effect on his mind and none at all on his senses. But next day, when he was about to return to his fair sweetheart's house to discuss the laws of nature and convention with her, His Honour the magistrate informed him with insolent glee that she was in a convent.

'Well, then,' he said, 'I'll go and discuss them with her in the convent.'

'That is not possible,' said the magistrate.

He explained to him at great length what a convent was, and how the word came from the Latin 'conventus', which means assembly; and the Huron failed to understand why he could not be admitted to the assembly. As soon as he learnt that this assembly was a sort of prison in which young girls were kept locked up, something horrible and quite unknown to the Hurons and the English, he became as furious as Hercules his patron was when Eurytus, King of Oechalia, a no less cruel person than the Abbé de Saint-Yves, refused him the fair Iola his daughter, a no less beautiful person than the Abbé's sister. He wanted to go and set fire to the convent and carry off his sweetheart or be burnt to death with her. Mlle de Kerkabon, horrified, gave up all hopes of seeing her nephew become a sub-deacon, and tearfully declared that he had the devil in him since he had been baptized.

CHAPTER 7

The Ingenu repels the English

THE Ingenu, plunged into dark and profound melancholy, went for a walk in the direction of the shore, with his double-barrelled shotgun over his shoulder and his big cutlass at his side, shooting the occasional bird from time to time and often tempted to shoot himself. But still he loved life, because of Mlle de Saint-Yves. One minute he would curse his uncle and aunt, the whole of Lower Brittany, and his baptism; the next minute he would bless them for having been instrumental in his meeting the one he loved. He would resolve firmly to go and burn down the convent, and then he would be brought up short at the prospect of setting fire to his sweetheart. The waters of the Channel are not more churned by the winds from east and west than was his heart by so many conflicting emotions.

He was striding along without knowing quite where he was going, when he heard the sound of a drum. He saw in the distance a whole crowd of people, of whom half were running towards the shore, and the other half running away.

There was much shouting on all sides. Curiosity and courage at once impelled him towards the place where all the noise was coming from. He reached it in a trice. The commander of the militia, who had supped with him at the Priory, recognized him immediately. He ran up to him with open arms.

'Look, it's the Ingenu! He'll fight for us.'

And the militiamen, who were dying of fright, took heart and also shouted:

'It's the Ingenu! It's the Ingenu!'

'Gentlemen,' he said, 'what's going on? Why are you in such a state? Have they put your sweethearts in a convent?'

Then a hundred voices shouted out all at once:

'Can't you see? The English are landing!'

'So?' replied the Huron. 'And fine fellows they are too. They never suggested making me a sub-deacon. They didn't run off with the one I love.'

The commander explained to him that the English had come to loot the Abbey of the Mountain, drink his uncle's wine, and perhaps carry off Mlle de Saint-Yves; that the small ship which had brought him to Brittany had only come to reconnoitre the coast; that the English were in the habit of carrying out acts of hostility without having declared war on the King of France; and that the province was in danger.

'Ah, well, if that's the case, they're breaking the laws of nature. Leave it to me. I've spent a long time among them, I can speak their language, I will talk to them. I don't believe they can be up to anything so wicked.'

During this conversation the English squadron was gradually getting nearer. Off rushed the Huron in their direction, jumped into a little boat, reached them, climbed aboard the admiral's ship, and asked if it were true that they had come to ravage this country without having properly declared war. The admiral and his crew all burst out laughing, gave him some punch, and sent him back from whence he came.

The Ingenu, piqued, now thought only of giving his former friends a good fight on the side of his compatriots and the good Prior. The local gentry were hastening to the scene from every corner: he joined forces with them. They had a few cannon: he loaded them, aimed them, and fired them one after another. The English came ashore: he ran up to them, killed three of them with his own bare hands, and even wounded the admiral who had laughed at him. His valour gave fresh heart to the whole militia: the English returned to their ships, and the whole shoreline echoed to the cries of victory.

'Long live the King! Long live the Ingenu!'

They were all embracing him, and everyone was eager to staunch the flow of blood from a few slight wounds he had received.

'Ah!' he was saying, 'if Mlle de Saint-Yves were here, she would put a compress on me.'

The magistrate, who had hidden in his cellar during the encounter, came to compliment him along with the others. But he was most surprised to hear Hercules the Ingenu saying to a dozen willing young men standing round him:

'Friends, saving the Abbey of the Mountain is nothing. There's a girl we must rescue.'

These words alone were enough to fire the young hot-heads with resolve. Other people were already flocking to follow the Ingenu, and they were all heading straight for the convent. If the magistrate had not informed the commander at once, and if people had not set off in pursuit of the jubilant horde, that would have been that. They took the Ingenu home to his uncle and aunt, who wept warm tears of tender joy over him.

'I can see you'll never be a sub-deacon, nor a prior,' his uncle said to him. 'You'll be an officer—an even braver one than my brother the captain, and probably just as poverty-stricken.'

And Mademoiselle kept crying and embracing him and saying: 'He'll get himself killed, just like my brother. It would be much better if he became a sub-deacon.'

The Ingenu, during the fight, had picked up a large purse full of guineas, which in all probability had been dropped by the admiral. He did not but doubt that with this purse he could buy up the whole of Lower Brittany and, more especially, make a great lady of Mlle de Saint-Yves. Everyone encouraged him to make the trip to Versailles, there to receive due reward for his services. The commander and the senior officers showered him with written testimonials. Uncle and aunt were in favour of their nephew making the journey: it ought not to be too difficult to be presented to the King, and that alone would give him prodigious standing in the province. The two good people added to the English purse a sizeable contribution from their own savings.

The Ingenu said to himself:

'When I see the King, I shall ask him for Mlle de Saint-Yves's hand in marriage, and I'm sure he won't refuse me.'

So he departed to the acclamation of the whole district, nearly hugged to death, bathed in his aunt's tears, blessed by his uncle, and asking to be remembered to the fair Saint-Yves.

CHAPTER 8

The Ingenu goes to court. He sups with Huguenots on the way

THE Ingenu took a stage-coach to Saumur, because at that time there was no other means of transport. When he reached Saumur, he was surprised to find the town almost deserted and to see several families moving out. He was told that six years previously Saumur had had a population of fifteen thousand inhabitants and that now there were not even six thousand. He did not fail to mention this during supper at his inn. There were several Protestants at the table. Some were complaining bitterly, some were shaking with anger, and some were weeping and saying: 'Nos dulcia linquimus arva, nos patriam fugimus'.* The Ingenu, who had no Latin, asked for an explanation of these words, which mean: 'We are leaving our sweet countryside, we are fleeing our homeland.'

'And why are you fleeing your homeland, gentlemen?'

'Because they want us to recognize the Pope.'

'And why would you not recognize him? Don't you have any godmothers you want to marry? Because I was told he was the one who could give permission for that.'

'Ah, sir, this Pope says he holds sway over the dominions of kings!'

'But what is your profession, gentlemen?'

'We are mostly drapers and mill-owners, sir.'

'If the Pope says he holds sway over your mills and your drapery, you do very well not to recognize him. But as far as the kings are concerned, it is entirely their affair. What are you getting mixed up in it for?'

Then a little man in black spoke up and gave a most knowledge-able account of the company's grievances. He talked about the Revocation of the Edict of Nantes with such passion and deplored with so much pathos the fate of fifty thousand refugee families, and fifty thousand more who had been converted by the dragoons,* that now it was the Ingenu's turn to shed tears.

'How is it then', he was saying, 'that so great a King, whose glorious renown reaches even the Hurons, can deprive himself like this of so many hearts who would have loved him and so many hands that would have served him?'

'It's because, like all great kings, he's not been told the truth,' said the man in black. 'He was led to believe that he had only to say the word and everyone would think as he does, and that he would make us change religion the way his musician Lully makes those rapid scene changes in his operas. Not only has he already lost five or six hundred thousand very useful subjects, but he is also making enemies for himself. And the present ruler of England, King William, has formed several regiments with these very same Frenchmen who would have fought for their monarch.

'Such a disastrous situation is all the more surprising when you think that the reigning Pope, for whom Louis XIV is sacrificing part of his people, is his declared enemy. For nine years now the pair of them have been having this violent quarrel. Things came to such a pitch that France finally wanted to see an end to the yoke which had been subjecting it to that particular foreigner for century after century, and above all to stop giving him money, that *primum mobile* of world affairs. It seems clear enough, therefore, that this King has been misled both about his own interests and about the extent of his power, and that they have even got at the magnanimity of his heart.'

The Ingenu, increasingly moved, asked who these Frenchmen were who were thus misleading a monarch so dear to the Hurons.

'It's the Jesuits,' he was told. 'Especially Father La Chaise, His Majesty's confessor.* One can only hope that God will one day punish them for it and that they will be hounded as we are being hounded. Can anyone be as unfortunate as we? Monseigneur de Louvois* sends Jesuits and dragoons after us on every side.'

'Right, gentlemen!' replied the Ingenu, who could contain himself no longer. 'I'm on my way to Versailles to receive due reward for my services. I will have a word with this Monsieur de Louvois. I am told he's the one who wages the wars—from his study, that is. I will see the King. I will make sure he has the truth. It is impossible not to acknowledge the truth of this matter once one has seen it for oneself. I shall soon be back to marry Mlle de Saint-Yves, and you're all invited to the wedding.'

These good people now took him for some grand nobleman who was travelling incognito by the stage-coach. Some took him for the King's fool.

There was at the table a Jesuit in disguise who acted as the reverend Father La Chaise's spy. He gave him an account of all this, and Father La Chaise informed Monseigneur de Louvois. The spy communicated in writing. The Ingenu and the letter arrived at Versailles at almost the same time.

CHAPTER 9

The arrival of the Ingenu at Versailles. His reception at court

THE Ingenu arrived in the kitchen courtyard in a 'chamberpot'.[1] He asked the chair-bearers when it was possible to see the King. The bearers laughed in his face, just as the English admiral had done. He treated them in the same way and hit them. They wanted to do the same back, and matters would have taken a bloody turn if an officer of the guard, a Breton gentleman, had not come past and dispersed the rabble.

'Sir,' the traveller said to him, 'you look like a decent sort to me. I am the nephew of the Prior of Our Lady of the Mountain. I have killed some Englishmen, and I have come to speak to the King. Please take me to his room.'

The guards officer, delighted to come across this good fellow from his home province who did not seem to be quite au fait with the ways of the court, told him that one did not speak to the King just like that and that you had to be presented by Monseigneur de Louvois.

'Well, take me to Monseigneur de Louvois then, and no doubt he will take me to His Majesty.'

'It is even more difficult to speak to Monseigneur de Louvois than it is to the King,' said the officer. 'But I will take you to M. Alexandre, who is senior official at the Ministry of War.* It's as good as talking to the Minister himself.'

So off they went to this M. Alexandre, the senior official. They were refused admittance: he was busy with a lady of the court and had left orders to let no one in.

'Oh, well,' said the guards officer, 'no harm done. Let's go and see M. Alexandre's senior official. It's as good as talking to M. Alexandre himself.'

The Huron, quite baffled, followed him. Together they waited for half an hour in a small antechamber.

'What is all this?' said the Ingenu. 'Is everyone round here unavailable? One has more chance of fighting the English in Lower

[1] This is a means of conveyance from Paris to Versailles which resembles a small covered tumbril.

Brittany than one has of getting to see people on business in Versailles.'

He passed the time by telling his compatriot all about his amours. But the chiming of the hour summoned the officer back to his post. They promised to meet again the next day, and the Ingenu remained a further half hour in the antechamber thinking about Mlle de Saint-Yves, and about the difficulty of speaking to kings and senior officials.

Eventually this key man appeared.

'Sir,' said the Ingenu, 'if I'd waited as long before repelling the English as you've made me wait for my audience, they would now be laying waste Lower Brittany to their heart's content.'

This remark made an impression on the official. At length he said to the man from Brittany:

'What do you want?'

'Reward,' said he, 'and here's my evidence.'

He laid all his papers out in front of him. The official read them and said that he would probably be given leave to buy a commission.

'Me! Give someone money because I repelled the English! Pay for the right to get killed for you while you sit here calmly giving audiences? You must be joking. I want a company of cavalry, and for nothing. I want the King to get Mlle de Saint-Yves out of her convent and to give her to me in marriage. And I want to speak to the King on behalf of fifty thousand families I mean to return to him. In short, I want to make myself useful. Give me a job, and pay me an advance.'

'What is your name, Mr Loudmouth?'

'Aha,' retorted the Ingenu. 'So you haven't read my papers, then? So that's the way things are, is it? My name is Hercules de Kerkabon. I have been baptized, I am staying at the Blue Dial, and I shall report you to the King.'

The official concluded, like the people at Saumur, that he was not quite right in the head, and did not take much notice.

That same day the reverend Father La Chaise, confessor to Louis XIV, had received the letter from his spy accusing one Kerkabon, a Breton, of being a Huguenot sympathizer and criticizing the behaviour of the Jesuits. M. de Louvois, for his part, had received a letter from the magistrate with all the questions, who depicted the Ingenu as a good-for-nothing who went round wanting to burn down convents and abduct young girls.

The Ingenu, after a walk in the gardens of Versailles, which he found boring, and after dining in a manner befitting a true Huron and Lower Breton, had gone to bed in the fond hope of seeing the King the next day, obtaining Mlle de Saint-Yves's hand in marriage, being given at least one company of cavalry, and stopping the persecution of the Huguenots. He was busy lulling himself to sleep with these pleasant prospects when the constabulary entered his room. The first thing they did was to seize his double-barrelled shotgun and his large cutlass.

They made a note of what money he had on him and led him off to the castle built by Charles V, son of Jean II, next to the Rue Saint-Antoine at the Porte des Tournelles.

Just how surprised the Ingenu was as they made their way I leave it to you to imagine. At first he thought it was all a dream. He still felt rather numbed. Then, all of a sudden, carried away by a fit of rage that doubled his strength, he grabbed two of his escorts by the throat, threw them out of the carriage-door, and hurled himself after them, dragging the third, who was trying to restrain him, along behind. He fell to the ground in the attempt, was caught and bundled back into the carriage.

'Well there you are,' he said to himself, 'that's what you get for running the English out of Lower Brittany! What would you say, fair Saint-Yves, if you could see me now?'

At length they reached the quarters which had been allocated to him. Silently they carried him into the room where he was to be locked up, as one bears a corpse into a cemetery. This room was already occupied by an old solitary from Port-Royal called Gordon,* who had been languishing there for the past two years.

'Here you are,' said the chief myrmidon, 'I've brought you some company.'

Whereupon they shot the enormous bolts on the thick door which was covered with broad iron bars. And so the two captives remained, cut off from the entire universe.

CHAPTER 10

The Ingenu imprisoned in the Bastille with a Jansenist

M. GORDON was a sprightly and serene old man who knew two great things: how to put up with adversity and how to comfort the unfortunate. He advanced towards his companion with an open and compassionate expression, and said as he embraced him:

'Whoever you may be, you who have come to share my tomb, rest assured that I shall always subordinate my own needs to the easing of your torment in this infernal abyss into which we are both fallen. Let us worship the Providence that has led us into it, let us suffer in peace, and let us hope.'

These words had the same effect on the Ingenu's soul as those English drops that bring a dying man back to life and make him reopen his eyes in surprise.*

After the preliminary courtesies were over, Gordon did not press him to reveal the cause of his misfortune but, by the gentleness of his words, combined with the interest that two unfortunates naturally take in one another, made him want to open his heart and unburden himself of all that weighed upon him. But the Ingenu could not quite put his finger on the reason for his misfortune. It all seemed to him like an effect without a cause, and the worthy Gordon was just as bewildered as he.

'God must have great things in store for you', said the Jansenist to the Huron, 'to have brought you from Lake Ontario to England and France, to have had you baptized in Lower Brittany, and to have placed you here that you might be saved.'

'To tell you the truth,' replied the Ingenu, 'I think the devil alone has had a hand in my destiny. My fellow Americans would never have treated me in the barbarous way I've been treated here. They simply wouldn't know how. People call them "savages". They are rough men of principle, whereas the people here are smooth villains. It's been rather a surprise, I must say, to have come all the way from another world only to be put behind bars with a priest in this one. But then I think of the enormous number of people who leave one half of the world to go and get killed in the other, or who are shipwrecked on the way and eaten by the fish. I don't see what God has been gracious enough to have in store for all of them.'

Dinner was served to them through a grating. The conversation turned on Providence, *lettres de cachet*,* and how not to fall victim to the various kinds of mishap to which everyone in the world is prone.

'I've been here two years now,' said the old man, 'with only myself and my books to comfort me. I haven't had a single moment's ill humour.'

'Ah, M. Gordon,' exclaimed the Ingenu, 'what you mean is, you're not in love with your godmother. If you knew Mlle de Saint-Yves as I do, you would be in despair.'

As he said this, he could not hold back the tears, and he felt a little easier in himself as a result.

'But why', he said, 'do tears bring relief? It seems to me that they ought to have the opposite effect.'

'My son, everything about us is physical,' said the kindly old man. 'All secretion is good for the body, and everything which relieves the body relieves the soul. We are the machines of Providence.'

The Ingenu who, as we have said many times, possessed deep reserves of good sense, thought carefully about this idea, the germ of which somehow seemed to exist within him already. Having done so, he asked his companion why his machine had been behind bars for the last two years.

'Because of efficient grace,'* replied Gordon. 'I am considered to be a Jansenist. I knew Arnauld and Nicole.* The Jesuits persecuted us. We believe that the Pope is simply a bishop like any other, and that's why Father La Chaise obtained an order from the King, his penitent, to deprive me, without any of the due processes of law, of man's most precious possession: my freedom.'

'It's very strange,' said the Ingenu. 'Everyone I meet who has suffered a misfortune has suffered it because of the Pope. As for your efficient grace, I can honestly say I don't understand a thing about it. But I do consider it to be by the great grace of God that I have ended up in my misfortune with a man like you, who is able to offer my heart comfort of a kind I never thought to feel again.'

Each day the conversation became more interesting and more instructive. The two cell mates were becoming soul mates. The old man knew a lot, and the young man wanted to learn a lot. By the end of a month he was studying geometry, and lapping it up. Gordon made him read Rohault's *Physics*,* which was still all the rage, and he had the good sense to find nothing but uncertainties in it.

Then he read the first volume of the *Enquiry after Truth*.* This new source of illumination enlightened him.

'What!' he said. 'Our imagination and our senses distort things to that extent! You mean our ideas are not formed by objects, and we cannot conceive them for ourselves unaided!'

When he had read the second volume, he was no longer as happy with the work, and he concluded that it is easier to demolish than to construct.

His fellow inmate, astonished that a young ignoramus should think something that should only occur to trained intellects, formed a high opinion of his intelligence and grew even fonder of him.

'This Malebranche of yours,' said the Ingenu one day, 'seems to me to have written one half of his book with his reason and the other half with his imagination and prejudices.'

A few days later Gordon asked him:

'So what do you think about the soul, and the way ideas come to us, and about the will, and grace, and free will?'

'Nothing,' the Ingenu rejoined. 'If I did think anything, it would be that we are in the power of the Eternal Being, just as the stars and the elements are; that he controls everything we do and are, that we are little cogs in the huge machine of which he is the soul; and that he acts in accordance with general laws and not as the fancy takes him. That much only, I think, we can understand. The rest is a dark void as far as I'm concerned.'

'But, my son, that would make God responsible for sin!'

'But, Father, your efficient grace would make God responsible for sin, too. For it is certain that all those to whom this grace was refused would be living in a state of sin, and whoever delivers us unto evil, is he not responsible for that evil?'

Such simplicity put the good fellow at a considerable loss. He had the feeling that his attempts to extricate himself from this morass were to no avail, and he piled up such a mountain of words that appeared to make sense and yet made none at all (rather like the doctrine of physical premotion)* that the Ingenu felt sorry for him. The question obviously involved the origins of good and evil, and so poor old Gordon had to go through the lot—Pandora's box, Ormuzd's egg being pierced by Ahriman, the enmity between Typhon and

Osiris, and lastly original sin. Thus did they grope in the dark: and not once did they see eye to eye. But in the end all this nonsensical speculation about the soul took their minds off their own wretchedness, and by a curious twist the host of calamities befalling the universe reduced their sense of their own troubles. They did not venture to bemoan their own lot when suffering was everywhere.

But in the calm of the night the thought of fair Saint-Yves banished all idea of ethics and metaphysics from her lover's mind. He would wake up, his eyes wet with tears, and the old Jansenist would forget about his efficient grace and the Abbé de Saint-Cyran and Jansenius* the better to comfort a young man he believed to be in a state of mortal sin.

After their reading and their discussions they would talk again about the things that had happened to them, and after they had talked about them to no purpose, they would then read, together or separately. The young man's mental powers grew steadily stronger. In particular he could have gone far with his mathematics, if it had not been for the distractions of Mlle de Saint-Yves.

He read some histories: they depressed him. The world seemed too full of villainy and human misery. For indeed history is but a tableau of every crime and catastrophe. On such a large stage the vast majority of innocent, peaceable human beings continually fade into the background. The leading characters are invariably depraved men of ambition. It is as if history only succeeds if it is like tragedy, which palls if it is not enlivened by passion and foul deeds and great disasters. Clio, no less than Melpomene, has need of a dagger.

Although the history of France is full of horrors, just like every other country's, it struck him nevertheless as being so revolting in its beginning, so dull in its middle, and ultimately so paltry, not excepting the age of Henry IV, as being so consistently lacking in major landmarks and so much a stranger to all the fine discoveries that have distinguished other nations, that he found himself having to fend off boredom if he were to read all the detail involved in the obscure calamities which had been packed into this one tiny corner of the world.

Gordon thought the same. They would both laugh with sheer pity when it came to the rulers of Fezensac, and Fesansaquet, and Astarac.* Studying them would, indeed, do no one any good—except perhaps their heirs, if they had had any. The great age of the

Roman republic made the Ingenu indifferent for a time to the rest of the world. He was full of the spectacle of a victorious Rome bestowing its laws on other nations. He would wax lyrical in contemplation of this people whose one guiding principle for seven hundred years had been an enthusiasm for freedom and glory.

So the days passed, and the weeks, and the months; and he would have thought himself happy in this house of despair had he not been in love.

His good nature was such that he still felt upset about the Prior of Our Lady of the Mountain and the sensitive Mlle de Kerkabon. 'What will they think when they don't hear from me?' he would often ask himself. 'They will take me for an ungrateful wretch.'

The very idea tormented him. He felt much sorrier for those who loved him than he did for himself.

CHAPTER 11

How the Ingenu develops his talents

READING nurtures the soul, and an enlightened friend brings it solace. Our captive was now enjoying these two advantages, not having hitherto known of their existence.

'I would almost be tempted to believe in metamorphosis,' he said, 'for I have been changed from a brute into a man.'

He built up a library for himself with a part of the money he was allowed to spend. His friend encouraged him to set his thoughts down in writing. Here is what he wrote about ancient history:

I imagine that the nations of the world were for a long time like me, that they came late to education, and that for centuries they attended only to the present moment with scarce a thought for the past and none for the future. I travelled five or six hundred leagues across Canada, and I never once saw a single monument. No one there has the faintest idea what their great-grandfather did. Is not man in his natural state like that? The human species of this continent seems to me superior to that of the other. It has added to the sum total of its being through the arts and through the pursuit of knowledge. Is this because it is a bearded species and God has denied a beard to the Americans? I do not believe so, for I see that the Chinese have almost no beard and that they have been cultivating the arts for more than five thousand years. In fact, if their records stretch back more than four thousand years, then the nation itself must have been unified and flourishing for more than fifty centuries.

One thing in particular strikes me about this ancient history of China's, which is that almost everything in it is believable and belongs to the real world. I marvel at it for being devoid of marvels.

Why have all other nations given themselves fabulous origins? The ancient chroniclers of French history, who are not in fact so ancient, have the French descending from one Francus, son of Hector. The Romans used to say that they sprang from a Phrygian, even though not one single word in their language had the slightest connexion with the language of Phrygia. Their gods had spent ten thousand years in Egypt, and their devils had been in Scythia, where they had given birth to the Huns. All I can find before Thuycidides are various unlikely tales reminiscent of the *Amadis* romances, and much less amusing; nothing but apparitions, and oracles, and prodigies, and sorcery, and metamorphoses, and interpreted dreams, and all of it deciding the fate of nations, from the greatest empire to the tiniest state. Sometimes animals speak, sometimes they are worshipped. Sometimes gods are transformed into human beings, sometimes human beings are transformed into gods.* Ah, if we must have fables, let them at least be the emblems of truth! I love philosophers' fables, and I laugh at children's. I hate those of charlatans.

One day he came across a history of the Emperor Justinian. This told how some dimwits in Constantinople had issued an edict, in very bad Greek, against the greatest leader of the age because this splendid man had uttered the following words in the heat of discussion: 'Truth shines with its own light, and the minds of men will not be enlightened by the flames around the stake.' The ignorant divines maintained that this proposition was heretical, indeed reeked of heresy, and that the contrary axiom was catholic, universal, and Greek: 'The minds of men will be enlightened only by the flames around the stake, and truth cannot shine with its own light.' The theological establishment condemned several of the leader's statements like this, each with an edict.

'What!' cried the Ingenu, 'edicts from people like that!'

'Well no, not edicts,' Gordon replied. 'In fact counter-edicts, which everyone in Constantinople laughed at, not least the Emperor. He was a wise ruler, and he had managed to reduce these dunderheads in cap and gown to being able to do nothing but good. He knew how these gentlemen, along with several other crook-bearers, had exhausted the patience of his predecessors as Emperor with their counter-edicts on rather more serious issues.'

'He was quite right,' said the Ingenu. 'One must lend one's support to the holy men and then keep them in their place.'

He wrote down many other thoughts, which left old Gordon thoroughly aghast.

'What!' he said to himself. 'To have spent fifty years of my life educating myself and to fear that I may never acquire the natural good sense of this child who's almost a savage! I'm afraid that I may simply have been erecting painstaking defences around my own prejudices. He just listens to the simple voice of nature.'

The good fellow had a few of those little books of criticism, or periodical pamphlets, in which people who are incapable of producing anything at all denigrate the work of those who can, in which the Visés of this world insult the Racines, and the Faydits the Fénelons.* The Ingenu looked through some of them.

'These people are just like certain types of gnat', he said, 'that lay their eggs up thoroughbreds' backsides. It doesn't stop them racing.'

The two philosophers scarcely deigned even to glance over this excrement of literature.

Presently they read the rudiments of astronomy together. The Ingenu had some globes brought: this great spectacle held him entranced.

'How hard it is', he would say, 'to be getting to know about the sky just when the right to look at it has been taken from me. Jupiter and Saturn are orbiting away in those vast spaces, millions of suns are casting light on to millions of worlds, and here, in this little corner of the Earth I've landed up in, there are living beings depriving me— me, a sighted, thinking being—of all the other worlds I could be seeing, and of the one God had me born into! The light that was created for the whole universe is lost to me. They did not keep it from me in those Northern parts where I spent my youth and early childhood. But for you, Gordon, I would now be in the darkness of the void.'

CHAPTER 12

What the Ingenu thinks about plays

THE young Ingenu was like one of those sturdy saplings which, having begun life in poor soil, soon spread their roots and branches when transplanted to more favourable ground. The extraordinary thing was that a prison should have been that ground.

Among the books with which the two captives occupied their leisure were some collections of poetry, some Greek tragedies in translation, and one or two French plays. The love poetry brought both pleasure and pain to the soul of the Ingenu. Every line spoke to him of his beloved Saint-Yves. The fable of the *Two Pigeons** rent his heart: he was very far from being able to return to his own dovecot.

Molière he found spellbinding. Through him he learnt about the Parisian way of life and about human nature in general.

'Which of his comedies do you prefer?'

'That's easy. *Tartuffe*.'

'I think so too,' said Gordon. 'It was a Tartuffe who threw me into this cell, and Tartuffes may well have been behind your misfortunes. How do you find these Greek tragedies?'

'All right for the Greeks,' said the Ingenu.

But when he read *Iphigénie*, *Phèdre*, *Andromaque*, and *Athalie*,* he was beside himself. He sighed, he wept, he learnt them by heart without even meaning to.

'Read *Rodogune*,'* Gordon told him. 'It is said to be the greatest play ever written. The rest of them, which you enjoyed so much, pale in comparison.'

On reading the very first page the young man told him:

'This is not by the same person.'

'How can you tell?'

'I don't quite know yet. But this verse doesn't do anything for me, not for my ear, nor for my heart.'

'Oh, don't worry about the verse,' replied Gordon.

The Ingenu objected:

'Why have it then?'

Having read the play through very carefully and with no other end in view but that of enjoying it, he looked at his friend in dry-eyed astonishment, not knowing what to say. Finally, when pressed to give an account of what he had felt, this is the answer he gave:

'I scarcely understood the beginning, I was revolted by the middle, and I found the last scene very moving, though barely credible. I did not find myself getting involved with any of the characters, and I can't remember more than about twenty lines of it, I who remember them all when I like them.'

'Nevertheless that play is considered the best we have.'

'If that is so,' he replied, 'perhaps it's like the many people who do not deserve the positions they occupy. But, well, this is all a matter of taste. Mine must be not properly developed yet. I may be wrong. But, as you know, I'm rather accustomed to saying what I think, or rather what I feel. I suspect that illusion and fashion and personal whim often have a lot to do with people's judgements. I said what I said with real life in mind. It may be that my idea of real life is far from perfect. But sometimes it may also be that the majority of people don't much bother to judge according to real life.'

Then he recited some lines from *Iphigénie*, which he was full of, and although he did not declaim very well, he put so much real and deep feeling into it that he reduced the old Jansenist to tears. He read *Cinna* next. He did not weep, but he did admire.

'What does make me cross, though,' he said, 'is the way this splendid girl keeps accepting rolls of coins every day from the very man she is trying to have assassinated. My advice to her would be what I read in *Les Plaideurs*: "for goodness sake, give the money back!" '

CHAPTER 13

The fair Saint-Yves goes to Versailles

WHILE our unfortunate was finding more to enlighten him than to console him; while his natural gifts, which had been stifled for so long, were beginning to blossom with such rapidity and vigour; and while nature, as it perfected itself within him, was avenging him for the outrages of fortune, what of the Prior and his good sister, and of Saint-Yves, the fair recluse? After a month they began to be worried, and by the third they were deep in despair. False conjectures and ill-founded rumours gave cause for alarm. At the end of six months they thought he was dead. Eventually M. and Mlle de Kerkabon learnt from a letter a guards officer had sent to Brittany some time previously that a young man who sounded like the Ingenu had arrived at Versailles one evening, but that he had been abducted during the night, and that nothing had been heard of him since.

'Oh, dear,' said Mlle de Kerkabon, 'I fear our nephew must have done something silly and got himself into trouble. He is young and from Lower Brittany. He has no way of knowing how one should behave at court. Brother dear, I have never seen either Versailles or Paris. Now's our opportunity. Perhaps we may even find our poor nephew. He is our brother's son. It is our duty to rescue him. Who knows, we may yet make a sub-deacon of him, when his youthful high spirits have moderated a little. He had a considerable aptitude for study. Do you remember how he used to argue about the Old and New Testaments? We are responsible for his soul. We had him baptized. His dear beloved Saint-Yves does nothing but spend her days weeping over him. We really must go to Paris. If he's hiding in one of those dreadful houses of pleasure I've heard so much about, we'll get him out.'

The Prior was moved by what his sister said. He went off to find the Bishop of Saint-Malo, who had baptized the Huron, and asked him for his support and advice. The prelate agreed to the journey. He gave the Prior letters of introduction to Father La Chaise, the King's confessor and the highest dignitary in the land, for Harlay, the Archbishop of Paris, and for Bossuet, the Bishop of Meaux.

At length brother and sister set out. But when they reached Paris, they found themselves completely lost, as if in a vast labyrinth without thread or means of egress. Their resources were limited. They had to hire carriages every day to carry out their search, but the search was fruitless.

The Prior called on the reverend Father La Chaise: he was with Mlle du Tron and unable to grant an audience to any prior. He went to the Archbishop's door: this prelate was in conference with the beautiful Mme de Lesdiguières on church business. He hurried to the Bishop of Meaux's country-house: he and Mlle de Mauléon were carrying out an investigation into Mme de Guyon's notion of mystical love.* He did, however, finally manage to speak to these last two prelates. Both of them told him that they could not become involved with the Prior's nephew, given that he was not a sub-deacon.

In the end he went to the Jesuits. One of this fraternity welcomed him with open arms, assured him that he had always held him in particularly high regard, not that he had ever met him, and swore blind that the Society had always had a soft spot for the people of Lower Brittany.

'But this nephew of yours,' he said, 'he wouldn't by any unfortunate chance be a Huguenot, would he?'

'Absolutely not, reverend father.'

'Nor a Jansenist?'

'I can assure Your Reverence that he is scarcely even a Christian. It's about eleven months since we baptized him.'

'Splendid, splendid. We will take care of him. Do you have a substantial living?'

'Oh, very modest, and my nephew does cost us a great deal.'

'Any Jansenists in the vicinity? You must be very careful, my dear Prior. They're even more dangerous than the Huguenots and the atheists.'

'Not a single one, reverend father. We don't know anything about any Jansenism at Our Lady of the Mountain.'

'So much the better. Off you go, there is nothing I wouldn't do for you.'

He dismissed the Prior with a fond farewell, and thought no more about him.

Time passed, and the Prior and his good sister were beginning to despair.

Meanwhile the cursed magistrate was urging the marriage of his great booby of a son to the fair Saint-Yves, who had been let out of the convent for the purpose. She still loved her dear godson every bit as much as she detested the husband that was on offer. The affront of having been put in a convent added to the fervour of her love. Being ordered to marry the magistrate's son was the final straw. Regrets, fond affection, and disgust seethed in her soul. Love, as everyone knows, is considerably more resourceful and bold in a young girl than is friendship in an old prior and an aunt turned forty-five. Moreover, she had learnt much in the convent from all the romances she had read on the sly.

The fair Saint-Yves remembered the letter that a guards officer had written home to Lower Brittany, and which had been the talk of the province. She resolved to go herself and make enquiries at

Versailles, to throw herself at ministerial feet if her 'husband' was in prison, as they said he was, and to obtain justice for him. Something gave her the secret inkling that at court a pretty girl is never refused: but she had yet to learn at what cost.

Her decision made, she felt much better. She calmed down, stopped rebuffing her idiot fiancé, welcomed the detestable future father-in-law, showed warmth to her brother, and was all sweetness and light throughout the household. Then, on the day appointed for the ceremony, at four o'clock in the morning, she left home in secret, with all her smaller wedding presents and everything else she had managed to lay her hands on. She had arranged things so carefully that she was already ten leagues off when they first entered her room towards midday. The surprise and consternation were considerable. The interrogating magistrate asked more questions that day than he had done all week. The bridegroom looked even sillier than ever. The Abbé de Saint-Yves angrily decided to rush off in pursuit of his sister. The magistrate and his son wanted to go with him. And thus did destiny bring to Paris almost the entire population of this canton of Lower Brittany.

The fair Saint-Yves had a shrewd idea that they would follow her. She was on horseback and, without giving the game away, she asked every passing despatch-rider if he had seen a fat abbé, a preposterous magistrate, and a young booby making haste along the road to Paris. Having learnt on the third day that they were not far behind, she took a different road, and was clever and lucky enough to reach Versailles while they were vainly searching for her in Paris.

But how should she proceed in Versailles? Young and beautiful, without counsel or support, unknown to anyone, exposed to dangers of every sort, how could she dare seek out an officer of the guard? She thought of consulting a low-ranking Jesuit. There were all kinds of them ready to cater for people of every station, rather in the same way as God, it used to be said, has provided different forms of nourishment for every species of animal. From Him the King had his own confessor, whom all those who were seeking church livings referred to as the 'Head of the Gallican Church'. Then came the confessors to the princesses. Ministers didn't have any: they were not so foolish. There were Jesuits for the junior officers in the royal household, and especially for the chambermaids, through whom their mistresses' secrets were known (a not insubstantial undertaking). The fair Saint-Yves consulted one of this latter category, who was known as Father All-things-to-all-men. She said confession to him, told him what had happened to her, about her situation and the danger she was in, and begged him to secure lodgings for her with some good lady of devout character who would keep her from temptation.

Father All-things took her to see one of his most loyal penitents, the wife of a royal cupbearer. From the moment she arrived she set about winning this woman's trust and friendship. She made enquiries about the Breton guards officer and requested him to come and see her. Learning from him that her lover had been abducted after speaking to a senior official, she rushed off to see this senior official. The sight of a beautiful woman melted his heart, for it must be allowed that God made woman solely that man might be tamed.

Duly mollified, the bureaucrat told her everything.

'Your lover has been in the Bastille for nearly a year and, but for you, might have spent the rest of his life there.'

The tender-hearted Saint-Yves fainted. When she had recovered herself, the official said:

'I lack the influence to do good. The only power I have is sometimes to do evil. Take my advice and go and see Monsieur de Saint-Pouange. He does both good and evil, and is the favourite cousin of Monseigneur de Louvois. This minister has two bosom companions. M. de Saint-Pouange is one. Mme du Belloy* is the other, but she is not in Versailles at the moment. So all you have to do is win over the protector I have indicated.'

Fair Saint-Yves, torn between partial joy and thorough anguish, between faint hope and sorry apprehension, pursued by her brother and adoring her lover, wiping away the tears and shedding yet more, trembling with exhaustion and taking fresh heart, hurried away to see M. de Saint-Pouange.

CHAPTER 14

The Ingenu's intellectual progress

THE Ingenu was making rapid progress in his studies, particularly in the study of man. The reason for this rapid intellectual progress lay as much in his education as a savage as in the natural cast of his personality. For, having learnt nothing at all in his childhood, he had not acquired any prejudices. His thinking, not having been warped by error, remained as straight as ever. He saw things as they are, whereas the ideas with which we are imbued during childhood make us see things our whole lives through as they are not.

'Your persecutors are abominable men,' he said to his friend Gordon, 'and I pity you for the way you have been oppressed. But I also pity you for being a Jansenist. All sects seem to me to be assemblies in error. Tell me, are there sects in geometry?'

'No, my dear boy,' said kind Gordon with a sigh. 'All men are agreed on the truth once it has been demonstrated, but they are only too divided about truths of a more obscure kind.'

'About false truths, you mean. If there had been one single truth buried away in that heap of arguments you've all been rehashing for so many centuries, it would doubtless have been discovered by now. And the whole universe would have been agreed on that one point at least. If this truth were necessary, as the sun is to the earth, it would shine forth like the sun, too. It is an absurdity, an outrage against the human race, an attack on the Infinite and Supreme Being, to say: "There is one truth essential to man, and God has hidden it".'*

Everything that this ignorant young man said on the basis of what nature had taught him made a deep impression on the mind of the unfortunate old scholar.

'Might it really be', he cried, 'that I have been making myself wretched for nothing? I am much more certain of my wretchedness than I am about efficient grace. I have spent my days debating the freedom of God and mankind, but I have lost my own. Neither St Augustine nor St Prosper will save me from this particular abyss.'

The Ingenu finally spoke his mind to the full:

'Shall I be absolutely frank with you? People who get themselves persecuted over these pointless arguments seem to me to be lacking in wisdom. Those who do the persecuting seem to me to be monsters.'

The two captives were absolutely in agreement about the injustice of their captivity.

'I am a hundred times more to be pitied than you,' the Ingenu would say. 'I was born as free as the air. There were two things I lived for, freedom and the object of my love. Then they come and take both of them away from me. Here we two are in irons, not knowing why we are here and not being able to ask. I lived among the Hurons for twenty years. People call them barbarians because they take revenge on their enemies, but they have never oppressed their friends. I had hardly set foot in France before I was shedding blood for it. I have quite possibly saved a whole province, and the only thanks I get is being stuck in this living tomb, where I'd have died in a frenzy of rage if it hadn't been for you. Doesn't this country have any laws?! People are condemned without a hearing! It's not like this in England. Ah, it wasn't the English I should have been fighting against.'

His increasingly philosophical turn of mind was thus unable to quell his inner nature, which had suffered this infringement of its foremost right; and it allowed full rein to his just anger. His companion did not contradict him.

Absence always strengthens the love that goes unsatisfied, and philosophy does not diminish it. The Ingenu spoke as often about his dear Saint-Yves as about ethics and metaphysics. The purer his feelings became, the more he loved. He read some of the latest novels. He found few that depicted the state of his soul. He felt that his heart always felt more than what he read about.

'Ah, all that most of these writers give you', he would say, 'is just wit and clever technique.'

And so in time the good Jansenist priest gradually became the confidant of these feelings of love. Previously he had known love only as a sin one accuses oneself of in confession. He now came to know it as a sentiment that is as noble as it is tender, that can uplift the soul as well as soften it, and that can sometimes even give rise to virtues. In the end, wonder of wonders, a Huron was converting a Jansenist.

CHAPTER 15

Fair Saint-Yves resists some propositions of a delicate kind

So the fair Saint-Yves, yet more loving than her lover, went to see M. de Saint-Pouange, accompanied by the friend with whom she was lodging, their faces well hidden by their hoods. The first thing she saw at the door was her brother, the Abbé de Saint-Yves, coming out. She found this unnerving, but her devout friend reassured her.

'It is precisely because someone has spoken against you that you yourself must speak. Make no mistake: round here accusers are always right if one isn't quick to confound them. Besides, if I am not mistaken, your presence here will have more effect than your brother's words.'

Give a woman who is passionately in love the slightest encouragement, and she is fearless. La Saint-Yves went to her audience. Her youth, her charms, and her love-filled eyes moistened with a few tears, attracted everyone's attention. Every courtier in the under-ministry momentarily forsook the idol of power to contemplate that of beauty. Saint-Pouange showed her into a private room. She spoke with feeling and elegance. Saint-Pouange was touched. She trembled. He offered reassurance.

'Come back this evening,' he told her. 'Your business deserves to be considered and discussed at leisure. There are too many people about at the moment. Audiences are rather rushed affairs. I must go over all this with you in more detail.'

Then, having complimented her on her beauty and on her fine feelings, he advised her to come at seven o'clock that evening.

She did not fail. The devout friend came with her again, but remained behind in the reception room and read the *Christian Pedagogue* while Saint-Pouange and fair Saint-Yves were in the private room at the rear.

'Do you really believe, mademoiselle,' he began by saying, 'that your brother came here to ask me for a *lettre de cachet* against you? To tell you the truth, I'd rather issue one to have him sent back to Lower Brittany.'

'Alas then, sir, there must be a very liberal supply of *lettres de cachet* in your offices if people come asking for them from the remotest corners of the kingdom just as if they were pensions. It is far from my intention to ask for one against my brother. I have many grounds for complaint where he is concerned, but I respect people's free-dom—and I am asking for that of a man I wish to marry, a man to whom the King owes the defence of a province, a man who can be of service to him, and who is the son of an officer killed in his service. What is he accused of? How can he have been so cruelly treated without a hearing?'

With this the under-secretary showed her the letter from the Jesuit spy and the perfidious magistrate.

'What! Can there be such monsters as this is the world! So that's how they intend to force me to marry that ridiculous son of that ridiculous and evil man! So this is the kind of evidence you rely on here to decide the fate of citizens!'

She threw herself to her knees and sobbed for the freedom of the brave man who adored her. In this position her charms appeared to their very greatest advantage. She was so beautiful that Saint-Pouange, losing all sense of shame, insinuated that she could have what she wanted if she would begin by granting him the first fruits of that which she was saving for her lover. Saint-Yves, aghast and deeply embarrassed, pretended for a long time not to understand him. He would have to speak more plainly. A word let slip at first with discretion led to one of a more forceful kind, which was followed by another still more explicit. Not only was the cancellation of the *lettre de cachet* offered, but also various rewards—money, hon-ours, establishments—and the more that was promised, the more did the desire not to be refused gain in strength.

Saint-Yves was crying and gasping for breath, slumped on a sofa and hardly able to believe what she was seeing and hearing. Saint-Pouange, for his part, threw himself to his knees. He was not unattractive himself and might not have caused such fright in a heart less prepossessed. But Saint-Yves adored her lover and thought it a horrible crime to serve him by betraying him. Saint-Pouange renewed his entreaties and his promises. In the end she had so turned his head that he told her it was the only way of securing the release of this man in whom she was taking such a violent and tender interest. This strange conversation continued for some time. The devout lady reading her *Christian Pedagogue* in the antechamber was thinking to herself:

'My God! It's been two hours now. What can they be doing in there? Monseigneur de Saint-Pouange has never given an audience as long as this before. Perhaps he's refused all this poor girl's requests, since clearly she must still be pleading with him.'

At last her companion emerged from the study, totally distracted, unable to speak, and deep in thought about the character of great and not-so-great men, who so casually sacrifice a man's freedom and a woman's honour.

She did not say a word on the way home. As soon as they reached her friend's house, she let go and poured out the whole story.

The devout woman made great signs of the cross:

'My dear friend, tomorrow we must go and consult Father All-things, our director of conscience. He has much influence with Monseigneur de Saint-Pouange. He is confessor to several maids in the household. He is a pious and accommodating man who is also director of conscience to ladies of quality. Put yourself in his hands, that's what I always do. I've never had cause to regret it. We poor women need a man to show us the way.'

'All right, then, my dear friend. Tomorrow I shall go and see Father All-things.'

CHAPTER 16

She consults a Jesuit

As soon as the fair, disconsolate Saint-Yves was with her confessor, she confided to him that a powerful and lustful man was offering to release her legal intended from prison, and that he was asking a high price for his services; that she found an infidelity of this kind horribly repugnant; and that, if it had simply been a question of her own life, she would sacrifice it rather than succumb.

'What an abominable sinner!' said Father All-things. 'You really ought to tell me the name of this villain. For it must surely be some Jansenist or other. I will denounce him to His Reverence Father La Chaise, and he will have him thrown into the very same cell as the dear person you are to marry is in now.'

The poor girl, after much hesitation and deep misgivings, finally named Saint-Pouange.

'Monseigneur de Saint-Pouange!' cried the Jesuit. 'Ah, my dear girl, that's quite different. He is a cousin of the greatest minister we have ever had, a man of parts, a defender of the good cause, a good Christian. He cannot have had such an idea. You must have misunderstood.'

'Ah, Father, I understood only too well. I am lost whatever I do. I can but choose between misery and shame. Either my lover remains buried alive, or I render myself unfit to live. I cannot let him perish, and I cannot save him.'

Father All-things tried to calm her with these sweet words:

'First, my daughter, never use the word "lover". It has something worldly about it which might offend God. Say "my husband", for even though he isn't yet, you regard him as such, and nothing could be more respectable.

'Secondly, although he is your husband by intention and in your hopes, he isn't your husband yet. So you wouldn't be committing adultery, which is an enormous sin that one must always avoid as far as possible.

'Thirdly, when the intentions are pure, no blame or malice attaches to the action. And nothing could be purer than wanting to free your husband.

'Fourthly, there are marvellous examples in holy antiquity which you can use to guide your conduct. St Augustine records that during the proconsulship of Septimius Acindynus, in the year 340 of our salvation, a poor man, unable to render unto Caesar that which was due unto Caesar, was condemned to death, as is just, despite the maxim: "Where there is nothing, the king's rights are as nothing." At issue was a pound of gold. The condemned man had a wife upon whom God had bestowed both beauty and prudence. A rich old man promised to give the lady a pound of gold, and even more, on condition that he might commit this foul sin with her. The lady did not think she was doing anything wrong in saving her husband's life. St Augustine is most approving of her generous submission. It is true that the wealthy dotard deceived her, and perhaps her husband was hanged just the same. But she had done everything in her power to save his life.

'You may rest assured, my daughter, that when a Jesuit quotes St Augustine at you, the saint *must* be right.* Not that I am advising you to do it. You are a sensible girl: it is to be assumed that you will seek to be of use to your husband. Monseigneur de Saint-Pouange is a man of integrity: he will not deceive you. That's all I can say. I will pray to God for you, and I hope that everything will turn out to His greater glory.'

Fair Saint-Yves, no less alarmed by what the Jesuit had said than by what the under-secretary had proposed, returned to her friend quite distraught. She was tempted to look to death as a means of escape from the horror of leaving her adored lover in dreadful captivity or from the shame of setting him free at the cost of her most precious possession, and of that which should belong only to the same unfortunate lover.

CHAPTER 17

She succumbs out of virtue

SHE begged her friend to kill her. But this woman, no less indulgent than the Jesuit, spoke to her yet more plainly:

'I'm afraid', she said, 'that this is the way things are mostly done here at court, for all its agreeable sophistication and renown. The most inconsequential of posts, as well as the most sought after, have often been filled only at the price being asked of you now. Listen. You have become my friend, and I trust you. I can honestly tell you that if I had been a stickler like you, my husband would not now have the benefit of the small post which brings him in a living. He knows it, and far from being upset about it, he regards me as his benefactress and himself as my creation. Do you think the prestige and wealth of those who have held positions of authority in the provinces, or even in the army, have all been due entirely to the service they have given? There are some who owe it all to their lady wives. The high ranks in the military have been sought with lovemaking, and the post has gone to the husband of the fairest.

'Your situation is much more promising. It is a matter of setting your lover free and marrying him. It is a sacred duty which you have to carry out. No one blamed the beauties and the fine ladies I'm talking about. People will applaud you. They will say you permitted yourself a moment of weakness only from an excess of virtue.'

'Ah, some virtue!' cried the fair Saint-Yves. 'What a maze of

iniquities! What a place! And how I am learning about the ways of
men! A Father La Chaise and a ridiculous magistrate have my lover
put in prison, my family persecutes me, and the only hand extended
to me in my hour of need is a hand intent on my dishonour. One
Jesuit has ruined a brave man. Another Jesuit wants to ruin me. All
around me nothing but snares and pitfalls, and I on the verge of
perdition! Either I must kill myself or I must speak to the King. I will
throw myself at his feet as he passes on his way to Mass or to the
theatre.'

'They won't let you near him,' her good friend told her. 'And if
you did have the misfortune to speak, Monseigneur de Louvois and
the reverend Father La Chaise could have you locked away in a
convent for the rest of your days.'

While this good woman was thus adding to the confusion in her
despairing soul and thrusting the dagger yet deeper into her heart,
along came a messenger from M. de Saint-Pouange with a letter and
two lovely pendant earrings. Saint-Yves tearfully refused them, but
her friend took charge of them.

As soon as the messenger had gone, our confidante read the letter,
in which the two friends were invited to a little supper that evening.
Saint-Yves vowed that she would not go. The devout lady wanted to
try the diamond earrings on her. Saint-Yves could not bear the idea
and refused all day long. At the last, thinking only of her lover,
overwhelmed, dragged against her will, not knowing where she was
being taken, she allowed herself to be conducted to the fateful
supper. Nothing had been able to induce her to wear the pendant
earrings. The confidante brought them along and forcibly put them
on her just before they sat down to eat. Saint-Yves was so embarrassed and agitated that she allowed herself to be teased, and the
master of the house thought this augured very well. Towards the end
of the meal the confidante discreetly withdrew. Saint-Yves's patron
then showed her the rescission of the *lettre de cachet*, a deed of gift
for a considerable sum of money, and a commission for a company in
the army. And he was fulsome in his promises.

'Ah, how I would love you,' Saint-Yves told him, 'if you did not
want to be loved quite so much!'

Finally, after long resistance, after much sobbing and protesting
and weeping, worn out by the struggle, utterly at a loss, and grown
quite faint and limp, she was obliged to yield. Her one resource

was to promise herself that she would think only of the Ingenu while the cruel man mercilessly enjoyed that to which necessity had reduced her.

CHAPTER 18

She delivers her lover and a Jansenist

AT daybreak she hastened to Paris, armed with the ministerial order. It is difficult to depict how she felt during this journey. Imagine a virtuous and noble soul, humiliated by her shame, intoxicated with love and tenderness, racked with remorse at having betrayed her lover, and full of pleasure at delivering the one she adores. Her bitter experiences, her struggles, her success, each had a part in her thoughts. She was no longer that simple girl whose mind had been narrowed by a provincial education. Love and misfortune had moulded her. Sentiment had developed as far in her as reason had in the mind of her unfortunate lover. Young women learn to feel more easily than men learn to think. Her adventure had taught her more than four years in a convent.

She was dressed extremely simply. She felt revulsion for all the finery in which she had appeared before her deadly benefactor. She had left the diamond earrings for her companion without so much as a backward glance. At once embarrassed and lovestruck, worshipping her Ingenu and hating herself, she finally arrived at the gate

> Of that dread castle, palace of vengeance,
> Which oft confined both crime and innocence.*

When the time came to step down from the coach, her strength failed her. People came to her assistance, and in she went, with pounding heart and furrowed brow, a tear in her eye. She was taken to the governor; she made to speak to him; her voice faltered; she showed her order, scarcely managing more than a few words as she did so. The governor liked his prisoner: he was very pleased he should be set free. His heart had not become hardened like that of some of those honourable gaolers, his colleagues, who, ever ready to live off the misfortune of others, thought only of the remuneration that attached to their custody of the captives, and so treated their victims as sources of income and were secretly filled with a ghastly joy at the tears of these unfortunates.

He had the prisoner brought to his apartment. The two lovers caught sight of one another, and both fainted. The fair Saint-Yves remained motionless for a long time, giving no sign of life. The other was soon himself again.

'It would seem she is your wife,' said the governor. 'You didn't tell me you were married. I am instructed that it is to her generous efforts that you owe your deliverance.'

'Ah! I am not worthy to be his wife,' said the fair Saint-Yves in a quavering voice, and swooned once more.

When she had recovered consciousness, she handed over, still trembling, the deed of gift and the commission of a company. The Ingenu, as surprised as he was touched, was awaking from one dream only to find himself in another.

'Why was I shut up in here? How have you managed to get me out? Where are the monsters who put me here? You are a goddess come down from heaven to rescue me.'

The fair Saint-Yves lowered her gaze, looked up at her lover, blushed, and then at once averted her eyes that were brimming with tears. Eventually she told him all she knew and of all she had been through, except for that which she would dearly have liked to conceal for ever, and at which anyone else but the Ingenu, someone more accustomed to the world and more versed in the ways of the court, would easily have guessed.

'Is it possible that a miserable wretch like that magistrate can have had the power to deprive me of my freedom? Ah! I see now that it is the same with men as it is with the lowest animals. All may do harm. But is it possible that a monk, a Jesuit confessor to the King, can have contributed to my misfortune just as much as that magistrate did, and without my having the faintest idea on what pretext the detestable villain has persecuted me? Did he make me out to be a Jansenist? And then you, how did you not forget me? I wasn't worth it. I was only a savage. To think of it! You have managed, without counsel or assistance, to undertake the journey to Versailles! There you appeared, and my fetters were broken! So beauty and virtue do possess an invincible charm that can break down gates of iron and melt a heart of bronze!'

At the word 'virtue', sobs broke forth from the fair Saint-Yves.

She did not realize just how virtuous she had been in committing the crime for which she reproached herself.

Her lover continued thus:

'O angel who has sundered my chains, if you had credit enough— how, I don't yet understand—to secure justice for me, secure it now also for an old man who has been the first to teach me to think, as you have taught me to love. Misfortune brought us together. I love him as a father. I cannot live without you, but nor can I live without him.'

'I! I beg a favour of the same man who . . . !'

'Yes, I want to owe everything to you, and I want never to owe anything to anyone but you. Shower me with your gifts and write to this powerful man. Finish what you have begun, finish your miracles.'

She felt that she ought to do everything her lover asked. She made to write, but her hand could not obey. She began her letter three times, and three times she tore it up. Finally she wrote, and the two lovers departed, having bid farewell to the elderly martyr to efficient grace.

Saint-Yves, at once happy and heartbroken, knew which house her brother was lodging in. There she went, and her lover took an apartment in the same house.

They had scarcely arrived when her protector sent her the order for the release of old Gordon, and demanded an assignation for the following day. So it was that, for every decent and generous thing she did, dishonour was the price. She viewed with absolute disgust this custom of trading in the misfortunes and happiness of men. She gave the order of release to her lover and refused the assignation with a protector whom she could never set eyes on again without dying of anguish and shame. The Ingenu was able to part from her only because he was going to deliver a friend. Thither he flew. As he carried out this task, he reflected on the strange events of this world and marvelled at the courage and virtue of a young girl to whom two unfortunates owed more than their lives.

CHAPTER 19

The Ingenu, the fair Saint-Yves, and their families are reunited

THE generously and respectably faithless girl was with her brother the Abbé de Saint-Yves, the good Prior of the Mountain, and the lady Kerkabon. They were all equally astonished, but their situations and sentiments were very different. The Abbé de Saint-Yves was making tearful confessions of guilt at the feet of his sister, and she was pardoning him. The Prior and his warm-hearted sister were also crying, but with joy. The villainous magistrate and his insufferable son were not there to spoil this touching scene. They had left at the first rumour of their enemy's release, and were scurrying home to the provinces to hide away their foolishness and fright.

Our four leading characters, stirred by a hundred different impulses, were waiting for the young man to return with the friend he had gone to set free. The Abbé de Saint-Yves dared not lift his gaze to meet his sister's, and good Kerkabon was saying:

'So I shall see my dear nephew again.'

'Yes, you shall see him again,' said the charming Saint-Yves, 'but he is a different man. His bearing, his tone, his ideas, the way he thinks, everything has changed. He has become as respectable as once he was naïve and found everything strange. He will be the honour and consolation of your family. Would that I too could be the honour of mine!'

'You're not the same either,' said the Prior. 'What can have happened to cause such a great change in you?'

In the middle of this conversation the Ingenu arrived, hand in hand with his Jansenist. The scene then became more novel and interesting. It started with tender embraces from the uncle and aunt. The Abbé de Saint-Yves almost threw himself at the knees of the Ingenu, who was an Ingenu no longer. The two lovers exchanged glances expressing all that they felt. Satisfaction and gratitude glowed in the face of the one: awkwardness and embarrassment were etched in the tender, faintly distraught gaze of the other. There was surprise that she should mingle sorrow with so much joy.

Old Gordon endeared himself to the whole family in a matter of moments. He had shared misfortune with the young prisoner, and that entitled him greatly. He owed his deliverance to the two lovers: that alone reconciled him to love. The asperity of his former opinions was fading from his heart. He had become human, just as the Huron had. Each of them recounted his adventures before supper. The two abbés and the aunt listened like children listening to ghost stories—or like grown-ups who love nothing more than a tale of woe.

'Alas,' said Gordon, 'there are possibly more than five hundred innocent people currently in the same chains that Mlle de Saint-Yves has broken. No one knows of their misfortunes. One can find plenty of hands raised against the throng of the unfortunate, but rarely a helping hand.'

So just a reflection made him feel all the more emotional and grateful. Everything added to the triumph of the fair Saint-Yves, and they all wondered at the greatness and steadfastness of her soul. This admiration was mixed with the respect one involuntarily feels for a person one believes to have influence at court. But from time to time the Abbé de Saint-Yves would say:

'How did my sister manage to gain this influence so quickly?'

They were about to sit down to an early meal when, lo and behold, who should appear but the good friend from Versailles, knowing nothing of all that had passed. She was in a coach and six, and there is no need to guess whose carriage it was. In she walked with that imposing air of someone from the court who has important business, made a very slight bow to the company and, taking the fair Saint-Yves to one side, said:

'Why do you keep people waiting so long? Come with me. Here are the diamonds you forgot to take.'

She could not speak these words softly enough for the Ingenu not to hear them. He saw the diamonds. Brother Saint-Yves was horrified, while uncle and aunt merely experienced the surprise of simple folk who have never seen such magnificence. The young man, who had improved his mind with a year of reflection, involuntarily reflected some more and appeared momentarily disconcerted. His lover noticed. A deathly pallor spread across her beautiful face. A shudder seized her, and she could scarcely stand up.

'Ah, madam,' she said to the fateful friend, 'you have ruined me! You have sent me to my death!'

These words pierced the heart of the Ingenu, but by now he had already learnt to control himself. He made no comment on them for fear of upsetting his sweetheart in front of her brother, but he too turned pale.

Saint-Yves, in anguish at the change she could see in her lover's face, dragged the woman out of the room into a small passage and threw the diamonds on to the floor.

'Oh, I was not seduced by these, and you know it. But the man who gave them to me will never see me again.'

Her friend picked them up, and Saint-Yves went on:

'He can take them back, or he can give them to you. Away with you. Remind me no more of my shame.'

The ambassadress finally departed, quite unable to understand the remorse to which she had been witness.

Fair Saint-Yves, weighed down by a heavy heart, and feeling as if some physical upheaval were choking the very breath from her body, was obliged to take to her bed. However, so as not to cause alarm, she kept her suffering to herself and, on the simple pretext that she was tired, she begged leave to go and rest—but this only after reassuring the company with kind, comforting words and after darting some looks at her lover that set fire to his soul.

Without her animating presence the supper was a gloomy affair at first, but the gloom was of that interesting kind which gives rise to absorbing and instructive conversations far superior to the frivolous merriment that people generally look for and which is usually no more than unwelcome clamour.

In a few words Gordon sketched out the history of Jansenism and Molinism,* of the persecutions which each side inflicted on the other, and of the bigotry of both. The Ingenu provided a commentary on this history and voiced his pity for those who, not content with all the discord sown by the pursuit of their own interests, bring further ills on themselves in the name of chimerical objectives and unintelligible absurdities. Gordon narrated, and the other analysed. The rest of the company were moved as they listened, and within them a new light began to shine. There was talk of the long duration of our misfortunes and the brevity of our lives. It was noted that each profession has one vice and one danger which are peculiar to it, and that, from the prince to the lowliest of beggars, everything seems to point to there being something amiss in nature. How is it that so many people, for so little money, are willing to become henchmen and be the persecutors and executioners of others? With what inhuman indifference a person in authority will consign a family to its ruin by the stroke of his pen, and with what even more barbarous joy hired hands will carry this out!

'When I was young,' said the excellent Gordon, 'I knew of a relative of the maréchal de Marillac* who had been hounded from his own province on account of that notorious unfortunate and was hiding in Paris under an assumed name. He was an elderly man of seventy-two. His wife, who was with him, was about the same age. They had a wastrel of a son who had run away from home at the age of fourteen. Having enlisted and then deserted, he had passed through every stage of debauchery and abjection. Finally, having assumed the name of one of the family estates, he had ended up in the bodyguard of Cardinal de Richelieu (for, like Mazarin, this cleric too had his bodyguard) and had risen to the rank of subaltern in this company of henchmen. This adventurer was ordered to arrest the old man and his wife, which he did with all the ruthlessness of a man who wants to please his master. As he was escorting them, he heard the two victims bemoaning the long series of misfortunes that they had undergone since the cradle. The father and mother counted among their greatest misfortunes the wildness and ruin of their son. He recognized them, and took them to prison all the same, insisting that His Eminence had to be served above everything else. His Eminence rewarded his zeal.

'I saw one of Father La Chaise's spies betray his own brother in the hope of a small living, which he didn't get. And I saw him die, not of remorse but of grief at being duped by one of the Jesuit fraternity.

'Being a confessor, as I was for a long time, gave me an insight into family life. I hardly came across one single family that was not steeped in bitterness, while outwardly it put on a façade of happiness and appeared to be positively brimming with joy. And I have always observed that the really great unhappinesses have been the result of our voracious greed.'

'For my part,' said the Ingenu, 'I think that a soul which is noble and sensitive and counts its blessings can live happily. And I certainly hope to enjoy undivided bliss with the fair and generous Saint-Yves. For I flatter myself,' he added, turning to her brother with a smile of friendship, 'that you will not refuse her to me as you did last year, and that this time I shall go about things in a rather more seemly manner.'

The Abbé lost himself in apologies for the past and in protestations of eternal friendship.

Uncle Kerkabon said that it would be the happiest day of his life.

The kindly aunt, in ecstasies of tearful joy, exclaimed:

'I always said you'd never be a sub-deacon. This sacrament's a much better one. Would to God the honour had been mine but, well, I'll be a mother to you instead.'

Then it was simply a question of which of them could outdo the other in praise of the tender, loving Saint-Yves.

The heart of the man she loved was too full of what she had done for him, and he loved her too much, for the business with the diamonds to have made any overriding impression on his emotions. But those words that he had heard only too clearly: 'You are sending me to my death', still secretly alarmed him and tainted all his joy, while the praises heaped on his fair sweetheart made him love her all the more. In the end they talked of nothing but her, and of the happiness the two lovers deserved to enjoy. They all arranged to live in Paris together and planned how they might become rich and famous, and they gave themselves over to such hopes as are so easily raised by the merest glimpse of happiness. But the Ingenu in his heart of hearts had a secret feeling that led him to reject this illusion. He reread the promissory notes signed 'Saint-Pouange', and the certificates signed 'Louvois'. He was told what sort of men they were, or were thought to be. Everyone spoke about the ministers and their ministries with that prandial freedom of speech which the French regard as the most precious freedom to be savoured in all the world.

'If I were King of France,' said the Ingenu, 'I know how I would choose the Minister of War. I would look for someone of the highest birth, for the simple reason that he has to give orders to the nobility. I would require that he had been an officer himself, that he had been promoted through the ranks, that he was at least a lieutenant-general, and that he was worthy to be a field marshal. Because it is essential, is it not, that he should himself have been a serving officer so as to have a better, more detailed understanding of the service? And the officers will be a hundred times happier, will they not, to obey a fighting man who has demonstrated his courage as they themselves have, rather than some functionary who, however intelligent he may be, can only guess at what is involved in a campaign? And I wouldn't mind if my minister spent freely, even if my First Lord of the Treasury did find it a mite awkward from time to time. I would like him to have an easy time of it, and even for him to be known for his debonair approach, because that is the mark of a person who is in control. The nation likes it, and duty seems less of a chore.'

He wanted ministers to have this sort of character because he had always found that an even temper is incompatible with cruelty. Monseigneur de Louvois might not, perhaps, have been content with all the Ingenu's requirements. His merits were of a different order.

But while they were at table the illness of the unfortunate girl was beginning to take a more serious turn. She had begun to run a temperature, and a raging fever had developed. She was in some discomfort and yet did not complain, being concerned not to spoil the enjoyment of those having supper.

Her brother, learning that she was not asleep, went to her bedside. He was taken aback at her condition. Everybody came running, and her lover arrived first after her brother. Doubtless he was the most alarmed and upset of all, but he had learned to add discretion to all the happy gifts which nature had showered upon him, and a ready sense of what is proper was beginning to dominate in him.

They summoned a local doctor at once. He was one of those doctors who visit their patients in a rush, confuse the illness they have just seen with the one they are currently attending, and blindly apply a science from which even all the mature reflection of a sound and discerning mind cannot remove the uncertainty and the dangers. In his haste to prescribe a remedy which was then in fashion, he made the illness twice as bad. Fashion even in medicine! That kind of madness was far too common in Paris.

The unhappy Saint-Yves was doing even more than her doctor to make her illness dangerous. Her soul was destroying her body: and the teeming thoughts that troubled her poured into her veins a poison yet more dangerous than that of the highest fever.

CHAPTER 20

Fair Saint-Yves dies, and what comes of it

ANOTHER doctor was summoned. Instead of assisting nature and allowing it to run its own course in a young person whose every organ was calling her back to life, this one was solely concerned to do down his colleague. The illness became fatal within two days. The brain, which is thought to be the seat of the understanding, was attacked as violently as the heart, which is said to be the seat of the passions.

By what incomprehensible mechanism are the organs of the body made subject to feeling and thought? How can one single, painful thought disrupt the circulation of the blood, and how in its turn can the blood and its irregularities affect human understanding? What is this fluid—which we have yet to identify but which certainly exists—that is more rapid and more active than light, that darts into all the channels of life in less than the blinking of an eye, gives us sensations and memory, sadness or joy, reason or delirium, recalls with horror what one would like to forget, and turns a thinking animal variously into an object of wonder or a subject fit for compassion and tears?

This was what the kindly Gordon was saying, and his perfectly natural reflection (and one which it rarely occurs to people to make) in no way detracted from the emotion he felt, for he was not one of those miserable philosophers who endeavour to remain beyond the reach of feeling. He was touched by the fate of the young girl, as a father might be to watch the lingering death of a beloved child. The Abbé de Saint-Yves was in despair. The Prior and his sister were in floods of tears. But who could depict her lover's plight? No language has the words to convey such an extreme of grief: languages are far too imperfect.

Aunt Kerkabon, herself almost lifeless, was holding the head of the dying girl in her frail arms, and her brother was on his knees at the foot of the bed. Saint-Yves's lover was pressing her hand, bathing them in tears and sobbing. He said she was his benefactress, his future, his life, one half of himself, his beloved, his wife. At the word 'wife' she sighed, gave him a look of ineffable tenderness, and let out a sudden cry of horror. Then, in one of those intervals when suffering is suspended, and the exhaustion of senses overwhelmed grants release and strength to the soul, she exclaimed:

'I, your wife! Ah, my dear love, that word, that happiness, that prize, they were not for me. I am dying and I deserve to. O God of my heart! O you whom I have sacrificed to infernal demons, it is all over. I have been punished. Live and be happy.'

These tender, terrible words made no sense, but they filled every heart with fear and pity. She had the courage to explain herself. Each word made all those present shudder in disbelief, and with pain and compassion. They all joined in execrating the man of power who had remedied a horrible injustice only by the perpetration of a crime, and who had forced the most respectable innocence into becoming his accomplice.

'Who, you? Guilty?' said her lover. 'No, that you are not. Crime is in the heart alone, and yours belongs to virtue and to me.'

He followed up this sentiment with words which seemed to bring the fair Saint-Yves back to life. She felt consoled, and was surprised to be still loved. Old Gordon would have condemned her in the days when he was but a Jansenist; now, having learnt wisdom, he esteemed her and wept.

In the midst of all these tears and apprehensions, while every heart was full of the danger this very dear girl was in, while all was consternation, a messenger from the court was announced. A messenger! And from whom? And why? He was come from the King's confessor for the Prior of the Mountain. It was not Father La Chaise who wrote: it was his valet, Friar Vadbled, a most important person at that time and the man who communicated the reverend father's wishes to the archbishops, the man who gave audiences, who promised livings, and who sometimes issued *lettres de cachet*. He was writing to the Abbé of the Mountain that 'His Reverence was informed of the adventures of his nephew, that his imprisonment had simply been a mistake, that minor mishaps like this often happened, that there was no need to be concerned about it and, lastly, that he was agreeable that he, the Prior, should come the following day and present his nephew to him, that he should bring good Gordon with him, that he, Friar Vadbled, would introduce them to His Reverence and to Monseigneur de Louvois, who would have a word with them in his antechamber'.

He added that the story of the Ingenu and his fight against the English had been told to the King, that the King would be certain to deign to notice him when he passed by in the gallery, and that he might perhaps even nod to him. The letter ended by expressing the hope, which he had been led to entertain, that all the ladies of the court would make a point of inviting his nephew to their levees, and that several of them would say 'Good day, M. Ingenu' to him; and that assuredly he would be a subject of conversation at the royal supper-table. The letter was signed: 'Your affectionate Friar Vadbled, SJ'.

The Prior having read the letter out aloud, his nephew, who was furious but managing for the moment to restrain his anger, said nothing to the bearer. Instead, turning to his companion in misfortune, he asked him what he thought of the style.

Gordon answered him:

'There you are, that's how they treat men like monkeys! First they beat them and then they make them dance to their own tune.'

The Ingenu, his true character showing itself once more, as it always does at moments of great upheaval in the soul, tore the letter into little pieces and threw them in the face of the messenger:

'There's my answer.'

His uncle was horrified and had visions of a thunderbolt and twenty *lettres de cachet* raining down upon him. He quickly went and wrote a letter to excuse as best he could what he took to be a young man's quick temper, but which was actually the outburst of a fine soul.

But matters of more sorrowful concern were taking possession of all their hearts. That fair unfortunate, Saint-Yves, could sense already that her end was nigh. She was calm, but it was that awful calm of prostration when nature no longer has the strength to fight.

'O my dear love!' she said in a faltering voice, 'death is punishing me for my weakness. But I die with the consolation of knowing that you are free. I adored you even as I betrayed you, and I adore you even as I bid you an eternal adieu.'

Not for her some vain show of strength. The paltry glory of having a few neighbours say 'she was courageous in death' never crossed her mind. Who at the age of twenty can lose her lover, her life, and what is called her 'honour', without regret and without anguish? She felt the full horror of her situation, and communicated it in dying words and glances of the kind that speak with so much authority. And then like the others she wept, in the moments when she still had strength enough to weep.

Let others seek to praise the ostentatious deaths of those who enter destruction with impassivity. That is the fate of animals. We die like them with indifference only when age or illness makes us similar to them in the dullness of our organs. Whoever feels a great loss feels a great regret. If he should repress it, he is carrying vanity into the very arms of death.

When the fateful moment arrived, all those present cried out and wept. The Ingenu lost the use of his senses: people of strong character feel things much more violently than others when they have a tender heart. Good Gordon knew him well enough to fear that he might kill himself when he recovered consciousness. They removed every possible weapon. The unfortunate young man noticed. He said to his family and to Gordon, without so much as a tear or a groan, or any other apparent emotion:

'Do you really think that anyone on earth has the right or the power to stop me putting an end to my own life?'

Gordon was careful not to rehearse the tiresome platitudes with which people try to prove that it is not permissible to exercise one's freedom to cease living merely because one is in terrible pain; that one should not go out simply because one cannot stand being at home any more; that man is on earth as a soldier at his post—as if it were of any consequence to the Being of Beings whether a few assembled bits of matter were in one place or another: so many powerless reasons that firm, considered despair disdains to hear, and to which Cato's only answer was a dagger blow.

The fearful, gloomy silence of the Ingenu, his dark eyes, his trembling lips, and the shuddering of his body filled the souls of the onlookers with that mixture of compassion and dread which holds every faculty of the soul in thrall, which makes all speech impossible, and manifests itself only in single words and broken phrases. The landlady and her family had arrived. They trembled at his despair. They kept watch over him and observed his every movement. Already the icy corpse of fair Saint-Yves had been taken downstairs, away from the gaze of her lover, who seemed still to be looking for her although he was no longer in a state to see anything at all.

In the midst of this spectacle of death, with the body displayed at the door of the house, and two priests standing by a stoup of holy water and reciting prayers with an absent air, and passers-by idly sprinkling a few drops of holy water on the bier, while others passed by quite unconcerned, and with the family weeping, and the lover ready to put an end to things, Saint-Pouange arrived with the friend from Versailles.

His passing fancy, having been satisfied on but the one occasion, had now become love. The rejection of his gifts had piqued him. Father La Chaise would never have thought to come to the house, but Saint-Pouange, with the mental picture of fair Saint-Yves daily before him, and burning to assuage a passion of which a single moment's enjoyment had planted the goad of desire within his heart, did not hesitate to come himself in search of her whom he might not, perhaps, have wanted to see more than three times had she come to him of her own accord.

Down he stepped from his carriage. The first object which presented itself to view was a bier. He averted his eyes with the simple distaste of a man who has been nourished on a life of pleasure and who thinks he ought to be spared any spectacle which may recall him to the contemplation of human misery. He made to climb the steps. The lady from Versailles enquired out of idle curiosity who was to be buried. The name of Mlle de Saint-Yves was proffered. At this name she turned pale and uttered a dreadful cry. Saint-Pouange spun round: surprise and pain gripped his soul. Good Gordon was there, his eyes filled with tears. He paused in his sad prayers to tell the courtier the facts of this horrible catastrophe. He spoke to him with the authority of grief and virtue. Saint-Pouange had not been born evil. The torrent of life's dealings and amusements had carried away his soul, a soul which had yet to know itself. He was not yet approaching old age, the old age which usually hardens a minister's heart. He listened to Gordon, his eyes fixed on the ground, and from these eyes he wiped away a few tears which he was astonished to shed. He knew repentance.

'I absolutely must meet this extraordinary man you have told me about,' he said. 'I feel for him almost as much as I feel for this innocent victim whose death I have caused.'

Gordon followed him to the room where the Prior, Aunt Kerkabon, the Abbé de Saint-Yves, and a few neighbours were reviving the young man after he had once more fainted.

'I have caused your misfortune,' the under-minister told him. 'I shall devote my life to its reparation.'

The first thing that occurred to the Ingenu was to kill him and then kill himself afterwards. Nothing could have been more fitting. But he was unarmed and closely watched. Saint-Pouange would not be put off by his refusals, accompanied as they were by all the reproach and scornful disgust which he justly deserved, and which were being heaped upon him.

Time is a great healer. Monseigneur de Louvois eventually managed to make an excellent officer of the Ingenu, who has since been heard of in Paris and in the army under a different name, to the general acclaim of all law-abiding citizens, and who has been both an expert on war and an intrepid philosopher.

He could never speak of what had happened without heaving a sigh, and yet to talk of it brought him comfort. He cherished the memory of the tender-hearted Saint-Yves till the very end of his days. The Abbé de Saint-Yves and the Prior were each appointed to fine livings. Good Kerkabon was happier to see her nephew with military honours than with a sub-deaconry. The devout lady of Versailles kept the diamond earrings and received a further handsome gift. Father All-things was given boxes of chocolate, and coffee, and sugar candy, and crystallized lemons, along with the *Meditations of the Reverend Father Croiset* and *The Flower of the Saints** bound in morocco. Good Gordon lived with the Ingenu in the closest friendship until his death. He too received a living, and forgot once and for all about efficient grace and concomitant concourse.* He took as his motto: 'It is an ill wind that blows nobody any good.' How many decent men and women in the world have been able to say: 'An ill wind blows nobody any good'!

THE WHITE BULL

*Translated from the Syriac by Mr Mamaki,
Interpreter of Oriental Languages to the King of England**

CHAPTER 1

How the Princess Amasida met a bull

THE young Princess Amasida, daughter of Amasis, King of Tanis in
Egypt, was walking along the Pelusium Way in the company of her
ladies-in-waiting. A deep sadness bore her down: tears welled from
her beautiful eyes. Everyone knows what caused her grief, and how
afraid she was of displeasing her father the King by this very grief.
Old Mambres, a former magus and eunuch to the Pharaohs, was at
her side. Indeed he almost never left it. He had been present at her
birth, he had raised her, and he had taught her of the science of
Egypt all that it was proper for a fair princess to know. Amasida's
intelligence was the equal of her beauty. She was as sensitive and
warm-hearted as she was charming; and it was this sensibility that
was now costing her such floods of tears.

The Princess was twenty-four years old, while Mambres the
magus was about thirteen hundred. He it was, as everyone knows,
who had that famous argument with Moses, when victory hung long
in the balance between the two profound philosophers. If Mambres
eventually gave best, it was only because of blatant interference on
the part of the celestial powers who favoured his rival. It had taken
gods to vanquish Mambres.*

Amasis had put him in charge of his daughter's household, which
office he performed with his customary wisdom. The sighs of the
fair Amasida moved him to pity.

'O my beloved! My young, darling beloved!' she would periodically exclaim. 'O greatest of conquering heroes, most accomplished
and handsome of men! How can it be? Almost seven years have
passed since you disappeared from the face of the earth! Which god
has taken you from your loving Amasida? You are not dead: the

learned prophets of Egypt are agreed on that point. But you are dead to me. I am all alone in the world. The world is empty and deserted. What strange marvel made you abandon your throne and the woman you loved? Your throne! The foremost throne on earth, but for you a mere trifle. But I who adore you, my dear Ne . . .'

She was about to finish.

'Tremble to speak that fateful name,' said wise Mambres, former eunuch and magus to the Pharaohs. 'You might be denounced by one of your ladies-in-waiting. They are all devoted to you, and doubtless every fair lady regards it as a point of honour to serve the noble passions of fair princesses. But, well, one of them might be indiscreet or, conceivably, even treacherous. You know your father the King has sworn to have your head cut off, fond as he is of you, if you speak that dread name which is forever on the tip of your tongue. Weep, but hold your peace. The law is indeed a harsh one, but you cannot have been brought up in Egyptian wisdom without having learnt to command your tongue. Remember how Harpocrates, one of our greatest gods, always has a finger to his lips.'

The fair Amasida wept and said no more.

As she was walking silently towards the banks of the Nile, she saw in the distance, in the shade of a grove washed by the river waters, an old woman dressed in grey rags who was sitting on a small mound. Beside her she had a she-ass, a dog, and a goat. In front of her was a serpent, who was no ordinary serpent, for its eyes were as tender as they were animated. It had a noble and interesting face, and its skin gleamed with the brightest and the softest colours alike. An enormous whale, lying half in and half out of the river, was not the least surprising member of this company. On a branch sat a raven and a pigeon. All these creatures seemed to be engaged in rather lively conversation.

'Alas,' said the Princess softly to herself, 'they're probably all talking about their amours, and here am I forbidden to speak the name of the one I love!'

In her hand the old woman was holding a light metal chain, some hundred fathoms long, to which was tethered a bull grazing in the meadow. This bull was white, plump, shapely, even nimble, which is most uncommon in a bull. The horns were of ivory. He was the most handsome example of his kind one could ever hope to see. Neither that of Pasiphae nor the one whose form Jupiter assumed for carrying off Europa came anywhere near this superb specimen. Even the charming heifer into which Isis was turned would scarce have been worthy of him.

As soon as he saw the Princess, he ran towards her, as fleet as a young Arab colt devouring the broad plains and rivers of ancient Saana to reach the silky filly that reigns supreme in his heart, and makes his ears prick up. The old woman was trying desperately to restrain him. The serpent appeared to be shooing him back with his hissing. The dog was chasing after him and snapping at his well-turned ankles. The she-ass kept cutting across his path and lashing out with her hind legs to make him turn back. The whale swam up the Nile and, leaping out of the water, threatened to swallow him whole. The goat remained motionless, rigid with fear. The raven flapped about the bull's head, as if it was trying to bring itself to peck his eyes out. Only the dove went with him, out of curiosity, and murmuring gentle encouragement to him.

Such an extraordinary spectacle gave Mambres serious pause for thought. Meanwhile the white bull, dragging chain and old woman behind him, had already reached the Princess, who was seized with astonishment and apprehension. He threw himself at her feet, kissed them, wept tears over them, and then looked up at her with eyes that were filled with an extraordinary mixture of anguish and joy. He dared not bellow for fear of frightening the fair Amasida. He could not speak. The limited vocal range that heaven had vouchsafed to certain animals had been denied him, but his every gesture was eloquence itself. The Princess found him most pleasing. She felt that a little light amusement might afford her some momentary respite in the midst of her most grievous sorrow.

'What an adorable animal,' she said. 'I would like to have him in my stable.'

At these words the bull went down on all four knees and kissed the ground.

'He understands what I say!' cried the Princess. 'He's showing me that he wants to be mine. Ah, most holy magus and eunuch divine, grant me this one consolation. Buy this beautiful cherub[1] for me. Agree a price with that old woman. I presume she must be the

---

[1] 'Cherub', in both Chaldaic and Syriac, means 'ox'.*

owner. I want this animal for my very own. Do not refuse me this harmless comforter.'

The ladies of the palace all added their entreaties to the pleas of the Princess. Mambres allowed himself to be persuaded and went to speak with the old woman.

CHAPTER 2

How wise Mambres, former sorcerer to the Pharaohs, recognized
an old woman, and how she recognized him

'MADAM,' he addressed her, 'you know how much young girls, and especially young princesses, need to keep themselves amused. The King's daughter has taken a mad fancy to your bull. I beg you to sell him to us. You will be paid in cash.'

'Sir,' replied the old woman, 'this precious animal does not belong to me. I, and all the animals you see here, have been set to keep careful watch over him, to observe everything he does, and to report on him. God forbid that I should ever want to sell such a priceless animal!'

Mambres, at these words, felt a faint glimmer of light begin to dawn on him, though he could not yet quite make things out clearly. He looked at the old woman in her grey cloak with renewed attention.

'Worthy lady,' he said, 'either I'm mistaken or I've seen you somewhere before.'

'Well, I am not mistaken,' replied the old lady. 'I saw you, sir, seven hundred years ago, on a journey I made from Syria to Egypt some months after the fall of Troy, when Hiram reigned in Tyre and Neferkheres in ancient Egypt.'

'Ah, madam,' cried the old man, 'you are the noble pythoness of Endor.'

'And you, sir,' said the pythoness as she embraced him, 'you are the great Mambres of Egypt.'

'O unforeseen encounter! O memorable day! O decrees of the Eternal One!' said Mambres. 'I feel sure it cannot have been without some order of universal Providence that we two should meet again here in this meadow on the banks of the Nile near the magnificent city of Tanis. What?! Is it really you, madam, and you so famous on the banks of your little Jordan river, and the very greatest in the world when it comes to calling up departed spirits?!'*

'What?! Can it really be you, sir, and you so famous for changing rods into serpents, and day into night, and rivers into blood?!'*

'Yes, madam, it is I. But my advanced age has meant some reduction in my lights and powers. I have simply no idea how you came by this white bull, nor who these animals are who are watching over him with you.'

The old woman collected herself, lifted up her eyes to heaven, and then replied in these terms:

'My dear Mambres, we belong to the same profession, but I am expressly forbidden to tell you about this bull. I can, though, satisfy your curiosity about the other animals. You will easily recognize them by their distinctive features. The serpent is the one who persuaded Eve to eat an apple and make her husband partake also. The she-ass is the one who spoke to that contemporary of yours, Balaam, in the narrow place. The whale that's always got its head out of the water is the one who swallowed Jonah some years ago. The dog is the one who followed the angel Raphael and young Tobias on their journey to Rages of Media in the days of the great Salmanazar. The goat is the one who bears upon himself all the sins of the nation. The raven and the pigeon are the ones that were in Noah's ark at the time of that universal catastrophe and great landmark in history which, to this day, almost no one on earth really seems to know very much about. So there you have it.* But as for the bull, you are not to know.'

Mambres listened with respect. Then he said:

'The Eternal One reveals what He will and to whom He will, my illustrious pythoness. All these animals that have been sent like you to guard the white bull are known only to your own generous and amiable race, which is itself almost unknown to the rest of the world. The wonders which you and yours have performed, as have I and mine, will one day give great cause for doubt and be a stumbling-block to faith among bogus sages. Fortunately, in one small corner of the world, these marvels will gain credence among the real sages, those who listen to their local seers, and that's all it takes.'

As he said this, the Princess pulled at his sleeve, and pleaded:

'Mambres, won't you then buy me my bull?'

The magus, now lost in a deep reverie, offered no reply, and Amasida wept anew.

She then spoke to the old woman herself, and said:

'My good woman, I beseech you by all that you hold most dear in the world, by your father, and your mother, and your wet-nurse, all of whom, I imagine, are still alive, to sell me not only your bull, but also your pigeon, who seems to be very fond of him. As for your other animals, you can keep them. But I warn you, I'm quite capable of having a fit of the vapours if you refuse to sell me this charming white bull. He will be the light of my life.'

The old woman respectfully kissed the hem of her gauze dress and said:

'Princess, my bull is not for sale. I have already told your illustrious magus. All I might be able to do for you is to bring him to graze near your palace every day. You would be able to stroke him, and give him biscuits, and bid him caper to your heart's content. But he must never go out of sight of any of the animals who accompany me and who are responsible for guarding him. As long as he does not try to escape, they will do him no harm. But if he tries to break his chain again the way he did when he saw you, then woe betide him! I would not answer for his life. That whale you can see would most certainly swallow him whole, and keep him longer than three days in his belly. Or else that serpent, who may have seemed quite gentle and amiable to you, might give him a deadly bite.'

The white bull, who understood perfectly everything the old woman was saying, but who could not speak, accepted all these terms with a submissive air. He lay down at her feet, lowed softly and, looking tenderly at Amasida, seemed to say to her:

'Come and see me sometimes on the grass.'

The serpent then intervened and said:

'Princess, I advise you to do exactly as Miss Endor has just told you.'

The she-ass also had her say and was of the same opinion as the serpent. It broke Amasida's heart that the serpent and the she-ass should speak so well, while a handsome bull with such noble and tender feelings was quite unable to express them.

'Alas,' she muttered under her breath, 'it's just the same at court. Nothing but handsome noblemen who haven't a word to say for themselves, or common boors with a gift for smooth talk.'

'This serpent is no boor,' said Mambres. 'Make no mistake. He is perhaps someone of the very greatest consequence.'

It was getting late. The Princess was obliged to return home, having promised faithfully to come back the next day at the same time. Her ladies-in-waiting were all agog and understood nothing of what they had seen and heard. Mambres was mulling things over. The Princess, remembering that the serpent had called the old woman 'Miss', drew the illogical conclusion that she must be a virgin, and felt it as an affliction to be yet one herself—a respectable affliction which she concealed as scrupulously as she did the name of her lover.

CHAPTER 3

How the fair Amasida held secret converse with a handsome serpent

THE fair Princess bid her ladies breathe not a word of what they had seen. They all promised to keep the secret, and indeed kept it for an entire day. As may be imagined, Amasida slept little that night. Some unaccountable charm repeatedly brought her handsome bull to mind. As soon as she could be alone with her wise Mambres, she said to him:

'O wise man! That creature has quite turned my head.'

'He rather occupies mine too,' said Mambres. 'It is quite clear to me that this particular cherub is a considerable cut above the rest of his species. I see too that there is a great mystery in all this, but I fear something awful is going to happen. Your father Amasis is a violent and suspicious man. This whole business requires that you proceed with the greatest possible prudence.'

'Oh, I'm too full of curiosity to be prudent. It is the only passion which can find room in my heart beside that which devours me for the lover I have lost. What? Am I then not to know what manner of thing this white bull is, that is causing such an uncommon stir within me?'

'Madam,' replied Mambres, 'I have told you before that my learning is diminishing as I grow older. But unless I am very much mistaken, the serpent knows all about that which you are so eager to discover. He is clever, he knows how to put things, and he has long been accustomed to taking a hand in ladies' affairs.'

'Oh, of course,' said Amasida, 'he must be that handsome

Egyptian serpent that puts his tail in his mouth and symbolizes eternity, the one who lights up the world when he opens his eyes and who casts it into darkness as soon as he shuts them again.'

'No, madam.'

'The serpent of Aesculapius, then?'

'Even less likely.'

'Jupiter perhaps, in the form of a serpent?'

'Absolutely not.'

'Oh, I know. It's that rod of yours that you once turned into a serpent?'

'No, I tell you, madam. But all these serpents do belong to the same family. This particular one has a considerable reputation where he comes from. He's said to be the cleverest serpent there has ever been. Consult him. But I warn you, it's a very dangerous business. If I were you, I would forget about all of them, bull, she-ass, serpent, whale, dog, goat, raven, dove, the whole lot of them. But passion has got the better of you. All I can do is pity you and fear for you.'

The Princess beseeched him to arrange a tête-à-tête for her with the serpent. Mambres, kind man that he was, consented; and, ever deep in thought, went off to find his pythoness. He put to her this latest notion of his Princess with such oblique subtlety that he persuaded her.

The old woman told him that on Amasida's head be it; that the serpent knew a great deal about life and living; that he was most polite with the ladies; that he asked for nothing better than to oblige them; and that he would attend their rendezvous.

The old magus returned to the Princess with this good news; but he remained afraid that something was going to go wrong, and he still thought his thoughts.

'You wished to speak to the serpent, madam. He awaits Your Highness's pleasure. Remember that you must flatter him a good deal. For all creatures are essentially vain, and no one more so than him. It is even said that he was once expelled from some lovely place or other on account of his excessive pride.'

'I've never heard that,' objected the Princess.

'That doesn't surprise me,' replied the old man.

He then told her all the various rumours that had circulated about this most celebrated serpent.

'But, madam, whatever strange things may have happened to him, you will not get his secret out of him unless you flatter him. In a nearby land he is said to have once played a thoroughly villainous trick on women. It is right that a woman should try to beguile him in return.'

'I shall do what I can,' said the Princess.

And so she set out with her ladies from the palace and the good eunuch-magus. At this time the old woman had set the white bull to graze quite some distance away. Mambres left Amasida on her own, and went to talk to the pythoness. The principal lady-in-waiting chatted with the she-ass. The other court ladies amused themselves with the goat, the dog, the raven, and the dove. As for the great whale, it was frightening everybody, so the old woman ordered it back into the Nile.

The serpent at once went up to Amasida in the grove, and together they had the following conversation.

THE SERPENT

You have no idea how flattered I am, madam, by the honour which Your Highness has deigned to do me.

THE PRINCESS

Sir, your great reputation, the delicacy of your features, and the sparkle in your eye quickly persuaded me to seek this tête-à-tête with you. I have heard it said among the people (if such a source may be relied upon) that you were once a great lord in the empyreal heaven.

THE SERPENT

It is true, madam, that I did once occupy rather a distinguished position up there. It is claimed that I was once a favourite and have since fallen into disgrace, but that's just a rumour that started in India. The Brahmans were the first to produce any substantial account of my adventures.[1] I have no doubt that the Northern poets* will one day write an exceedingly strange epic poem about them, for, in all honesty, there is very little else you can do with them. But I am not so fallen that I don't still hold very considerable sway here on earth. I would almost venture to say that I have the whole world in my hands.

[1] The Brahmans were indeed the first to imagine a revolt in heaven, and this fable served for a long time afterwards as the basis for a story about the war of the giants against the gods, and for a good few other stories as well.

THE PRINCESS

I believe it, sir, for it is said that you have a talent for persuading people of anything you wish. And to please is to reign.

THE SERPENT

I find, madam, as I look upon you and listen to what you say, that you hold over me that very power which I am supposed to have over so many other souls.

THE PRINCESS

You are, I think, an amiable victor. People say that you have won many ladies over in your time, and that you started with our common mother, whose name escapes me.

THE SERPENT

People malign me. I gave her the best advice in the world. She placed her faith in me, and my view was that she and her husband should gorge themselves on the fruit of the Tree of Knowledge. In suggesting such a thing I thought I should meet with the approval of the master of things. It seemed to me that a tree that was so essential to the human race had not been planted to serve no purpose at all. Would the master have wanted to be served by idiots and illiterates? Was the mind not created that it might enlighten itself, might improve itself? Is it not necessary to know both good and evil that we may do the one and avoid the other? There is no doubt about it, I should have been thanked.

THE PRINCESS

Yet they say that in your case no good came of it. It would seem that it's since then that so many ministers have been punished for giving good advice, and that so many real men of learning, so many great minds, have been persecuted for writing things that are useful to the human race.

THE SERPENT

It would seem, madam, that my enemies have been telling you tales. They go about proclaiming that I have fallen from favour in the court of heaven. Proof that I still have considerable influence up there is that they themselves admit that I was on the council when there was that question of putting Job to the test; and that I was afforced to it again when they took the decision to play a certain little King called Ahab false.[1] That noble commission was entrusted to nobody else but me.

THE PRINCESS

Ah, sir, I cannot believe that you are one to play a person false. But since you are still a member of the council, may I ask if you would grace me with a favour? I hope that such an amiable lord as yourself will not refuse me.

THE SERPENT

Madam, your wish is my command. What are your orders?

THE PRINCESS

I beg you to tell me about this white bull, for whom I am filled with such incomprehensible feelings which both melt my heart and strike terror into my breast. I have been told that you would be kind enough to explain things to me.

THE SERPENT

Madam, curiosity is an essential part of human nature, and especially among the members of your delightful sex. Without it people would remain sunk in the most shameful ignorance. I have always sought, to the best of my ability, to satisfy the curiosity of the ladies. People accuse me of being so ready to oblige merely to spite the master of things. I swear to you that my one object would be to oblige you also. But the old woman must have warned you that there is some danger for you in the revelation of this secret.

THE PRINCESS

Ah, but that's what makes me all the more curious.

THE SERPENT

Then you are just like all the other fair ladies to whom I have been of service.

---

[1] 1 Kings 22: 20–2; 'And the Lord said, Who shall persuade Ahab, that he may go up and fall at Ramoth-Gilead? . . . And there came forth a spirit, and stood before the Lord, and said, I will persuade him. And the Lord said unto him, Wherewith? . . . And he said, Thou shalt persuade him, and prevail also: go forth, and do so.'

THE PRINCESS

If you have any feeling at all, if it is true that people should help each other, if you will have pity on a poor unfortunate, do not refuse me.

THE SERPENT

You are breaking my heart. I must satisfy you. But do not interrupt me.

THE PRINCESS

I promise.

THE SERPENT

Once upon a time there was a young King, a King as handsome as a picture, and he was in love, and was loved . . .

THE PRINCESS

A young King! Handsome, handsome as a picture, in love, loved! And by whom? And who was this King? How old was he? What has become of him? What's his name?

THE SERPENT

There you go interrupting me already, you see, when I've scarcely begun. Be careful. If that is all the self-control you have, you are lost.

THE PRINCESS

Oh, sir, I am sorry. I shall not be so heedless again. Do go on, I beg you.

THE SERPENT

This great King, the most amiable and valorous of men, a conquering hero wherever he took up arms, used to dream a lot, and when he couldn't remember his dreams on waking, he would require his magi to remember them for him and to tell him what it was he had dreamt. Failing which, he would have them all hanged, for nothing could be fairer than that. Well, almost seven years ago, he had this lovely dream which he couldn't remember when he awoke, and after a most expert young Jew had interpreted his dream for him, the amiable King suddenly turned into an ox.[1] For . . .*

---

[1] Throughout antiquity the terms 'ox' and 'bull' were used interchangeably.

THE PRINCESS

Ah, it's my dear Nebu . . .

She was unable to finish. She fainted. Mambres, who had been listening in the distance, saw her fall and thought she was dead.

CHAPTER 4

How they wanted to sacrifice the ox and exorcize the Princess

MAMBRES hastened to her side in tears. The serpent was distressed. He was unable to cry, but he was hissing lugubriously, and he cried out:

'She's dead!'

The she-ass repeated after him:

'She's dead!'

The raven repeated it too. The rest of the animals all seemed stricken with grief—except for Jonah's whale, that is, who always was rather unfeeling. The principal lady-in-waiting and the other court ladies all arrived on the scene and started tearing their hair out. The white bull, who was grazing some way off, heard the commotion and rushed to the grove, dragging the old woman along behind him and bellowing resoundingly. In vain did the ladies sprinkle the dying Amasida with their smelling-bottles full of rose-water and carnation-water, and myrtle-water, of friar's balsam and Mecca balsam, of cinnamon and amomon, of clove, musk, and ambergris. She showed not the slightest sign of life. But as soon as she felt the presence of the handsome white bull at her side, she recovered her senses and looked pinker and more beautiful and more alive than ever. She showered a hundred kisses upon this charming animal, as he rested a languid head upon her alabaster bosom. She called him 'My master, my King, my heart, my life'. She wrapped her ivory arms about his neck, a neck yet whiter than snow. A wisp of chaff clings less firmly to its amber, or the vine to its elm, or the ivy to its oak, than she did. One could hear the soft murmur of her sighs. One could see her eyes now glowing with a tender flame, now misting over with the precious tears of love.

As one might imagine, all this caused Amasida's lady-in-waiting and other companions some considerable astonishment. As soon as they had returned to the palace, they all told their lovers of this strange adventure, each of them adding different details of a kind to enhance its singularity, which is what lends variety to all stories.

When Amasis, King of Tanis, was informed, his royal heart was filled with righteous anger. Such was the wrath of Minos when he learnt that his daughter Pasiphae* was bestowing her favours on the father of the Minotaur. Thus did Juno quiver when she saw her husband Jupiter caress the fair heifer Io, daughter of the river Inachus.* Amasis gave orders for the fair Amasida to be locked in her chamber and placed a guard of black eunuchs at her door. Then he summoned a meeting of the Privy Council.

Mambres, the Grand Magus, presided, though he no longer enjoyed quite the influence he once had. The ministers all came to the conclusion that the white bull was a spellbinder. (Quite the reverse was true: he was spellbound. But people at court are always getting these delicate matters wrong.) It was decided on a majority vote to exorcize the Princess and to offer up the bull and the old woman as sacrifices.

Wise Mambres did not want to go against the views of the King and Council. But it was his prerogative to carry out any exorcisms, and he had a very plausible pretext for a postponement. The God Apis had just died in Memphis. (Bull gods die just the same as any other.) No exorcism was permitted in Egypt until another bull had been found to replace the departed. It was therefore agreed by Council that they would wait for the nomination of a new god that was due to take place in Memphis.

Kind old Mambres was alive to the peril of his dear Princess's position. He saw full well whom it was she loved. The syllables 'Nebu' which had escaped her lips had revealed the whole mystery to the eyes of the sage.

At that time the dynasty[1] of Memphis was in the hands of the Babylonians. They still retained this vestige of the conquests they had once made under the leadership of the greatest King on earth, the same that was also Amasis's mortal enemy. Mambres had need of

---

[1] 'Dynasty' literally means power,* so one may use the word in this sense, despite Larcher's cavilling. 'Dynasty' comes from the Phoenician 'dunast', and Larcher is an ignoramus who knows neither Phoenician, nor Syriac, nor Coptic.

all his wisdom to steer a safe course in the midst of so many difficulties. If King Amasis discovered the identity of his daughter's lover,
she was as good as dead, for he had sworn an oath to this effect. The
great, young, handsome King with whom she was in love had
dethroned her father, who had recovered his kingdom of Tanis
almost seven years previously only because no one knew what had
become of the beloved monarch, that conqueror and idol of nations,
who was the charming Amasida's generous and tender-hearted lover.
But, on the other hand, sacrificing the bull would certainly mean that
fair Amasida would die of a broken heart.

What could Mambres do in such thorny circumstances? Off he
went, the moment the Council meeting was over, to find his fair
ward, and said:

'My dear child, I shall do all I can for you. But I tell you again,
they will cut your head off if ever you should speak the name of the
one you love.'

'Ah, what is my neck to me,' said the fair Amasida, 'if I cannot put
my arms around the neck of Nebuchad . . . ! My father is a very
wicked man! Not only did he refuse to give me in marriage to the
handsome prince I worship, but he then declared war on him, and
when my beloved overcame him, he found a way of turning him into
an ox. Has there ever been a more dreadful piece of malice? If my
father were not my father, I don't know what I might not do to him.'

'It wasn't your father who played that cruel trick on him,' said
wise Mambres, 'it was a man from Palestine, one of our old enemies,
the inhabitant of one tiny country among all the host of nations
that your royal lover brought under his yoke the better to civilize
them. Anyway, metamorphoses like that ought not to surprise you.
You know how I used to do some rather better ones myself in my
time. At one stage there was nothing commoner than such transformations, though they raise a good many eyebrows among the wise
men of today. Those true stories that you and I used to read
together told us how Lycaon, King of Arcadia, was changed into a
wolf. The fair Callisto, his daughter, was changed into a she-bear; Io,
our own venerable Isis, daughter of Inachus, into a heifer; Daphne
into a laurel; and Syrinx into a pipe.* And fair Edith, wife of Lot, the
best, the most loving father that ever was, did she not become—not
far from here, moreover—a great big pillar of the finest and most
flavoursome salt, retaining all the marks of her sex, and having

regular periods every month,[1] according to the testimony of the great men who have been to see it?* I used to see transformations like that myself when I was young. I once watched five great cities, situated in the driest, dustiest part of the world, being transformed into a beautiful lake in a matter of moments.* In my young days you couldn't move for metamorphoses.

'In short, madam, if hearing examples of what has happened to others may help to lessen your pain, remember that Venus changed the Cerastes into oxen.'*

'I know,' said the unhappy Princess, 'but are the examples of other people really any comfort? If my lover were dead, would I find consolation in the fact that all men die?'

'Your troubles may not last for ever,' said the sage. 'Since your fond lover has become an ox, you can see, can you not, that from being an ox he may very well become a man again. As for me, I deserve to be turned into a tiger or a crocodile if I don't use what little power I have left on behalf of a Princess who is worthy to be worshipped by the entire world, on behalf of fair Amasida whom I dandled on my knees, and whose fateful destiny it is to suffer such cruel ordeals.'

CHAPTER 5

How wise Mambres acted wisely

HOLY Mambres, having offered the Princess every possible word of comfort, and brought her none at all, at once hastened to see the old woman.

'My dear comrade,' he said, 'ours is a fine profession, but it is also a very hazardous one. You are in danger of being hanged, and your ox of being burnt, or drowned, or eaten. I don't know what people will do to your other animals, for, prophet that I am, I really know very little. But keep the serpent and the whale well hidden. See that the latter keeps his head under water and that the other fellow

---

[1] Tertullian, in his poem *De Sodoma*, writes:

> Dicitur et vivens alio sub corpore sexus
> Munificos solito dispungere sanguine menses.

St Irene, book IV, has: 'Per naturalia ea quae sunt consuetudinis feminae ostendens.'

doesn't leave his hole. I will put the ox in one of my stables in the country. You can both be together there, since you say you're not allowed to leave him anywhere. The scapegoat will come in useful as a means of expiation. We'll send it away into the wilderness bearing the sins of the whole company. It's accustomed to the ceremony, and it'll do it no harm at all. And as you know, a goat that walks is a goat that works. All I ask is that you will shortly lend me Tobias's dog, that most agile hound, and the she-ass of Balaam, who can run faster than a dromedary, and the raven and the pigeon from the ark, both of them swift in flight. I want to send them on a mission to Memphis on a matter of the utmost importance.'

The old woman answered the magus:

'My lord, you can do what you like with Tobias's dog, and the she-ass of Balaam, with the raven and the pigeon from the ark, and the scapegoat. But my ox cannot lie in a stable. It is written that he must be tethered by a chain of metal, 'that his body shall be wet with the dew of heaven, that he must be fed with grass like oxen, and that his dwelling shall be with the wild asses'.[1] I have been put in charge of this: I must obey. What would Daniel, Ezekiel, and Jeremiah think if I entrusted my ox to others? I can see that you already know who this strange animal is, so I can't be blamed for letting you in on the secret. I am going to take him far away from this unclean land, towards Lake Sirbon, and far away from the cruel attentions of the King of Tanis. My whale and my serpent will defend me. I fear no one when I serve my master.'

Wise Mambres answered thus:

'My good woman, may God's will be done! Provided that I know where to find our white bull, I don't care whether he's at Lake Sirbon or Lake Moeris or Lake Sodom. I simply want to help him, and you too. But what have Daniel, Ezekiel, and Jeremiah got to do with it?'

'Oh, my noble sir,' the old woman rejoined, 'you know as well as I do the interest they took in this important business. But I have no time to lose. I have no wish to be hanged. I don't want my bull burnt, or drowned, or eaten. I'm off to Lake Sirbon, that is by Canope, with my serpent and my whale. Goodbye.'

---

[1] Daniel 5.*

The bull followed her, all pensive, having first given the beneficent Mambres to understand how grateful he was to him.

Wise Mambres was sore perplexed. He could see that Amasis, King of Tanis, being in despair at his daughter's mad passion for this animal, and believing her to be under a spell, would have the wretched bull pursued all over the place, and that the latter would inevitably be burnt as a sorcerer in the public square of Tanis, or else given to Jonah's whale, or roasted and served up at table. He wanted to spare the Princess this particular unpleasantness, whatever it took.

He wrote a letter to his friend, the High Priest of Memphis, in holy script and on Egyptian paper* (this was in the days before it was widely used). Here is his letter, word for word:

Light of the world, earthly agent of Isis, Osiris, and Horus, and chief of the circumcised, whose throne is raised, as is most meet, above all other thrones, I am apprised that your god, the Bull Apis, is dead. I have another here at your service. Come hither quickly with your priests to recognize and worship him, and to lead him away to the stall in your temple. May Isis, Osiris, and Horus watch over and keep you, and may they watch over you, my brothers and priests of Memphis!

Your affectionate friend,
Mambres.

He had four copies made of this letter, in case of accident, and enclosed them in cylindrical cases of hardest ebony. Then, summoning four couriers he had chosen to take this message (they were the she-ass, the dog, the raven, and the dove), he said to the she-ass:

'I know how faithfully you served my colleague Balaam. Serve me likewise. There is not an onager* alive as can outstrip you. Off you go, my dear lady, deliver my letter personally, and return.'

The she-ass replied:

'As I served Balaam, so shall I serve my noble Lord. I shall go and I shall return.'

The sage placed the ebony baton in her mouth, and she was away like an arrow.

Then he summoned Tobias's dog and said to him:

'Faithful cur, swifter in the chase than Achilles that was fleet of foot, I know what you did for Tobias, son of Tobit, when you and the angel Raphael accompanied him from Nineveh to Rages of Media, and from Rages to Nineveh, and when he brought his father back the ten talents[1] which Tobit had lent during his captivity to the slave Gabael, for these slaves were very rich.* Carry safely to its destination this letter that is more precious than ten talents of silver.'

The dog replied:

'My Lord, as once I followed Raphael the messenger, so may I run your errand just as well.'

Mambres placed the letter in his mouth. He spoke likewise to the dove. It replied:

'My Lord, as once I brought an olive branch back to the ark, so shall I bring you your reply.'

It took the letter in its beak. In an instant all three of them had disappeared from sight.

Then he said to the raven:

'I know how once you fed the great prophet Elijah[2] when he was in hiding by the brook Cherith, so renowned throughout the world. Every day you brought him fresh bread and plump fowl. All I'm asking you to do is to take this letter to Memphis.'

The raven answered with these words:

'It is true, my noble sir, that I did take the great prophet Elijah the Tishbite his dinner every day, and that I saw him ascend into the air on a chariot of fire which, though it is not the fashion, was drawn by four horses of fire.* But I always ate half the dinner myself. I shall happily carry your letter for you, as long as you promise me two square meals a day and payment in cash in advance for my pains.'

Mambres, much angered, told this animal:

'You sly glutton, I'm not surprised that, where once you were as white as a swan, Apollo should have turned you as black as a mole, that time on the plains of Thessaly when you betrayed the fair Coronis, the unfortunate mother of Asclepius.* So, tell me then, did you eat lark and chicken every day when you spent those ten months on the ark?'

'We ate very well, sir,' the raven retorted. 'Roast meat was served twice a day to all winged creatures like me who live only on flesh, to all vultures, kites, eagles, buzzards, hawks, kestrels, falcons, horned owls, barn owls, and the whole countless host of birds of prey. Much larger quantities were laid out for the lions, leopards, tigers, pan-thers, ounces, hyenas, wolves, bears, foxes, martens, and all them

---

[1] Twenty thousand French silver ecus, at current rates.
[2] 1 Kings 17.

four-legged carnivores. There were eight persons of rank on the ark—indeed they were the only persons left in the world at all—and they were continually kept busy looking after our table and our wardrobe: to wit, Noah and his wife, who were hardly a day over six hundred, and their three sons with their three wives. It did one's heart good to see how clean and tidy those eight servants of ours kept the place while they provided for four thousand guests with extremely large appetites, not to mention the enormous problems caused by ten to twelve thousand other individuals, from the elephant and the giraffe to the silkworm and the fly. The only thing that surprises me is that our provider, Noah, should be unknown to every nation whose stem he is. But that's no concern of mine. I had already been to a feast like that before at Sisutrus's, the King of Thrace's.[1] It's the sort of thing that happens to us crows and ravens from time to time by way of a lesson. In a word, I want good grub and to be well paid in cash.'

Wise Mambres forbore to entrust his letter to so particular and garrulous a beast. They parted company thoroughly displeased with one another.

He had, meanwhile, to find out what was going to become of the handsome bull, and not to lose track of the old woman and the serpent. Mambres gave orders to some intelligent and trusty servants to follow them, and he for his part proceeded in a litter along the banks of the Nile, as deeply absorbed in his cogitations as ever.

'How is it', he mused, 'that this serpent is master of almost the entire world, as he is always bragging he is, and as so many learned men say he is, and yet he does as an old woman tells him? How is it that he is periodically summoned to the council up above, while down here he must go upon his belly? How can he possess people all the time by virtue of his own person, while so many sages claim it takes words to drive him out again? And why does one small nation not far from here suppose him to have been the ruination of the human race, and yet the human race knows not a thing about it? I've reached a ripe old age and I've studied all my life, but all I can see here is a whole host of contradictions which I cannot reconcile. I

---

[1] Berosus, the Chaldean writer, does indeed record that the same thing happened to Sisutrus, King of Thrace. The event was even more marvellous, for his ark was five stadia long by two stadia wide. A great controversy has arisen among men of learning as to which of them is the more ancient, King Sisutrus or Noah.

cannot explain the things that have happened to me, nor the great feats I performed once upon a time, nor those I have witnessed. All things considered, I am beginning to suspect that the world actually works on contradictions. "Rerum concordia discors", as my master Zoroaster used to say in his own tongue.'*

While he was lost in these metaphysical speculations which, like all metaphysics, tended to the obscure, a boatman singing a drinking song moored a small boat by the bank. Three grave personages alighted from it, half-clad in dirty, torn rags, but still managing to maintain beneath this livery of destitution the most majestic and august of airs. It was Daniel, Ezekiel, and Jeremiah.

CHAPTER 6

How Mambres met three prophets and gave them a good dinner

THESE great men, whose faces shone with the light of prophecy, recognized Mambres as one of them by the few rays of such light that still remained to him, and prostrated themselves in front of his palanquin. Mambres, too, recognized them as prophets, though more by their clothing than by the streaks of fire darting from their august heads. He had a shrewd idea that they had come to find out about the white bull; and with his usual caution he stepped down from his conveyance and walked a few paces towards them in a manner which combined courteous welcome with dignified reserve. He helped them to their feet and gave orders for tents to be pitched and dinner prepared, for he judged the three prophets to have great need of both.

He sent an invitation to the old woman, who was as yet only five hundred paces off. She accepted the invitation and arrived, still leading the white bull on a tether.

Two soups were served, one a bisque, the other a chicken broth. As entrées they had carp's tongue tart, liver of burbot and pike, chicken with pistachios, some young pigeon garnished with truffles and olives, two turkey pullets in a coulis of crayfish, with agarics and morels, and an onion stew. The main course consisted of young pheasant, partridge, grouse, quail, and ortolan, accompanied by four salads. In the middle stood a centrepiece in the most exquisite taste.

Nothing could have surpassed the delicate flavour of the entremets, nor could one have hoped for a more magnificent, more eye-catching, or more imaginative dessert.

Moreover, Mambres had discreetly seen to it that the meal contained no boiled silverside or roast sirloin or ox-tongue or palate of beef, nor a single cow's udder, lest the unfortunate monarch, who was watching the dinner from a distance, should think they meant him any offence.

This great, unhappy Prince was grazing by the tent. Never had he felt more cruelly the fateful turn of events which had deprived him of his throne for seven long years.

'Alas,' he thought to himself, 'there's Daniel who turned me into a bull, and that witch of a pythoness who watches over me, both enjoying the choicest fare one could ever wish to eat, and here am I, the sovereign ruler of all Asia, reduced to eating grass and drinking water!'

They drank liberally of the wines of Engedi, Tadmor, and Shiraz. When the prophets and the pythoness had become somewhat the worse for wear, conversation began to flow more freely than it had during the earlier courses.

'I must say,' said Daniel, 'I certainly didn't eat half as well as this when I was in the lions' den.'

'What, sir, they put you in the lions' den?' said Mambres. 'And how is it they didn't eat you?'

'You know perfectly well, sir,' said Daniel, 'that lions don't eat prophets.'

'In my case,' said Jeremiah, 'I've spent my whole life starving to death. I'd never eaten a proper meal before today. If I had to be born again and I could choose what as, I would much rather be a tax-inspector or a bishop in Babylon than a prophet in Jerusalem, I can tell you.'

Ezekiel spoke:

'I was once ordered to lie on my left side for three hundred and ninety days, and throughout that entire time to eat barley cakes, millet, fitches, lentils, and wheat covered in . . .[1] I dare not say what. The only concession I managed to extract was that it could be cow-dung. My lord Mambres serves rather daintier fare, I don't mind

---

[1] Ezekiel 4.

telling you. But being a prophet isn't all bad. You've only to look at the hundreds of us who do it.'

'Talking of which,' said Mambres, 'would you mind explaining to me what your Aholah and your Aholibah had to do with anything, and why they were so keen on horses and asses?'*

'Oh them,' Ezekiel replied, 'they were just rhetorical flourishes.'

After these frank unburdenings of the heart, Mambres got down to business. He asked the three pilgrims why they were come unto the kingdom of Tanis. Daniel answered first. He said that the kingdom of Babylon had been in a state of great upheaval since Nebuchadnezzar had disappeared; that the prophets had all been persecuted in line with normal court practice; that they spent half the time with kings lying prostrate at their feet, and the other half receiving a good thrashing; and that in the end they had been obliged to seek refuge in Egypt for fear of being stoned. Ezekiel and Jeremiah also spoke at length and in a very fine style, but no one really understood what they were saying. As for the pythoness, she continued to keep a watchful eye on her beast. Jonah's whale was in the Nile, opposite the tent, and the serpent was playing in the grass.

After coffee they went for a walk along the Nile. Then the white bull, catching sight of the three prophets who were his enemies, bellowed fearsomely, charged them, and caught them with his horns; and as prophets are generally nothing but skin and bone, he would have run them through and gored them to death. But the master of things, who sees all and puts everything to right, at once changed them into magpies; and they went on talking just as before. The same thing happened again subsequently with the Pierides,* so closely has fable imitated history.

This latest incident gave wise Mambres further food for thought.

'There you are,' he said, 'three great prophets turned into magpies. That'll teach us not to talk too much, nor to speak out of turn.'

He concluded that wisdom is more precious than eloquence and was busy mulling this over, in his usual way, when a great and terrible spectacle presented itself to his gaze.

CHAPTER 7

The King of Tanis arrives. His daughter and the bull are
to be sacrificed

GREAT whirlwinds of dust could be seen approaching from the
south. There came a sound of drum, trumpet, fife, psaltery, dulci-
mer, and sackbut.* Several squadrons and battalions were on the
march, and Amasis, King of Tanis, was at their head, riding on a
horse caparisoned in a cloth of scarlet and gold brocade. And the
heralds were crying out:

'Seize the white bull. Bind him, and cast him into the Nile, and let
Jonah's whale feed on him. For the King, my lord, who is just, will
be avenged on the white bull who has put a spell upon his daughter.'

Good old Mambres thought harder than ever. He saw clearly that
the sly raven had gone to tell the King everything, and that the
Princess was in great danger of having her head cut off. He said to
the serpent:

'My dear friend, go quickly and comfort the fair Amasida, my
ward. Reassure her that there is nothing to be afraid of, whatever
happens, and tell her a few of your stories to charm away her fears.
Because girls like listening to stories, and telling stories is the only
way to get on in the world.'

He then fell on his face before Amasis, King of Tanis, and said
to him:

'O King, may you live for ever! The white bull must be sacrificed,
for Your Majesty is always right. But the master of things has said:
"This bull shall not be eaten by Jonah's whale until Memphis shall
have found a god to replace the god that is dead." Then shall you be
avenged, and your daughter will be exorcised; for she is possessed.
You are too pious a man not to obey the orders of the master of
things.'

Amasis, King of Tanis, thought for a while. Then he said:

'The Bull Apis is dead. May God have gathered his soul unto
Him! When do you think they'll find another bull to reign over
fertile Egypt?'

'Sire,' said Mambres, 'I ask but one week.'

The King, who was very religious, said:

'I grant it you. I shall remain here for a week, at the end of which I shall sacrifice my daughter's seducer.'

And he summoned his tents, his cooks, and his musicians, and remained one week in this place, as it is written in Manethon.*

The old woman was in despair that the bull in her keeping had only a week to live. Every night she had departed spirits appear to the King in order to deflect him from his cruel purpose. But in the morning the King never remembered about the spirits he had seen in the night, just as Nebuchadnezzar had once forgotten his dreams.

CHAPTER 8

How the serpent told stories to the Princess, to comfort her

MEANWHILE the serpent was telling stories to the fair Amasida to ease her pain. He told her how he had once cured an entire nation of the bites of certain little serpents, simply by displaying himself at the end of a stick. He told her of the exploits of one hero, who had behaved in such marked contrast to Amphion, the architect of Thebes in Boetia. This Amphion used to have his building stones fetched to the sound of a violin: a rigadoon and a minuet were enough to build an entire city. But the other fellow could destroy cities to the sound of a trumpet. This man also hanged thirty-one kings who were very powerful and ruled a canton some four leagues long by four leagues wide. He had great stones rain down from heaven on an enemy battalion fleeing before him; and having slain them this way, he then bid the sun and the moon stand still in broad daylight so that he could smite them again between Gibeon and Ajalon on the road to Bethoron (just like Bacchus, who once stayed the sun and the moon on his journey to the Indies).*

The wisdom and caution that every serpent must possess prevented him from telling fair Amasida the one about Jephthah, that mighty son of an harlot, who cut his daughter's head off because he had just won a battle. This particular story might have inspired rather too much terror in the Princess. But he did relate the adventures of the great Samson who slew a thousand Philistines with the jawbone of an ass, tied three hundred foxes together by the tail, and then allowed himself to be caught in the snares of a girl less fair, less tender, and less true than the charming Amasida.*

He told her of the unhappy amours of Shechem and the delightful Dinah, aged six, and of the rather happier amours of Boaz and Ruth, of the amorous liaisons of Judah with Tamar, his daughter-in-law, of Lot with those two daughters of his who did not want the world to end, of Abraham and Jacob with their handmaids, of Reuben with his mother, of David and Bathsheba, of great King Solomon, anything, in short, that might dissipate the grief of a fair Princess.*

CHAPTER 9

How the serpent brought her no comfort

'I FIND stories like that boring,' remarked the fair Amasida, who had both intelligence and good taste. 'All they're good for is having commentaries written about them by Irishmen like that lunatic Abbadie, or Frenchmen like that phrase-monger of a Houteville.* The sort of story that might once have been told to the great-great-great-grandmother of the great-great-great-grandmother of my grandmother will no longer do for me, educated as I have been by wise Mambres, and having read the *Essay concerning Human Understanding* of our Egyptian philosopher Locke, not to mention the *Widow of Ephesus*.* I require a story to be essentially plausible, and not always sounding like the account of a dream. I prefer it to be neither trivial nor far-fetched. I particularly like the ones which, from beneath the veil of the plot, reveal to the experienced eye some subtle truth that will escape the common herd. I am tired of suns and moons that old women do as they please with, and mountains that dance, and rivers that flow back to their source, and dead people coming back to life.* But, worst of all, when this sort of nonsense is written in an inflated and incomprehensible style, I find it dreadfully tiresome. As you can appreciate, a girl who is afraid of seeing her lover gobbled up at any moment by a great whale and of having her head cut off by her very own father, does need something to keep her amused. But try to amuse me in a manner to suit my taste.'

'That's rather a tall order,' replied the serpent. 'Time was when I could have helped you while away many a happy hour. But latterly my imagination and my memory have not been quite what they were. Alas, where are the days when I used to entertain the girls? Still, let's see if I can remember some moral tale to please you.

'Twenty-five thousand years ago King Gnaof and Queen Patra sat upon the throne of Thebes, city of a hundred gates. King Gnaof was very handsome, and Queen Patra even more beautiful. But they were unable to have children. King Gnaof offered a prize for the person who would show them how best to carry on the royal line. The faculty of medicine and the college of surgeons both produced excellent treatises on this important question: not one led to success. The Queen was dispatched to take the waters. She fasted and said novenas. She gave a considerable sum of money to the temple of Jupiter Ammon, who gave us ammonium chloride. All to no avail. Finally a young priest of twenty-five came before the King and said to him:

' "Sire, I think I may know the sacred words which will produce that which Your Majesty so ardently desires. It will be necessary for me to have a private word in Her Majesty your wife's ear. And if she does not conceive, you can hang me."

' "I accept your proposal," said King Gnaof.

'The Queen and the priest were left alone together for a quarter of an hour. The Queen conceived, and the King would dearly have hanged the priest.'

'Dear God,' said the Princess, 'I can guess what's coming next. Your story is much too common. I would even say that it alarms my maidenly modesty. Tell me a fable that is perfectly true and well attested, one that really is moral, and that I haven't heard before, one "to complete the education of my heart and mind",* as our Egyptian pedagogue Linro would say.'

'Here's one then, madam,' said the handsome serpent, 'and there's none more authentic.

'There once were three prophets, each of them as ambitious and dissatisfied with his lot as the other. Their folly was to want to be kings; for there is but one step from the rank of prophet to that of monarch, and man forever aspires to climb every rung upon the ladder of fortune. Otherwise their tastes and interests were as different as could be. The first used to give marvellous sermons to his assembled brethren, who would applaud. The second was desperately fond of music. And the third had a passion for young ladies.

The angel Ituriel came to speak to them one day as they were sitting at table discussing the delights of being royal.

' "The master of things has sent me to you", the angel told them, "to reward your virtue. Not only will you all be kings, but you will also all find constant satisfaction in your ruling passion. You, the first prophet, I make you King of Egypt. You will be able to hold meetings of the Council whenever you like, and they will applaud your eloquence and your wisdom. You, the second prophet, you will reign in Persia. You will be able to spend the entire time listening to heavenly music. And you, the third prophet, I make you King of India, and you can have a charming mistress who will never leave you."

'The one who was allocated Egypt began by summoning his Privy Council, a body of a mere two hundred sages. He harangued them at length, as protocol required, and was much applauded; and the monarch tasted the sweet intoxication of praise untainted by flattery.

'After the Privy Council came the Council for Foreign Affairs. This was a much larger body; and his new speech met with even greater eulogies. And so it went on with the other councils. There was not a moment's respite from the pleasures and glory of being the Prophet King of Egypt. The noise of his eloquence spread to the four corners of the earth.

'The Prophet King of Persia began by having an Italian opera staged for himself, in which the choruses were sung by fifteen hundred castrati. Their voices moved his soul to the very marrow of his bones (which is where, in fact, it is located). This opera was succeeded by another, and the second was followed by a third, without interval.

'The King of India closeted himself with his mistress, and there knew sensual pleasure to perfection. He regarded it as a sovereign felicity to have constantly to be caressing her, and he pitied the sad fates of his two colleagues, of whom one was reduced ever to keeping his own council, and the other to being always at the opera.

'Some days later all three of them heard some woodcutters outside their window, who were leaving an inn on the way to do some woodcutting in a nearby forest, each one with a little lady-friend on his arm that he could swap as the fancy took him. Our kings begged Ituriel to be kind enough to intercede for them with the master of things and to make them woodcutters.'

'Well,' interrupted the tender Amasida, 'I have no idea whether the master of things granted their request or not, and I don't much care. But I do know that I should want nothing of anybody if I were closeted alone with the one I love, with my dear Nebuchadnezzar.'

The vaults of the palace ceilings echoed to the sound of this great name. First Amasida had said only 'Ne', then 'Nebu', then 'Nebuchad', but finally passion had got the better of her, and she had uttered the fatal name in full, despite the solemn promise that she had made her father. All the ladies of the palace repeated 'Nebuchadnezzar' after her, and the sly raven did not fail to go and inform the King. The countenance of Amasis, King of Tanis, grew troubled, for he was troubled also in his heart. And that is how the serpent, the most wise and most subtle of all the beasts of the field,* was for ever bringing harm to women when he thought only to do them good.

Now Amasis, full of wrath, gave orders on the instant for his daughter Amasida to be fetched by twelve of his alguazils, those men who are ever ready to perform all manner of dirty deed at the King's command, and then say in their own defence: 'It's what we're paid for.'

CHAPTER 10

How they wanted to cut off the Princess's head, and how they did not cut it off

As soon as the Princess arrived, all trembling, at the camp of her father the King, he said to her:

'My child, you are aware that it is customary to put to death any princess who disobeys her royal father. A kingdom cannot be governed properly otherwise. I forbade you to speak the name of Nebuchadnezzar, your lover and my mortal enemy, the same that dethroned me nearly seven years ago and that then disappeared from off the face of the earth. In his place you have chosen a white bull, and you have cried out "Nebuchadnezzar". It is right that I should cut off your head.'

The Princess answered him:

'Father, may your will be done, but grant me time at least to bewail my virginity.'

'That is only fair,' said King Amasis. 'It is a well-established usage among all prudent and enlightened princes.* You shall have one whole day to bewail your virginity, since you say you still possess it. Tomorrow, which is the last day of my week's encamping, I shall have the white bull swallowed by the whale, and I shall cut your head off at nine o'clock in the morning.'

And so the fair Amasida went for a walk along the banks of the Nile there to bewail, in the company of her court ladies, such virginity as remained to her. Wise Mambres meditated at her side, counting the hours and the minutes.

'Well, my dear Mambres,' she said, 'you once changed the waters of the Nile into blood, in the time-honoured fashion, but now you can't even change the mind of my father Amasis, King of Tanis! Are you going to let him cut off my head at nine o'clock in the morning?'

'It will all rather hang', replied the meditative Mambres, 'on the diligence of my messengers.'

Next day, as soon as the shadows cast by the obelisks and the pyramids indicated the ninth hour of the day, they bound the white bull with rope the better to throw him to Jonah's whale, and they brought the King his great sword.

'Alas and alack,' said Nebuchadnezzar privately to himself, 'I am the King, and yet I've been an ox for nigh on these seven years. And hardly am I reunited with the woman I love than they feed me to a whale.'

Never before had the wise Mambres thought so long or so hard. He was immersed in his sorry reflections when, lo, in the distance, he espied all that he had been waiting for. A huge crowd was approaching. The three figures of Isis, Osiris, and Horus were advancing together in unison, borne upon a litter of jewel-studded gold by a hundred senators of Memphis and preceded by one hundred maidens playing upon the sacred sistrum. Four thousand priests, their heads shaven and crowned with flowers, accompanied them, mounted each upon a hippopotamus. Further back, and no less resplendent, came the ewe of Thebes, Bubastis's dog, Phoebe's cat, Arsinoe's crocodile, Mendez's goat, and all the lesser gods of Egypt, who were come to pay homage to the Great Bull, to the great god Apis, who was as powerful as Isis, Osiris, and Horus put together.*

In the midst of all these demigods, forty priests were carrying an enormous basket filled with sacred onions,* which were not quite gods but looked very much as if they might have been.

On either side of this long line of gods, and of the countless throng that followed, marched forty thousand warriors, helmet on head, scimitar at the left hip, quiver over the shoulder, and bow in hand.

All the priests were singing in chorus, and in a harmony such as both touched and uplifted the soul:

> Our ox is dead and done,
> We'll find ourselves a better one.

And with each pause in their song could be heard the sound of sistrum, castanet, tambourine, psaltery, bagpipe, harp, and sackbut.

CHAPTER 11

How the Princess married her ox

AMASIS, King of Tanis, surprised by this spectacle, did not cut his daughter's head off: he replaced his scimitar in its scabbard. Mambres said to him:

'Great King! A new order has begun. Your Majesty must set the example. O King! Go quickly and untie the white bull yourself, and be the first to worship him.'

Amasis obeyed and prostrated himself, he and his whole people with him. The High Priest of Memphis offered the first handful of hay to the new Bull Apis. Princess Amasida festooned his handsome horns with roses, anemones, buttercups, tulips, pinks, and hyacinths. She took the liberty of kissing him, albeit with great reverence. The priests strewed palms and flowers along the way as they led him back to Memphis. And wise Mambres, still cogitating, whispered to his friend the serpent:

'Daniel turned the man into an ox, and I have turned the ox into a god.'

They returned to Memphis in the same order of procession. The King of Tanis, somewhat dazed, followed in their train. Mambres, looking calm and collected, walked at his side. The old woman followed them, lost in admiration. She was accompanied by the serpent, the dog, the she-ass, the raven, the dove, and the scapegoat. The whale swam up the Nile. Daniel, Ezekiel, and Jeremiah, who had been changed into magpies, brought up the rear.

When they reached the frontier of the kingdom, which was not far, King Amasis took his leave of the Bull Apis and said to his daughter:

'My daughter, let us return unto our lands that I may cut off your head, even as it has been resolved in my royal heart that I shall, because you spoke the name of Nebuchadnezzar, my enemy, the same that dethroned me seven years ago. When a father has sworn to cut off his daughter's head, he must fulfil his promise; otherwise he is cast into hell for ever, and I have no wish to be damned for love of you.'

The fair Princess answered King Amasis in this wise:

'My dear father, you can go and cut the head off anyone you please, but you're not cutting off mine. I stand upon the territory of Isis, Osiris, Horus, and Apis. I will not leave my handsome white bull. I shall kiss him all along the way until I have seen his apotheosis in the great stable of the holy city of Memphis. A girl of my station may surely be indulged in such a fancy.'

Hardly were the words out of her mouth than the Bull Apis exclaimed:

'My dearest Amasida, I shall love you till I die.'

This was the first time anyone in Egypt had ever heard Apis speak in all the forty thousand years they had worshipped him. The serpent and the she-ass cried out:

'The seven years are over.'

The Egyptian priests all lifted up their hands to heaven. Suddenly everyone noticed that the god was losing his two hind legs. His two front legs became human legs. Two fine, solid, muscular, white arms emerged from his shoulders. His bull's muzzle gave way to the features of a charming hero. He turned back into the handsomest man on earth, and said:

'I would rather be Amasida's lover than be a god. I am Nebuchadnezzar, King of Kings.'

This latest metamorphosis astonished everybody, apart from the meditative Mambres. But what surprised no one was that Nebuchadnezzar married the fair Amasida there and then in the presence of this large gathering.

He let his father-in-law keep the kingdom of Tanis, and established some generous foundations for the she-ass, the serpent, the dog, the dove, and even for the raven, the three magpies, and the whale, thereby demonstrating to the whole world that he could pardon as well as conquer. The old woman received a fat pension. The scapegoat was sent off into the desert for a day that all past sins might be expiated; after which they gave him twelve she-goats as a reward. Wise Mambres returned to his palace to think things over. Nebuchadnezzar, having embraced him in fond farewell, reigned in peace over the kingdoms of Memphis, Babylon, Damascus, Balbec, and Tyre, over Syria, Asia Minor, and Scythia, over the lands of Shiraz, Mosok, Tubal, Madai, Gog, Magog, and Javan, over Sogdiana, Bactria, the Indies, and the Isles.*

Every morning the peoples of this vast realm would chant:

'Long live great Nebuchadnezzar, King of Kings. No longer a dumb animal he!'

And ever afterwards it was the custom in Babylon, each time a ruler (having been grossly deceived by his satraps, or his magi, or his treasurers, or his wives) recognized the error of his ways and duly mended them, for the entire populace to shout out at his gate:

'Long live our great King who is no longer dumb!'

EXPLANATORY NOTES

CANDIDE

3 *epigraph*: this pastiche of the traditional fictional device of the lost manuscript has no basis in fact. The ungermanic name of Dr Ralph is a
mystification, though it is true (if irrelevant) that Minden is in
Westphalia.

7 *The King of the Bulgars joined battle with the King of the Abars*: the King
of the Bulgars constitutes a veiled allusion to Frederick the Great of
Prussia, whose homosexuality is suggested by his fictional nationality. As
in all Voltaire's stories, however, the allegory transcends its possible top-
ical basis. Similarly, the war in question is partly the Seven Years War
(1756–63) but also all European wars before or indeed since.

9 *a worthy Anabaptist named Jacques*: Voltaire has in mind a sect of the
Protestant Reformation that originated in Holland and Germany in the
sixteenth century, and whose members set great store by simplicity and
the sharing of goods. Hence Jacques's charity. From the Greek *ana* +
baptizein, meaning to baptize again. Anabaptists were—and are—noted
for their advocacy of adult baptism (on the grounds that infant baptism is
invalid because not voluntarily sought). That Jacques should die by
drowning is thus a piece of Voltairean irony, as is the fact that his death
results from saving another man's life.

13 *Four times I've trampled on the crucifix*: after the expulsion of all Europeans (and Christians) from Japan in the seventeenth century, Dutch
merchants were allowed to continue trading with Japan if they carried
out this act of abjuration. It is also mentioned in *Gulliver's Travels*.

The city of Lima . . . last year: Lima was destroyed by an earthquake
in 1746.

14 *guilty of marrying his fellow godparent*: the Roman Catholic Church
regarded godparents as having entered into a spiritual relationship with
one another with which the physical relationship of marriage was
incompatible. For the same reason it forbade marriage between godparent and godchild. The correct English term for fellow godparent is
'gossip', but the relationship now suggested by this word is no longer
exactly one of deep spirituality.

had removed the bacon when eating a chicken: Voltaire mocks anti-Semitic
persecution with a characteristic *reductio ad absurdum*.

15 *san-benito*: a scapular, or long strip of sackcloth with simply a hole for the
head. Those who admitted their guilt, whether or not under torture,
wore ones with the flames pointing downwards, which indicated that
they were to receive a lesser punishment than being burnt at the stake.

Those who remained unrepentant, and were to be burnt, had flames pointing upwards. The presence or absence of devils' tails and claws would appear to be a whimsical Voltairean refinement.

21 *Holy Hermandad*: the agents of the Holy Brotherhood of the Inquisition.

22 *a fleet was being fitted out . . . San Sacramento*: the mission settlements in Paraguay, then a much larger territory than it is today, were about to be partitioned between Spain and Portugal, but the Jesuit missionaries who governed them declared their independence, whether for their own gain or, as they claimed, to protect the Paraguayans from slave-traders. Between 1754 and 1757 combined Spanish and Portuguese forces were sent to crush the rebellion. The Jesuits were finally expelled in 1767.

26 *O che sciagura d'essere senza c . . . !*: 'O what a misfortune to be without b[alls]!'

28 *Robeck*: born in Colmar in 1672, and moderately notorious, he preached the absurdity of living (particularly in Sweden, it seems). He waited until 1739 before he actually disposed of himself by drowning.

30 *the Cordelier with the loose sleeves*: in 1581 the Franciscan order was riven by a dispute about the design of its habit, in particular about the nature of the sleeves and the hood. Hence the order was a favourite butt of Voltaire's anticlerical humour. Cordeliers are Franciscan friars, so called because they wear a rope-belt. Since the Franciscan order began as a group of mendicant friars who set particular store by poverty, the use of the loose sleeve in a manner akin to the poacher's pocket has particular edge.

36 *Journal de Trévoux*: an influential Jesuit periodical of the time, and noted for its opposition to the *Encyclopédie* published from 1751 onwards by D'Alembert (1717–83) and Diderot (1713–84) with the collaboration of many writers including Voltaire.

38 *the Lobeiros*: in French 'les Oreillons': after the Spanish name 'Orejones' given to a particular tribe with large, long-lobed ears which had been described in Garcilaso de La Vega's *Histoire des Incas du Pérou* (1704). The auricular deformity may, it has been suggested, have been attributable to the weight of their earrings. In French the name is the more comic for also meaning 'mumps'. It may be noted that the cannibalism of Voltaire's Lobeiros would seem to be no worse—indeed, in some respects, it is more discriminating—than that of the Turkish aga and his janissaries who survive a siege on lady's buttock.

45 *the law courts*: the French includes the term 'parlement', which was a supreme judicial body quite unlike a modern elected assembly and, roughly speaking, combined the functions of a high court and a court of appeal. It was also part of its function to register royal edicts as they passed into law. The 'parlements' exerted greater and greater power under the reign of Louis XV (1715–74), much to Voltaire's dismay. For Voltaire, part of the perfection of Eldorado lies in having an enlightened,

constitutional monarch whose power is not eroded by his judiciary. See Introduction, p. xxxix.

51 *a Socinian*: a follower of the Siennese uncle and nephew Lelio and Fausto Sozzini (in Latin Laelius and Faustus Socinus) who founded a sect of antitrinitarians in the sixteenth century. Like the modern Unitarian Church they denied the divinity of Christ but asserted the superiority of his moral teaching. Essentially theirs was an attempt to found religion on reason, and as such they were of considerable interest to Voltaire.

52 *I am a Manichaean*: see Introduction, p. xiii.

53 *There was more joy in Candide at finding this one sheep*: a parody of Christ's parable of the lost sheep (Matthew 18: 12–14; Luke 15: 3–7).

54 *the religious convulsions crowd*: Voltaire has in mind those Jansenist fanatics who, between 1729 and 1732, publicly went into allegedly 'miraculous' trances and convulsions, particularly in the Saint-Médard cemetery where the Jansenist deacon Pâris was buried. Jansenism was a religious doctrine derived from the works of St Augustine by Cornelius Jansen, or Jansenius (1585–1638), Bishop of Ypres in Flanders. In a manner akin to that of Calvinism, it repudiated the efficacy of the human will and asserted predestination, claiming that divine grace would be granted to the elect rather than earned by good works. Like Calvinism it was characterized by moral austerity. It had a strong popular following as well as many powerful adherents in the law courts or 'parlements'.

56 *a confessional note . . . the other world*: this refers to a practice prevalent in the 1750s whereby the last rites would be performed only on presentation of a note from one's confessor attesting that one had subscribed to the Papal Bull *Unigenitus*, issued in 1713 and condemning certain aspects of Jansenism as heretical. See below, note to p. 190 of *The Ingenu*.

a little abbé from Périgord: an abbé was far from being an abbot as we understand that term. He was one who was entitled to wear ecclesiastical dress by virtue of some theological study, but who did not necessarily belong to the clergy. Such study was usually the only way to receive higher education unless you were a member of the aristocracy or higher gentry: hence there were a large number of abbés. Some received a church living but did not carry out any of the incumbent's duties, which were delegated to a curate. As Theodore Besterman puts it: 'nearly all of [them] lived exactly like everybody else, except that they did not usually marry; their conduct therefore tended to be even more irregular than that of laymen' (*Voltaire*, 29 n. 24).

57 *she was buried alone . . . nobly*: actors and actresses were automatically excommunicate in France and therefore denied a Christian burial (just as, for obviously different reasons, Don Issacar the Jew is denied a dignified interment in Chapter 9). Voltaire has in mind the famous actress Adrienne Lecouvreur (1692–1730) who had played the part of Monime in Racine's *Mithridate*. She had also taken the leading role in some of his own plays.

58 *a Fréron*: Élie Fréron (1718–76), an implacable and not always unjustified critic of Voltaire's tragedies.

59 *Master Gauchat . . . Archdeacon T . . .*: both Gauchat and the Archdeacon T . . . (in fact the abbé Trublet) were opponents of Voltaire and the *Encyclopédie*. The former wrote twelve volumes of supposed refutations between 1753 and 1763, and the latter was author of the *Journal chrétien*. This section on the visit to the Marchioness of Dubelauchwitz and its accompanying discussion of the theatre was added by Voltaire after 1759.

61 *Molinists*: Louis Molina (1535–1600) was a sixteenth-century Spanish Jesuit who had been the author of the Jesuits' doctrine on the question of free will. Here 'Molinists' is a synonym for 'Jesuits' but implies that the Jesuit quarrel in this case is with the Jansenist doctrine of predestination. Père La Chaise, Louis XIV's confessor who features in *The Ingenu*, was a Molinist.

64 *a wretch from Atrabatia . . . what this was all about*: Atrabatia is the Latin name of the province of Artois, the birthplace of Robert-François Damiens (1714–57) who attempted to assassinate Louis XV in 1757. Henri IV was assassinated by François Ravaillac (1578–1610) in 1610, an unsuccessful attempt on his life having been made in 1594.

65 *so as to encourage the others*: Admiral Byng had been in command of British naval forces when they were defeated by the French (under Admiral Galissonnière) off Minorca in 1756. Court-martialled for his irresolute conduct in the engagement, he was acquitted of the charge of cowardice but found guilty of dereliction of duty and, on 14 March 1757, executed by firing squad on his own quarterdeck. Voltaire had met Byng when he was in England and vainly interceded on his behalf with a letter written in Byng's defence by the duc de Richelieu, a Marshal of France and Voltaire's friend since his schooldays, who had played an important part in the engagement.

67 *a young Theatine monk*: the Theatines were a Roman Catholic brotherhood co-founded in 1524 by Gian Petro Carafa, Bishop of Chieti (in Latin *Teate*), later Pope Paul IV.

72 *his journey to Brindisi . . . the stars in the heavens*: Horace, *Satires*, i, 5; ii. 8; i. 7 (Horace has Rupilius, not Pupilus); *Epodes*, v. 8, 12; *Odes*, i. 1.

77 *carnival in Venice*: respectively the six kings are: (1) Sultan Achmed III who ruled over Turkey from 1703 to 1730. He was deposed after a military coup by the janissaries and died in 1736; (2) Ivan VI of Russia who was dethroned in favour of Elizabeth, the daughter of Peter the Great. He was imprisoned and later put to death in 1764 on the orders of Catherine the Great; (3) Charles Edward Stuart, the Young Pretender (1720–88), grandson of James II of England and son of James Stuart, the Old Pretender, who died in Rome in 1766; (4) Augustus II, King of Poland and Elector of Saxony, who was dispossessed of his Saxon lands by Frederick of Prussia in 1756. His father Augustus II of Poland had been dethroned by Charles XII of Sweden in 1703 but later reinstated

after Charles XII was defeated by the Russians at the battle of Poltava in 1709; (5) Stanislas Lesczinski, King of Poland from 1704 to 1709, and whose daughter Marie married Louis XV in 1726. On the death of Augustus III in 1733 he had tried to regain the throne but eventually, in 1735, returned to France where he was granted the Duchy of Lorraine which he ruled until his death in 1766; (6) Théodore, one-time adventurer in the service of Sweden, and later representative of Charles VI, Emperor of Austria, in Florence, who then helped the Corsicans in their revolt against their Genoese masters and was proclaimed King of Corsica on several occasions. He was subsequently imprisoned as a debtor in England, where he died in 1756. Needless to say, these six kings could not all have been in Venice at the same time.

78 *an ex-ruler called Ragotsky*: Rákóczy (1676–1735), Prince of Transylvania, subsidized by Louis XIV and supported by the Turks, had instigated a Hungarian uprising against the Emperor Joseph I in the early years of the century. The uprising was quelled, and he took refuge in a palace on the Sea of Marmara near Constantinople.

81 *a young icoglan*: icoglans were young boys employed in a sultan's seraglio.

83 *the plenum and materia subtilis*: see Introduction, p. x.

85 *the Sublime Porte*: the Ottoman or Turkish court.

MICROMEGAS

89 *twenty thousand French feet*: in French a 'pied de roi', which measured 0.324 metres, as opposed to a 'pied anglais', which measured 0.305 metres. The 'pied de roi' was divisible into 12 'pouces' (lit. 'thumbs'), which in turn were divisible into 12 'lignes' (lit. 'lines'). A 'toise', translated as a 'fathom', was the equivalent of six 'pieds de roi'.

90 *or so his sister says*: Mme Périer, in her *Vie de M. Pascal* (1684). Blaise Pascal (1623–62) was indeed a precociously gifted mathematician. He defended Jansenism (see above, note to p. 54) in both his *Lettres provinciales* (1656–7) and his fragmentary *Pensées* (published posthumously).

at the end of his telescope: the Reverend William Derham in his *Astro-Theology, or a Demonstration of the being and attributes of God from a survey of the heavens* (London, 1715).

91 *Lully's music*: Jean-Baptiste Lully (1632–87), influential court musician and composer to Louis XIV, renowned especially for his operas and ballets.

Secretary of the Saturnian Academy . . . long calculations: Voltaire has in mind Fontenelle (1657–1757), who was Secretary of the Académie des Sciences in Paris from 1699, a Fellow of the Royal Society, and author of the *Entretiens sur la pluralité des mondes* (*Conversations on the plurality of worlds*), in which he emphasizes the insignificance of man and the planet Earth in relation to the universe as a whole. Fontenelle appears in a better light at the end of the story (though this, apparently, did little to placate the man himself).

94 *a celebrated inhabitant . . . predicted it would be*: the Dutch astronomer Christian Huygens (1629–95) in his *Systema saturnium* (1659).

95 *two moons*: Père Castel (1688–1757) was a Jesuit scientist who had attacked Voltaire's *Éléments de la philosophie de Newton* (1738). In his *Traité de la pesanteur universelle* (*Treatise on Universal Gravitation*; 1724) he had sought to defend the Cartesian model of the universe against the Newtonian. Mars's two moons were not finally observed until 1877, but their existence had been predicted by Kepler on the basis of analogical reasoning.

97 *a flock of philosophers . . . anyone else to make*: Pierre-Louis Maupertuis (1698–1759) and other scientists left Dunkirk on 2 May 1736 to take measurements of a terrestrial meridian (by the method of triangulation) in the Arctic Circle. Having completed these observations early in 1737, they set out on the return journey to France on 10 June, but the ship was badly damaged by storms on the coast of the Gulf of Bothnia (which lies between Sweden and Finland). After being repaired, it resumed its voyage on 18 July. Maupertuis's measurements, replacing earlier, inaccurate ones taken in France itself, proved a resounding vindication of the Newtonian theory that the Earth was flat at its two poles. Maupertuis also brought back with him two young Lapp women who, as might be expected, created something of a stir in Paris.

99 *Leeuwenhoek and Hartsoeker . . . discovery*: Antonie de Leeuwenhoek (1632–1723), the Dutch naturalist and microscopist noted for his work on the circulation of the blood and on spermatozoa. Nicolas Hartsoeker (1656–1725), his compatriot and fellow-naturalist, also worked on spermatozoa.

'I have caught nature in the act': a phrase from one of Fontenelle's works which had been notoriously quoted by Lord Bolingbroke (see below, note to p. 192 of *The Ingenu*) on the occasion of the discovery of Fontenelle himself in a compromising situation with the marquise de Tencin (1682–1749), a leading salon hostess (and mother of the illegitimate D'Alembert, whom she abandoned as a baby on the steps of a church).

102 *that fable nonsense of Virgil's . . . Swammerdam . . . Réaumur*: Virgil, *Georgics*, iv; Jan Swammerdam (1637–80), the Dutch anatomist and entomologist, author of *Biblia naturae sive Historia insectorum*; René-Antoine Réaumur (1683–1757), French physicist and naturalist, inventor of the Réaumur scale (1730) and author of a six-volume natural history of insects (1734–42).

animals in turbans: an allusion to the Russo-Turkish War (1736–9).

104 *Ἐντελέχεια ἐστι*, etc.: Aristotle, *De anima*, ii. 2.

The soul . . . never know again: a reference to the Cartesian theory of innate ideas.

105 *Malebranchist . . . nothing to do with it*: Nicolas Malebranche (1638–1715) was an Oratorian theologian, scientist, and philosopher. His brand of Christian rationalism made a strong impression on Voltaire in his early years, and he returned to many aspects of it with sympathy in his last decade. Among many other things, Malebranche sought to resolve the Cartesian dualism of mind and matter by arguing that God is the sole cause both of what we think and of what happens in the material world, and effects a kind of correspondence between the two.

the hand of a clock . . . clear: a caricatural version of Leibniz's system of pre-established harmony. See Introduction, p. xiv.

I do not know how I think . . . people think: a faithful, if simple, version of some of the ideas in John Locke's *Essay concerning Human Understanding* (1690). Locke rejected the notion of innate ideas and argued that we know the world only through our senses.

a little animalcule in academic dress: Voltaire has in mind a doctor of theology from the Sorbonne.

ZADIG

109 *Thalestris . . . made the journey*: Thalestris, Queen of the Amazons, was said to have sought out Alexander the Great that he might father a child by her. Similarly, of course, it was the Queen of Sheba who made the journey to see King Solomon.

Sadi: The name of a real Arabic writer whose work had been translated into French in 1634 and again in 1704.

110 *Zadig*: Voltaire may have derived the name from the Arabic word for 'the truthful one' or from the Hebrew for 'the just man'. He may also have known of Handel's *Zadok the Priest*.

114 *a Babylonian called Arnou . . . around the neck*: there was at that time a Parisian called Arnoult who could, according to the advertisements in the *Mercure de France*, cure and prevent all forms of apoplexy with a sachet hung around the neck.

115 *he did not spend his time . . . broken bottles*: these are all allusions to seriously proposed scientific projects of the first half of the eighteenth century. Swift had already satirized this kind of thing in the section of *Gulliver's Travels* relating to Gulliver's visit to Balnibarbi.

138 *the land of the Gangarides*: situated on the east bank of the Ganges, this land is sometimes evoked by Voltaire, as in *The Princess of Babylon*, as a kind of Garden of Eden.

139 *'the Widow's Pyre'*: we know it by the Hindi term 'suttee'.

142 *Cambalu*: the capital of Cathay, i.e. Beijing.

143 *Teutates*: a druidic god to whom human sacrifice was made.

145 *the tower upon Mount Lebanon*: cf. Song of Solomon 4: 4: 'Thy nose is as the tower of Lebanon which looketh towards Damascus.'

148 . . . *set me apart from other men*: Voltaire has in mind the political theories of Thomas Hobbes (1588–1679).

153 *A basilisk*: a fabulous reptile reputedly about a foot long and able to kill men, but not women, with a look.

     Ogul: apart from being a genuine Middle Eastern name, this is also an anagram of *gulo*, the Latin word for glutton.

176 *'boopis'*: 'having large or cow-like eyes'. Voltaire may have confused this with another Greek term relating more specifically to colour. This whole episode is a veiled allusion to Louis XV's relationship with Mme de Pompadour.

WHAT PLEASES THE LADIES

178 *good King Dagobert*: see Introduction, p. xxviii.

     agnus dei: wax tablets blessed by the Pope and stamped with the figure of a lamb (the Lamb of God).

     paladins: strictly one of the twelve peers of Charlemagne's household, but more broadly a knight errant or paragon of knighthood. The same term is used in Voltaire's original French.

     Lutetia: the Latin name for Paris.

179 *Saint Denis*: King Dagobert was famed for his patronage of this abbey for Benedictine monks, which he founded in 630 and which is situated in the small town to which it has given its name, some four miles north of Paris. St Denis (Dionysius) was the first bishop of Paris and was martyred in 270 on the hill now known as Montmartre (Martyr's Mount). Having been executed by decapitation, so the legend has it, he picked up his head and walked several miles, simultaneously preaching a sermon. The place where he stopped became a small shrine and later the site of the Basilica of Saint Denis (and a burial place for the kings of France).

     Bertha, my wife: see Introduction, p. xxviii.

185 *his loving Baucis*: an allusion to the myth, related in Ovid's *Metamorphoses*, of the elderly couple who welcomed the two gods Zeus and Hermes, travelling in disguise as humble wayfarers. Despite their own poverty the couple showed themselves to be more hospitable than their rich neighbours, whose land Zeus then flooded before also turning Philemon and Baucis' modest cottage into a sumptuous temple. Zeus further gave them one wish, and they chose to live together for ever (as priest and priestess of the new temple). Thus on their death they were changed into an intertwining pair of trees, an oak and a lime.

186 *Clovis needed for his christening*: Clovis I (*c.*466–511)—also Chlodwig (whence both Louis and Ludwig)—is by popular tradition considered the first King of France. As King of the Salian Franks, a Germanic people living in the area of the present-day border between France and

Belgium, he extended Frankish rule eastwards by conquest and marriage, and converted to Christianity to secure the allegiance of his new subjects. He was baptized in the cathedral at Rheims on Christmas Day 496, and a subsequent legend had it that the sacred oil, or chrism, with which he was anointed was delivered from heaven by a dove.

189 *From Apelles' brush . . . not Lemoine*: Apelles (*c.*352–308 BC), renowned Greek painter of the ancient world, celebrated by many writers for his paintings of Alexander the Great; Phidias (*c.*490–*c.*430 BC), regarded as the finest sculptor in ancient Greece; Carle Van Loo (1705–65), distinguished contemporary painter ennobled by his patron Louis XV; Jean-Baptiste Pigalle (1714–85), leading French sculptor who in 1776 completed a statue (now in the Louvre) of a very elderly, nude Voltaire; and Jean-Louis Lemoine (also Lemoyne) (1665–1755), famous French sculptor and father of Jean-Baptiste Lemoine or Lemoyne (1704–78), another sculptor. Voltaire's simple mention of 'Lemoine' may designate either, but not François Lemoine (1688–1737), who was principally a painter.

THE INGENU

190 *Father Quesnel*: Père Quesnel (1634–1719) was the leading Jansenist after the death of Antoine Arnauld (1612–64). His *Réflexions morales sur le Nouveau Testament* were first published in 1671, and the Papal Bull *Unigenitus* was a condemnation of one hundred and one propositions extracted from it. The fictional attribution is appropriate because of the anti-Jesuit nature of the story, as well as being humorously incongruous since a rather risqué *conte* is about the last thing the austere Quesnel would ever have written.

St Dunstan: Dunstan (924–88) was an Englishman who had been educated by monks in Ireland and who became Bishop of Worcester, then London, and finally Archbishop of Canterbury.

191 *Barbados water*: 'a cordial flavoured with orange and lemon peel' (*OED*).

192 *The magistrate and the tax-collector . . . guests*: given recent events in Brittany the magistrate and the tax-collector were two key political figures. See Introduction, p. xxxix.

'nihil admirari': Lord Bolingbroke (1678–1751) was a Tory minister and sceptic whom Voltaire had met in 1722, who may have introduced him to the works of Newton and Locke, and whose brand of deism had exerted some influence on him. The motto is from Horace, *Epistles*, i. 6.

193 *'Huguenots'*: as Voltaire was aware, the name derived from the German 'Eidgenossen' meaning companions united by oath, or confederates. The term was applied to Protestants in Geneva and subsequently gallicized.

194 *Reverend Father Sagard Théodat, the famous Recollect missionary*: Gabriel Sagard Théodat published his *Grand Voyage au pays des Hurons . . . avec un dictionnaire de la langue huronne* (*Great Journey to the Land of the Hurons . . . together with a dictionary of the Huron language*) in 1632 and a

history of Canada in 1636. The Recollects were a reformed Franciscan order (suppressed in 1790) who sought detachment from the created and recollection in God. They found much to admire in the life of the Hurons, a small tribe who had become allies of the French and were later almost wiped out by the Iroquois. See also Introduction, p. xxxii.

200 *'Confess your faults to one another'*: Epistle of St James 5: 16.

202 *baptized in a stream*: Acts of the Apostles 8: 26–39.

203 *wine rejoices the heart of man*: Ecclesiasticus 40: 20.

204 *Judah the Patriarch . . . blood of grapes*: Genesis 49: 11.

Hercules: Voltaire is implicitly poking fun at Cardinal de Fleury (1653–1743), who had been Louis XV's chief minister for several decades up until his death and whose given names were the Christian 'André' followed by the rather less Christian 'Hercule'.

206 *Marrying one's godmother is not allowed*: see above, note to p. 14 of *Candide*.

213 *'Nos dulcia linquimus arva, nos patriam fugimus'*: Virgil, *Bucolics*, i. 3–4.

converted by the dragoons: see Introduction, p. xxxi.

214 *His Majesty's confessor*: Père François de La Chaise (1624–1709) was confessor to Louis XIV from 1675 to 1709 and enjoyed considerable political as well as ecclesiastical influence. The famous cemetery in Paris is named after him.

Monseigneur de Louvois: the marquis de Louvois (1639–91) succeeded his father as Minister for War and, after the death of Colbert in 1683, became the most powerful of Louis's ministers.

215 *M. Alexandre . . . Ministry of War*: a real historical figure who served as the equivalent of Permanent Secretary to Louvois's deputy, the marquis de Saint-Pouange. Saint-Pouange continued to hold office in the Ministry after Louvois's death in 1701 until his own in 1706. A reader of 1767 might have seen in Voltaire's portrait of Saint-Pouange some reference to the contemporary Secretary of State, the comte de Saint-Florentin, who was known for his religious intolerance, for his despotic abuse of *lettres de cachet* (see below, note to p. 219), and for what some commentators term his 'lax morals'.

217 *an old solitary from Port-Royal called Gordon*: Port-Royal monastery was the centre of Jansenism from 1635. It was closed down by Louis XIV in 1709 and destroyed in 1712. Why Voltaire chose the name Gordon is unclear. Possibly it constitutes a reference to Thomas Gordon, the Scottish opponent of Catholicism and High Anglicanism and author of the *Independent Whig*, who had died in 1750. Voltaire admired him as one of the great figures of British rationalism. It is also the case (according to Arthur Young's *Travels in France and Italy*, 1792) that a man called Gordon was imprisoned in the Bastille for thirty years until an English diplomat secured his release after the authorities were unable to say why

he had been imprisoned in the first place. There is no evidence that Voltaire knew this, but the parallel suggests he may have.

218 *English drops ... surprise*: known as 'Goddard's drops' after their inventor, they were akin to smelling salts and consisted largely of ammonia.

219 *lettres de cachet*: these were orders, signed by the King and countersigned by a minister (later by bishops and other governmental and ecclesiastical officials), for the imprisonment without trial of anyone who had incurred official displeasure. It was a key instrument of unjust repression and used (or abused) even more widely in the eighteenth century than in the seventeenth.

efficient grace: the Jansenist theory of efficient grace is expounded notably in Pascal's *Écrits sur la grace* (*Writings on Grace*).

Arnauld and Nicole: for Arnauld see above, note to p. 190. Pierre Nicole (1625–95), one of the Port-Royal group, was co-author with Arnauld of the *Logique de Port-Royal*.

220 *Rohault's Physics*: Rohault's *Traité de physique* (*Treatise on Physics*; 1671) was essentially a version of Cartesian physics, with which Voltaire, as an admirer of Newton, had no sympathy.

Enquiry after Truth: Malebranche's *La Recherche de la vérité* (1674–5). See above, note to p. 105 of *Micromegas*.

doctrine of physical premotion: the theory that God acts on human will through physical causes.

221 *Abbé de Saint-Cyran and Jansenius*: see above, note to p. 54 of *Candide*. The Abbé de Saint-Cyran was Jean Du Vergier de Hauranne (1581–1643), a friend of Jansenius and head of Port-Royal.

Fezensac, and Fesansaquet, and Astarac: three extremely small areas in the Armagnac region in the south-west of France which, in the Middle Ages, had been independent territories.

223 *... transformed into gods*: this whole section adumbrates *The White Bull* and is an indication of part of the satirical point of that story. As its heroine's name suggests, the events befalling Princess Amasida, daughter of King Amasis, are not far removed from the world of the *Amadis* romances. The latter probably began as a fourteenth-century cycle of chivalric romances written in Portuguese by Vasco da Lobeira (who died in 1403), though the only known texts are fifteenth century and Spanish. Known under the title *Amadis de Gaule*, many of the romances were translated into French in the sixteenth century, and more in the seventeenth.

224 *the Visés ... the Fénelons*: Jean Donneau de Visé (1640–1710) founded the *Mercure galant* (later the *Mercure de France*) in 1672. A second-rate writer and critic, he attacked several of the major authors of his day, including Jean Racine (1639–99). Faydit (1640–1709), an Oratorian, published his *Télémachomanie* in 1700, an attack on Fénelon (1651–1715) and his

didactic romance *Télémaque* (1699), which propounded humane and liberal principles.

225 *Two Pigeons*: by Jean de La Fontaine (1621–95).

Iphigénie . . . Athalie: by Racine.

Rodogune: by Pierre Corneille (1606–84), as is *Cinna* (1640). *Les Plaideurs* (1668), mentioned at the end of the chapter, is Racine's one comedy. There the point concerns a discreet reference to money in Act II. i of *Cinna*, which Voltaire deemed vulgar and unworthy of a classical tragedy.

227 *the Archbishop's door . . . mystical love*: François de Harlay de Champvallon (1625–95) was Archbishop of Paris from 1671 and played an important part in the Revocation of the Edict of Nantes. He had also refused a Christian burial to Molière (who was an actor as well as a playwright). None of this endeared him to Voltaire, who exploits the Archbishop's reputation for philandering and recalls the rumour that the Archbishop had died ('the death of a happy man') while making love to Mme de Lesdiguières. Bossuet (1627–1704) was Bishop of Meaux from 1681. He had been tutor to the Dauphin between 1670 and 1680. He was a theologian and historian, and particularly noted for his sermons. He was said to have entered into a legal contract of marriage with a Mlle Desvieux who later changed her name to de Mauléon when, with her 'marriage' settlement, she bought a small property of that name just outside Paris. Madame de Guyon (1648–1717) was the principal exponent in France of Quietism, the belief that religious perfection may be attained, without the sacraments, by the passive and continuous contemplation of the Deity. It was condemned in 1696 by a commission over which Bossuet presided. Père La Chaise was also notorious for his philandering: but the identity of Mlle du Tron is not known, and she may be entirely fictitious.

230 *Mme du Belloy*: thought to be a reference to Mme du Fresnoy, who was Louvois's mistress and for whom Louvois obtained a position as Lady of the Royal Bedchamber. On Saint-Pouange see above, note to p. 215.

231 *'There is one truth . . . hidden it'*: a reference to the Jansenist and Pascalian doctrine of the *deus absconditus*, according to which God has withdrawn from the world he created with the result that his presence cannot be observed and that his existence cannot be proved by pure reason.

236 *the saint must be right*: because it was the Jansenists rather than the Jesuits who looked to St Augustine as an authority. While Voltaire is here parodying Jesuit casuistry, it is true that St Augustine does approve of the wife's action, as does Voltaire when he uses the anecdote as the basis of one of his first stories, *Cosi-Sancta* (written in 1715 or 1716, and published in 1784). Pierre Bayle had condemned the wife's action in his *Dictionnaire historique et critique* (in the article entitled 'Acindynus'), and Voltaire, in his own *Dictionnaire philosophique*, criticizes Bayle for the severity of his condemnation. Nevertheless the tragic manner in which the action is treated in this story suggests a different attitude on Voltaire's part.

239 *Of that dread castle ... innocence*: a quotation from Voltaire's own epic poem *La Henriade* (1723), canto iv, 455–6.

244 *Molinism*: See note to p. 61 above.

245 *the maréchal de Marillac*: Marillac (1573–1632) was implicated in plotting against Cardinal Richelieu and executed.

253 *Meditations ... The Flower of the Saints*: Père Croiset was the Jesuit author of four volumes of *Méditations ou Retraite spirituelle pour un jour de chaque mois (Meditations or Spiritual Retreat for one day of each month*; 1694–1710). For Voltaire the work epitomized unintelligent narrow-mindedness. *Flos sanctorum, o Libros de las vidas de los Santos (The Flowers of the Saints*; 1599) was a popular Spanish work, often translated into French, by another Jesuit, Pedro Ribadeneira.

concomitant concourse: the doctrine that God bestows divine grace in the course of human actions as man struggles to avoid sin.

THE WHITE BULL

254 *epigraph*: again an entirely fictional attribution. The only Mamaki Voltaire might have heard of was a teacher at the Jesuit college in Rouen, who in 1759 had set his pupils as the subject of their Latin verse composition the story of a happy brigand who ceases his brigandage. (Cf. the figure of Arbogad in *Zadig*.)

It had taken gods to vanquish Mambres: cf. 2 Timothy 3: 8; and Exodus 8: 19.

256 *footnote*: Voltaire is mocking Dom Calmet, the Benedictine author of a *Commentaire littéral sur tous les livres de l'Ancien et du Nouveau Testament (Literal Commentary on all the books of the Old and New Testaments*; 24 vols., 1707–16) and a *Dictionnaire historique, critique, chronologique, géographique et littéral de la Bible* (4 vols., 1730). These two erudite but literal-minded works were a rich source of ammunition for Voltaire. Here he has in mind Dom Calmet's comment in the *Dictionnaire* that 'the term "Cherub" in Hebrew sometimes means calf or ox'.

258 *... departed spirits*: 1 Samuel 28: 7–25.

... rivers into blood: Exodus 7: 8–2; 10: 21–3.

The serpent ... there you have it: Genesis 3; Numbers 22: 21–35; Jonah 1: 17–2; 11; Tobit (in the Apocrypha) 5: 5–6, 16; Leviticus 16: 7–10, 20–2; Genesis 8: 6–12. Salmanazar was King of Assyria from 728 BC and died in 714 BC.

262 *Northern poets*: an allusion to John Milton (1608–74). His epic poem *Paradise Lost*, written in blank verse and based on the Book of Genesis, was first published in 1667 and then in a revised and expanded version in 1674.

265 *This great King ... ox. For ...*: Daniel 2: 1–13; 4: 4–33.

267 *his daughter Pasiphae*: in fact, his wife. Phaedra was their daughter.

267 *Thus did Juno quiver . . . Inachus*: Ovid, *Metamorphoses*, i. 588–624.

 'Dynasty' literally means power: Voltaire had used the word 'dynasty' in
 this sense during a previous polemical exchange with Larcher, an ancient
 historian (see below, note to p. 283). Its derivation from the Greek word
 for 'dominion' or 'power' was his justification, but in French (as in
 English) its sense of 'a succession of kings of the same family' was
 too entrenched to permit of such usage. Larcher delighted in mocking
 Voltaire on the point, and Voltaire responds here with a welter of false
 erudition and a particularly careful use of the word 'cavilling' in its
 etymological sense of 'specious pedantry' . . .

268 *Lycaon . . . pipe*: Ovid, *Metamorphoses*, i. 209–43; ii. 401–95; i. 588–624; i.
 548–56; i. 689–712. The point, of course, is that the Old Testament is no
 less fabulous than Ovid.

269 *fair Edith, wife of Lot . . . see it*: Genesis 9: 26—for the pillar of salt. The
 rest of this extraordinary account derives from Dom Calmet's credulous
 commentary on the supposed miracle. His sources, given in Voltaire's
 note, are unreliable: the poem *De Sodoma* is a fourth-century work by an
 unknown writer and not by Tertullian, while the second-century Greek
 text of St Irene is known only in a suspect Latin translation. Voltaire
 particularly enjoyed this example of exegetical lunacy.

 five great cities . . . a matter of moments: Genesis 19: 24—for the destruction of Sodom and Gomorrah. Dom Calmet provided the other three
 cities and the lake.

 . . . Cerastes into oxen: Ovid, *Metamorphoses*, x. 220–37.

270 *Daniel 5*: in fact an adaptation of Daniel 4: 23, 25 and 5: 21.

271 *Egyptian paper*: i.e. papyrus. Voltaire is parodying the anachronisms of
 the Old Testament since the story is set in the reign of King Amasis of
 Egypt (568–26 BC) and papyrus was believed to have been first used under
 Alexander the Great (356–323 BC). There is the further implication that
 a considerable amount of time elapsed before the oral history of Old
 Testament events was finally recorded in writing, which in itself would
 be a clear source of anachronism and other errors.

 onager: Voltaire uses the term 'onocrotale' which Rabelais had used in
 Gargantua (chapter 8) to denote a large bird. It is likely that he may have
 intended the French word 'onagre'.

272 *. . . slaves were very rich*: Tobit 1: 14; 4: 1, 20; 5: 1–9; 9: 1–5.

 . . . four horses of fire: 2 Kings 2: 11.

 . . . mother of Asclepius: Ovid, *Metamorphoses*, ii. 596–632.

274 *'Rerum concordia discors' . . . own tongue*: or rather as Horace wrote in
 Epistles, i. 12, 19.

276 *. . . horses and asses*: Ezekiel 23.

 . . . with the Pierides: Ovid, *Metamorphoses*, v. 670–8.

277 *Great whirlwinds . . . sackbut*: Daniel 3: 5, 7, 10, 15.

278 *Manethon*: a historian of the Pharaohs, but only fragments of his work are known, and at second hand. This is not one of them.

. . . *journey to the Indies*: for this paragraph see Numbers 21: 8–9; Joshua 6: 1–20; 12: 24; 10: 11–14.

279 . . . *the charming Amasida*: Matthew 10: 16; Judges 9: 1, 30–40; 15; 4, 15; 16: 4–20.

. . . *a fair Princess*: Genesis 24; 47: 28 (the joke derives from a retro-spective chronology based on Jacob's age); Ruth 2–4; 46: 15; Genesis 38: 6–26; 19: 31; 16: 1–4; 30: 3–13; 35: 22; 49: 4; 2 Samuel 11: 2–27.

that lunatic Abbadie . . . Houteville: Abbadie, a (French) Protestant, had written a Christian apologetic entitled *Traité de la vérité de la religion chrétienne* in 1684, which was republished several times and used also by Catholics. The abbé Houteville had published his *La Religion chrétienne prouvée par les faits* in 1721. Voltaire mocked them for using the 'canni-bals' fables' of the Old Testament as witness to the coming of Christ.

the Widow of Ephesus: a tale by La Fontaine, based on an episode in Petronius' *Satyricon*. The story is the source of the Widow Cosrou scene in *Zadig*, Chapter 2.

. . . *dead people coming back to life*: Horace, *Epode*, v. 45–6; Psalms 114: 4; Joshua 3: 14–17; 2 Kings 4: 32–7.

280 *'to complete the education of my heart and mind'*: see Introduction, p. xxxiv.

282 . . . *all the beasts of the field*: Genesis 3: 1.

283 *a well-established usage . . . enlightened princes*: Judges 11: 37: 'And she [Jephthah's daughter] said unto her father, Let this thing be done for me: let me alone two months, that I may go up and down upon the mountains, and bewail my virginity, I and my fellows.'

the ewe of Thebes . . . together: the Theban cult of the ewe comes from Herodotus, ii. 42. Bubastis, an Egyptian goddess and the town named after her, was associated with a cat, not a dog. Phoebe's cat arises from Voltaire's misreading of his source about the cult of Bubastis: Phoebe was not a place. Arsinoe was, and the crocodile was worshipped there. So was the goat in Mendez, according to Herodotus, ii. 46. (Voltaire's claim in his *Philosophie de l'histoire* that it was granted the favours of the ladies of that town was what sparked the row with Larcher: see above, note to p. 267.)

284 *filled with sacred onions*: the notion that onions might have divine status can be traced back to Juvenal (*Satire* xv). Voltaire airs it with glee in several of his works.

286 *Memphis . . . the Isles*: Genesis 10: 2, 5.

The Oxford World's Classics Website

www.oup.com/uk/worldsclassics

- Information about new titles
- Explore the full range of Oxford World's Classics
- Links to other literary sites and the main OUP webpage
- Imaginative competitions, with bookish prizes
- Articles by editors
- Extracts from Introductions
- Special information for teachers and lecturers

www.oup.com/uk/worldsclassics